THE DOOR TO THE ladies' room swung open and Hank Madison swooped in. Standing at the marble-topped vanity that featured four sinks, and clutching her damp white hand-towel to her chest, Maddie gasped.

"Hank!"

He looked around at this female territory he'd invaded. "Nice." Then he focused on her, his gaze roving over her face. "We need to go. We need to begin the meeting."

"Yeah, I know. That's why I'm in here. I told you I suffer from stage fright."

"Maddie, Maddie, Maddie," Hank said slowly, sensually, "I can't make you go out there. And right now I don't care if you do or if you don't. I'm happy just to be in here with you."

He approached her with a slow, rolling gait that had Maddie involuntarily tensing When Hank stood directly in front of her, he looked down into her eyes.

"Maddie, I want to—"

"Me too," she breathed, grabbing his tie and pulling him to her. She raised her face for his kiss. And Hank obliged, lowering his head until her mouth met his.

&

"Cheryl Porter writes with charm, wit and imagination. A wonderful storyteller, a wonderful story. This book is a delight to read—don't miss it!"
—Heather Graham, *New York Times* bestselling author

Mad About Maddie

CHERYL ANNE PORTER

St. Martin's Paperbacks

MAD ABOUT MADDIE

Copyright © 2001 by Cheryl Anne Porter.

All rights reserved. No part of this book may be used or reproduced in any manner whatsoever without written permission except in the case of brief quotations embodied in critical articles or reviews. For information address St. Martin's Press, 175 Fifth Avenue, New York, NY 10010.

ISBN: 0-312-97895-2

Printed in the United States of America

St. Martin's Paperbacks edition / September 2001

St. Martin's Paperbacks are published by St. Martin's Press, 175 Fifth Avenue, New York, NY 10010.

10 9 8 7 6 5 4 3 2 1

To Pup . . . who is the most wonderful and most beloved kind of creature, you know.

Mad About Maddie

PROLOGUE

FUNERALS AREN'T SUPPOSED TO be funny. And this one, by anyone's standards, wasn't. But seated in the small and crowded church's front pew, as befitted her status as chief mourner, Maddie Copeland sat appalled at her own behavior. This nervous silliness was so unlike her. She'd heard of the phenomenon, an "inappropriate laughter" response, but she'd never experienced it before. Certainly she was saddened by the passing of her very elderly friend, James. And she'd cried. A lot. But today—in the church, during the funeral, with the Reverend Hobbs delivering the eulogy—all she could think about were the funny moments during her three-summer-long friendship with James Madison.

Maddie stifled yet another guffaw by digging her fingernails into her palms. Yes, she told herself, it was healing to think of the good times. To celebrate a life. To remember the fun. *Just don't sing and dance at the man's funeral, Muddle. Get yourself under control.* She was trying to do that. Yet even picturing how disrespectful a belly-busting guffaw into this hushed atmosphere would be didn't sober her. Instead, the very idea that she *might* laugh out loud made the possibility all the more real that she *would*.

Awash in an embarrassed heat, Maddie put a hand to her forehead and rubbed. *Dear God, I have got to get a grip.* That darned James, the dearly departed. Maddie allowed herself a surreptitious grin. James Henry Madison, Sr.—eighty years senior, to be exact. He had been so funny. Suddenly the word *funny* seemed funny, triggering yet another rising tide of hilarity that rumbled its way up from deep inside Maddie. She all but stuffed her lace hanky into her mouth. Her shoulders shook and tiny choking noises escaped her. *Please, God, let everyone think I'm crying.*

Focusing purposefully on her black-clad lap, Maddie

took several deep breaths and tried to concentrate on the eulogy. She couldn't. Into her mind popped the words "lobster clock." She held a fist against her mouth and pressed hard. *Don't think about the stupid lobster clock or you'll embarrass yourself for life. Think about anything that's not funny. Your surroundings. The weather.*

Maddie willed herself to take her own advice. *Okay, weather.* It was a brilliant August day in her hometown, the coastal village of Hanscomb Harbor, Connecticut. A time of year when life was languid and good. *Unless you're dead.* Horrified, Maddie choked back a traitorous chuckle. *Stop that. People will think you've lost your mind.* In desperation, Maddie pinched herself hard on the arm until the pain sobered her. She breathed in a huge gulp of air.

There. That's better. Poor James—and his lobster clock. *Go back to the weather.* Warm and sunny and muggy. As Maddie had seen on the way to church, hordes of gleeful tourist-locusts lolled on the broad swathe of pristine beach. Their children happily thronged the game arcade. Still other visitors crowded the various eateries and shops that nestled side by side on the boardwalk upshore from the cool waters of Long Island Sound.

There. Sanity. Feeling more in control of herself now, Maddie again directed her attention to the Reverend Hobbs, who was endlessly holding forth in a religious way from the pulpit. Within moments, though, Maddie had once more lost the thread of the eulogy, impersonal as it was since the preacher had never met James, a summer resident only. Maddie smiled to herself. Dear, sweet James. She recalled first meeting him three summers ago when he'd rented one of those ramshackle cottages from Mr. Cotton Hardy.

James. Always cheery, always sweet, with no mention of his illness or the pain he had to have been enduring. So stoic. So brave. And now he was gone. Maddie felt herself tear up, this time with the appropriate emotion. She sniffed away tears as her mind leapt back three days to that horrible ride in the back of the ambulance with James. They'd sped toward the small community hospital in the next township over. It had been awful. But not as awful as the ride today with her in the limo behind James's casket in the hearse ahead.

From there, Maddie's mind made a natural leap back to a cold day five years ago when she'd buried her parents. A car wreck on an icy road had taken their lives. And this was the same church where she'd sat through that sad affair. The church hadn't changed any. Tucked away on a cobblestoned side street, the structure sat surrounded by a Kelly-green lawn and bright, blooming flowers. The white-painted building, with its tall steeple that pierced the treetops, contained hardwood pews, a simple altar, and a reverent congregation.

Maddie dabbed at her eyes with her hanky and tucked that too, too painful memory back into her mind's vault. What she ought to be focusing on, she told herself, was James's impending cremation. An involuntary expression of squeamishness claimed her features. *Forget that.* She skipped forward to the point where she could visualize herself retrieving his ashes from the funeral director. A solemn moment. Mistake. Sadness ended right there, and the wacko images again took over. Maddie put a shielding hand over her eyes as if that would stop the renewed fit of giggles that lurked right behind her sadness.

Why had she ever promised James that she would honor his last wish? Maddie doubted seriously if she could bring herself to pour her friend's fine-ground ashes into the hollowed-out belly of that hideous, red-glazed ceramic monstrosity of his: a souvenir lobster clock he wanted as his urn. Over a foot tall, the broad and hefty thing stood balanced on its fan of a tail. Its claws were raised over its head and clutched in them was a cheap clock that ticked loudly. It took both hands to even hold on to the darned thing. To Maddie it looked like a cartoon version of Atlas holding up the universe. And that lobster face. Could it be worse? A big cheesy grin and huge black cheerful eyes painted on its face.

In Maddie's estimation, the clock certainly was not an appropriate vessel to be used as an urn. But James had been adamant that this tacky Hanscomb Harbor souvenir be his final resting place. All she had to do, he'd said cheerfully while showing her how, was unscrew the cap on the back of the lobster's head and, using a funnel, pour his ashes into the hollow interior. Originally, he'd explained proudly, that space had held bath salts.

Bath salts, for heaven's sake. Maddie put a hand to her aching forehead. How . . . undignified. She could just see herself now, there in her kitchen and handling James's ashes. What if she dropped them and they scattered everywhere? Could she bring herself to take a broom and sweep him up into a dustpan? Or what if she sneezed at a crucial moment and blew James all over the countertops? Was she really supposed to dust him up with a rag? Or what if the darned lobster clock got broken? Or stolen? The nightmares were endless. A shudder for the possibilities shook her.

"I just knew it, Maddie. You're shivering again. I told you to bring a sweater. But do you listen to me? No."

Celeste's whispered words, with their undertone of genuine if fussy concern, brought Maddie back to the moment. Leaning toward her elderly friend and employee who sat at her side on the hard pew, she whispered back, "I'm not cold, Celeste. I was just thinking about . . . well, cremation. It seems so . . . icky, somehow."

With every white hair in place in a soft bun at the back of her head, and with a sympathetic expression lighting her sweet and grandmotherly face, Celeste McNeer gave Maddie's hand a pat. "Not the least bit icky, dear. Pretty efficient, if you ask me. Get cremated and save the little pitchforked devils of hell the trouble of having to cook up some brimstone to fry you with. Seems to me they'd appreciate that so they could get on with the uglier torments. Like gouging out your eyes."

Maddie's mouth opened in indignant shock—everyone's usual response to Celeste's outrageousness. "Celeste! James is *not* going to hell."

Celeste pursed her lips. "Haven't you been listening to the Reverend Hobbs? Hellfire and brimstone. What an old puritanical patoot he is. I tell you, this is one tough and stringy eulogy to have to digest. And long, too. 'Kingdom come' could already have come and been long gone before he's done."

"You're terrible," Maddie hissed, hiding her amusement and thinking how James would have enjoyed this conversation. "We're supposed to be mourning here."

"Well, then, wail and sob a bit and I'll comfort you— anything to drown out that man's ranting up there." Then, with a sudden softening of her expression, Celeste whispered, "I mean it, though, honey. You and James were dear friends, so cry if you feel like it. I sure did when my Angus passed on, God rest his soul."

With a surge of affection, Maddie gently squeezed the bony, freckled, and blue-veined hand of her incorrigible friend. "I know how much you miss Angus," she whispered. "He was a wonderful cat. But to tell you the truth, I was just . . . well, picturing everything that could go wrong when I'm trying to get James's ashes into that silly lobster clock of his."

Celeste soberly nodded, as if Maddie's were the most natural of comments in the world. As if everyone at some time or another had faced this same dilemma. "That's a poser, all right. I expect this will be the first time a lobster's ever ingested a man. Outside of Jules Verne, that is."

Caught off guard, Maddie burst out laughing. Quickly, guiltily, she slapped both hands over her face and shook with the force of her emotion. Even though she had to know Maddie was laughing, Celeste put an arm around her and patted her shoulder. Maddie's embarrassed ears told her the church was deathly quiet except for the ragged sounds *she* was making. Even Preacher Hobbs hesitated.

Celeste took control, announcing loudly for the benefit of the supremely uncomfortable congregation, "There, there, honey. You let it all out now. *Crying*'s good for what ails you." She pounded Maddie's shoulder mercilessly. "You're *supposed* to be crying."

Choking and coughing, Maddie wailed . . . with disguised laughter.

Over this, Preacher Hobbs proceeded, every bit as loudly and with great determination, to harangue the mourners with some cryptic verse from the Bible.

It was hopeless. The more Maddie tried not to laugh, the worse sounds she made. She was sure of only one thing: James would have loved this. He'd probably have laughed right along with her. But she doubted that most of the people packed with her into the small church would understand. Or approve. Especially Miss Lavinia Houghton, tyrant librarian, who sat directly behind Celeste and had already twice sniffed loudly and tut-tutted disapprovingly. Why, if she knew Maddie was laughing, she wouldn't hesitate to have her burned at the stake.

Fearing a raging case of the hiccups, Maddie struggled for a composure that was slow in coming. When she finally wiped at her eyes, her only thought was to thank God that real tears stood in them.

Celeste poked at Maddie with her elbow and nodded her head not so subtly toward the strait-laced woman in the pew behind them, and whispered heatedly, "If Lavinia shushes us one more time or snorts at us through her big beak of a nose, I'm going to turn around and wallop her. Just give her a bloody nose. Let's see if she can sanctimoniously sniff at us around that, the old biddy."

Fearing Celeste would actually pop Lavinia Houghton in the nose—and right here in church—Maddie quickly gripped her employee's hands in hers and lifted her chin toward the man in the pulpit. "I believe Preacher Hobbs is finally winding down."

"Well, hallelujah. There is a God, and He made that man shut up." Celeste's whisper was more of a hiss as she got in the last word before joining Maddie in paying attention to the closing remarks.

For her part, and as the preacher called for the mourners

to begin filing past the casket, Maddie sighed soberly and took a last look at the man whose body reposed in the open coffin.

Goodbye, James, my friend. I wish we'd had more time together before you had to go. I loved you for all the wacky things you did, although I didn't always understand your reasons. But you always displayed a kindness and generosity of spirit. How rare is that? And I thank you for how interested you always were in listening to me talk about myself. Hope I didn't bore you to death. Maddie's eyes popped open wide. She put a hand to her forehead. *God, sorry. Poor choice of words. But . . . goodbye. Oh, one last thing: I wish there were more men around like you, James. Only more my age. No offense.*

CHAPTER ONE

THE BIG STRETCH LIMO slowly snaked its attention-grabbing way through the small fishing village of Hanscomb Harbor. In the spacious and luxurious passenger cabin behind the chauffeur reposed James Henry "Hank" Madison, III. Accompanying him was his very recently deceased grandfather's longtime friend and family attorney, Jim Thornton, a man only a little younger than James Senior had been at the time of his death less than a week ago.

This was no social outing, which was just as well because Hank was in no mood to enjoy anything about this trip. Not the usually pleasurable ride in his Learjet, which he sometimes piloted. Not the beautiful countryside they'd passed by on their way here. Certainly not this damn backwater village. And especially not one particular woman who lived here.

"I swear, Jim, I don't know whether to laugh or cry. This is just like the old man to pull a stunt like this."

"Stunt? How in God's name could his sudden death be a stunt, Hank? This just happened. It wasn't planned."

Hank exhaled, feeling guilty. "I didn't really mean that. It's just unfair, dammit. I wanted to be here when this happened. But there I was in Australia. Halfway around the world."

Jim sat forward to give Hank's knee a quick and comforting pat. "Now, don't beat yourself up, son. You got back here as quick as you could. Think of this as a sad and unfortunate event of timing. No one saw his end coming this quickly. Not even his doctors."

"I know that. I've settled that in my mind. But what about the rest of it, Jim? What do I do with that? If I'd known at all that he'd die and rush his own funeral in some out-of-the-way town I'd never heard of before, I wouldn't have gone to Australia. Hell, I would have stepped in a lot earlier and put a stop to things with that woman."

"I know you would have." Jim Thornton, a bulldog of a man more than forty years Hank's senior, bore many titles, among them the presidencies and chairmanships of many political and charitable foundations. But today he rode along in his capacity as trusted family friend as much as senior partner in an internationally famous law firm that handled the affairs of the rich and famous, both of which Hank was. "You look exhausted, son."

Hank rubbed at his gritty-tired eyes. "I am. Over thirty hours of flying time just to get to the East Coast. I barely had time to shower and catch a meal."

"We didn't have to come here today, Hank. You could have rested."

"No," Hank said stubbornly. "We had to come here today. The sooner the better. I just want to meet this woman, see what I'm up against, and then we can get out of here."

Jim exhaled dramatically. "It's not that simple."

"Nothing ever is where my grandfather is concerned." Hank shook his head. "Or was. Did you know about this place, Jim? Or this woman? Before now, I mean. Hell, did anyone know what was going on with him?" Hank beat himself up with the guilty judgment that *he* should have known. But how could he? James Senior had been, to put it mildly, eccentric.

"Your grandfather and I were friends, Hank. I wasn't his keeper or his nursemaid. He didn't owe me—or you—an explanation for his whereabouts or his activities. But, hell, I thought he was at his house on Long Island and under the eye of his housekeeper. I had no idea he was slipping away to come here. In fact, I only found out about this place when he was rushed to the hospital in Indian Neck, like I told you."

"That's right. How did you know he was in the hospital? Or even which one?"

"Gerta. James asked a nurse to call her so Gerta could send for me."

"I don't get it. Why call his housekeeper? Why didn't he just have the nurse call you directly?" Jim's beetling expression clearly communicated his desire not to answer the question. But Hank wouldn't let him off that easily. "Come on, Jim, it can't be any worse than it is now."

Jim exhaled gustily. "All right. He called Gerta because he didn't bring Beamer with him this time, and he wanted to . . . say goodbye to his dog."

Hank chuckled fatalistically. "Well, there you have it. The old man's priorities."

"Now, don't do that, Hank. Your grandfather spoke mostly of you at the end."

"What did he say? 'Take care of the dog'?"

"That's not funny. He said to tell you how much he loved you. If you'd been in New York, he would have called for you. You have to know that."

Hurt and grief warred with guilt inside Hank. "I don't know. But maybe."

Jim leaned forward, toward Hank. "I know you've suffered a huge loss whether you want to act like it or not. We all have. Hell, James was my best friend for over fifty years. Like a brother to me. But that doesn't mean I couldn't see his faults, too, Hank. We all know what he was like."

Hank's chuckle had nothing to do with humor. "So we're going to call his antics 'faults'?"

"Okay, so the old coot was crazier than a loon about some things. But his heart was good and he loved you. He did some funny things, that's for sure." Jim chuckled and prodded Hank to join him. "He was like Elvis. Giving away money and cars and houses to strangers. And yes he was open to all kinds of scams. But he had a good heart, Hank, and he never did any harm."

Thinking of the reason for this visit, Hank remained unamused. "No harm, Jim? Then why am I here now? Who is this woman? And what has my grandfather done this one final time that I'll have to straighten out?"

Jim was suddenly the attorney. "I'm bound by your

grandfather's wishes, Hank. Until the reading of the will, my hands are legally tied."

"I just hope mine aren't." Hank waited, but Jim had no comeback to that. That was not good.

Hank directed his attention out the limo's tinted window and worried. What in the hell had the old man gotten himself into? All Hank knew was there was a woman at the end of this ride who needed to be present at the reading of his grandfather's new will. His *new* will. In Hank's book, that could only mean one thing. His sweet old grandfather, former business tycoon who'd made a huge fortune in the advertising business, on both Madison Avenue and Wall Street, and who had possibly been going benignly senile, had been taken in by a gold digger with a sob story. *Great. Just lovely.* Jim kept denying that, but Hank thought he knew better. After all, it had happened before. And more than once. How many times had Hank had to pay some scheming woman off in order to extricate James Senior from her clutches? Three? Four?

Dammit. It looked like number five was around the bend. Hank took a deep breath and exhaled it slowly. But it did nothing to calm him. He turned to Jim, only to realize the older man had been watching him with a grin and a speculative expression on his face. "All right, Jim, what's so funny? You keep looking at me as if you can't wait to see what happens next."

Jim chuckled. "That's because I can't."

"That answer is wearing thin here. Come on, talk to me. I have a right to know. Who is this woman we're going to meet? What was she to my grandfather? What's he done?"

Jim held up a hand. "Patience, my boy. Patience. You'll know in due time."

Hank hated condescension almost as much as he hated a mystery, especially one that involved his family and his livelihood, if not his fortune. That being so, he spoke more harshly, and more crudely, than he ever had before to Jim. "Spare me the client–attorney privilege crap, okay? He may have been your client and even your friend, but he was *my* blood, Jim. Mine. Not yours. So tell me what the hell is up."

Jim's face darkened, his eyebrows veed down over his nose. "You're hurting right now, Hank. I'm going to keep that in mind. But don't tell me I'm not family. I held your mama when you were just a baby and she cried over your daddy getting killed in Vietnam. Hell, I even diapered your bottom. And I'm the one who made trips out to California to check on the two of you after she moved you there. *And* I gave you your first flying lessons when you came back East at eighteen. Don't you go forgetting any of that history."

Hank had gone over a line and he knew it. "I'm sorry, Jim. I shouldn't have said what I did. You are family. You and Mary, both. Like parents to me. I mean that. It's just, well, you know how the old man was. Damn, I could never relax. It seems I've spent about half my time dealing with his disasters. Cleaning up after him was like fighting wildfires. You never knew when or where the next one would crop up. Mother says he was always that way. Goodhearted yet crazy as hell. She said it took more energy than she had just to be around him."

Jim's laugh said he'd let go of his anger. "I hear you. The old man was all that and more, wasn't he? Never met a stranger for whom he didn't open his wallet. Now, speaking of your mother, have you told her yet about this woman and the will?"

"Please. You know what Lady Lillian is like. She's another one who needs an adult to be in charge of her."

Jim's gaze roved over Hank, and his expression softened. "You never got to be a kid, did you, Hank? All your life you've had to parent your mother and your grandfather. Always be on guard. It's no wonder you never relax."

Hank shrugged off Jim's observation. "It wasn't all that bad. I had fun. When I was a kid. But about Mother, I'll tell her later. She tends to go off like a rocket. And right now I just want to do this myself and in my own way."

Jim's grunt made as much of a point as did his words

that followed it. "James Senior said the same thing to me. He wanted to do this himself, his own way. That stubborn, independent streak does run strong in the Madison blood. I've certainly seen plenty of evidence of it over the years."

Hank chose not to respond to that. Instead, he again gazed out the tinted window to his left. His mind chose to show him a scene from his past . . . him making the decision as a skinny, uncertain high school graduate to leave his mother and California to come back East and attend Harvard. Sixteen years ago. In that time, Jim had guided him, had talked easily with him of such manly things as women, boating, malt liquors, women, business, golf, women, sports, the stock market, women, things like that.

Jim had shown him how to be a man. It was that simple. And Jim's wife Mary had spoiled Hank terribly. Still did. With no children of her own, she called him her adopted son. What would he have done without her? She was warm, loving, stable, sweet, where his real mother was flamboyant and impossible—but a tiger where he was concerned, that was true. She fiercely loved her only child. So did Mary. And so did Jim. They were a family. Not by anyone else's definition, maybe. But a family nonetheless—

"It's beautiful here, isn't it?"

Jim's cheery comment yanked Hank back to the moment. "I hadn't noticed. Too damned tired, I guess."

"Or too deep in thought," Jim said. "Look around you. My God, it's great here. I can see why James Senior loved Hanscomb Harbor. I wouldn't mind spending some time here myself. How about you?"

"Don't bet on it. I won't be staying here any longer than I have to. And after that, I'll never be back, Jim."

"Never say 'never,' son."

Again, Hank heard nothing there that required a response. He sank back against the tufted leather of the seat and lapsed into silence as he stared out his window and watched the picturesque village slip by in seeming slow motion. They had no choice but to proceed at a snail's pace. Given the narrowness of the curved lanes, some of them cobbled, his chauffeur Burton was forced to maneuver the stretch limo with great care. Surprising Hank was the realization that suddenly the harbor town on the other side of the darkly tinted window was capturing his attention. He hadn't expected that it would.

Hank had been to many New England fishing villages in his life. But this one was different somehow. Charming and picturesque, yes. But to the point of surreal. It was disconcertingly like a theme park come to life. Clean, well kept, orderly. There should have been a fence around it and someone in a booth at the town's entrance who was taking money and handing out tickets. Actors should have been walking around in period clothing. He looked for a sign telling visitors what time this place closed. *Just look at this.* The quaint buildings and shops, the weathered boats, and the crusty old fishermen, even the tourists, looked handpicked for realism.

It was too much. There was even the requisite town square with its gazebo, the bait and tackle shop that offered fishing excursions, the expected tavern, many brightly painted houses, and even two steepled churches. And a lighthouse. It looked more like a movie set of a New England fishing village than it did an actual town. Hank believed he wouldn't have been surprised had some movie director stepped up to yell, "Cut!"

"I really wish you would have waited until the reading of the will, Hank, to meet her," Jim said into the silence. "This trip is unnecessary and ill-advised."

"I think that's about the fourth time you've said that since we left New York. I heard you on the ride to the airport, then during our flight, again when we landed, and now here. So, point taken, all right?"

Jim sat forward and ran a hand over his round and balding head. "I'm not so sure it was, Hank. You hear me, but you're not listening. I told you yesterday that I sent Miss Copeland a letter notifying her that the reading of the will is set for next Tuesday. She wouldn't even have gotten my notification until today. And may not even know about it yet, if her mail hasn't come."

"I promise you that late mail will be the least of her problems after today. And this Miss Copeland woman, what do we know about her? Don't tell me something stupid like my grandfather married her right before he died."

"No. Nothing as lock, stock, and legal barrel as that. I believe they were just friends. But I am sorry you found out about her before next Tuesday."

Hank stared at Jim's heavy-boned, jowly face. Though he loved and respected this man, he'd always thought Jim's head was too big for his body. "You're sorry I found out about her? What were you going to do? Just spring her on me on Tuesday?"

"That was how James Senior wanted it done, yes."

Exasperation ate at Hank. Could his grandfather have been more quirky? "Why? What's the need for all this secrecy? I don't get it. I'm just glad that your junior associate—what's his name?"

"John Carouthers."

"Right. John Carouthers. I'm just glad that he told me."

"Well, you're the only one. Carouthers has a lot to learn before he becomes a partner. If he becomes a partner. Look, I saw how the news hit you when he let it slip that he'd been at the hospital in Indian Neck with me the night your grandfather died. And that's why I insisted on coming along today, Hank. I think it only fair to tell you before you meet Miss Copeland that what James did and how he handled his affairs . . . well, it wasn't like you make it seem."

"Oh, I think it is, Jim. I think it's exactly how it seems."

"And I'm telling you that it isn't. I've met her. You haven't."

"So you keep saying."

Planting his elbows atop his knees, Jim knit his fingers together into one fist and held them against his lips. For long silent moments, he stared at Hank across the leather-seated, thick-carpeted, luxurious car. Finally he moved his hands and spoke. "I advised him against his course of action, Hank, just as I advised you against this one. There was no real need for you to come here just to see what she's like. But James Senior didn't listen to me any better than you are right now. All I can tell you is that he loved you very much. And he did what he's done out of love for you."

Hank's strong emotions had him sitting forward. "Jim, he did what he's done, as you put it, because he was nuts. I loved him, but he wasn't even on the chart. Neither is my mother. Which makes me worry about myself. But the point is, we should have had him declared incompetent years ago."

"But he wasn't."

"Well, it certainly seems so from where I'm sitting. That would have at least given me a reason, something to point at when I try to understand why he behaved the way he did."

Jim exhaled softly. "I do know what you mean. I can't pretend that I ever understood him, not in his later years. I sometimes wonder, though—and I don't mean to hurt you—if he did the things he did to get more of your attention, Hank."

Startled by that, Hank sat back. "Mine? I saw him every day unless I was . . ." He didn't want to say the word, but he was too honest. "Busy." The emotions hit him like a blow. "Unless I was too busy. Damn, Jim. What's wrong with me? Did I ignore him?"

"If you did, it was because you had to, son. Hell, you took over Madison and Madison—one of the largest advertising firms in the world—when you were right out of college. And you've worked your butt off since then to make it even more successful. There's only one of you, so don't be hard on yourself. I was just talking out the side of my mouth. Ignore me."

Hank wanted to, but he couldn't. Retreating into his troubled thoughts, he wondered if maybe Jim was right. Maybe—

"I have to tell you, Hank," Jim said, breaking into the silence between them, "that I hope you haven't come here to take out your frustrations with James on this unsuspecting woman."

"Unsuspecting? Like hell she is. She's evidently a major player here. Still, give me some credit. I'll behave." Hank searched his mood, then added, "I think. Maybe. It depends."

"Oh, Christ. Depends on what?" Jim's brow wrinkled with obvious concern.

"On whether or not she's another gold digger who took advantage of my grandfather."

"She's not."

"Now how the hell do you know that? She had to know who he was and what he was worth."

"Oh, I'm sure she did. But I don't think it mattered to her. I really don't."

The cynical side of Hank had him all but snorting. "Now, how would you know that?"

"Because I've met her twice. Once at the hospital and then briefly at the funeral the other day. And I talked with James about her. She didn't strike me as a gold digger at all. Remember, I deal with that kind of thing all the time with some of my clients. So I know one when I see one."

"Maybe."

Jim pinched his lips into a stubborn pucker. "We'll see soon enough, Hank. But I think you'll be surprised. Pleasantly so."

"Right."

Just then, an electronic whisper of sound alerted Hank that Burton had pushed the button to lower the darkened privacy window that separated the chauffeur from his passengers. The glass smoothly disappeared into its casing, showing Hank the back of Burton's head and George's head. Sandwiched between the two brawny bodyguards was a glimpse of the bright day outside. Hank could see that the cobblestoned street meandered off to the right, taking with it the land. Ahead of them and to their left was only ocean and sky.

Looking into the rearview mirror, Hank met his driver's gaze looking back at him. "We're here, Mr. Madison."

"Thank you, Burton." Hank returned his attention to Jim Thornton. And suddenly saw a balding sad old man who'd just lost his best friend ever and his first client. A man whose suit swallowed him like it was a too-big sack. He saw a man he'd known and cared about all his life. A man who'd had a hard job to do and had been caught in the middle. The messenger. They always kill the messenger. "Jim," Hank began, "I'm sorry if I'm taking this out on you. And I'm glad you're here today to keep me from behaving like such an ass."

Jim smiled. "You're a good man, Hank. And I know you'll do the right thing." He sat forward, gesturing excitedly to the outside. "Come on, I'll introduce you to Miss Copeland. Give her a chance. You might find that you like her as much as James Senior did."

"I doubt it," Hank said sourly, a last vestige of resistance wriggling about inside him. She was probably some middle-aged sharpie who'd latched on to a rich old dying man in order to secure her own future. Give her a chance? Hell, he'd give her a payoff, was more like it, and never see her again. He had a nice round number in mind, something in the low seven figures. It had worked before and it would work now. Having ordered that in his mind, Hank felt ready to meet this Miss Copeland. He directed his attention to his driver. "All right, Burton. Let's do it."

"Yes, sir." Burton and George exited the limo, closed their doors, and opened the back doors for Hank and Jim to step outside into the warm sunshine of the summer day.

With Jim at his back, Hank stepped out of his limo and onto a narrow strip of tree-shaded, slightly buckled sidewalk that fronted the perfect gift shop for this town. He checked out this territory with the sharp eye of a marauding knight about to lay siege to an embattled castle. Bay window for displays. An array of summer and beach items colorfully graced the window. The building itself was shingled with pinkish weathered wood. A low gabled roof. Beveled-glass panes in the door. A sign constructed of a heavy plank of wood hung from two big brass hooks. Maddie's Gifts, it said. Not very inventive. But still, she was a shop owner, so Hank could applaud her entrepreneurial spirit, if nothing else.

"What do you think?" Jim said, sounding like a hopeful, helpful realtor. "This place has potential, if you ask me."

Hank turned to his grandfather's friend. "Potential for what?"

"Real growth development, Hank. Come on, use your creative eye here. You're the wonder kid of advertising. This whole town could use a dose of savvy publicity, don't you think?"

"A dose of something, all right," Hank muttered, his hands planted at his waist as he squinted judgmentally at the storefront. Just then he caught a glimpse of a bobbing white head attached to an elderly woman inside the shop. As he watched, she crossed from one side of the display window to the other—in the direction of the door. Hank turned to Jim. "Let me guess. *That*'s Miss Copeland, right?"

Before Jim could answer, the shop door opened with the musical accompaniment of a tiny tinkling bell. The grandmotherly woman in a parrot-green pantsuit called it a "stupid ass of a freaking bell" and then poked her white head outside to glare at him and Jim. "Well, are you coming in or not?" she wanted to know. "The suspense is killing us."

Oh, Lord, what now? At the back of her shop, behind the jewelry counter where the cash register resided, Maddie abandoned the account books spread in front of her and stared at her employee's back. Celeste had just called out rudely to the people exiting a black limo. Maddie's field of vision was partially blocked by the many gift-laden display units that crowded between her and the shop's front bay window. But from what she could see, there were two men. Two really big humorless men with bull necks and football shoulders. And they were advancing on her shop.

They had guns under those suit coats. Maddie couldn't see any weapons, but she just knew the men were carrying guns—guns they would probably use to shoot Celeste before this little exchange was over. The prospect didn't frighten Maddie. She knew mere bullets would only bounce off that ornery woman who was also able to leap tall buildings in a single bound.

Maddie felt it only fair that she should rescue the unsuspecting men from Celeste. She hurried out from around the counter. But as with most well-intentioned acts, she was too late. She stopped. The men were inside. Their crew cuts, aviator's sunglasses, and dark suits did nothing to alleviate Maddie's tension. Silently they looked the shop's interior over. Automatically Maddie did the same, wondering what they expected to find. She couldn't detect anything amiss or the least bit threatening. Well, except for Celeste. Maddie again faced the men, who had yet to speak. Who were these guys? Were they gangsters? Were they from the government? It was hard to tell the difference these days.

Then, apparently satisfied that everything was okay, and with their feet apart and their hands folded together loosely in front of them, they stared impassively down at Celeste. She stood about as high as their belt buckles, yet hadn't backed down one inch. Her arms were crossed under her bosom as she flagrantly looked them up and down. She then pivoted to look over her shoulder at Maddie. The older woman's brown eyes were widened in wonder. "Just look at the size of the pair of them, will you? I saw pillars in the Coliseum in Rome that weren't this big."

"Dear God." Maddie rushed forward, grabbing Celeste by the arm and tugging her back as she fussed into the older woman's ear. "You have never been to Rome. Not even Rome, Georgia. Now let the nice men inside to look around." She smiled at the nice men. "Please. Come in. Look around. Let me know if I can help you with anything."

The two men didn't move or speak. Maddie's eyes rounded with the mystery of it all.

Just then, Celeste clutched Maddie by the bib on her red shop-apron and pulled her closer. "See those bulges there under their coats?" she whispered loud enough to be heard several blocks away at the noisy arcade. "Those aren't their happy meters, I'll wager. No, ma'am. Those are guns."

Breathless with shocked embarrassment, Maddie frantically whispered into Celeste's ear. "I know they are. So will you stop digging our graves with your words, please?"

Celeste pulled back, her mouth already opening with a retort that was never spoken because the two big men suddenly and silently moved apart, one to each side, and allowed—surprise!—two other men to enter the shop single file.

Maddie gasped. She recognized the first man advancing through the door. "I know you," she said, releasing Celeste as she went to greet him. "You were at the hospital. And James's funeral, weren't you?"

The older man approached her, smiling, his big hammy hand held out to her. "Yes, Miss Copeland, I was. Jim Thornton. It's nice to see you—"

"Oh, wait just a damned minute here."

Startled by the other, younger man suddenly pushing his way between her and Mr. Thornton, even as he interrupted their conversation, Maddie took a step back and stared the way of the interloper. And forgot how to breathe. *Zing!* went the suddenly alive strings of her heart. They fairly vibrated with awareness. Maddie had to stiffen her knees. The man standing in front of her was some serious *GQ* cover-model material. How in the name of every female hormone that was supposed to be on the job could she have overlooked him?

This man, whoever he was, with his athletic good looks and his dark hair and piercing black eyes, reeked of affluence and sensuality. To say she had trouble breathing, much less standing, was an understatement. In fact, she had all she could do not to look up to the ceiling and mouth, *Good job, God.*

Yes, the man was all that. And he was mad, too. Despite being entranced by his physical self, Maddie could only stand helplessly by as he railed at Mr. Thornton. "Are you kidding me here, Jim? And you said this wasn't what I thought. Like hell it isn't. I know exactly what this is. Look at her." The Adonis jerked a thumb Maddie's startled way. "She's young, a blue-eyed blonde and gorgeous. No wonder James Senior raced here every summer. Christ, I would, too."

Maddie didn't know whether to be complimented or insulted.

But Celeste did. "Hey, easy now, young fella. You can't come in here calling Maddie a gorgeous blue-eyed blonde. You take that back—or you'll answer to me."

Maddie tugged her little bulldog employee back to her side. "It's okay, Celeste. Those aren't bad things he said, honey. I'll take it from here." She smiled at the younger man, who didn't return it, and felt a bit disconcerted. "I don't think we've met, yet you seem to know me. So I'm going to take that to mean your being here today has nothing to do with souvenir shopping. And since you're here with him"—she indicated the older man—"maybe this has something to do with James?"

The handsome man nodded, looking hard and angry. "You guessed right. James Senior was my grandfather."

His words bludgeoned their way into Maddie's consciousness. "Ohmigod. *Your* grandfather? You're Hank? *You're* James's little grandson?"

"Well, I'll be a son of a bitch," Celeste slowly intoned, crossing her arms over her bosom.

Everyone ignored her in favor of staring at Maddie, who felt compelled to explain. "I'm sorry, but that's how James described you, you know. His little grandson. But you're not little at all, are you?" The flames already in her cheeks burst with renewed heat. "I mean, you're certainly not what I expected."

"I guess I'm not." His expression hardened. "But you are. You are exactly what I expected. Don't think this hasn't happened before or that I don't know how to deal with women like you. Because I do." The disgust for her that he felt was evident in his words, but he compounded the insult by giving her a look meant to shame her.

"Excuse me?" As suddenly over him as she had been captivated by him, Maddie bristled with insult. "Not that I owe you an explanation, but James was my friend. And that's all. So I don't think I like your insinuations."

"Neither do I," Celeste said. "Insinuations won't cut it around here, young man. If you got something dirty to say, you just say it right out loud where we can all hear it. I know I want to."

"Celeste, please," Maddie fussed while tugging her X-rated employee back to her side. "I'll take care of this." She then proceeded to do just that. "You," she said to James's grandson, "can show some respect, or you can take these two big men here and this man—" Exasperation warring with anger, she turned to the balding man whose head appeared to be too big for his body. "Who *are* you, anyway?"

He again held out his hand for her to shake. "Jim Thornton. I'm the late James Senior's friend and attorney, Miss Copeland."

Ingrained manners prevailed. Maddie shook his hand and nodded civilly. "Pleased to make your acquaintance." She then rounded on the grandson. "I'm sorry for your loss. Your grandfather was a wonderful man. Now leave."

Hank Madison bristled, his eyebrows lowering like thunderclouds over his deep-set eyes. "I don't think you are in a position to be dictating terms here."

"And yet I am." Maddie's heart pounded with the strong emotions of the moment. Despite her anger and her insult, she felt energized and alive in ways she hadn't been for a long time. She feared it had way too much to do with Hank Madison. "This is my place of business. My property. Hence, my terms, Mr. Madison."

"Miss Copeland, please," Jim Thornton soothed, even as he took James's grandson by the elbow. "We didn't come here today to upset you."

"Well, you've done exactly that. Because I am very upset. Nor do I have any idea what is going on here or even what this is all about."

The attorney turned to the younger man. "See? I told you she didn't. And I told you not to come here today, didn't I? I told you no good would come of this, Hank. But would you listen to me? No. And now you've upset her."

Hank Madison's dark eyes narrowed. "That's not all I'm going to do."

A frisson of fear slipped over Maddie's skin. She eyed the big men with the guns. They hadn't moved. Still, she exchanged a worried glance with Celeste. For once the tiny little terrier of a woman had nothing to say. That scared Maddie worse. And because it did, she planted her hands at her waist and forced herself to speak calmly and quietly. "Are you threatening me, Mr. Madison?"

"Hardly. I'm talking about legal options. I'll see you on Tuesday." With that, he pulled his arm from Mr. Thornton's grip, wheeled around, and signaled to the two hit men or whatever they were. "Let's go." They fell in behind him, then one slipped around him to open the tinkling-bell door.

Maddie addressed the remaining man, the attorney, who was clearly distraught. "What does he mean, he'll see me on Tuesday? What's going on?"

Jim Thornton looked from her to the limo outside. Maddie followed his gaze and saw one of the really big men standing on the sidewalk and holding open the back door of the limo. He made a show of checking the time on his watch. An obvious signal that the attorney needed to hurry. Mr. Thornton exhaled and turned back to her. "Has your mail come today?"

"What? My mail? No."

Celeste clucked her tongue. "That Mr. Canardy. I swear he brings the mail around when he gets good and ready. Like it's an imposition on his time. Mind you, it's not a large post office here, and he is the only one that runs it. But it keeps him busy and out of his poor wife's hair. She doesn't have much of that, you know. Hair, I mean. She's losing it. Could be stress."

Maddie joined the attorney in quietly staring at Celeste. "Dear, I don't think Mr. Thornton really cares about all that."

"Well, he was the one who asked about the mail."

Mr. Thornton took it from there, addressing Maddie. "I am so sorry all this happened, Miss Copeland. James never meant for it to be like this."

"James never meant for *what* to be like this? I still don't know what's going on."

"I know you don't." He glanced outside again before speaking hastily to Maddie. "Look for a packet from me in your mail. You should get it today. It's an official notification of the reading of James's will on Tuesday."

"His will? What does that have to do with me?"

"You're named in it."

"I'm named in James's will?"

"Most definitely. Also in the packet you'll get is your itinerary."

"My itinerary? What do I need an itinerary for?"

"Your trip to New York City. In case the packet from me isn't delivered today, let me give you my card. You call me." He reached into an inside pocket of his suit coat, pulled out a business card, and pressed it into her hand. "See you Tuesday."

Maddie glanced at the card and then at the man. "What has James done? He's really upset his grandson, whatever it is."

Jim Thornton chuckled softly. "Yes, he has. But, you know, Miss Copeland, I think James was right. You *are* perfect. I'll see you on Tuesday." With that, the older man turned and hurried out of the shop.

He almost collided with Mr. Canardy coming in with the mail.

CHAPTER TWO

❧

THE LAW OFFICES OF Thornton Cowling Drake Silverman and Hodges et al. were presidential, palatial. The offices occupied several floors of a midtown Manhattan high-rise. Surrounding Maddie on that Tuesday afternoon in Mr. Thornton's office were polished woods and gleaming marble. Entire pillars of marble. Valuable antiques. Thick rugs. A massive desk dominated the room. Wainscoted walls and elegant appointments rounded out the impression of wealth and power. Real power. This was an office from which you'd expect a head of state or a monarch to rule over an entire country.

As Maddie waited—she was early—she tried not to be overawed or intimidated by her surroundings. She sat on an elegant couch that was part of an intimate suite done in muted earth tones. She faced a huge marble fireplace set between two floor-length windows, which were covered in dark-cherry draperies. These were drawn back with gold tasseled cords.

Maddie crossed her ankles and tried to relax. She set her purse next to her as if she were afraid to take up too much room. From this vantage point, she surveyed Mr. Thornton's world. She couldn't even imagine such wealth as lay behind all this. Why, the president of the country should have it so nice. In fact, there on a wall was his picture with Mr. Thornton. *Great.* Maddie took a deep breath and swallowed. She wished this ordeal would hurry up and be over. It was nerve-racking. Not because of what might be in James's will with regard to her, she admitted, but because of the prospect of seeing Hank Madison again. *God, he is fabulous. And really, really mad at me.*

Maddie quirked her mouth for what would never be. She and Hank Madison. Not going to happen. Because, from what she could gather, given his anger and his insinuations last week while in her shop, he believed his inheritance was threatened by something she'd done. Maddie shook her head. Like what, for example? And he'd also said he knew how to deal with women like her. Maddie felt her temper rise. What was that supposed to mean? Could she be more in the dark here?

Thus disheartened, Maddie flopped backward on the sofa in a sprawl of arms and legs. In a fit of defiance, she kicked her pumps off. Her feet were killing her. She just lay there, staring absently at the fabulous painting across the way, which she deemed to be a priceless original. She could thus deem such things, since she'd majored in art history at Columbia and had worked for three years in the research department of the Whitney Museum here in New York.

A sudden prick of unease told her she'd better sit up and take stock of herself. "Right." In her efforts to right herself she knocked her purse off the sofa. The contents went everywhere. Lipstick, keys, compact, wallet, everything in its own direction. "Oh, lovely. Just great," Maddie fussed in a whispery voice as she went down on all fours and crawled around, quickly scooping up each item and dumping it back into her purse.

A sudden perverse thought occurred to her, there on her hands and knees. *Now would be a perfect moment for someone to come in, wouldn't it?* Spooked and certain an entire pantheon of attorneys were at this moment staring at her bottom, Maddie popped upright, somewhat like a prairie dog coming out of its hole. She looked all around. Still alone. A relieved sigh escaped her. She put a hand over her hammering heart. "Okay, so things like that only happen in Doris Day movies and not in real life."

Clutching her purse, Maddie struggled to her stocking feet and this time sat decorously on the sofa's overstuffed cushions. She thought to put her shoes back on, but that was also the instant when she spied the wet bar.

Chewing on a thumbnail, she looked all around. Still alone. She turned toward the bar again, this time hearing its siren song. Well, she had been told by that Mrs. Crane executive assistant woman to make herself comfortable. With such permission, the temptation became deed as, shoeless still, Maddie padded across the thick carpet over to the bar and sorted through everything while she talked to herself. "Hmmm. A German Riesling. Chilled. Uncorked. That says 'drink me.' "

Maddie plucked the dark bottle out of its bucket of ice and studied it. Had Mr. Thornton planned to serve this wine following the reading of James's will? Probably. She shrugged. So she'd get an early start. She plucked a wineglass from a hanging rack and poured herself a healthy measure of the white wine. The first sip was nirvana. Feeling better now, she stepped over to one of the floor-length windows that afforded her with—naturally, in these surroundings—a magnificent view of the city.

Allowing her gaze to wander where it would over the skyline, she set her mind to wondering what today was really all about. And how the coming revelations in this very office would affect her life. For better? Or for worse? Obviously there was money involved. Obviously James had kept things from her. A lot of things. Like that little grandson of his. Maddie put a hand to her steadily warming face. "Little, hell. What am I going to do about him?"

She hated admitting it to herself, but she couldn't lie to her own conscience. Yes, she'd spent the last three days thinking about Hank Madison. She hadn't wanted to think about him, but there he'd been—a fully grown and handsome red-blooded American male. Maddie shook her head slowly in appreciation of the man. "Just when you don't want one, there one is. Wow. What a perfect example of the whole breed he is."

But Maddie didn't trust herself with such men. After all, she'd thought she loved another fine example. Stanton Fairchild, M.D. No, she *had* loved him. He hadn't loved her. And he'd left her standing at the altar a little over a year ago. So there she'd been in her white dress with a church full of people, all shifting uncomfortably in their seats as she'd faced them and told them that the man she'd thought she'd spend the rest of her life with simply hadn't shown up. And everyone could go home. Which was what she'd done. Gone back home to Hanscomb Harbor. Thank God she hadn't moved to New York City yet. And so could just return to her house, where it was safe and where her heart was safe. Until Hank Madison.

"Dammit." At this point in her life she didn't even want to think about some red-blooded American-male type. Or any other type. Right now she was off them. Men. A woman couldn't count on them. "Oh, ha. Tell that to the hormonally charged hussy who controls my thoughts."

It was embarrassing. When she was awake, her mind kept replaying her confrontation with Hank Madison in her shop on Saturday. How many times since then had she startled herself with the realization that she'd paused her mental video in mid-argument so she could visualize him at her leisure? So she could linger over such details as his dark eyes, his darker hair, how broad his shoulders were, how his hands might feel on her. And when she was asleep, well, her little tart of a brain hadn't minded showing her how she really thought of the man . . . naked.

"I have *got* to stop doing this," she warned herself, forcing his handsome image from her mind. With an act of will, she focused on the wonderful reality of New York City on the other side of the window's glass. *Look at this place.* She couldn't help comparing it to Hanscomb Harbor. *Talk about a world apart.* No one had to tell her, though, that these two worlds were about to collide, that her immediate future most likely was somehow tied up with Hank Madison's. *Great.*

Suddenly angry with herself for being so captivated by a man who'd been nothing but arrogant and insulting with her, Maddie gulped at the Riesling. And glared out the window. Sure, she had to see him today. But after this, she could just stop thinking about him. It was that easy. Just refuse him access to her thoughts. Tell him to butt out of her dreams, tell him to take a flying—

"May I join you?"

Maddie shrieked and jerked around. The half-full wine-glass flew from her suddenly nerveless fingers—and hit Hank Madison, who was standing right behind her, in the middle of his chest.

"I'll take that as a yes." Unsmiling, Hank meant to play it cool with this little gold digger. Show her that he wasn't susceptible to her wiles and her charms. So why had his gaze locked with Maddie Copeland's frozen and horrified one? Damn. She was as beautiful as he remembered. Fine-featured. Delicate. Fair-complected. Full sensual mouth. Wide blue eyes. Arresting figure.

Stop right there. Think, man. All those things are her arsenal of weapons. You're smarter than this. You're not a frail eighty-year-old man. Resist. Hank gave himself a mental shake and again became aware that some expensive—and cold—vintage from Jim's stock of fine wines was soaking into his shirt and dripping down his slacks, right onto his Italian loafers. Funny how he hadn't really noticed, even though he could certainly feel its chill on his skin.

"I am *so* sorry," the blonde said. "I didn't know you were there. God, you startled me."

Hank pulled his handkerchief out of an inner pocket of his suit coat and dabbed at his shirtfront. "Obviously."

"I'm serious. I didn't even hear you come in. What'd you do—just appear in a puff of smoke?"

Hank met her gaze—and willed himself not to be moved by the deep blue and the silver lights of her eyes. "You mean like a magician—and not the devil, right?"

She cocked her head in an arch way that suggested she was on to him. "I don't know. Your choice."

Hank hoped his answering grin conveyed his let-the-games-begin attitude. "So, what were you so deep in thought about over here that you didn't hear me enter?"

"You, mainly. Well, no, I mean your grandfather. This place. What it all means; that will. And you."

"I see." This was good. She was concerned about his reaction to her being in his grandfather's will. She'd damned well better be. Hank pinched his wine-soaked shirt and pulled it away from his chest. "For future reference, I prefer my wine in a glass."

"I am so sorry."

He ignored that, keeping the game going. "So, what are we drinking here? I already know it's chilled." He smelled his now damp handkerchief and spied the wine bottle on the bar. "Mmm. Nice bouquet. A Riesling, perhaps? From one of the fine vintners in Germany?"

She looked impressed. "That's amazing. You got all that from a handkerchief?"

"I wish. But no. You left the bottle sitting out."

She confirmed this with a glance over her shoulder to the bar. Then she faced him again. "Cheater." She surprised him by plucking his handkerchief from him and dabbing roughly at his custom-made white dress shirt. "This is awful. Seriously. I feel so clumsy. I just can't believe—"

"Maddie." He grabbed her hand, holding it hostage. He'd startled himself by using her first name. It had come to him so easily. Hank realized rationally that he was standing there, holding her hand, and staring down into her upturned and sensual face. But rationality lost out to senses, which were shouting that her skin was soft, warm, electrifying. That her hand felt small and fine-boned. That nothing had ever felt so right as her nearness to him. Hank wanted only to pull her to him and kiss her deeply, soundly.

No. He meant he wanted to push her away and tell her to stay the hell away from him. With the old man gone, did she think it was time to work on the young man? He wanted to tell her that her feminine wiles were wasted on him, that she could stop the sexy-but-helpless-blonde routine.

Then she said, "Hank." Just the one word. His name . . . on a breathy exhalation.

Good sense fled. Hank dipped his head down to hers

and claimed her lips with a hunger that shook him. A current of tiny shocks abraded his lips the moment his mouth met hers. Forgotten in his moan of desire for her was the spilled wine, their surroundings, his suspicions regarding her, and everything else in the world except for the feel of her surrendering to him. She melted against him. His arms encircled her, crushing her to him. He deepened their kiss. Hungry, questing, probing the heat and the wetness of her mouth. She whimpered against him, and Hank was undone. He gripped her arms, breaking their contact, pulling back, peppering her face with kisses fueled by intense desire. "Maddie, God, you're all I can think about—"

"Oh, Hank, we shouldn't—"

"We should. I want to lay you down right here and take you." He held her to him and nuzzled her neck, practically growling his words into her skin. "I want you in the worst way. Christ, do you have any idea what you've been doing to my dreams lately? I can't think. Can't eat—"

"Hank, wait. Please." Maddie stiffened, pulled back. Finally hearing "no," Hank instantly throttled down and held her more gently, slightly away from him. He noticed her breaths were shallow, her lipstick smeared, and her pupils dilated. "This is insane. What are we doing? Look where we are."

"Where?" Hank couldn't think. All the blood had apparently left his head. He looked around. "Oh, man. Jim's office." He let go of Maddie as if she were hot. She was hot. So was he. Very hot. In fact he was surprised to realize that the wine that still soaked his shirt hadn't sizzled and steamed itself dry against his desire-racked body.

Maddie looked down at her wine-dampened blouse and pulled it away from her skin. "Oh no, now I'm all wet."

That was a line Hank wasn't about to touch with a ten-foot pole. Then he thought . . . what the hell. "If you weren't, I'd think I was slipping."

It took her a second, but she got his drift. Her cheeks flamed red with embarrassment as she looked away from him and began straightening her clothing, her hair, anything to avoid looking at him. She pushed his handkerchief into his hands. "Here. This is yours. Sorry."

Hank exhaled his regret at his actions. "Look, Maddie, I shouldn't have kissed you. I'm sorry. I had no right. Let's just call it a draw and pretend it never happened, okay? Because it's not going to go any further than this."

She drew back as if surprised. "Excuse me? Do you even hear yourself? I mean are you always this arrogant? Of course it's not going any further. And I don't know what made you think I wanted it to. Because I didn't kiss you, remember. You kissed me."

"And you kissed me back. But let me ask you your own question. Does *this* always work for you?"

As if totally confused, she shook her head, setting her golden blond hair swirling about her shoulders in such a way that Hank, despite everything, itched to stroke it. " 'This' what? I have no idea what you're talking about."

"All right, Maddie, look, drop the act, okay? It's going nowhere. Maybe we should just retreat to our corners and wait for Jim to come in."

"There is no 'act.' But fine. Separate corners work for me." She stepped past him, careful not to touch him.

Hank turned, watching her and hating himself for his lapse in resolve and then this behavior around her. She'd gotten to James Senior, but she wasn't about to get to him. That was his promise to himself. Yet here he was watching her slender, swaying hips as she headed for the couch, where he could see her purse atop a cushion. No doubt she intended to repair the damage to her makeup that he'd done with his kiss. *Oh, man, it wasn't supposed to be like this.* He really didn't want to like her. And he certainly didn't want to be charmed by her. Exhaling sharply, Hank busied himself with folding his damp handkerchief.

Perhaps his exhalation caught her attention, but whatever had, Maddie turned to face him. "I just want you to know that I've never done anything like that before. Kissing a man I hardly know, I mean."

Exactly what he would expect any gold digger to say. "Right."

"I'm serious. I'm not that type of woman."

"What type of woman is that?" He shoved his handkerchief back into his inner coat pocket.

"The kind who throws herself at a man. That's not me."

"If you say so."

"I do. And I wish you'd believe me."

"All right. I believe you."

"No you don't."

"Sure I do. Besides, you didn't throw yourself at me. I pretty much threw myself at you, as you reminded me. But I still say we both liked it."

She had no comeback to that. She just looked down and away and then opened her purse, pulling out a tissue and compact, which she opened and held up to her face as she wiped at her smeared lipstick. Fascinated despite himself with this feminine ritual that was somehow sensual, Hank watched her—and she caught him doing so. "You might want to consider cleaning your face, too, Hank."

She was right. He pulled out his handkerchief again and wiped at his mouth, all the while denying how much he liked her using his given name. He then happened to look down at her feet. "You're not wearing shoes."

Maddie's gaze followed his. She wriggled her toes. He couldn't stop the chuckles that had him shaking his head. Nor could he stop himself from wondering if she might be, could possibly be, as unspoiled and innocent as she appeared. What shook him the most was how much he realized he wanted that to be true.

Just then, the sound of a door opening behind him captured Hank's attention. "Sorry to keep you waiting. Had a client with an emergency. She has got to quit carrying a gun. Or improve her aim, one or the other."

Jim had spoken, calling out from the next room over, but first through the door was Mrs. Crane, the attorney's executive assistant. In her arms was a very thick file that no doubt contained the last will and testament of James

Henry Madison, Senior. Hank felt his heart rate pick up. In those papers was written his future. The efficient brown-haired woman set the paperwork on Jim's desk, smiled politely, and left the office.

Then Jim came in. He wasn't alone. The leash he held had at its other end a beautiful golden retriever. Hank brightened, recognizing Beamer, his grandfather's dog. Perfectly groomed but with her head and tail down, she padded into the room, a living picture of dejection. Hank's heart went out to her. She had to be missing her owner, the poor thing. Though a little surprised to see the dog here of all places, Hank nevertheless was grateful for the distraction she would supply. He called out to her and clapped his hands together. "Hey there, Beamer. What you doing, girl?"

Up came the dog's head and her ears. Recognition dawned in her big brown eyes. Grinning now, her whole demeanor transformed, she tugged against her leash and whined happily. Laughing, Jim released its catch from her collar. "Just what the doctor ordered. Go on, girl. Go say hi to your kid."

Hank grinned as the seventy or so pounds of sweet-natured canine energy bounded his way. He crouched down in anticipation of her boisterous greeting. "That's a girl. Come here."

To Hank's surprise, the dog tore past him, spinning Hank around in her wake. "Beamer! Where are you going, girl? Come here!"

But she wouldn't. Thoroughly excited now and yapping to prove it, the dog headed straight for Maddie, who stood frozen and wide-eyed in front of the couch. "Watch out," Hank warned, a hand extended to her.

"Ohmigod, no," Maddie gasped, both of her hands held out in front of her. As if that could ward off Beamer's enthusiastic greeting. "Oh, no, please. Get her away. I'm afraid of dogs."

Too late. Already airborne, Beamer pounced on Maddie, eliciting from her a hair-raising yell and sending her flying backward helplessly onto the couch's cushions.

"Oh, hell." Hank tore for the couch. "Get off her, Beamer! Get off! Down, girl!"

No such luck. With Maddie thoroughly pinned under her weight, the friendly dog whined and licked her victim all over her face. From under the dog, Maddie fought every show of affection coming her way, shrieking and tugging at the dog's fur. "Help me! Get her off!"

With Jim right on his heels and then helping him, Hank straddled the big, determined dog around her furry middle and tugged her backward. "Come on, now. Get off. Bad Beamer. Down. Where are your manners?"

Manners? As if Hank's had been any better a few minutes ago when he'd all but attacked Maddie, too, and kissed her. A thinking part of Hank's mind wanted to know what it was about this woman that had gotten to all the Madisons and made them act like idiots.

In only a moment, he and Jim had Beamer off Maddie. Jim leashed the excitedly barking dog and was diligently urging her back and away, two directions she clearly didn't want to go. The retriever lunged unsuccessfully in Maddie's direction. For his part, Hank went to Maddie's rescue as she struggled—all arms and legs and run nylons and disarrayed clothing and dog-kiss-wettened face and wild hair—to sit up or stand up, or whatever she was trying to do. It was hard to tell, exactly, what with her fighting his help and crying out.

Finally, Hank got her to her feet and held onto her arms as he put his face in front of hers. "Maddie, it's me. Hank." Not that he was a calming presence to her, he realized. But at least he wasn't the dog. "Look at me, Maddie. You're OK. Do you hear me?"

Clearly in shock from being accosted, Maddie stared blankly up at Hank. While he sympathized with her, he had to fight back a threatening chortle of laughter. Apparently more than one of Beamer's slurpy kisses had essentially moussed Maddie's hair out at a wild angle from her temple. She looked like a mad scientist whose lab had just exploded. Then she blinked and her vision cleared. Recognition of Hank shone from her eyes. She promptly burst into tears and melted against him. Encircling his waist with her slender arms, she held onto him for all she was worth.

Startled, meeting Jim's clueless gaze over the top of Maddie's head, which rested under his chin, Hank saw Jim shrug his shoulders as he held the dog's leash with both hands. Straying blond hairs of Maddie's tickled Hank's nose. With a nod of his chin, Jim silently urged Hank to comfort her. So, with really no choice, Hank put his arms around Maddie and awkwardly patted her slender back and said inane but hopefully comforting things.

After a moment, and as Hank tried not to feel her breasts mashed against his chest, Maddie said, "I'm sorry. I feel so silly, but I can't help it."

"Hey, no need to explain. Beamer attacked you." Could he sound more supportive and in her corner? This meeting was not going at all like he'd planned. He'd told himself beforehand that he'd undo her with cool and calm and reserve. And yet here he was comforting her and apologizing to her—after he'd already kissed her. He was no better than the dog. "I don't know what got into me. Her. I mean her. She's not usually like that."

"Well, she is with me," Maddie sobbed. "Every time she sees me, she knocks me down and licks me all over."

"Well, I can't fault her for wanting to do that," Hank heard himself admitting out loud. Maddie abruptly stiffened in his arms and pulled back, staring accusingly into his face. Hank immediately switched tactics. He turned, pointing at the golden retriever. "Terrible manners, Beamer. You know better. Apologize."

Standing four-square and flat-footed at the very end of her taut leash as it was still held valiantly by Jim Thornton, and singularly unimpressed with Hank's berating of her, Beamer lowered her ears and tail . . . and showed Hank her teeth. Not in a nice way.

A bit taken aback by that display, Hank focused again on Maddie, still so pleasantly ensconced in his embrace, and adopted a droll expression. "See? You have nothing to be afraid of. She minds every word I say."

Still looking frazzled, Maddie ignored all that. "You have to understand that a big stray dog bit me when I was a little girl. And I had to take rabies shots. I've been afraid of dogs ever since. Or of being bitten by one, I guess is more accurate."

"But Beamer doesn't bite," Hank assured her. "As you've seen, if you hold still long enough, all she'll do is lick you skinless."

"Excuse me, Maddie, but did James Senior know you were afraid of dogs?" This was Jim cutting in.

Nodding yes, Maddie finally pulled out of Hank's embrace and fussed self-consciously with her hair and clothes as she faced Jim. For his part, Hank tugged at his slacks' waistband and generally tried to act as if he hadn't been affected so greatly by Maddie's nearness.

"Of course James knew," Maddie assured Jim. "When he would visit my shop, he always had her with him. But he left her outside. It was that or have her break everything in my shop as she jumped on me and licked me to death. I must put out a pheromone or something that draws her to me."

Hank wondered—this time silently—if he'd reacted to that same pheromone just a few minutes ago when he'd been drawn to her and had kissed her with such abandon.

By now Beamer had calmed down enough to sit, although she watched Maddie's every movement with her big brown and adoring eyes. Hank caught the odd, bemused expression on Jim's face and said, "What?"

Jim blinked, shook his head. "Nothing. Or everything. This complicates matters even more. And I didn't think that was possible before now."

Instantly alert, again recalling why they were really here, Hank blurted, "Why? What's complicated?"

"Everything," Jim said. Then he frowned and really focused on Hank and then Maddie standing next to him. "Why are your clothes wet?" His glance fell to Maddie's stocking feet. "You're not wearing any shoes." He turned an accusing glance Hank's way and waited.

Exhaling a breath, and feeling busted, about like he was ten years old, Hank heard himself saying, "I don't know about the shoes. But we spilled some wine on us. Nothing more."

Jim's expression further wrinkled with confusion as he glanced the way of his wet bar and then back at Hank and Maddie. "So what'd you do—throw it at each other?"

"Hardly." Totally over this scene, which could only get more ridiculous, Hank signaled Maddie to precede him over to the chairs that faced Jim's desk. "Let's just get this will read and get on with our lives, shall we?"

CHAPTER THREE

⌾

"No, Celeste, I am being serious. Listen to me: this is not a joke. Okay, one more time and in a nutshell. The will." Maddie took a deep breath, preparatory to launching into the details. On the phone with her employee, she was stretched out that next evening in the hammock in her very own backyard in Hanscomb Harbor. Twilight was deepening. The air was warm and sweet and filled with the sounds of insects tuning up for their nightly serenade. And her life was totally screwed. "I know it's confusing. I keep trying to get a handle on it, but it's too big. The numbers, I mean. Astronomical. Yes, like light-years. But here we go.

"So, okay, James left me everything that was his, Celeste. Everything. Money. Billions of dollars of it. Houses. Cars. Airplanes. Helicopters. An actual airline. Real estate holdings in most states of the union. Entire cities. Farms. Banks. Malls. Stocks. Bonds. Portfolios. A globally known *Fortune* Five Hundred company—Madison and Madison Advertising, to be exact. And his dog, Celeste. Let's not forget the dog. I hear you. But how was I to know James was *that* Madison? He never said. I agree: you'd think it would have come up.

"No, I can't quit my job and sell the shop and the house and go on a shopping spree with you. No I can't. No I can't. Now, stop that and let me explain. I have no access to anything for six weeks. Because there's a big 'if' attached, that's why. Hank Madison? Is he pissed? Wouldn't you be? Exactly. He's all that and more. So here's what *he* has to do. I hope you're sitting down, Celeste. Good. The will stands—meaning everything is mine—unless Hank takes a *vacation* of no less than six weeks. No, honey, not a *vaccination*. A vacation. You heard me right. And it had to start yesterday. Yep. The very day of the reading of the will.

"Totally. Just drop everything, here's your packed bag, and go relax in, of all places in the world, Hanscomb Harbor. For six weeks. And while he's here, he can't perform any Madison-business-related work, either. No phone calls. No faxes. No meetings. Can't sign anything. Nothing. In fact, he can't even leave Hanscomb Harbor—or he loses everything to me.

"Quit cheering, Celeste. It's not cool. No it isn't. You need to know I don't want the money or any of the rest of it. I am serious. I don't want it. Because it's all too mind-boggling and complicated and it's not really mine. I wouldn't want it at another person's expense. Yes, I know I'm too nice for my own good. But I just think it's rightfully Hank's. So I don't want any of it. Not the money and especially not the dog. I know she's a sweet dog. But I don't *like* dogs. Remember those rabies shots I had to take as a kid? Haven't forgotten them or the dog that bit me.

"Now, don't sidetrack me because there's more. No, not more money, sweetie. More details. Guess what? I'm in charge of him. Hank Madison has to report in to me every day for six weeks. Exactly. Oh, he's very happy about that. Ecstatic." Maddie pressed the heel of her free hand to her throbbing temple as she listened to Celeste at the other end of the phone line. "Certainly it's insane. I mean, a vacation? How hard can that be? Why? Well, all I know is what Jim Thornton said. He's that attorney who came to the shop that day. Yes, the one who looks like a bulldog. Anyway, he said James had a lot of regrets about his life and believed that the Madison men are workaholics who don't learn, sometimes until it's too late, what is important. Exactly. All the mushy stuff. Families and love and companionship. Rest and relaxation. Time to smell the roses. All of those things. So this will was James's way of freeing his grandson from making the same mistakes he did.

"What? Why involve me? I guess because he liked Hanscomb Harbor and I live here and he liked me and trusted me to carry out his wishes. That's it. Seriously. Again, because I'm nice. Yuck. Anyway, if Hank stays here for an uninterrupted period of six weeks and doesn't work, he wins. And if he doesn't, everything is mine. No. I think it's awful. I do. For the same reason I would have hated it if my parents had left everything to a total stranger.

"No, Mr. Thornton tells me I can't just sign it all back over to Hank, should he fail and everything goes to me. It's more complicated than that. How? Well, if I don't agree to participate, or if Hank doesn't agree, then everything Madison will be put in some kind of megatrust something that I don't understand and Hank can't get to it. Right. Mind-boggling. So, the bottom line is, if I don't do my part, Hank loses. And if he doesn't do his part, he loses. *But* at the end of the six weeks—say Hank does his time here—then he gets his life and his holdings back. And I get James's personal fortune. Stop cheering and listen to me. Are you listening? Neither one of us can walk away. I agree. It's either insanely brilliant. Or brilliantly insane. I don't know which, Celeste. And it's all giving me a big headache. Look, honey, I'm going to go for now. I'll talk to you tomorrow, okay? Thanks for listening. Bye."

Maddie pressed the off button on her cordless phone and tossed it carelessly onto the hammock with her. Then she lay there, swinging gently and trying not to think. Even though she wore only denim shorts and a tank top, the August air felt warm as it caressed her skin. Overhead, a full moon flirted with the lengthening shadows of the day. In the blue-black velvet of the sky, starry night-lights coyly twinkled on. As if it were a game of tag, Maddie tried to catch them in the process but was unsuccessful. Smiling, taking a deep breath, she reached over to a small table next to the hammock and retrieved her iced tea.

Just then, the cordless phone rang, startling her into all but jackknifing and nearly spilling her drink. Fighting the suddenly unstable swing of the hammock, and limited to using only her one hand, since her other hand held her slippery glass steady, Maddie fished around under her body and finally came up with the phone on the third ring. She didn't have caller ID, but she suspected who this was. Hank Madison. Time for the prisoner to check in. Maddie took a deep breath for calm, blew it out, and answered. "Hello."

"Maddie? It's me. Hank Madison."

Maddie felt the hairs rise on the back of her neck. What a voice. It was as if he'd taken lessons to get that smooth, deep, pearls-rolling-around-in-whiskeyed-cream timbre to it. Maddie's nerve endings sent gooseflesh darting over her skin. "Hello," she said again, striving for his tone—cool and civil and businesslike. After all, this was no social call. Then she heard herself blurting, "Look, let me just say that I know you have to call me. But I'm also totally aware that I'm the last person you want to talk to, under the circumstances. And I don't blame you. I really don't. But I just wanted that said up front."

She heard a heavy sigh at his end. Somehow she knew he was running a hand through his hair. At least, that was what she pictured him doing. "I appreciate that," he said. "But I'm calling for more than one reason."

More than one reason? Maddie's grip on the phone tightened. "Okay. So what are they? No, wait. Hank, this is really hard. I had no idea what James was up to. None. I swear. I didn't even really know who he was—I mean, one of *the* Madisons. I thought he was just *a* Madison."

"So you keep saying."

Maddie firmed her lips at his tone. "I keep saying it because it's the truth." Hank responded with a silence that unnerved her and had her prodding him. "That's all I have to say. Your turn."

"Thank you."

His tone of voice, so cool and superior, really made her mad. How did he do this? One second she was apologizing to him. And in the next she wanted to tell him off, which meant she would again have to apologize to him. Like she needed this. Then she remembered that his life, not hers, was the one in the can right now. The emotional basement. Hadn't the guy had enough trauma and drama in the past week without her laying into him? Not that he didn't deserve it, but she just couldn't bring herself to smack him around right now. Maddie suppressed a sigh, hating that she never could stay mad at people. What was wrong with her? But she knew. She was nice. It was like a curse. "Are you still there, Hank?"

"Yes. Is there someplace here in Hanscomb Harbor where we can get a drink? One you won't throw on me, that is."

Bam. Her temper flared. "That was an accident."

"I remember. Will you have a drink with me?"

He was waiting for her to say yes. Maddie realized she was tempted to join him, if for no other reason than the privilege of feasting her eyes on him. But uncertainty on another score assailed her. Should she talk to him without a lawyer present? What if he tried to talk her into signing something or tried to get her to agree to some legal something she really shouldn't? Given how her libido behaved around him, she just might weaken and do it. "You're kind to ask," she settled on saying, erring on the side of caution. "But I'm not sure that would be such a good idea."

"Really? Why not? I think we could both use a drink, if you ask me."

"Well, you could be right about that." Still, she hesitated. She heard his breathing in her ear. Maddie told herself she was not affected. Yeah, right. Not affected by the man who was a major heartthrob and probably, in his circle, the most eligible bachelor on the planet, as well as one of the richest men on earth. Or had been until yesterday. *Thanks, James,* was Maddie's droll and defeated thought.

"So what do you think? Yes or no?"

Blinked back to the moment by the sound of his voice, Maddie considered the question at hand. A drink and where to get one. Then she thought of something else. "Did you bring your hit men with you?"

"My hit men? Oh, you mean George and Burton. No, they're not with me. Part of the agreement in the will."

"Oh. Right. I forgot." The will. It would always be between them. The realization had her stumbling badly and babbling. "Well, anyway, if they were, I would have been forced to bring Celeste with me."

"Celeste?"

That one word, the way he said it. He thought her an idiot and still she couldn't leave off this attempt at levity gone awry. "My employee. The little white-haired lady in the bright green suit. You remember her. Rude. Weighs about twelve pounds."

"Ah, yes. Vividly. But Maddie, you don't have to worry. Yes, I'm upset." He chuckled, but it wasn't because he was amused. "Now *that* had to be the understatement of the millennium. But I'm not violent. Besides, getting rid of you would only complicate matters and revert my inheritance to that trust. So, you're safe."

Was he kidding her or what? "You say that so calmly."

"Because I know I'm not violent. Or homicidal. If I were going to be anything, it would be suicidal. But I'm not that, either. Because if I offed myself, you'd win. And I hate to lose."

Maddie swallowed. No more Mr. Nice Guy, obviously.

"So will you meet me for a drink tonight?"

"Gee, how could I say no after all that? Such a heartfelt invitation."

"This is business."

"It sounded like it."

"Jesus, Maddie, can you cut me a little bit of slack here? Yesterday was the icing on a three-layer cake of one huge personal shock after another."

"You have every right to be off balance, Hank. I'll give you that. But you don't have the right to take it out on me."

Another humorless chuckle. "My apology. I can see how you're totally innocent in all this."

That did it. "You know what? You've checked in with me. Fine. You've fulfilled your obligation here. I'll write down your call in my notebook—"

"You're keeping a notebook?" He sounded incredulous.

"Oh, tell me you wouldn't. There's a lot at stake here.

And you know what else? If I were you, I'd be nice to me. I didn't ask for any of this, whether you believe it or not. But you do need me now. And that's not some power trip talking. I'm just saying you're in a hard place and—"

"And a man who finds himself already in a hole should quit digging, right?"

"Exactly."

Silence ruled the airwaves for several ticks on the clock. Hank spoke next. "All right. You're right. Truce? Let me buy you a drink? Remember, my grandfather thought I worked too hard and needed to relax. This is me relaxing."

Maddie rubbed at her temple. "Let's talk about that for a minute. I mean, I don't know you, but I don't get what's so hard about taking time off. So James wanted you to take a vacation. Obviously, this was a point of contention between you. Why don't you just take one and get on with your life? All you have to do is sit around on the beach. It's not like he said you have to go bear hunting with a stick or wrestle live alligators."

"I may as well because sitting around will kill me quicker. I can't do it. We Madisons are workaholics. And he knew that. He'd been one, too. I know you don't understand, Maddie. He was my grandfather. I loved him, but he was totally nuts."

"He was not. He was a sweet old man and—"

"I agree. But how would you like to chair a stockholders' meeting at Madison and Madison?"

"What?"

"According to my grandfather's will, you're the new chairwoman of the board. That means you get my life."

"Yeah, but only for six weeks. I don't have to really do anything—"

"Wrong. There's a stockholders' meeting next week in New York City."

That sent a cold feeling to the pit of Maddie's stomach that had nothing to do with her glass of iced tea. "Oh, God. He was nuts."

"That's what I've been saying."

Riding the wave of her panic, Maddie blurted, "So James just gives *me* a *Fortune* Five Hundred company and about a billion dollars in cash and tons of real estate and all the headaches that go with them—and *you* nothing because you worked too hard? Why in God's name didn't you simply take a vacation now and then, man? We could have avoided all this."

"Like I said, I can't, that's why. Not 'won't.' Can't. Well . . . couldn't."

"Help me understand this," Maddie wailed in desperation.

"I will. This would be easier in a smoky bar over drinks, but okay. I could never relax before, partly because my grandfather was like Elvis Presley."

That silenced her. Then she said, "You're going to have to help me here, Hank."

"I don't mean the music and the outfits. I mean every time my back was turned, he gave things away to strangers. Big things. Like cars. Money. Like Elvis did."

Maddie gave in. "I need a drink. I'll meet you at the Captain's Tavern. It's at the end of the boardwalk by the water. Give me thirty minutes."

"You got it. See you there. Bye."

"Bye," Maddie said, but he was already gone. She hit the off button on her cordless and gave herself over to her troubled thoughts. Just what did Hank think could come of their having a drink together? Obviously he wanted to discuss the will and that made her uncomfortable. There was nothing either one of them could do to change it. Jim Thornton had made that very clear. And surely Hank realized that she was the pawn here and not him. Surely.

Must be locals night, was Hank's guess. A couple of tourist types sat self-consciously at the long wooden bar inside the Captain's Tavern and chatted up the bartender. But for the most part, everyone here looked as if they'd answered a casting call. Rough-looking men, brawny types who were probably fishermen, Hank surmised, owned the pool tables and peppered the atmosphere with their boisterous talk. A few couples sat at the tables scattered around the place, and a friendly waitress moved among them, smiling and taking orders. Creating background music was the clinking of glasses and the bursts of laughter that rose above it all.

Hank realized that he liked it here. This establishment could become a trendy watering hole if the right people discovered it, he decided, viewing it with his advertising mogul's eye.

Seated alone at a table with his whiskey and soda, he looked around now with a touch of poignancy and a sense of loss. Had his grandfather come here? Had he maybe sat at this very table, the crazy old coot? Hank finally admitted it. He missed the old guy. Or would, once he got over being mad at him for his damned will. Hank shook his head at his grandfather's antics. Before this will debacle, Hank had really only been amused by his grandfather freely giving away things of great value. The money was, after all, from James's personal fortune and his to do with as he saw fit.

Of course, the grasping women out to rook James Senior had been another matter. When that happened, Hank had stepped in. But overall, what James Senior had done was merely be generous and kindhearted and make other people's lives better. Couldn't fault a man for that. Until this punch in the gut masked as a legal document. Hank raised his drink in a subtle and silent salute to his grandfather. *Thanks, old man. I never saw this one coming. But I've never been one either to walk away from a challenge. And you know that.* His sort-of toast completed, Hank took a healthy swig of his drink and watched the entrance to the bar. Any minute now his problem and its solution, all rolled into one pretty woman, would walk through that door.

As if he'd willed her to appear, she did so right on cue. Suddenly she stood framed in the doorway. Hank's heart all but stopped. *Damn.* And then he believed his hearing followed it. Because there wasn't a sound in the place. *What the hell?* Just then, the place erupted in called greetings, all of them addressed to Maddie. "Maddie, girl, how're you doing?" "Hey, Maddie, good to see you." "How you holding up, honey?" "Maddie, my kid said his first word today. He said da-da. Smart like his old man, eh?" "Maddie, buy you a drink?" And on and on. It was like *Cheers* and she was Norm.

Laughing and accepting the room's accolades, like some kind of queen, Maddie waved to everyone, shook her head no, and indicated Hank sitting there at his table. Mock groans and catcalls filled the air. Not knowing what to make of this, Hank shook his head and turned back to Maddie. Blond, slender, arresting, looking fresh and casual in jeans and a white shirt, she made her way over to him and said, "Hi. Sorry about all that. I grew up here."

"I figured." Hank surged to his feet, only to realize he was grinning and had a hand held out to her. As if he meant to pull her into a hug and kiss her cheek. The realization hit him like a brick wall and stopped him cold. Maddie stopped just as abruptly in leaning toward him. Her expression faded into a grimace of confusion as she searched his face. Hank suddenly realized she'd been intent on the same greeting. Now, that was interesting.

Maddie recovered first. "I'm sorry I kept you waiting. I had to change clothes and then the phone rang and it was Celeste—and I'm babbling and you probably don't care about all that, do you?"

"No problem." Hank stepped hastily around the small table to pull out a chair for her. He wished she hadn't mentioned changing clothes. All he could see now in his head were her long, firm limbs and the slender roundness of her wonderfully feminine proportions, scantily clad. *Easy, Hank. She's your jailer and possibly the enemy here.*

As she sat down, her perfume's flowery-musky scent, warmed by her body's heat, wafted up to fill Hank's senses. His blood threatened to leave his head and travel south. Behind her, Hank could only stand there, lost in his desire and hating himself because he wanted her. Christ, he couldn't believe this. The one woman in the world he didn't dare want, and yet he did. And she held his whole future in her slender hands. One wrong move from him, one wrong word, and he was done for. Boy, it didn't get any better than this.

Hank roused himself enough to return to his chair. He thought to signal to the dark-haired waitress but saw she was already on her way over to their table. Hank directed an inquiring look Maddie's way, wanting her drink order.

But the waitress usurped him. "Hi, Maddie."

He should have known. Hank sat back and watched the exchange.

"Hi, Stephie. How's your mother?"

"Good. She's out of the hospital now."

"Oh, I'm so glad to hear that. But she should know better than to eat anything Mrs. Hardy sends her. The woman is lethal."

"Honey, Mrs. Hardy brought the muffins right to Mama herself. What could she do but sample one?"

"Oh, God. Poor thing. Still, tell her I asked after her. And Bill, how's he?"

The pretty waitress grinned self-consciously and pointed secretively over to the pool tables. "Here every night, playing pool and talking trash to me."

"He hasn't proposed yet?"

Stephie all but sat down with them. "No, girlfriend, I tell you, men nowadays. Afraid of commitment? I guess. They think because they got the milk for free, they don't have to buy the cow—"

"Excuse me," Hank cut in, seeing how this could sour in a hurry. Both women gave him their attention. "Would you like a drink, Maddie?"

Stephie waved an apologetic hand at Hank. "Oh, sorry." She turned to Maddie. "Your usual, hon?"

Her usual? For some reason that made Maddie all too human to Hank. He had a sudden sense of a real, live person here who had existed with a full life of her own before she'd ever popped up to bedevil him. Of course, rationally he'd known that was true anyway. But still, confirmation of her life before now left him feeling jealous. As if until now he'd been left out of something fun. And still could be. *Goddamn will.* Yet he was acutely aware that without it, he most likely never would have met Maddie. Curious, that.

Then Hank heard Maddie's order. "I think a nice big glass of some chilled white wine will do."

"Very funny," he told her.

Sober of expression, essentially ignoring his comment, she looked him up and down. "In a glass big enough to cover an area, oh, I don't know, approximately sixteen and a half by thirty-four, I'd guess."

Amused despite himself, Hank looked down at his maroon knit shirt tucked into his khaki slacks and grinned. "Good guess." He turned to soberly address the cocktail waitress. "Bring me another whiskey and soda. And a white wine in my shirt size for the lady. Oh, and a couple of dry towels for me, please. I think I'm going to need them."

"Probably will with Maddie," Stephie chirped as she executed an about-face and flounced away, heading for the bar.

Maddie grinned at Hank. "I'm sorry. I couldn't resist."

He gestured his forgiveness. "Don't hold back on my account. So what's your usual here? Drink, I mean."

"Rum and Coke."

"Ah. A real drinking woman."

"I was. Not so much anymore."

"Really?"

"Yes. I finally got over a few things, let's say."

"Drowned your sorrows?"

"In a way. More like I washed that man right out of my hair."

"Anyone I know?"

She shook her head. "No. Not your grandfather. Although I do miss him and am sad at his passing."

Hank focused on his drink, then met Maddie's gaze. "Me, too."

She smiled sympathetically. "I can tell you loved him, even if he did drive you crazy."

A burst of sorrow tinged with momentary bitterness and anger swept over Hank. He swallowed, as if by doing so he could rid himself of the unfairness of it all. "I only thought he drove me crazy before, Maddie. He topped himself this time."

"I agree. And I think you think I had something to do with that. I certainly didn't."

Hank wanted to believe her. She seemed warm and genuine and intelligent . . . or she was a really good actress. He just didn't know which yet. He slouched against his chair's back and stared at her. "Maybe you did. Maybe you didn't."

Maddie threw her hands up as if defeated. "Where is this coming from, Hank? You act like I took James for his money. Or your money, I guess. Nothing could be further from the truth."

"Not in my experience."

Maddie started to make some comment but her friend Stephie made her appearance at their table with her laden tray. "Here we go." She put the wine in front of Maddie, the whiskey and soda in front of Hank, next to his previous one—and two fluffy white towels in the middle of the table. "You kids play fair now," she chirped, smiling big and moving on to the next table.

Maddie picked up her wineglass and sipped at it. Hank downed his old drink and set the squat little tumbler aside, pulling the fresh one in front of him. "You were getting ready to say something," he prompted Maddie, ignoring the tug on him of her deeply blue eyes.

"Yes, I was. But it can wait. You asked me here for a drink. And here I am. So . . . what'd you want?" Then she held up a hand. "As long as it's not about the will or legal business."

"It's not," Hank assured her, knowing better. But that was all right. He could go down this conversational side street for now. "It's about Beamer."

Maddie's expression fell. "The dog? What about her?"

"Gerta, my grandfather's housekeeper in Long Island, is

bringing her to town on Friday. She's yours now, you know, thanks to my grandfather's largesse."

Maddie's expression was remarkable for lack of expression. "I have no comment."

All Hank could see in his mind was Maddie in Jim's office with her hair spiked up with dog spit. He tried not to laugh. "Well, I just thought you might want advance warning so you could lay in a supply of kibble."

Maddie rubbed a hand over her face. "Oh, God. What am I going to do with a dog?"

"Well, you have to walk her, for one thing."

Maddie dropped her hand to her lap. "I know that much. I have just never wanted a dog after being bitten by one. And especially not a great big one who adores me."

"That's the best kind, from what I hear."

"So you say." Then she narrowed her eyes at him. "Mr. Thornton could have called me to tell me that."

"That's true." Surprising Hank was the realization that he was enjoying himself and didn't really want to bring up anything confrontational right now. "Okay, so the real reason I called you and asked you to meet me was . . ." He cast about for something. "That kiss yesterday."

"Oh. That." She looked everywhere but at him.

Hank watched her profile, wanting only to kiss her again. "Yes. That. I'm sorry it happened."

She cocked her head now and stared at him without blinking. "Well, thank you. You couldn't say that over the phone? You had to see my face to say you're sorry you kissed me? Great. I'm sorry you kissed me, too, by the way."

This wasn't going well. "I didn't mean it that way. The kiss was great. I just meant that I'm sorry if I surprised you with it. I shouldn't have done that."

"Oh. Well. Then . . . it was okay, I guess. The kiss, I mean."

Now Hank was insulted. Time to get back to business. "Before Stephie came over with the drinks, you were going to make some comment."

"I was? Oh, yes, I was. Well, I said no business, didn't I? But here I go. I was going to ask you what *your* experience has been that makes you think I used an old man to gain a fortune I don't want."

Hank shrugged. "Everybody wants a fortune."

"Not me."

Up until this point he'd been prepared to believe her. Everyone wanted a fortune. Everyone. But then she'd overstated her case. Or understated it. "Look, say you did, uh, use your feminine wiles—"

"Oh, stop right there. He was eighty years old, for God's sake. And a sweet little man—"

"The last woman was two years ago and she was twenty-three."

Maddie jerked forward, her mouth open with surprise. "What last woman? What are you talking about?"

"The woman my grandfather was going to marry because she 'loved' him." Hank said it sarcastically. "She'd already knocked off her first elderly husband a year before that. And she wasn't even the first one to try to get to James Senior. Not that they all wanted to kill him. But she was the fourth one. They saw an easy mark in my grandfather."

Maddie sat back abruptly and sipped at her wine. "This is incredible. I had no idea James was so vulnerable."

"Well, he was. But not a one of them got a dime."

Maddie's face colored. With guilt, anger, or embarrassment, Hank couldn't say. "Until me, right? And I got it all. That's the way you see this, isn't it?"

"You know, I want to. It would make everything else a lot easier. But I just can't really buy it myself."

"Why not?"

"Because this is a temporary situation. I sit for six weeks and then I'm out of here."

"Providing you can do it."

"I can do it. How are you going to feel when I do?"

"Relieved. I know you don't believe me, but that's the truth. I'm not like those other women, Hank. James was someone I saw in my shop or around town for about six weeks every summer. We were summer friends. So he didn't tell you about me because there was nothing to tell you. And no one could have been more surprised than me at the reading of his will yesterday. No one."

"Except me."

Maddie saluted him with her wineglass. "Of course."

Not blinking, holding her gaze locked to his, Hank allowed the silence between them to stretch out.

After about six ticks on the clock, Maddie's expression fell. "You still think I'm a gold digger."

"I didn't say it. You did. And I'm serious. Four other women. All blond. And that's my experience with my grandfather. And in my own life? Two. Women want us for our money."

"For God's sake. Either you're selling yourself short, Hank Madison, or you need to work on your personality. Or maybe you need to have someone else pick women for you."

Hank slouched back against his chair. "Suits me. Know any *nice* women?"

Maddie crossed her legs as she set her wine down atop the table. "Yes, I know a nice woman. Me. But you shouldn't equate nice with weak. And I think you do. I also think you're behaving like a spoiled brat. I mean big whoop. You have to take a vacation. Learn to slow down. From where I'm sitting, James did you a favor."

Hank shook his head. "No, he didn't. He totally disrupted my life, and you know it. But what he didn't know, and couldn't know, was the timing. I mean, his dying, as hard as that sounds, couldn't have happened at a worse time for Madison and Madison."

"What do you mean? What's wrong?"

Hank exhaled. "Two things. And I'm only telling you all this because I have to, since you're the chair right now." Totally undone by just the enormity of what could go wrong, Hank ran a hand over his face and muttered, "Christ Almighty." Then he focused on Maddie, figuring he looked as haggard as he felt. "Anyway, there's the stockholders' meeting next week. You have to chair that."

She slowly shook her head no. "Oh, I really don't want to do that."

"And I really don't want you to, either. But there's more. I've been working for two years on a major deal with a company in Japan. Major. Huge. I've been trying to get these guys to the table forever. And now, they're ready to talk. So how's your Japanese?"

"Oh, God." Her eyes rounded, her mouth turned down.

"Exactly." Hank leaned over the table toward her. "It's not about being a spoiled brat, Maddie. I think you can see what a tough spot I'm in. The timing couldn't be worse. I'm hoping you can see that I can't stay here and play these games my grandfather put in place. I just can't. If I don't show up at the office next week, there may not be a Madison and Madison to go back to. If nothing else, the documents require my signature. Aside from that, the stockholders are going to be spooked once the news of this damned will gets out. And that spookiness could kill the other deal if everyone starts dumping their stock. If that happens, then everything will tumble like a house of cards."

Maddie now looked as frantic as he felt inside. She'd leaned forward in her chair and her blue eyes were big and rounded. "But how's that possible? I mean, there's so much of everything. It can't all be tied up in this deal."

"James's personal fortune, everything you would get, no. But all of my assets, yes."

Maddie exhaled weightily. "I see. Wow. Sorry about that spoiled-brat thing. This is a tough spot you're in. But what do you want me to do about it? What *can* I do about it?"

Hank picked up his drink, brought it to his lips, and eyed her over the rim of his glass. "That's why I asked you here tonight, Maddie. Pretty much, I need to break the deal. I *have* to take care of this. And then we can start over."

Maddie picked up her wine and began drinking in earnest. Then she thunked the glass down on the table. "But if you do this—sneak away to New York . . . I assume you're intending to keep this from Jim—then you'll lose Madison and Madison anyway, Hank."

"I don't intend to lose my company, Maddie. Not by any means. All I'm asking for is a few days. And you can go with me. I'll broker the deal and you can chair the stockholders' meeting, all on the same day. Then we can come back here and relax."

"Until the next crisis. And after having already cheated and broken the provisions of your grandfather's will."

He was losing her. Hank started to feel too warm. "I see. Your sense of honor is involved."

She looked as if he'd insulted her. "Isn't yours?"

"Yes, dammit," he all but spit out. "It is." He ran a hand over his mouth and chin. "I could have simply gone, Maddie, and not told you and got back here without you ever knowing. I could have lied and cheated, but I didn't."

"It obviously occurred to you to do so."

"Yes, it did. It would to anyone, I think."

"You're probably right. But Hank, do you see that you're asking me to do those things now? Lie and cheat, I mean."

"I don't see it that way at all. For either of us. I see it as a couple days' reprieve. An aboveboard thing. We'll even get Jim's opinion, if that would make you feel better. All I'm asking for is a temporary stay of execution. Or vacation." He grinned and raised his eyebrows hopefully.

"Stop that," she cried, laughing at him. "Now you're trying to manipulate me."

Hank set his glass down and spread his hands wide. "Would I do that?"

"In a heartbeat you would."

Hank impulsively reached across the table and took her hand. He remembered its feel. So warm and small, yet elegantly long-fingered. "Come on, Maddie, work with me here. All I'm saying is I don't deserve to lose everything I've worked so hard for because my grandfather, whose company I was running, came unhinged on his deathbed, as cruel as that sounds."

With her gaze on his hand atop hers, she shrugged. "Well, it's a mess, I'll give you that. And you were pretty much blindsided by all this. Just as I was."

She was softening. Hank's heart rate picked up at this first sign of hope. "Are you saying you'll do it, Maddie?"

She shook her head and Hank's heart plummeted. "No. But I will think about it. I want to talk to Jim first."

Hank adjusted, releasing her hand, sitting back. "All right. That's fair. Talk to Jim."

Now she looked worried. "What do you think he'll say?"

" 'No' would be my guess. He's a real stickler. And an attorney."

"Yikes. Then what will happen?"

"That would be up to you."

Maddie frowned. "I swear I could just beat James for involving me with you Madison men. And God, I hate money and all the problems that come with having it."

Two strikes against him. He was a Madison man. And he came with the money. Therefore, he was one of those problems she'd rather not have. What surprised him was how that made him feel. Bad. Real bad.

"All right," she said, breaking the silence between them and standing up to leave. "So I'll think about it, talk to Jim, and let you know in the next day or so. Until I've made my decision, well, I don't want to see you. Just call me to check in, leave a message or something, okay? It will just be easier for me to do it this way. Thinking about this is all I can promise you, Hank."

He smiled, meaning it sincerely, and stood, too. "Then that's all I'll ask you for, Maddie." His appraising and masculine gaze slid over her. *For now,* he added to himself.

CHAPTER FOUR

❧

THE JOVIAL THURSDAY-EVENING CROWD of tourists packing the boardwalk frustrated Maddie in her efforts to find just one specific tourist. With frantic calls of "Excuse me!" she darted this way and that, skirting around people or bravely weaving her way through their thronging midst. *Where the devil is he?*

Then, miraculously, there he was up ahead. *Thank you, God.* Relief washed over Maddie, weakening her momentarily. Clutched in her hand was the man's money, plus some. She hurried to catch up to the tourist family who'd left her shop several minutes ago. They were now entering the open-air game arcade on the boardwalk. Maddie entered right behind them. Assaulting her senses were the bright lights, the dings and bleeps of the games, the children's happy shrieks, and the carnival music from the antique merry-go-round.

With her red bib apron still over her skirt and blouse, Maddie valiantly threaded her way through this even more densely packed crowd, desperate to keep the back of her target's head in her sight. "Sir? Yoo-hoo? Excuse me, sir? The man with the sack from Maddie's Gifts? Hello? There's been a mistake."

Hearing her call out and seeing her pointing at the man in the checkered shirt, more than one stranger got his attention and pointed back at Maddie. The man and his family stopped, turning to face her. "Are you talking to me?" the man said, his expression open and curious.

With a hand to her chest, as if that would stop the exercise- and fear-induced fluttering of her heart, Maddie nodded and swallowed. The crowds of people surged to and fro around her and the family whose evening of fun she'd just interrupted. "Yes, I am. I'm sorry to bother you, but a mistake was made at my shop."

The wife clutched at the man's sleeve. "What kind of mistake?" he said, not looking so friendly now. His fist closed tighter around the heavy gift bag from her shop. "I gave you the correct amount of money, didn't I?"

This was going to be a delicate transaction, Maddie could tell. "Yes, sir, you did. Correct as far as what my clerk told you was the price."

"You can't change the price on me."

Maddie was quick with a conciliatory smile. "Oh, no, sir. I'm not going to do that. In fact, I want to buy back your purchase from you, if I could."

The man exchanged a glance with his wife, who gathered up their three small children and headed with them toward the merry-go-round. "Buy it back?" he wanted to know, his gaze flitting to the curious onlookers stopping and listening. "Why would you want to buy it back? Aren't you in business to sell things? I didn't know your store was a swap meet."

"I understand your confusion, sir. I do. And I'd like to make it up to you. You see, the mistake was my clerk's. That particular item she sold you isn't for sale. What I'd like to do is refund to you the purchase price, plus twenty dollars for your trouble. Please." Maddie held the money out to the man, making sure that her pleading heart was in her eyes.

The man, a dark hairy brute wearing a Hanscomb Harbor souvenir fishing hat, eyed the money and then Maddie. "Well, that's real nice of you. But I want the lobster clock. I've never seen another one like it."

Oh, God. Maddie wet her lips and took a deep breath. The people pressed curiously around her and the tourist were being jostled by passersby. In turn, they bumped into her and the tourist, who was now in legal possession of James's ashes. Still, Maddie focused on not letting the big man lose face with the crowd around him. "You're absolutely right. It's a wonderful clock, and there isn't another one like it. Let me tell you why. You see, my friend died recently—"

Sympathetic *oh*s from the interested bystanders interrupted her. "Thank you. He'd lived a good long life," she said, acknowledging them before again focusing on the tourist, who was looking decidedly uncomfortable now. "And I hate to do this to you because, believe me, I know how it sounds. But, you see . . . well, my late friend's ashes are in that lobster's belly."

Disgusted *ooh*s and *ugh*s from the crowd now filled the air.

"Hey, it's not like it was my idea, okay?" Maddie announced to everyone around her.

"Good God, lady," the poor customer blurted. "Your friend's in this thing? Here. Take it." He shoved the fat, heavy bag—Celeste always went nuts with tissue wrapping—into Maddie's hands. "And keep the money. I don't want it." He rubbed his hairy hands on his black shorts as if they'd somehow been tainted.

Clutching James and his clock in one hand, Maddie held out the money with her other. "Please. Take the money. I insist. It's yours. And the extra twenty dollars." He shook his head no, "For your kids, then. Buy them an ice cream on me. I'm really sorry for this inconvenience and distress."

The man eyed her, the money, and the watching people around them. "All right," he said, dragging his words out and grabbing for the money. "For the kids. And thanks. That was nice of you. Sorry if I upset you."

Elated at the outcome—she had James back and perhaps hadn't lost any customers into the bargain—Maddie shook the man's sweaty hand and smiled. "I'm not the least bit upset. And I hope you're not. I just want to thank you for your understanding and wish you and your family a wonderful stay in Hanscomb Harbor."

With a big smile plastered on her face, Maddie groaned inside. Even to her own ears, she'd sounded as if she were the mayor or the president of the chamber of commerce. But her words had the desired effect. The tourist was clapped on the back and smiled at and told what a big person he was. Off he went with his new friends and in search of his family. For her efforts, Maddie received similar treatment, as well as a few more condolences on her loss, as she turned and made her way out of the arcade.

Maddie now stood on the relatively uncrowded sidewalk and off to one side of the arcade's busy entrance. She took a deep breath of the wonderful night air, an aromatic soup of seaside scents stirred with the fragrance of summertime itself. Thus fortified, she turned her gaze toward her shop. Her eyes narrowed murderously. *And now . . . to go kill Celeste.*

She hadn't gone more than ten steps before she heard, "Maddie!"

She turned around and spotted him. Her heart stuttered. "Hank." Her fingers closed spasmodically around the heavily wrapped package in her hands. Hank wasn't alone. "And Beamer. Oh, no."

The retriever spotted Maddie. Her furry floppy ears perked up with joy. She began howling and barking and tugging against her leash, straining in Maddie's direction. Tourists grabbed up their children and instantly cut the lunging animal a wide berth—clearing a path for the dog straight to Maddie.

"No. Uh-uh," Maddie warned, fearing she'd be trampled first by the dog and then the crowd in these close quarters. She tucked the lobster clock close against her side like a football and held her other hand out defensively toward Hank and Beamer. "It's not Friday. You said Friday."

Hank, using both hands to control the dog, blurted out, "Run, Maddie. I don't think I can control her. Go!"

She couldn't believe he was telling her to run. Was he kidding her? But still, horrified of being licked into submission—and in public—Maddie backed up another step as she glanced over her shoulder. She feared any moment her heel would strike one of the buckled squares of old sidewalk and send her reeling. It would be just her luck to have rescued James from the tourist, only to drop him herself and scatter him across the sidewalk and over unsuspecting tourists. Her nightmare come to life.

"I'm serious, Maddie. Go. Beamer's never been to obedience school. And she loves you. I don't think I can hold her much longer."

The dog lunged with great bounding happiness and nearly tore loose from Hank. Maddie forgot dignity as she shrieked and jerked around, running for all she was worth, running as if a whole clown-carload of circus dogs was on her heels. Clutching James's stupid lobster clock to her chest, she broke a few land speed records getting away, fearing as she did that any moment Beamer would tackle her and knock her to the ground and thoroughly slurp her to death.

"Well, great. You're really cool," Hank said, speaking to the suddenly docile and forlorn-looking golden retriever at the other end of the leash from him. Beamer turned big moist brown doggie eyes up to him and whined. "No, that's not going to work. Forget it. I thought big glossy dogs like you were supposed to be chick magnets, not repellents."

Beamer's flattened ears and narrowed brown eyes quickly brought him around. The lady was clearly offended. She sat there regally—facing away from him.

"Great. First Maddie. And now I've insulted the dog," Hank muttered. "I'm batting a thousand here with females." He tugged on the leash. "Come on, Miss Congeniality."

Apparently over her snit, Beamer obeyed, ambling along at Hank's side, the two of them headed companionably in the direction of Maddie's Gifts. "This doesn't change anything, you know," Hank said to Beamer. "I mean between you and Maddie. You're still her dog."

If Beamer had an opinion on that, she kept it to herself.

So, without further canine mishaps Hank and Beamer reached the front door of Maddie's shop. Inside, the lights were bright and customers milled around like off-duty ants. But it was the No Pets Allowed sign that stopped Hank with his hand on the big brass doorknob. *What now?* He exchanged a glance with the dog. But apparently Beamer knew where she was and what she was to do. Taking advantage of the slack in the leash, she padded over the few steps she needed to put her under the display window. She lay down like a sphinx and stared back at him, as if to say her being kept out of a place of business was a clear-cut case of dog abuse.

"Oh, stop it. It was your idea to go over there. What are you going to do? Call the SPCA?" Hank shook his head at being bested by a dog.

Then his gaze shifted to what sat on the sidewalk in front of Beamer's furry bulk. A big doggy water bowl of stainless steel. *Interesting.* Hank assessed the situation, seeing in his mind's eye his grandfather leaving Beamer out here when he visited Maddie. Suddenly feeling a little undone, and with his throat threatening to close, Hank peered into the shallow bowl. There was no water. Only dried bits of leaves and some dust. A shred of ribbon. And a tiny plastic spoon like you'd get with a sample from an ice-cream parlor.

The bowl had been empty for a while. Driven by a sudden need to set things right, he looked around and then took the few steps over to the side of the building. Given the night's darkness in the driveway between Maddie's shop and the next store over, a drugstore, he couldn't see a spigot anywhere and didn't feel as if he should trespass to hunt for one.

Acute frustration ate at Hank. Still, he felt compelled to wash the bowl out and put fresh water in it for the dog. But he was honest enough to admit it wasn't only for Beamer that he needed to do so. He needed to do it too for his grandfather. And for himself, so his grandfather wouldn't seem so . . . far away.

Just then, and behind him, the door to Maddie's Gifts opened. Hank expected maybe departing customers. Maybe even Maddie herself. No doubt by now he and the dog had been seen by someone inside. But the person standing in the doorway was none of the above. It was that tiny Celeste woman, garbed in a shocking array of orange satin and polyester under her red bib apron that matched the one he'd just seen Maddie wearing. So bright was Celeste's outfit that it hurt the eyes to look at her without squinting ... which Hank did.

"Well?" she greeted him, smoothing back from her wrinkled brow a stray lock of snow-white hair. "You coming in or not? The dog will be fine out here. She's used to it."

"She doesn't have any water," Hank heard himself saying.

"Then hand the dish to me," Celeste groused irritably, holding her age-gnarled hand out to him.

"Yes, ma'am," he said, stooping to pick it up and then shaking the debris out of it. He wanted to ask about Maddie but couldn't bring himself to do so.

"Hurry it up there. I've got a shop full of customers all to myself. I can't keep an eye on them and you too."

All to herself? Then Maddie hadn't come back to the shop just now? "Here you go." He handed her the bowl. She wrinkled her nose at its condition. "Thanks, uh ..." All Hank knew her by was Celeste, but he didn't feel he should call her that unless she invited him to do so.

"Celeste McNeer, one of the downtrodden masses forced to toil unto the brink of death. Now unclip that leash and bring it in with you. Beamer will stay put. Don't worry about her."

But Hank did. He worried. He looked from Celeste to the dog and back to Celeste.

Her heavy sigh was clearly one of impatience. "We don't aim to air-condition the outside here, son. You coming in or not? Much longer and my boss's electric bill will be more than the gross national product of Tahiti. Which is where I'm going to retire in my old age and wear a grass skirt. And don't you make the first senior-citizen joke about that, either."

"I wasn't going to." Fighting a grin, and instantly liking this woman, Hank turned away to unclip the leash. He then ruffled Beamer's ears with an affectionate swipe, and turned to go inside with Celeste. She stepped out of his way so he could come inside and then allowed the door to close behind her. The place was a mob scene of browsers and shoppers.

"Like I said, it's busy. Here." She gave him back the water bowl. "Go back there where that curtain is. There's a bathroom in there. Don't make a mess, or you'll be cleaning it up. Get the dog some water and take it to her. And then you can make yourself useful around here."

"Yes, ma'am." Like a mannerly little boy, Hank nodded his understanding of his orders. It had been a long time since he'd allowed anyone to dictate to him. But it amused him to see how readily he did the bidding of the tiny and fearsome Celeste McNeer. Not that he was afraid of her. He wasn't. It was just that discretion was, after all, the better part of valor. "Can I ask you something, Mrs. McNeer?"

"Anything but my age or how old I was my first time."

The chuckle broke free of Hank. He quickly covered it with a discreet cough. "No, ma'am, nothing like that. I just don't see Maddie here anywhere."

"That's because she's not. I already told you that. You slow or something, boy?"

"No, ma'am. I, uh, should tell you that Maddie probably won't want me here."

Celeste looked him up and down. "Then what are you doing here? You a troublemaker of some sort?"

Hank thought of his corporate image. "In some circles."

"Well, not in this one. And don't you worry about Maddie. I can handle her with one hand tied behind my back."

Hank's private opinion was that Celeste McNeer could probably handle three or more countries of medium size with one hand tied behind her back.

"Well?" Celeste arched her thin gray eyebrows at him and pursed her lips. "You coming or not? And don't act like Maddie's absence isn't your fault, either. Because I know better. And so do you, young man. Now, get that dog some water, and then the two of us, me and you, are going to do some serious work."

Locked in her house that was attached to the back of her shop and clutching James's still-wrapped lobster urn to her chest, Maddie sat in her favorite chintz-covered chair and tried not to be so angry or humiliated. But in fact, she was both. *Damn that Hank Madison, anyway.* He'd made her cry. She swiped at her nose with her wad of tissues. *The big jerk.* In the space of one week, he'd met her, accused her of being a hussy for money, kissed her, lost his fortune and his company to her, asked her out for a drink, had told her he was sorry he'd kissed her, then asked her to be his co-conspirator, and now here he was tonight—with a dog in tow that she didn't want.

And James. *Can we go there, huh?* What was he thinking with his new will, leaving her everything and his grandson nothing? How screwy was that? She didn't want to be a chairwoman of the board of anything. She didn't want to make this decision about allowing Hank to defect for a few days. And she didn't want James's dog. Or his grandson.

Yes she did . . . maybe the grandson, anyway

"No I don't." Maddie shifted to a hopeless flop, causing the gift-wrapped lobster to tip over to one side. Stubbornly, as if trying to push her out of the chair, the darned thing wedged itself between her and the upholstered chair arm. Maddie inhaled a shuddering breath. Evidently she was done crying because no more tears fell. All she knew was she didn't dare risk leaving Celeste alone in the shop with an evening full of customers. The ramifications were too hideous to contemplate.

Maddie knew that Celeste, left to her own devices, would give away the entire store, building and all. Maddie slouched down into the chair's comforting cushions and pronounced herself to be in a complete funk topped by a pout. A major dose of feeling sorry for herself. She hated it. "All right, girlfriend," she urged herself. "Pull yourself together and get yourself back to work. Right now."

With that, she struggled up from the chair and straightened her clothes. She eyed the wrapped urn. She straightened it, setting it upright in the chair. Leaving it tipped over seemed disrespectful.

With that settled, Maddie stepped over to a framed mirror above the tiny buffet in her diminutive dining room. She stared at her reflection in the glass. A groan escaped her. Her neck was red and splotchy. "Mirror, mirror on the wall, I am *not* the fairest of them all. Great." Her eyes were swollen. Streaks from her tears marred her makeup. Her mascara had run. And her hair was a mess. "Well, aren't I the embodiment of loveliness?"

Maddie went into the closet-sized bathroom with its 1920s fixtures and repaired what she could of her appearance. Within a few minutes she was opening the common door from her house into her shop and was stepping over the threshold into the storeroom. She closed the door behind her, pulled a ring of keys from her apron pocket, found the correct one, and locked the door.

Returning the keys to her apron, she made her way around the boxes and shelves of merchandise that stood between her and the heavy curtain that separated the storeroom from the shop floor. She stopped and looked at her watch. Good. The store would close in an hour. She could do this. Thus fortified, she resolutely walked to the curtain, pasted a smile on her face, and tugged the curtain back.

The sight that greeted Maddie stopped her where she was, the curtain still clutched in her hand. Her mouth opened, her pulse rate picked up.

Not twenty feet away, standing in profile to her and wearing a much-too-small red bib apron like hers and Celeste's, was Hank Madison. The man was waiting on her customers. Every female customer, that is. He was surrounded. It was like December, the women were children, and he was Santa Claus. He was enjoying every minute of it, too, she could see, if one could judge by his bright grin and his easy manner. As she watched, he pointed hither and yon to various displays. He described the merit of each item held out to him by one of the smitten ladies. He even went so far as to check a price and the future availability of an item.

Enchanted and bemused despite herself, Maddie finally let the curtain fall behind her and just stood there, her arms crossed under her breasts, and watched him. She couldn't really blame the women because she was a bit star-struck herself. All a woman could do, when she first saw him, was take in the whole package, consider the whole man. Only after a bit of staring could she begin to pick out individual features. Like his dark and wavy hair, cut short and stylish. His high forehead, those deeply black eyes, the aquiline nose, and that sensual mouth. The way he carried himself, his athletic physique, the way his clothes fit him. The way he smiled down at each woman who clamored for his attention.

A heavy sigh escaped Maddie. There was no doubt about it. Hank Madison was a major heartthrob. Just then, as if he'd read her thoughts and knew she was there and checking him out, Hank turned and caught sight of her. His gaze locked with hers. Maddie's breath caught, her bones melted. Something deep within his eyes softened yet seemed to heat up. He winked at her and turned his attention again to the middle-aged woman who was coyly batting her eyes at him and hanging on every word he said. Maddie shook her head. The man could sell these women the very rolls of toilet paper out of the bathroom.

And if he did, judging by the cacophony off to Maddie's right, Celeste would ring it up on the cash register for them. The tiny woman was like an army general directing troops. She had the crowd of customers in a single file formed to the left, their selections and their money in their hands as they stood out of the way of the shoppers in the aisle. The poor people in line appeared shell-shocked, yet pleasantly so, as if they considered themselves to be insiders, part of some frenzied buy-up in the shop that the general public didn't yet know about.

Looking from one to the other of them, Maddie put a

hand to her mouth to hide her grin of amusement. She wondered if she should wade in or stay out of the way. While Celeste and Hank certainly didn't seem to need her help, it was her shop. Just then Hank made up her mind for her. He caught her attention by calling out her name. Maddie turned his way and saw him waving her over. She stepped around several children searching through a big plastic bin of beach toys and finally made her way over to her new shop employee, Hank Madison, erstwhile advertising tycoon and business mogul.

"Yes, Hank?" she asked, her professional smile firmly in place and giving away nothing as she stared up at his handsome face. "How can I help you?"

"Well, actually," he said just as seriously, acting as if his very rent payment depended on making this sale, "you can help me with Mrs. Wainwright here from Rhode Island."

"Hello." Maddie nodded, not able to ignore the shocking layers of makeup the woman wore. And we aren't even going to talk about that shoe-polish–black hair. "I'm Maddie Copeland, the owner of the shop. What can I do for you?"

But it was Hank, the consummate salesman, who answered for the customer. "She's interested in this handbag here. But she wants it in silver. We only have it in gold here on the floor. I was wondering if that shipment of purses came in on my day off and might be in the stockroom?"

He was dead serious. Or seriously mocking her and the entire working public. Not sure if she was outraged or amused, or both, Maddie, just as dead-seriously, smiled up at him. "I'm not sure. Come with me to the back, *Hank,* and we'll both look." He was going to protest, she could see it in his face. So she gave him no way out. "Excuse us a moment, Mrs. Wainwright. We'll be right back. Hopefully, with that silver purse for you."

Maddie grabbed Hank's arm, refusing to be impressed by the hard muscle of his bicep, and propelled him past protesting females all the way back to the stockroom. The divider curtain had no sooner fallen back in place than Maddie released him and whirled to face him. "What do you think you're doing, Hank Madison?"

"Shhh," he cautioned, a finger to his lips. "That's a pretty thin curtain. Everyone can hear you."

Maddie lowered her voice. "What do you think you're doing, Hank Madison?"

"Where were you just now, Maddie?"

"You can't just come in here and put on an apron and start waiting on people! It's not that simple."

"I saw the water dish you left out front. Couldn't bring yourself to pick it up, could you?"

"I have laws and things I have to abide by with employees, you know. Applications, background checks, insurance, things like that."

"I'm sorry I made you cry. I didn't mean to."

Maddie had her retort all ready but then she finally heard him. And herself. She raised her hands, saying, "Wait a minute. We're having two different conversations here. And you did not make me cry."

"Your eyes look like you've been crying."

"That's because I have."

"You said you haven't."

"I said *you* didn't make me cry. I didn't say I wasn't crying."

"Well, what were you crying about?"

"That's really none of your business."

"I think it is."

Maddie exhaled sharply. "It's not, but fine. No big deal. I was crying about nothing. I'm allowed to, you know. I'm a woman. We cry. We don't have to have a reason."

"I'm sorry, Maddie. I never meant to make you cry."

He said it so quietly. Maddie felt terrible. She didn't know what to say, where to look.

Then, in the pregnant silence that filled the bit of space between their two bodies, Maddie suddenly became aware of how Hank's presence dwarfed everything in this close little room. Of how dusty the air was. How mercantilelike it smelled. Or maybe it was just that Hank was standing so close to her. And what that did to her nerve endings angered her. He had no right—and the man was standing over her like a vulture, she angrily decided, taking a step back. To her utmost shock, Hank advanced a step on her. She stepped back again. He came forward. A thrill of emotion shot through her.

She swallowed. Her heart was pounding. "What are you doing?"

"Exactly what you said. Looking for that shipment of silver purses."

"Oh, you mean the ones that came in on your day off? Please."

He grinned. "Just trying to help, ma'am."

"*Why* are you trying to help? The last time I saw you I told you I didn't want to see you—"

"Until you made your decision regarding my fate. I remember."

"Good. But I haven't decided yet."

"I didn't ask if you had."

He had her there. "So what are you doing here?" She pointed to his red bib apron. Doggone him, the man looked wonderful in it. "And what makes you think I need your help?"

"I didn't think you did. Celeste did. I came looking for you. She got me some water for Beamer—"

Maddie's gasp cut off his words. She barely stopped herself from looking around desperately. "That's right. The dog. I will *not* be slurped in my own shop. I won't. I just fixed my hair and my makeup."

"It's okay. She's outside. With the water dish."

Relief flooded through Maddie. She clasped her hands over her heart. "Thank God."

Hank's expression was bemused. "That dog really loves you. Are you sure you're afraid of her? I wouldn't think she would act like she does if you hadn't given her some encouragement."

Maddie tried not to look guilty. So she'd bought the dog a rawhide bone or two in the past. And a stainless-steel water dish. So they'd played a game or two of fetch the stick. What was the big deal? "Well, I don't encourage her. And I am afraid of dogs. In the same way that most people are afraid of sharks, I'm afraid of dogs." She thought about that. "Well, and sharks, too. But they're more easily avoided."

"That's true." His gaze roved over her face, leaving Maddie self-conscious about her haphazard repair job on her makeup. "Well, don't worry. She's outside. Anyway, Celeste was here alone, and the store was filling up with people."

With no warning, he reached out to her and straightened her blouse's collar. Maddie stiffened as his warm fingers brushed her neck, leaving scorch marks where he'd touched her. But he kept on talking as if he weren't aware that he'd done such an intimate thing. "So she tossed me an extra apron and told me to get to work. I did what anyone would have done to save his skin. I put the apron on and got to work. The rest you know."

Maddie lowered her gaze, not sure she knew anything anymore. Except how this man's nearness affected her.

"Maddie? Are you okay?"

She looked up, seeing the question in his black eyes. "Of course. I was just thinking of how we, well, ended things the other night. I think I'm just overwhelmed, Hank. And I know you are. I don't know what to make of it all."

"How about we just consider ourselves victims of a will left by a sweet but loony old man we both cared about and who cared about us?"

Maddie brightened. "I like that. It puts things in perspective. But I would like to talk to you some more before I make up my mind. I have about a billion questions."

He grinned. "One for each dollar?"

"Oh, don't remind me. It boggles the mind. And makes my stomach sick."

"You'll get used to it. Mine stays that way." Then his

dark eyes fairly gleamed with awareness of her as a woman. "Maddie, I've been a big jerk. I'd like to make that up to you." He moved as if he meant to take her in his arms—

But the curtain behind him was jerked open on its metal rod. Maddie jumped and Hank spun to face it. In stepped the wrath of Hanscomb Harbor. Celeste McNeer. Her face was pruned up to show her displeasure. The divider curtain fell into place behind her. "I got a lady out here who looks like she pulled a heist at a makeup counter and wants to know what happened to the two of you and her silver purse. She says you've been back here for ten minutes."

Stung with sudden remembrance, Maddie put her hands to her too-hot cheeks. "Ohmigod. Mrs. Wainwright." She shoved at Hank's back. "Go out there and appease her."

He balked like a stubborn mule. "What should I tell her?"

"Tell her anything. She doesn't really want a purse, you goose. She wants your time and attention. Give it to her."

"Whatever you say. You're the boss." With that, Hank shrugged his shoulders and tidied his apron, still managing to appear very masculine. "Cover me. I'm going in." With that he pulled the curtain aside and stepped out.

Grateful female voices chirped at his appearance. The curtain swung back into place. Maddie stared at the disapproving Celeste. And dared to smile.

"Don't you smile at me, young lady. You just told your employee to go out there and use his body to make a customer happy. That's sexual harassment."

"I did no such thing." Then she thought about it. "All right, I did. But I didn't mean it like that, Celeste. Do you really think I'm guilty of sexual harassment?"

Celeste considered this for a bit. "No, on second thought, maybe not. After all, he doesn't really work for you." Her expression brightened. "He works for me. You think he'd let me sexually harass him a bit?"

"Celeste McNeer, don't you even think about it. And I won't—"

The curtain was ripped to one side. Startled, Maddie and Celeste gasped and grabbed each other. It was Hank. His black eyes were deadly serious. "That lady left, so I went outside to check on Beamer. And she's gone, too."

CHAPTER FIVE

❧

"TURN RIGHT UP THERE at the next street."

Hank nodded. As he and Maddie, in his Lincoln Navigator, searched the night-darkened streets of Hanscomb Harbor, Hank had the distinct impression that Maddie knew where Beamer might have gone. She hadn't said as much, but she was giving him pretty specific directions to turn here and go straight there. To him, this seemed more like a definite route than it did a random pattern of guessing.

"How are you doing out here on your own? I mean in Hanscomb Harbor," Maddie asked out of the blue. "I know you're used to having people do for you."

Hank maneuvered his vehicle around the corner and onto the street she'd indicated. "Well, I've only been here a couple days. Had some trouble finding a room. All the tourists. But if you mean can the poor little rich boy do things for himself, yes I can. I can take care of myself."

"Of course you can."

"You don't believe me."

She shook her head. "No. Not until you believe me about not being a gold-digging bimbo."

Ah. So that's where this line of questioning was coming from. "A gold-digging bimbo. Man, that sounds crappy when you say it out loud."

"I know." She looked defensive and triumphant at the same moment.

"Okay, so I had that coming. But all right. Deal? I won't think of you as a gold-digging bimb—"

"You won't *think* I am? I'm not."

"Okay, you're *not* a gold-digging bimbo, and I can take care of myself. How's that?"

"I don't know. Do you really believe it?"

"About you? Yes I do. I do believe that you're not."

"What changed your mind?"

"Jesus, Maddie, am I going to need my attorney?"

She sighed, gesturing with her apology. "No. I'm sorry. I'm just glad you can see I'm not that way. At least, I hope you can. Because I'm not."

"I conceded the point, Okay?"

"Good."

After that, they drove along in silence. Hank couldn't help but notice how empty the streets suddenly were. Not an hour ago they'd been mobbed with tourists. And the whole boardwalk area overlooking the beach had thrummed with the atmosphere of a carnival. But now? You could hear crickets. It was eerie. He glanced over at Maddie. "Where did everyone go?"

Sitting on the passenger's side, she shrugged against the restraint of her seat belt. "Well, most businesses have closed for the evening. But there are a few indoor things to do. Mr. Bailey shows an early movie over at the community center. Some are at the Captain's Tavern. But my guess is the families have probably taken their tired children back to the beach cottages or the Harbor Inn Motel, wherever they're staying. Family time. Time for baths and bedtime stories."

"I can vouch for the motel being full of kids. That's where I finally found a room," Hank commented automatically as his mind worked on the wistful way she'd spoken of children and families. He glanced over at her. She wasn't looking his way. Instead, she stared solemnly out at the night. Hank was struck by how delicate, how fragile she looked. Was it her blond coloring? Her blue eyes? Her slenderness? Or a combination of them all? Whatever it was, she'd gotten to him. Hank realized he wanted nothing more than to reach over, take her hand, raise it to his lips, and kiss it reassuringly. But he couldn't. They didn't have that kind of relationship. Or much of any other kind, either. A sigh escaped him. *That damned will.*

He faced the road ahead now, but his troubled mind would not let him be. All he could think about was the fact that he had to stifle his urge to touch her. Hank's grip on the steering wheel tightened as he thought how unfair it all was to him and Maddie. What his grandfather had done— bequeath to Maddie what was rightfully Hank's and then essentially put her in charge of seeing that Hank carried out the provisions or risk losing everything for them both—had maybe been done in good faith and because of a kind heart, if not a slightly wacky one.

But well intentioned or not, James Senior had made a big mess of things, God love him. Hank knew that if he and Maddie had met under other circumstances, they might have had a chance together. A really good chance. Because there was no denying that he was attracted to her. As if he needed proof of that, he relived again their passionate kiss in Jim's office—*before* the reading of the will that had put them in their present adversarial position. *Damn.*

Troubled by the direction of his thoughts, Hank chose to take up their conversation where it had left off. He spoke into the silence punctuated by the cold air blowing on them from the SUV's air-conditioning vents. "So, how do you feel about having kids, Maddie?"

She chuckled as if caught off guard by his question. "Wow." She adopted a thoughtful pose. "Okay. Well. How do I feel? I don't know. I suppose people should have them if they want them. Why?"

Hank grinned at her. "Did I sound like I was taking a poll? I meant someday would *you* like to have kids?"

"Oh. Me. Well, sure. Someday. How about you?"

Hank divided his attention between her and the ribbon of road ahead. "Yeah. I would. With the right woman."

"Ah. The right woman." Her tone was teasing. "And what would she be like?"

"Don't know. Someone who could stand to put up with me for more than five minutes would be nice, for starters."

Maddie chuckled. "Are you all that hard to get along with?"

"You can answer that better than I can."

"Really? Okay." She thought about it longer than a mere moment. "I guess you're all right."

"Whoa. A ringing endorsement."

Maddie's grin widened. "You shouldn't go fishing for compliments."

"I'll remember that." It felt good, this banter between them. But it only confirmed for Hank that without the will and the angry scene that had followed its reading and their subsequent wariness, he and Maddie might have had something good together. Hank sobered a bit, pulling away from her emotionally. "I can't get over this place, Maddie," he said, seeking safer conversational ground. "It's not even nine o'clock and already the sidewalks are rolled up for the night. How do you stand it here year-round?"

"Well, I don't think it's a matter of standing it. I love it here. It's home. And it's my refuge."

Her sharp intake of a breath alerted Hank that she'd revealed more than she intended. That only sharpened his curiosity—and maybe a tiny lingering doubt—about her. "Your refuge? From what? You're not running from the law, are you?"

"Hardly. Not unless you sic them on me."

"Like you said: hardly. But okay, you're not a felon. Aren't you a little young to be seeking refuge?"

She shrugged. "It has nothing to do with age. More like emotional bruises. Or a failed relationship, whatever." She exhaled sharply. "I really don't want to talk about him, Hank."

Him. Hmm. "Okay. No problem. I didn't mean to pry. I guess I just never expected to find someone like you in a place like this. I mean, you have 'big-city girl' written all over you. And let's face it, Hanscomb Harbor is not a big city."

"No, it isn't. But for the record, you didn't find me. I was pretty much thrust onto you."

He couldn't let that pass. Grinning devilishly, he said, "Hey, thrust onto me. I like that. A great visual. But I know what you mean. Because I was thrust onto you, too. Sucks, huh?"

She chuckled. "In some ways, yes. In others, not so much."

"I'm going to take *that* as a compliment. And one I didn't go fishing for."

"Whatever," she said, shaking her head and smiling.

Since they seemed to be getting along so well, at least for the moment, Hank chose then to voice a concern. "On another subject, are you sure Mrs. McNeer will be okay alone at the shop?"

Maddie shot him a look of amused disbelief. "Celeste? Not fine? Are you kidding? Save your worry for the customers."

"That's what I meant: will she wreak havoc on them?"

"Probably. Oh, take this right turn here."

Hank shot her a questioning look as he rounded the corner onto a cobbled lane called Queen Street. "Is she that bad? I mean Mrs. McNeer."

"Of course," Maddie said cheerfully. "But there're only about fifteen more minutes before closing time. Usually she needs longer than that to spawn a disaster the proportions of a tidal wave."

"Hmm." Hank glanced over at Maddie. Her expression said she wasn't kidding. "So why does Mrs. McNeer still work? Does she have to? I mean, she's pretty old to still be holding down a job."

"Oh, please say that to her, about her being old, will you? But before you do, give me some advance notice so I can set up bleachers and sell tickets to that show. And here's a clue—you'll need a whip and a chair."

"Ah. Touchy about her age, huh?"

"Oh, yes. A Gray Panther. A senior citizens' advocate. Not about to be pushed aside or told she's not a vital person."

"Yeah, I think I had a taste of that attitude earlier. Well, good for her. And good for you for hiring her."

"Hold the congratulations. I didn't hire her. She came

with the shop since it used to be hers. I bought it from her and changed the name. So she essentially adopted me and sees it as her right and her duty to terrorize me."

Grinning, hearing the note of true affection underlying Maddie's words, Hank stole another look at her. An oncoming car's headlights cast a silvery reflection onto her golden hair. The effect was breathtaking. Hank felt himself tighten with an overwhelming desire for her. *Cool it, man. Get it under control.* Right. Hank said the first thing that popped into his mind. "So, if you were a dog, where would you be?"

Maddie tsked. "God, under heavy sedation because I'd be afraid of myself."

Her droll retort had him laughing. "Okay, unfortunate phrasing."

Just then he pulled up to a stop sign. Queen Street had dead-ended. Ahead of them was the infinity of the ocean. Bright moonlight glanced off the water, and gentle breakers fell onto the rocky shoreline ahead. Hank looked left, then right, and focused on Maddie. "And your best guess would be . . . ?"

"Left. Go left."

But he didn't. Stopping him was the way she'd said it, how certain she sounded. With a wrist flung loosely over the steering wheel and his other elbow resting atop the console between them, Hank looked into Maddie's eyes. "You know where the dog is, don't you?"

She lowered her gaze from his. "I have an idea. But I could be wrong."

Hank's jaw worked as he considered her body language. He then looked out the window on his left and saw that the paved road disappeared around a bend about a quarter-mile down. In the middle distance, though, he could see a half-moon–shaped strand of beach lit up by a bright light atop a power pole. The crescent of sandy land supported a scattering of small cottages. From here, they looked to be the one-room kind that usually had rustic amenities and old brass beds covered in threadbare quilts. His grandfather would have loved something like this. Hank turned again to Maddie. "So. What's all that out there?"

Her expression gave nothing away. "Just some rental cottages owned by Mr. Cotton Hardy."

"I see. Did my grandfather rent one of them? Is that why you think the dog's out there?"

Maddie stared forlornly at him. Then he saw her throat work convulsively and her chin quiver.

A bit alarmed, Hank tensed. "Hey, what's wrong?"

Moonlight revealed tears standing in her eyes. "Oh, Hank, I'm just so sorry for your loss."

Hank felt his chest tighten with emotion. "I know you are, Maddie." He cleared his throat. "So," he said a little too loudly. "You think Beamer's out there at my grandfather's cottage, huh?"

"I do. It makes sense she would go where she feels close to James. And she's certainly not anywhere else. But I . . . well, it's only now occurred to me how being here might affect *you*. I should have thought of—"

"No, you shouldn't have. It's not your job. And I'm fine, okay?"

She nodded. "I didn't mean to step on your toes."

"You didn't. Which of those cottages was his?"

"Hank," she said quietly, sincerely, "it's all right to be sad."

Afraid he'd crumple right here, Hank closed his eyes and rubbed at them. "I know that. I said I'm all right." Then, grim, feeling ragged, he focused on her. "Which cottage was his, Maddie?"

She shook her head. "I don't know. I never came out here. He always got a ride into town. I just know he stayed here."

"All right. I guess we'll know which one was his when we find the dog, right?"

Staring at her hands in her lap, she nodded. "Yes. But Hank, I just want to say that I'm sorry you didn't know your grandfather died, that you couldn't be here at the end, and that you missed his funeral. It all happened so fast and no one could find you. Mr. Thornton told me how he tried. It's all so sad. And I just think it sucks, the whole thing. I include the will in that. I just wanted to say that to you, that I'm aware of what you're going through. So there, I said it. And now I'll shut up."

Raw emotions played tug-of-war with Hank's mood. He cleared his throat and sniffed. "You don't have to shut up. And thank you for what you said. Now, shall we go do this?"

Her smile was soft, sympathetic. "Sure. You need to turn left, Hank."

To his surprise, Hank realized that he wanted very much, at this quiet moment of some new kind of communication between them, to pull her to him and kiss her sweet mouth.

"Hank, did you hear me? You have to turn left. There's a car behind us."

It took a moment for her words to sink in. There was a car behind them. "Oh, hell, sorry." Regretting the kiss that never was, Hank shifted in his seat and peered into the rearview mirror and then the sideview mirror. Sure enough, a compact sedan sat behind them . . . patiently, expectantly. Hank looked in both directions, saw the road was clear, and turned left, as he'd been directed.

As Mr. Hardy's rental cottages loomed larger, Maddie rode along in silence with Hank. She wanted to kick herself for having said so much. She'd stepped over a line with him, and he'd let her know about it. His grief was private. He wasn't open to discussing it with her. No more than she wanted to talk to him about Stanton Fairchild, her absent groom, the big jerk. Still, Maddie was glad she'd expressed her condolences to Hank. It was how she felt, and he needed to hear it since he was given to jumping to conclusions about her.

It occurred to Maddie then that they'd covered quite a bit of ground. She meant conversationally speaking as opposed to actual road miles. The amazing thing to her, though, was that she'd been able to carry on a conversation at all with him, given the electricity that crackled in the air between them. God, he was so close to her. Every breath she took was scented with his aftershave and warmed by his body's heat. And his body? The man worked out, that was evident. Maddie couldn't deny how her heart pounded when she stared at his profile. His appeal to her was so deep as to be on some cellular level. And her response to him could only be called primal, beyond rational comprehension, really. Okay, he was *such* a man. To the tenth power. Just innately attractive to women. Who knew why?

But it was more than physical. She'd met handsome men before and not been affected this deeply. Certainly, she'd admired them, had even lusted. All of that held true with Hank, too. But from the first moment she'd seen him, even though they'd been in each other's faces, she'd felt something beyond anger. Something she had yet to explore, mainly because she didn't want to. Not until she saw how all this other stuff with the will, et cetera, worked out. And not before she felt ready to trust again. After all, Stanton had got her as far as the altar, where he'd dropped her. A woman didn't get over something like that quickly. Maybe not even slowly.

And maybe it didn't matter a bit. Because who said Hank felt anything for her? Wasn't she just opening herself up to a world of hurt by just thinking along these lines? Yes, she supposed she was. It was best, then, she concluded, to just think of him simply as someone she was thrown together with for a finite period of time. Someone who was so out of her league that they weren't even in the same solar system. Sure, Hank had manners and a lot of class. And she could really, really like him. But it was crazy to even go there. As if he would ever reciprocate with someone like her—a small-town nice woman with no aspirations to world renown.

Still, she saw the way he looked at her. The way he watched her mouth when she spoke. Okay, so the sex between them would probably be beyond wonderful. There was no denying that. After all, she knew how she felt when he'd leaned over toward her with his elbow resting on the console. He'd been close enough that she had only to lower her head to kiss him. And she'd wanted to. Very much. But then they'd talked about James and she'd remembered Hank's loss and how sad that was—

See? Intimacy died a quick death in the face of recent loss. Couple that with all the legal wranglings between them . . . and yes, getting past it all to what lay underneath would be an incredibly tough job. Not that she was sure she wanted to explore her surging pulse, she reminded herself again, or give a name to the crazy beating of her heart when she thought of him. Or the way she found herself pulled to him by an invisible rope. Or even the way she wanted to throw herself wantonly at him.

Now, how stupidly ironic was this, anyway? A little over a year ago, Stanton had scarred her for life. Or so she'd thought. And that was why she was here in Hanscomb Harbor. To get away from all those memories. To lick her wounds. To forget men, darn it. The single guys here in town had certainly come around, flirting, asking her out. But they were her friends from high school. She knew them too well. They knew it, and she knew it. And her girlfriends from high school . . . well, they were married and, though friendly, pretty much didn't want her, a young single woman, around their husbands. All of this meant her circle of friends was small. Then James had come around and—

"Maddie? Where are you? I said we're here."

"What? We're here? Where?" she said somewhat stupidly as she snapped out of her reverie and looked around. When had they left the pavement and pulled onto the tire-rutted trail between low dunes that led to Mr. Hardy's cottages? Maddie felt disoriented, as if she'd been shaken awake to find herself in a different location from where she'd gone to bed. She blinked and reality sorted itself out, assuming familiar shapes. "Oh, the cottages. Of course."

"You all right? You look lost or something."

"Oh. No, I'm fine. Sorry. I was just thinking."

"Care to share?"

Share what? That she couldn't believe that he'd popped into her life just when she really didn't want someone to pop into her life, only to have him turn out to be someone she really couldn't have because he was totally out of her league? She thought all that, but what she said was: "No."

He nodded *fair enough* and said, "Then how do you want to do this? I don't want to get shot. Or have the cops called."

"Don't worry about that. The police, I mean. There are only two and, well, they're harmless."

"Like in Mayberry? Sheriff Andy and Deputy Barney?"

"Ha-ha, big-city boy." Maddie raised her chin with mock offended pride. She wasn't about to admit to him that he wasn't far off the mark with Chief Brickman and Deputy Louie.

Maddie opened her car door and heard Hank opening his. The warm night air grabbed her and wrapped her in its cocoon embrace. The soft whooshing of the waves grasping at the shoreline reassured her somehow that everything would be fine. Still in the SUV, she turned to Hank. "I guess the best thing to do is be as quiet as we can and just look for her. I mean, a dog that big should be easy to spot."

"Assuming she wants to be spotted. If she doesn't want to be . . . in this dark and with these dunes and the cover of all those cottages?" Hank shrugged, shaking his head. "Could be difficult. And we're only assuming she's here."

"She has to be here, Hank. She certainly isn't anywhere else. Anyway, I think we should start with that one." Maddie pointed to a darkened cabin that sat a forlorn distance from the others, much like the new kid at school no one wanted to sit with at lunch.

"Why that one?" With his question, he leaned over toward her, opened the glove compartment, and pulled out a flashlight. His hand was within inches of her knee. Maddie caught her breath. Hank stared into her eyes. She had to fist her hand to keep from stroking his cheek and leaning forward to kiss his mouth. "You never know when you might need one," he said, grinning, winking at her. He then flipped the compartment door closed, sat up, and waited.

For what? Maddie honestly couldn't remember. She desperately cast about in her mind for the thread of their conversation. The man did the funniest things to her ability to pay attention. She couldn't believe she was acting like this. Was there such a thing as sexual dementia? You just got berserk around the one who turned you on? You did and said stupid things? And stared? And lost your mind? And couldn't keep up with simple conversations?

"Maddie?"

Blessedly, the sound of his voice popped her sanely back to the moment. "Oh. Sorry. That cottage there. Yes. I think I remember James saying the one he always rented was situated beyond the others. That one certainly is. And there's no car out front and the lights are off. It might be the safest one to start with, if nothing else."

"True." That was all he said as he opened his door and climbed out, closing the door behind him.

Maddie was suddenly assailed with a sense of being totally alone in her own world. It was awful. Sad. Lonely.

"Oh, God," she said softly to herself. *I have got to quit feeling these things. I don't need it. And Hank certainly doesn't, either. I am pretty much the enemy right now. I have control of everything that he has ever worked for. And he could lose it all. And I could never see him again, win or lose.*

Unable to stand her own thoughts, Maddie exited the Navigator, untied her bib apron, and tossed it onto the seat. She then realized that the fine, dry sand under her feet had poured into her sandals. *Ick.* She shook her feet, one at a time, trying to rid them of the sand. Finally, with a tsk of annoyance, and holding her long and silky peasant skirt up with one hand, she slipped out of her shoes, bent to pick them up, and shook them. With a careless toss of her wrist, she flipped them onto the SUV's floorboard and closed the car door.

She turned. Moonlight revealed Hank standing there watching her. Something deep inside Maddie awakened again. She stilled and met his gaze. The look on Hank's face said he'd been standing there a while. Obviously he'd skirted the back of his vehicle, only to catch her engaged in a moonlit ritual of shoe-shedding . . . with her skirt raised well above her knees. She should probably say something. "It's just easier for me in the sand when I'm barefooted."

He nodded, staring at her as if she'd performed some intensely intimate rite in front of him, one she'd had no right to do, a thing that had unnerved him.

With her face heating up from embarrassment, Maddie blessed the relative darkness she stood in. "What?"

"Nothing." He flicked on the flashlight, pointed it at the ground in front of them, and said, "After you."

"All right. But I think we should go the back way here. Behind these other cabins so we don't scare the tenants."

Hank nodded and leveled a battery-powered beam of light in the direction she'd indicated. He directed it over the landscape and said, "Okay. But how are you going to get over those dunes? They aren't as navigable as the beach route, I'll bet." He now flashed the light on her bare feet. "Look. Your skirt is long and you're barefooted. It could be tough going for you."

Maddie refused to look down at her feet. She could feel her toes, the traitors, wriggling their agreement with Hank. "I'm used to this terrain. I did grow up here, you know. I'll be fine."

"Whatever you say." His careless shrug said she would fall flat on her face not ten feet out from the car.

Maddie pursed her lips but refused to rise to the bait. And so they proceeded in slow and stumbling steps. The sand was maddeningly thick and fine. And hot and shifting. And uneven. So, of course, Maddie finally fell face-first, in a helpless belly flop, onto the surprisingly hard mound of sand. Her air left her in a surprised squawk of outrage, and she lay there stunned, not quite believing yet that she was on the ground.

She heard Hank sigh as he gripped her around the waist and pulled her to her feet. So surprisingly strong was he, so easily did he lift her, Maddie felt as if she were being pulled backward through a vortex of air. She expected her ears to pop. She then realized he'd lifted her with one arm wrapped around her. His other hand still held the flashlight.

"Are you okay?" Amusement laced his voice.

Stung and embarrassed, Maddie barked, "I'm fine. Just stand back while I dust myself off, okay?" She angrily rubbed at her arms and then shook out her skirt. "And don't you dare say 'I told you so,' Hank Madison."

"I wasn't going to." He backed off a few paces and stood facing her. His back was to the moonlight as he held the flashlight's beam on her so she could see what she was doing.

Such geographical placement meant Maddie couldn't see his face to see if he was still laughing at her. It was just as well, given how her dignity smarted. Because if she could see he was enjoying this, she'd probably push him down hard just to show him how it felt. At last she was as sand-free as she was going to get, and they set off again.

Blessedly, the dunes leveled out some toward the deep stretch of sandy beach. The going was a bit easier. But apparently Hank wasn't taking any chances. Without a word, he'd taken her elbow and guided her along. Maddie's first thought was that she should protest and pull away. But she didn't. Because to do so would be a silly thing, she told herself. Not the least bit expedient or reasonable. Why fall on her face again if Hank's grip—Hank's strong, warm grip—could help her? There was a time to be aloof and a time to be smart. This time was the latter.

"Maddie," Hank said out of the blue . . . or the black of night, she supposed. "You do remember this is Beamer we're looking for, right?"

"Of course I do. Why would you ask that?"

"Sorry. Watch that grassy tuft there." He'd knocked into her, forcing her to clutch at him for support. They righted themselves. He still gripped her elbow. "I mean, you're not going to run screaming into the ocean when we find her, are you?"

I might, was her thought. But what she said was: "Of course not. Don't be silly. No one ever died from being licked. I know that."

Hank stopped. His hand on her elbow forced her to do the same. He stood facing her now, the flashlight held down at his side. Its light illuminated her bare feet and his jogging shoes. To strangers they would appear to be on the verge of a romantic embrace. "Wait a minute. I want to ask you something."

"Okay." Maddie's stomach did a flip-flop. All she could see was Hank's profile, the side of his face lit by the moon. He was so incredibly handsome, so stirring, that Maddie's breath caught.

"When we were in Jim's office, at the reading of the will, why did you sign those papers?"

His question functioned like a cold shower, dousing Maddie with reality. Her knees stiffened and her heart thudded dully. "Which ones specifically? I signed a lot of papers."

"The ones to do with my business."

"I didn't think I had a choice in the matter, Hank," she replied cautiously, levelly. "Not any more of one than you did. I mean, your grandfather just left it all to me. In the same way someone might bequeath Aunt Tillie's brooch to little Mary."

"It's a little more complicated than that."

"Only in size. The effect was the same. But let me ask you something. Why do you think he did this to you? And why did he include me? That's the part I don't get. Gosh, if it's a vacation he wanted you to take, why not in Rome or in the Caribbean? Why me? And why Hanscomb Harbor? Sure, it's my hometown, and I love it. But it's pretty much off the beaten path for someone like you and your set."

Hank shrugged. "I don't know that I have a set, but still, I couldn't agree more. I'm sure he had his reasons, ones that made sense to him. Although they certainly don't to me."

Maddie licked at her lips. "Do you think maybe he . . ." She couldn't get the words out. It was a crazy thought she should never have attempted to voice.

"Do I think maybe he what?"

Struck shy and reluctant, afraid he'd laugh at her or really think she had designs on him, Maddie studied the pattern in the sand she was designing with her big toe. In the background, the steady whoosh-whoosh of the waves hitting the shore reminded her of a giant beating heart, one about the size hers felt whenever she was this close to Hank Madison.

Finally, she faced him. "Okay, here it is. Either James was totally nuts, which we both agree he probably was—"

"Jim doesn't think so. And he did redo my grandfather's will based on his state of mind in his last hours."

"True. Okay, so that aside. But James naming me and Hanscomb Harbor? And forcing you to be here, where I am? Well, do you think his last hope could have been that we—you and I—might get together . . . or something?"

Hank stiffened and sucked in air like someone had hit him in the stomach with a two-by-four. Maddie wanted to die for having spoken her mind. "No," Hank blurted, sounding stubborn. "I don't. Not at all. Let's go find the dog."

CHAPTER SIX

❧

MADDIE HELD HER SKIRT up and stumbled along beside Hank as he hurried them toward the rental cottage. When she could, when all her faculties weren't needed to help her keep her feet, she owned up to being so embarrassed right now that she'd like to throw herself headlong into the ocean. Why had she said that about them getting together? Why? He had to be thinking "gold digger" again.

She got no farther than that in her thoughts before she saw they'd successfully navigated their way to the back of the little square cottage set away from the others. Hank aimed his flashlight toward the front and Maddie saw a tiny screened-in front porch attached to the one-room weathered-wood structure. It didn't have the look of being occupied. In fact, it didn't have the look of a dwelling that could be safely occupied.

Hank stopped and turned to her. "Why don't you let me go first? In case Beamer is here. Or in case she isn't and someone human is. You never know."

"Okay. But, look, Hank, what I said back there at the car—"

"Drop it. Forget it."

"You really need to quit flattering yourself. I don't have designs on you."

"Good. Wait here."

Boy, he really didn't want to talk about it. Maddie's temper surfaced. "All right. Fine. Go ahead."

"I will."

"Good. Fine. Go."

"I am."

"I believe you."

"Wait here."

"I said I would."

Towering over her, Hank looked up and away from her. Perhaps he was asking for patience. He swung his gaze back to hers. "You do understand that if Beamer is here, I'm going to have to put her in the back of my car for the ride back to town, right? You know that?"

Maddie swallowed and pronounced herself the first person in history to actually feel her face growing pale—not that she was going to let him know that. "Great. She'll have me licked hairless by then. Oh, God."

"Jesus," Hank said as if that were the appropriate response in a litany they were reciting. He rubbed at his mouth and jaw, but didn't say anything else. He just stood there staring down at her. "Maddie, there's no other way. Why didn't you just tell me about this place and stay in town?"

"Because I . . . well, I just didn't think about that until now." *And because I pretty much wanted to be with you, you conceited hunk.*

"All right. Neither did I," Hank conceded. "But here we are now." He stared at the cottage, then inhaled deeply. "It's not like this little run-down beach house holds a lot of memories for me." Maddie wondered who he was trying to convince. "And it's not like this is the family home and he lived here for fifty years."

"I believe you. And where is that, by the way? Your family home."

"Long Island." His dark eyes accused her. "You ought to know. You own it now."

"I do?"

"You didn't read what you were signing the other day?"

"No. There had to be a hundred pages. I'd still be there."

"Right." Hank turned away.

"No." Her involuntary cry stopped him and had him turning to face her. "I've changed my mind. I don't want to be out here alone. I've seen that movie. The girl left behind always gets killed by the monster."

Hank stared at her. "For God's sake, Maddie, there is no monster. Only a dog. Besides, Beamer probably isn't even here. I'd think if she was, she'd have barked or come running around the corner when she heard us."

"That's true," Maddie said to his departing back, and hating it about herself that all she could do was admire his broad shoulders and narrow hips.

Then he went around the corner, out of view. Maddie began her vigil. She had to physically stop herself from whistling nervously. To her, standing there alone in the moon-silvered dark, it seemed as if he'd already been gone for hours. Of course, he'd only just left. Maddie crossed her arms under her breasts and hummed to herself, toeing the sand. Slowly the sounds around her began to encroach . . . and to comfort her. The wonderful salty scent of the briny water. The feel of the sand between her toes. The cool air on the bare skin of her arms. The way the breeze lifted her hair. The sound of the waves hitting the shore, relentlessly, patiently . . .

The cold, wet thing behind her that had just poked against her leg.

Maddie froze, much as if someone had stuck a gun in her back. She prayed that the thing behind her would be a squid that had taken several recent giant steps up the evolutionary ladder and could now walk on dry land. Or maybe a hideously large Jules Verne–esque crab. Or a 1950s horror-movie lobster that had crawled through some nuclear-disaster vapor cloud and was now fifty feet tall. That wouldn't be so bad. Anything but the dog with the slurpy tongue and the tremendous affection for her. Please. Not that.

An idle woof behind her put the lie to any but the dog theories. It was the dog. And it was behind her. And she was alone with it. And it loved her. No.

"H-Hank?" Maddie stuttered. She wet her lips and tried again, this time out loud. "Hank? Come here please." Well, it was a little louder. Still, no answer and no Hank. Maybe that was because she was facing the wind. Which meant the sound of her voice would carry in the opposite direction. Behind her. Where the dog was. Was all of nature against her tonight?

The good news was that the cold wet thing, the doggy nose most likely, was no longer poking at her leg. The canine had retreated. But how far? And what was it doing? Maddie tensed, her hands fisted. She was about one second away from panicking and running, screaming into the night. Then she heard herself. She was being silly. It was a dog, one that had never bitten her. And it loved her. And wanted to share its love in doggy kisses. How awful was that?

Maddie frowned, trying to find courage. Okay, this was her chance to take control and make the dog behave. Right here, she would draw a line in the sand. She felt the sand under her feet. And drew a line in it with her toe. So far, so good. Determined, yet with her heart pounding, with her pulse vibrating in her ears, and alive with adrenaline, Maddie whipped around. She pointed in a very commanding way, arm stiff and her face grim. "Stay, Beamer," she ordered. "Sit."

Which was pretty silly because the dog already was. Sitting, that is. Beamer's ears jerked erect—no doubt with surprise—when Maddie spun around to face her. But the golden retriever remained sitting. The result of Maddie's mastery over her? She decided yes and started getting cocky. *That was easy. Cool.* Maddie eyed the dog right back, absorbing other details.

"You're all wet," she heard herself say. "Nothing personal. It's just that you are." She was. She was soaked. And dotted with clumps of sand that stuck to her fur. Obviously she'd been swimming. And rolling in the sand.

As if being spoken to were a cue, Beamer got up and, grinning, padded toward Maddie.

"Oh, God." Maddie began backing up, a hand held out defensively toward the advancing dog. "No, Beamer. Sit. Stay."

She should have been more specific. Because Beamer didn't sit or stay, not until she stopped directly in front of Maddie, where she planted her four legs and vigorously shook herself all over, slinging excess salty water and sand all over Maddie.

Maddie put her arms up in front of her face and screamed.

Hank froze, his flashlight still illuminating the locked screen door to the cabin's ramshackle porch. He stared straight ahead, unseeing, as his mind replayed the sound. *That was Maddie, all right.* Somehow he knew the reason why she had screamed, too. *Beamer.*

Maddie had found or had been confronted by the dog. All of this flashed through his mind in a split second. In the next one, he rounded the front of the cabin and headed for the spot where he'd left Maddie alone. Hank aimed the flashlight's brightness at anything that moved. Which was a considerable feat because most everything was moving. He stopped cold, staring. *What the hell . . . ?*

He hadn't been the only one to heed Maddie's cry. A score of vacationers in various states of dress and undress had poured out of their rented cabins. With flashlights in hand, they were everywhere. Running, looking, holding small children and pets back in lighted doorways, pointing, and calling out what was the matter. The scene was that of a Keystone Kops fire drill gone awry.

In the center of the maelstrom of late-evening seaside activity were—no surprises here—Maddie and Beamer. Hank could see them through the gaps in the space between some of the concerned citizens. With a hand covering her mouth, Maddie's expression could only be called sheepish. Sheepish for having screamed, no doubt. For her part, Beamer stood her ground close to Maddie and barked her intent to protect the woman she adored from the unwanted advance of those bent on coming to rescue her from the dog.

"Great," was Hank's opinion. Wedging a shoulder between a skinny man in cut-off jeans and a grandmotherly lady in curlers, Hank worked his way through the crowd coalescing around Maddie and the dog. "Excuse me. Pardon me. Thank you. Yes, I know them. Everything is under control. The dog just startled her. No, it's not my dog. It's her dog. I know she screamed. No, there's no need for the police. Step back, please. She'll be fine. Just give her some air. Thanks."

In that way, Hank loosened the knot of titillated onlookers and insinuated himself into the center of the circle. He immediately gripped Beamer's collar and warmly encouraged her to step away from Maddie. The dog obeyed—with Hank helping her to retreat several paces away. The cabin dwellers did likewise, warily eyeing the dog. Beamer sat alert and grinning as she watched these human proceedings with great interest. Hank turned to the crowd. "Thanks. We appreciate your concern and your good citizenship. But it's over now. And you can return to your cabins."

"Hey," the man in the cutoffs called out, using his flashlight as a pointer and aiming it at Hank. "You look like that rich guy in the paper whose grandfather died. It was all over the news." He turned to his companions. "That's him, isn't it?"

They all agreed it was. A conversational buzz went through the gathering. He'd been discovered. Hank exhaled and met the openly curious stares directed at him and tried to dissuade them. "It's just a coincidence that I look like him."

"No. You're him," the older woman in curlers chimed in with great authority. "I saw you about a week ago on that news show with all those reporters around you. I never forget a handsome face. Now, tell the truth, son. You're Hank Madison, aren't you?"

What to do? He could either tell the truth, as the lady suggested, or he could engage in further and damning questioning. Hank's jaw tightened. This was about the last in a long list of things he needed. He was only too aware of Maddie's nearness, her silence, and his surprising desire to protect her from these well-meaning but interfering people. "Yes, I am," he finally replied. "Now, if you'll excuse me . . . ?"

"Can I get your autograph?" The curler woman held out a napkin and a crayon to him. Hank stared at them in disbelief. "I was drawing with the kids when I heard the young lady here scream," the woman explained.

Hank nodded, then shook his head about the autograph. "I'm sorry, but there's really no reason to have my autograph. I'm not a celebrity of any sort."

"Sure you are. You were on the TV."

The very definition of celebrity. Hank snapped his fingers for Beamer to come, which she did, and he then gripped Maddie's elbow. "Now, if you'll excuse us, the lady and I need to—"

"Hey, what about the young woman? Who's she? Is she anybody?"

"No. I mean yes. Certainly she's somebody. She's just not—"

"I know her. That's the lady who runs the gift shop in town."

"I don't do autographs, either," Maddie said quickly.

Hank was about one second from turning Beamer loose on the crowd. But instead of fangs, he decided on diplomacy. "Look," he said with authority, addressing those around them, "thank you for your concern here tonight. Now if you'll excuse us, we need to be moving along. And we'll let you get back to your evening, too. Good night, all."

Not brooking any arguments, Hank turned Maddie with him, put an arm around her shoulders, and again snapped his fingers for Beamer to follow them. Which, again and surprisingly, the dog did, opting to pad along obediently beside Maddie instead of attacking her. It was amazing, really, how the big golden retriever was completely mad about her. Hank didn't think he'd ever seen an example of such devotion before as the dog exhibited. And apparently with no encouragement from Maddie.

But Beamer wasn't the only one. Apparently his grandfather had been especially fond of Maddie, too. Fond? That was the understatement of the year. He'd bequeathed her the entire holdings of Madison and Madison, a *Fortune* 500 advertising firm, all his property, stocks, bonds, cash, art, real estate holdings . . . the list went on.

Amazing. Hank felt her warmly and quietly at his side. With every step they took together, she bumped gently against him. It was a very troubling feeling. Because she felt so right there. So damned right. Hank began to worry. Was he falling under her spell, too? Was she like those sirens of legend who perched on rocks and sang and lured sailors to their deaths? Could be. Or was she the kind of woman whom people—men, women, children, animals— just fell in love with and showered with affection and gifts? It was possible. The evidence was mounting. So, would he eventually lose his mind and his fortune, assuming he got it back, to her? Would he just throw himself at her? Would he one day be mad about her?

No. Hank told himself he most certainly would not. He was immune. Yet he still walked with his arm around her . . . all the way back to his SUV.

Two days later, and late in the afternoon of a pleasant Saturday, the bell over the front door of Maddie's Gifts tinkled as it closed. A smiling customer and her children walked off, visible through the display window, with their wrapped and bagged purchases. Before she passed out of sight, the woman outside waved cheerily at Celeste, who stared peevishly out the window.

When the woman was gone, Celeste wasted no time in puckering her lips and rounding on Maddie. "While I'm as grateful for the business as you are, if one more person comes in here and asks for you or that dog, I'm going to cheerfully choke them. You sure you and Hank Madison and Beamer didn't do something the other night out at the beach that makes everyone suddenly think you're celebrities?"

Across the store from Celeste, at the back counter where the register resided, Maddie looked up from tallying the day's receipts. "I certainly don't think of myself as a celebrity. But Hank may be. Evidently the news people, and the tabloids, got wind of James's death and the odd will and the money involved. And, smelling a scandalous story, they hounded Hank in New York."

This news brightened Celeste. "Will he be in *People* magazine? Or maybe on *Entertainment Tonight*?"

"I have no idea." Maddie frowned, seeing mental images of herself being linked to him and then being mobbed and having to wear dark shades as she was hustled to a waiting car. "God, I hope not."

"How about on Jerry Springer's show?"

"*Not* if there's a God."

"Well, you should be getting *some* of the attention," Celeste grumbled, clearly disillusioned with Maddie. "Why should Hank have all the fun? You're the one who got everything."

Maddie exhaled. "I didn't get anything. Not yet, anyway. And not all of it, either." Then, thinking of her decision regarding Hank's wish to go to New York on business, she muttered under her breath, "Maybe none of it." Out loud again to Celeste, she said, "I thought of that, the media interest in me, I mean. I imagine it's only a matter of time before they track me down."

"Won't be too hard, what with Hank being here."

"I asked him that, too: if we can expect an influx—"

"Sounds like some kind of bowel disease."

Maddie sent Celeste a censuring stare. "Thank you for that image. Nevertheless, I brought that up with Hank, about the town being overrun with news services. He said he didn't think so. He obviously got out of New York City without the reporters knowing it. Which explains why we still have peace and quiet here, I suppose."

"Peace and quiet won't feed the bulldog around here."

"What do you mean?"

"Sales, Maddie. You've got the receipts right there. We're barely making it. Even in tourist season. What are we going to do come winter when the store's closed? We need those reporters here and the curious folks they'll bring.

Lots of them. City people with dollars. People wanting anything with your name on it."

Maddie knew where this was coming from—Celeste's fears for her "old age"—and her heart softened. "We'll be fine, Celeste. You've forgotten about the money James left me." Guilt assailed Maddie because she knew she may not get it. Or deserve it. "I know it's hard to think about, honey, because it's so fantastic. But it could be that we'll soon have all the money we'll ever need, thanks to James."

Celeste crossed her arms and puckered her lips. "Not if Hank lives up to his end of the will. Then he gets it all back."

"No he doesn't. James left his personal fortune to me. I just don't get it until Hank has, well, pretty much served his time here."

"If he does."

"He will."

"How do you know?"

"I just know."

"You don't. But he would if you'd be nice to him."

Maddie folded her hands together atop the thin stack of receipts on the countertop. "Define 'nice,' Celeste, as you're using it. I dare you."

Celeste demurred coyly. "You know what I mean. Nice. Pay the man some attention. That's all."

"It's kind of hard to do that under the circumstances. Not that I want to. I don't."

Celeste tsked her opinion of that. "You still fretting over that doctor jerk? I never did like that Stanton Fairchild, not from the first time you brought him around. Stuck on himself, I said. But you've had a year now, Maddie, to get your thoughts in order and see that the problem was his and not yours, honey. Quit hiding."

"I'm not hiding, Celeste. I'm just—"

"You are hiding. Your friends—Margie and Susan—have quit calling you and asking you to do things with them."

"Oh, please. They keep trying to fix me up with someone I've known since third grade because they're afraid their husbands might look at me. Trust me, *not* interested."

"Well, you need to get interested. You know what they say: if you don't use it, you'll lose it."

"That's disgusting, Celeste. But you're sweet to care. And—"

"Sweet has nothing to do with it. I love you and worry about you, that's all." She said this with great ferocity and glaring.

Maddie grinned, bright and silly, at this tiny old woman she loved so much. "You're sweet, like it or not." Then she sobered. "But I know what you mean, Celeste. You're right about me needing to move on. I want to. I will. It's just, well, with Hank, with this silly stuff to do with James's will, I just think anything personal should be put on hold for now, that's all."

Celeste grumpily crossed her arms under her bosom. "You're going to let that man get away, aren't you? And we'll be poor all the rest of our lives."

It tickled, warmed, and irritated Maddie, all at the same time, that Celeste believed that her fortunes and misfortunes were directly tied to Maddie's own. "We're not poor, Celeste. How many meals have you missed? How many times has your electricity been cut off?"

Celeste looked everywhere but at Maddie. "Now you're going to pick on a helpless old woman."

"And who exactly would that be?"

"Hmph." Dressed in shocking pink with a chiffon scarf tied around her white bun at the nape of her neck, and apparently done tormenting Maddie, Celeste went to pet a contented Beamer. "Do you need me to call the SPCA, honey? Did they abuse you at the beach? Did they beat you and drag you to the car, baby?"

Beamer whined and thumped her tail on the hardwood floor as if to tell Celeste that yes she'd been sorely mishandled and the call to legal authorities was long overdue.

Maddie rolled her eyes, not believing any of this. The dog now completely obeyed Celeste. She never had before, not when James had been alive and would bring the dog along with him. But now? For whatever reason, the two were boon companions. *Watch out, world.* This development brought Maddie both distress and delight. Distress because there really was no reason now why the dog couldn't be with them during the day in the store. And delight because, as long as Celeste was around to tell her no, Beamer wouldn't attack Maddie affectionately.

All in all, a good arrangement since Hank had officially turned the dog over to her two nights ago when they'd got back to her house. And then the darned obedient man had done exactly as she'd directed him to do—he hadn't come around and had called her house to leave his daily message that he was alive and relaxed in Hanscomb Harbor. How impersonal and unsatisfying . . . except for the thrill of getting to play and replay his voice on her tape. Maddie heard herself sigh dreamily—and immediately popped to attention, lowering her gaze to focus on the receipts under her hands. *I have got to stop thinking about that man. This has heartache written all over it. And I don't need that again.*

But he could call, her stubborn hormones argued. Or he could come by. What else did he have to do? He couldn't work while he was here. He had to relax. Well, she certainly hoped he was, Maddie argued right back with herself. Because she hadn't been able to, knowing he was so close by somewhere in town, and she could just run into him at any moment.

And yet she hadn't. Not at the grocery store. Or the library. The Captain's Tavern. On the boardwalk. At the beach. Not that Maddie had gone to all those places hoping to see him. She hadn't. She'd had official business to attend to at each of those places. And it just so happened that he hadn't been at any of them, damn him. Maddie realized that she'd abandoned the receipts and was drumming her fingernails on the glass countertop and stewing.

Celeste, who had been scratching Beamer under her chin until now, much to the dog's delight, looked up and said, "That's a sign of sexual frustration, you know."

Maddie's cheeks instantly flamed with embarrassment. She stopped drumming. "It is not. I am not."

"Uh-huh. You know, you ought to run off somewhere fun and take Hank with you. A change of scenery and a man like that could do you a world of good."

"We're back to that, are we? I told you I don't—" Maddie took a deep breath. "Need a man."

"Oh, hell, honey, no one *needs* one. We might want one, but we don't need one. In my case, I wanted four and married them all. One at a time, of course. Buried them, too. One at a time. But before you go getting your feminist britches in a wad, just remember that your generation wasn't the first one to figure out men. But still, as the breed goes, Hank's one of the good ones. And I'm betting he could unknot some of those kinks in you and put some zing into your step."

"Celeste! I have plenty of zing in my step. And that's enough about that."

"Yep," Celeste told Beamer, "sexual frustration."

Beamer eyed Maddie, raising a doggie eyebrow. Then woofed gently at Celeste, who nodded her agreement. It was a conspiracy. Then, because Maddie studiously ignored the two, a companionable silence cast its quiet spell over them. Maddie had lost count again with the receipts and had to start over. Celeste continued her adulation of the dog. Then, out of the blue, she said, "What the heck do you think James was thinking, Maddie? You think he really believed that staying here in Hanscomb Harbor for six weeks would change Hank's ways?"

"I don't know. Maybe. Obviously James was concerned enough to put Hank through all these hoops."

"Hmph. Flaming hoops, if you ask me. Being here won't make him want to do anything but get right back to his real life. A man like Hank can't sit around. He'll blow up. Just like you read about in the papers. Those people who spontaneously combust. One minute they're sitting there, pretty as you please, eating their tuna salad sandwich and then *ka-boom.* Nothing left of them but some ashes and their shoes."

Ashes! Maddie jerked around, needing to see for herself the shelf behind her. There it was. She sighed her relief. There was the hideously ugly lobster clock. Celeste hadn't managed to sell it today. She then addressed Celeste's silly assertion about people just catching fire for no apparent reason. "That's ridiculous. You have never read that in any respectable paper. It doesn't happen."

Giving Beamer a final pat, Celeste stood up slowly, all creaking joints, and stretched. Then she gasped and pointed. "Maddie! Heads up. Look outside. Mr. Fireball at three o'clock."

Maddie looked where Celeste pointed. "What? Who?" Then she saw and her heart jumped, her pulse raced, and she felt hot. It was Hank. "Ohmigod."

She nervously ran her hands through her hair and straightened her apron. But she could have saved herself the effort. Hank walked right on by. He didn't stop, glance in, wave, anything. Just kept going. Taken aback, and much more disappointed than she cared to acknowledge, even to herself, Maddie stood there frowning.

"I saw you preening for him."

Maddie jerked her attention to Celeste. "I did not," she lied, wishing her face didn't feel so hot.

"Did too."

"I did not."

"Did too."

"Stop it. This is childish."

"Is not."

"It is too." Maddie heard herself and exhaled for calm. "Don't you have something to do? Something the gainfully employed might engage in during working hours?"

Celeste squinted at her. "Beg pardon?"

This was going nowhere. Maddie glanced at her watch. It was nearly five o'clock. "Quitting time. You go on, Celeste. And I'll close up."

Her employee shrugged and began untying her apron.

"Don't have to tell me twice. There's a hot bingo game tonight at the community center." Celeste lifted her apron over her head and went to hang it on its wooden peg by the storeroom curtain.

Maddie watched her. The minute Celeste's back was to her she stared longingly, pleadingly, out the display window.

"Ha. Caught you."

Maddie jumped guiltily. "Caught me what? I wasn't doing anything."

"Were too. You were staring out that window and wishing he'd come back." Maddie's protest rode her lips but Celeste held up a hand, cutting her off. "Now don't you go denying it. I see you mooning around here and your look of hope every time that door opens and that little bell tinkles."

Maddie felt rooted to the spot. Was she that obvious? "I do not."

Celeste puckered her features prunelike. "I'm not playing that again."

Before Maddie could say anything, the roar of a motorcycle pulling up at the curb outside caught her attention. Even with his helmet on, Maddie recognized Teddy Millicum. Suspicion became certainty. He was here for Celeste. Maddie turned to the pink-clad Day-Glo dynamo, who was innocently gathering up her purse and sweater. "Celeste McNeer, shame on you. He's in high school. He's a child."

Suddenly all prim and proper, Celeste preached, "Now look who's got a dirty mind. Teddy's a sweet boy and a neighbor. He's giving me rides until my car is fixed. And that's *all*, Miss High-and-Mighty. I swear, you and Lavinia Houghton. If you don't watch out, you're going to be a tight-assed old biddy just like her one day." Celeste pulled one arm and then the other through her sweater's sleeves and straightened it around her. She then bent to pat the dog goodbye.

"Oh, please, Celeste, don't play Miss Innocent with me.

Your car was fixed days ago. You just like riding on the back of that boy's motorcycle, don't you?"

Her nose in the air, Celeste strolled toward the front door. "Could be. Good night now." She opened the door, soundly cursed the tinkling bell, and stepped outside, pulling the door closed behind her.

Maddie hurried over to the door, standing a bit to the side of it and watching as the high-school-aged boy handed Celeste a helmet and waited for her to put it on. She did—with practiced ease—and climbed on the motorcycle, settling in behind Teddy. She wrapped her arms around him. With her purse slung over a shoulder, she grinned brightly and, as Teddy pulled away, waved at Maddie. The stinker had known she'd be watching.

Absolutely scandalized, and embarrassed to be caught peeping, Maddie crossed her arms and turned away from the beveled-glass panes set in the door. "I cannot believe that woman." Maddie heard herself. "Great. Now she has me talking out loud to myself." Then she remembered: she wasn't alone in the shop. Half fearful, Maddie glanced around and found the dog.

Beamer lay in front of the card table where Maddie had kept a jigsaw puzzle for James to work while he visited with her. Under the table was a box of James's belongings from the cottage that Mr. Hardy had brought her, not knowing at the time what else to do with them. Though her heart felt tender at the remembrance of James, Maddie brightened with the realization that she needed to give his things to his grandson, namely Hank Madison. Was that not the most perfect excuse to go looking for him?

Just then Maddie noticed that the dog's great golden head lay upon a wadded-up old sweater of James's. Had Beamer pulled it out? Or had Celeste? Maddie sighed, feeling something in her heart soften. The poor dog was grieving. She missed her owner. Come to think of it, she'd barely moved from that spot all day, except for the few times she or Celeste had let her out to attend to her doggy business. Beamer now stared up at Maddie and gave a cautiously hopeful thump of her tail.

A sigh escaped Maddie. "You poor thing. You miss James, don't you? That's why you went out to his cottage the other night. Well, I'm sorry for your loss, Beamer. I really am."

Beamer raised her head. With her ears perked up, she woofed politely at Maddie as if to say thank you. Maddie smiled. "Well, good. At least we got that settled—"

Behind her, the bell above the door tinkled maniacally, alerting Maddie to its being opened. Beamer came to her feet, alert now, her tail wagging. Maddie turned around, the words *I'm sorry but we're closed* on her lips. She never said them. Instead, her knees felt weak, her heart thumped. "Hank."

CHAPTER SEVEN

❧

"HI." HANK CLOSED THE door behind him, removed his sunglasses, then jerked a thumb over his shoulder, pointing to the great outdoors. "Was I seeing things, or was that Mrs. McNeer on the back of that kid's motorcycle that just went by?"

Over the din of her traitorous heart's happy singing, Maddie noted Hank's relaxed attire. Khaki shorts, a T-shirt from the arcade, and leather sandals. He'd donned the protective coloration of a tourist. "It was Celeste, all right. Can you believe it?"

"Of her? Yes." He folded his sunglasses and secured them in his T-shirt pocket. Then he spied the dog and grinned, nearly sending Maddie to her knees, even though the bone-melting smile wasn't directed at her. "Hey, Beamer. How's it going, girl?" Hank squatted down on his haunches and ruffled the dog's head and ears as he spoke affectionately to her. Beamer wriggled her joy and licked at Hank's hands.

Drinking in the sight of him, giddily happy and mad at herself for being so, as well as half terrified she was only moments away from behaving exactly as Beamer was, Maddie said, "Too bad you can't keep her with you at the motel."

"I'm not at the motel anymore. They had some people with reservations come in. I had to move."

"I see. Um, where'd you move to?" she pried, tucking a lock of her hair behind her ear and smiling, faking the attitude of someone merely being polite and only mildly curious.

He looked up at her, his expression unreadable. "Out to that cottage we went to the other night."

Maddie's smile faded. "Oh." He was staying where his

grandfather had. "Good." She didn't know what else to say, so she ended up saying everything. "Well, I understand you can have pets out there. Obviously. I mean James had Beamer out there. And we saw those other dogs, too. You and I, I mean. So would you like to keep her for a bit with you? She obviously wants to be out there. And now you're out there." *You're babbling like an idiot. Shut up.* "I just thought you might keep each other company. Or not."

Hank didn't say anything. He rubbed the dog's ears and managed to give the impression that he was thinking and avoiding Maddie's gaze. Maddie took this opportunity to take a deep breath and to drink in his athlete's physique and the smooth and graceful way he squatted on his haunches in front of the dog. Then he suddenly looked up at her, causing her to blink. "Thank you for the offer. But I don't think that would be a good idea, Maddie. I think it would confuse her when I leave. She needs to know her home is with you now."

Maddie felt thoroughly chastised. "Of course you're right. It was just a thought."

His gaze roved assessingly over Maddie's face, causing her to tense with wondering what he sought to see. Then he nodded, looking away from her to again pet the dog. After a few quiet ticks on the clock, he said, "So, how'd you do after I left the other night?"

Determined to sound intelligent and sophisticated this time, Maddie breezily said, "Well, there was no bloodletting, if that's what you mean. And I thank you again for giving her a bath while I went to the store for dog food. If you hadn't taken control, Beamer would probably still be yucky with sand. And starved, as well." She laughed breezily, today's modern woman. And caved. "Oh, who am I kidding? The truth is we were both miserable after you left."

Hank arched his eyebrows. Maddie choked with realization—that whole "we were both miserable after you left" remark. She felt her face heat up. "What I meant was I couldn't sleep." She pointed to the dog. "She wanted to sleep with me."

Hank chuckled, then his dark-eyed gaze bored suggestively into hers. "She's not the only one around here who does. But probably for different reasons."

Maddie's hormonal pulse skyrocketed. She didn't know where to look, but she did totally ignore his comment and keep right on talking, a bit too loudly. "So it took me a while, but I coaxed her onto the screened-in back porch. But, boy, she let me know how much she hated that." Hank grinned at her, revealing a mouthful of white, even teeth that looked as if they could chew her up. Darn him, he knew the effect he was having on her. "Okay," Maddie said. She pulled at her red apron, fanning herself. "Why is it so hot in here? Did the air-conditioning go out or something?"

Hank looked up and around assessingly, then held a hand out, palm up, as if feeling for the flow of air. "No. It's on," he said, maddeningly calm as he slowly raked his gaze up and down her figure . . . then looked her right in the eye again.

Self-conscious, her mouth dry with want, Maddie crossed her arms under her breasts. "So, it's nice to see you," she said pleasantly, desperately. "Did you get all moved in at the cottage?"

He shrugged. "It wasn't much of a move. Just my clothes out to a rickety old beach cottage. You ought to see it inside."

"I'd love to," Maddie heard herself blurt. She blinked rapidly and fought to keep a friendly smile, and no more, on her face.

Too late. Hank grinned . . . like a wolf seeing supper. "Yeah? Well, maybe we can arrange that soon. Right now it's not presentable for company."

"I bet. You poor man." Grateful for this relatively neutral topic of discussion, Maddie stood by benignly and watched Hank and Beamer together. She suddenly became aware of how the two of them filled her shop with their healthy presence. With them here, everything seemed . . . okay. Good. And warm. Just right, somehow.

Yet she felt like the outsider in this picture. She had to face it: she had no idea how to relate to either one of them, but especially Hank. How was she supposed to think of him? *Was* she supposed to think of him? And what about all this sexual innuendo, all the things that were not spoken but clearly suggested? The mouth-watering looks. The eye contact. That one hot kiss. The way he always leaned in toward her when they talked. The way she felt when he touched her, when he was simply in the same room with her. The sudden awkward silences . . . much like this one.

Clearly, they were attracted to each other. Then what was so hard?

But she knew. First and obviously was a lack of trust. She never felt certain Hank's overtures had as much to do with her personally as they might have to do with him flirting to influence her decision about his going, or not going, to New York to close that business deal and chair the stockholders' meeting. Whew. It was out in one breath. And too, she had that whole thing with Stanton and being jilted. She was still in retreat from relationships because of that. More out of injured pride, at this point, than lost love, she could now acknowledge. But still, there it was, a real thing in her life.

And on Hank's part, he had his grief over his grandfather's passing. The total upheaval of his life. And he'd thought her a gold digger at first. Then he'd found out she was something worse—a threat to him because of his grandfather's will. And neither one of them had a clue why James had done as he had. Or how this would all work out. So, yeah, Maddie decided, they had some things between them. Big things. Hard things.

Just then, Hank looked up, his gaze locking with hers as he caught her staring. She smiled too brightly and chirped, "So. How *are* things out at the cottage?"

Hank chuckled and pushed up to his feet. Beamer sat down beside him, as if she'd chosen sides. "I thought we'd discussed that already. But terrible, thanks. That is one ratty place."

"But more quiet than at the motel with all those kids." She was remembering their conversation in his SUV as they'd hunted for Beamer.

"Quiet it's not. I've had more visitors today than the White House, I'll bet."

"Oh, no. Not reporters?"

"No. The other tenants. Apparently I've been adopted into their community. They're nice people. And I appreciate the food and all the beer and the magazines—"

"Dear God."

"Exactly."

Then, out of the blue, the thought becoming words at the same instant, Maddie blurted, "I've made my decision about New York, Hank."

He sobered, his gaze searching her face for clues. "Okay. But not here, Maddie." He spread his hands, looking around, as if casting about for an idea. "Look, your sign outside says you close at five today. It's after that now. So how about the Captain's Tavern again? Dinner's on me. We can talk there. It's more neutral, I think. Better for both of us."

He suddenly looked so young, so vulnerable. Maddie's heart went out to him, and she smiled to reassure him. She then experienced a sudden appreciation for the fact that this man's life, his work, the way he thought of himself, were in her hands. But only as long as he allowed it to be. That got her. It was true. After all, and as he'd already told her, he could just say the hell with her and go to New York. He could have kicked about the will, too, and contested it, done something legal to get out of it. Yet he hadn't. Why? What was really keeping him here? What did he hope to find?

All that took her about three seconds to think. She realized he was still waiting for an answer . . . while she stood there nervously fiddling with her nametag. "So. The Captain's Tavern it is."

* * *

A preserved two-story wooden building painted a bright red, the Captain's Tavern, with its outside umbrella-covered tables, occupied the broad circular end of the relatively new boardwalk that had been built to link the tourist attractions. The popular watering hole itself overlooked the rocky border that fronted the low sea-grass-topped dunes that in turn led down to the sloping beach. Come the sunset, twinkling rows of tiny lights strung along the overhanging eaves of the weathered building promised a merry time for all, as did the carnival music of the nearby carousel. Add to that the soft glow of an early summer evening and the salt-tinged scent of a gentle breeze, and you had the perfect setting for romance.

But romance had nothing to do with Hank's bringing Maddie here tonight to a crowded yet neutral setting. Yet romance was all he could think about, despite the gut-tightening drama of what he thought of as her pending New York decision. But here, in this setting, his mind and his body were not thinking of the bottom line. They were seated outside at one of the tables, which Hank had snagged for them when two couples got up to leave. The table had been quickly bussed and Stephie, the waitress, had again greeted them. In front of Hank now sat a chilled stein of dark beer. Maddie had a white wine.

All of that was good. The problem, though, was that Maddie sat facing the beach. That put the sunset behind her, over her shoulder . . . her bare shoulder. Hank ached to stroke her skin. He knew how it would feel. Soft. Silky. Warm. He couldn't take his eyes off her. And it sure as hell didn't help that her golden hair reflected the sun's rays and lent her the breathtaking appearance of having a halo. Watching her, and filtering the rise and fall of cheerful conversations around them, Hank could barely swallow. After closing her shop, and while he'd fed Beamer and put her in Maddie's backyard, she'd changed into a spaghetti-strapped sundress that did nothing to hide her curves. In a complete froth now with wanting her, and feeling as if he were on fire, Hank chuckled self-deprecatingly and shook his head.

"What's so funny?" Maddie grinned expectantly.

"You, Maddie." With both hands he gestured dramatically at her. "Look at you. Damn."

Her smile faded. She looked down at her dress, pulling at it. "What's wrong? Is something showing that shouldn't be?" She raised her head, showing him an anxious, embarrassed expression.

"No. Nothing that shouldn't be. But still . . . everything. You just don't quit."

"So, I'm thinking some of these are compliments, right? But you have to help me out here, Hank. What are you saying?"

Hank assessed her. Should he tell her how she affected him? After all, they were at a pretty delicate juncture right now. One wrong word and . . . poof. His life as he knew it was gone. Instant rebellion flared in his heart. Sort of an "Oh, really? Well, then, what the hell?" thing. He leaned in over the table, closer to her, and grinned. "You'll probably shoot me for this—and rightly so—but you look like some kind of a sun goddess. I swear you make my mouth water. And I would like nothing better than to, uh, worship you right now."

With her mouth open as if she had trouble catching a breath and her blue eyes wide, Maddie sat back abruptly. "Well, I wasn't expecting that."

"No, I don't suppose you were. But there you have it. That's how I feel."

Her face colored a pretty pink, yet she looked troubled. "I cannot believe you are saying these things. Especially now."

"I know what you mean. I've wrestled with this. And I mean how to tell you exactly how you affect me without making you wonder at my motive. But then I decided what the hell, just say it. So the truth is, you've taken me completely by surprise, Maddie. I was prepared to fight you tooth, nail, and claw. And I thought I had you pegged. But

I couldn't have been more wrong. In fact, I think my grandfather—"

"Stop right there." She underscored her words with a hand held up, palm out to him. "Please don't say anything more."

Hank's passion for her, and speaking it aloud, made him bold. "Why? What's wrong? You're not going to tell me that you don't feel this whatever it is between us, are you? Because I've kissed you, and I think I know better."

Maddie sat up straighter, very serious, her mouth a thin line. "Look, I need to tell you that I'm not sure I trust any of this, Hank—any of what I'm feeling, what you might be feeling. Not in light of what brought us together. And not in light of what we came here to discuss."

"Okay." Shot down, Hank sat back and crossed his legs, an ankle resting atop the opposite knee. "So we have nowhere to go with this?"

Maddie sighed dramatically. "Oh, Hank, I don't know. This is the biggest mess. I hate it." Frowning, she rubbed at her temple and focused on him. "Okay, here's the thing. And this is hard for me to say. I feel vulnerable. And I hate that buzz word. I do. But it's how I feel. And I'm afraid that the only reason you're flirting with me is . . ." Her voice trailed off. She stared at her hands in her lap. "Is to try to manipulate me into making the decision you want." She met his eyes now. "There. I've said it."

Hank rubbed a hand over his mouth and chin and then exhaled. "I appreciate your honesty. But I think you sell yourself short. And me, too. You're a gorgeous, desirable woman in your own right, Maddie—"

"I've been told that before, only to be left at the altar. There I was, wearing a white dress and facing a church full of people. Alone. That blessed event was only a year ago, Hank. A very short year ago. And I'm not over it."

"Damn, Maddie. I had no idea. But you have to know I'm not that guy."

"Of course I do. But you are *a* guy, if you get my meaning."

"Yeah. You're battle-scarred. No one stands a chance with you. Bitter. Angry. I've been there myself. Not as far as the altar, but there."

She shrugged. "Then you know how hard it is."

"I do." He really had no idea what else to say.

Maddie cocked her head, giving him a considering look. She lifted her rounded goblet of wine and sipped at the spirits. "On another subject, where were you going this afternoon when you passed the shop just before Celeste left?"

Glad for this respite from intense subjects, Hank drank from his beer and set it down. "I was on my way to the hardware store. But it apparently closes early, too, on a Saturday."

Maddie nodded. "Most things do around the town proper. They'll remain closed tomorrow, too. Except for the businesses here on the boardwalk." She set her wineglass down. "So what were you going to get at the hardware store?"

Hank chuckled. "If you can believe it, a hammer and nails to pound some stability into the walls of that cottage."

"Hank, that's work. You're not supposed to work."

"No it isn't. It's my new hobby." He grinned widely. "And hobbies aren't work." She was still seriously grim. "For God's sake, Maddie, if I don't do something I'll explode. I'm a workaholic, remember? I need to be busy."

"Which defies the whole point of the will, Hank. Your grandfather wanted you to relax."

"Well, in light of that will, Maddie, it relaxes me to pound things with a hammer, okay? And why doesn't Mr. Hardy fix those old cottages up or tear them down and build new ones?"

"You're changing the subject, but he doesn't because he believes that his cottages are one of the few places around here that people who don't have a lot of money but deserve a nice vacation can afford. So if he went to the expense of fixing them up, or even built new ones, then he'd have to charge more. And that would shut out the very people he wants to serve."

Chagrined, Hank could only stare at her. "Well, don't I feel like Little Lord Fauntleroy with my 'let them eat cake' attitude."

Maddie laughed at him. A silvery sound somewhat like the tinkling bell above her shop's door. "Don't you mean Marie Antoinette?"

"Probably. But I don't stand a chance of passing that physical."

"No one with a head would."

"That's true."

She was intelligent and warm and funny and . . . everything a man could want in a woman. She was also in complete control of his life. Hank took a long draw of the rich, dark brew in front of him while Maddie sipped again at her wine. If he had any sense at all, he'd jump up from here and go hole himself up in that cottage for the next six weeks. If he lasted that long out there. If he didn't end up running screaming down the beach or right into the water. Back to nature and solitude wasn't all it was cracked up to be. Thoreau he wasn't, with all that Walden Pond madness.

Just then Maddie looked out toward the water and smiled some secret smile as she inhaled the salty tang of the air. The tilt of her head, the slender curve of her neck. This sultry setting. Hank swallowed, entranced again despite himself. His body tightened with its aching for her. "You really do love it here, don't you, Maddie?"

She gave him a dreamy smile that further unhinged him. "Yes. I was born and raised here. Sure, I left for college. Then work. Did the whole 'big city' thing. Most of the kids here do. But some of us come back and stay."

"Obviously. Here you are." Hank became aware again of the socializing adults on the tavern's deck with them and of the happy shouts of children in the nearby arcade. But he only had eyes for Maddie. "So tell me about college and work. What was that?"

"Columbia. Art history. Then I worked at the Whitney Museum in the research department. A completely lackluster three years."

"Then there was the big hurt at the altar with that guy?"

"Yes. Dr. Stanton Fairchild." She rolled her eyes.

Hank grinned at her expression, then shaded his eyes against the sunset. "Sorry. The sun's blinding right there on the horizon."

She smiled . . . a teasing, sexy smile. "Well, you could put on your sunglasses. But they may not help if it's really my radiance as a sun goddess that's blinding you."

"Oh, man." Hank ducked his head and put a hand to his forehead. "You're not going to let me forget that remark, are you?"

She laughed. "Not any time soon."

They were doing it again. Flirting. And he was on fire for her, dammit. Hank sent her a sidelong glance and acknowledged to himself that he couldn't get enough of looking at her. She had the most delicate jaw and the cutest little nose. And this was getting him nowhere. "Hey, I promised you dinner. Yet we've been sitting here for over an hour talking and drinking. And that's good. I like it. I'm having fun. But—"

"But we need to get down to business, right?"

"I like how you think."

"Before you go carving that in stone, I want to ask you something."

Hank spread his hands wide. "Fire away."

"All right. How'd you know the other night that this business deal of yours had come to a head? I mean, you were already here in Hanscomb Harbor and presumably not in touch with your company. The stockholders' meeting I understand. I assume they're scheduled way in advance?"

"Exactly. But about the other, I had just found out that morning of the will reading that it would all come together quickly. I just didn't know when."

"Until . . . ?"

"Until I went back to the office that afternoon and was informed." Hank began to wonder where all this was headed.

"You went back to the office before Jim whisked you here?"

"I did. No matter how unreasonable my grandfather's will is, Maddie, Jim isn't. He knows he couldn't just cart me away and not tell everyone where I was. And he knew I had to go back and talk with my board of directors and explain things. Thank God I have a supremely competent board that I can trust. But where's this coming from, Maddie? What's your point?"

"I just wanted to be sure that you've been actually relaxing and not working. You know: phone calls, faxes, people flying in and out."

He chuckled but not because anything was funny. "You don't trust me."

"I just want to do a good job," she demurred. "And make sure that, in light of this development and up until now, you've been living up to your end of the bargain."

"You sound like a lawyer. But I have been, Maddie. It's just me and the sun and the surf."

"Good. So how *are* you holding up with all this relaxing?"

Hank shrugged. "Like I said, I should be dead inside of a couple weeks. But don't start counting the money yet. I might pull through."

"That isn't funny."

Hank crossed his arms atop the table. "Well, what do you expect from me? I don't like being questioned like this. And you have to understand that in my normal life I don't answer to anyone on a daily basis. Just a couple times a year to stockholders."

"In my normal life I wouldn't be asking you any of these questions. They'd be none of my business. But being in the same boat with you right now, well, I'm trying not to rock it. So if you say you're not working, you're not working."

"Thank you."

"You're welcome."

"So what do we do now?"

"I tell you my decision, I guess."

"Okay." Hank stared intently into her blue eyes. His heart pounded dully in anticipation of her answer.

She grinned. "I say yes."

Hank sat up straight, tense, his heart pounding. "Yes? What does yes mean, Maddie? I don't want to make a mistake here."

"I'm saying that I think you should go to New York. For the stockholders' meeting and to ink your business deal."

He was afraid even to breathe. He gripped the table and stared at her. "And if I do—'no harm, no foul' with respect to the will?"

She shook her head. "No." Then frowned. "I mean yes. Yes, there will be no harm, no foul. Is that clear?"

"Very clear." Sheer relief robbed Hank of strength, or he would have jumped up and hugged her and swung her around. "Thank you, Maddie," he said simply. She didn't say anything, just stared at him. Suddenly troubled, maybe even alarmed, Hank sobered. "Wait. What am I missing here, Maddie? Something to do with your decision? Something you haven't told me yet?"

"No. I told you my decision."

Hank thought about the way she said that. Her voice was flat of tone. She didn't like her decision. And he didn't like that she didn't. "Okay, Maddie. Tell me where you are in your thinking. What brought you to this decision, I mean. I need to know."

"I don't know why you would. What difference does it make?"

He was right. She hated her decision—and most likely him for forcing it on her. Hank wanted very much to take her hand, yet he didn't dare. "It makes a lot of difference to me, Maddie."

She focused on her wineglass, which she was gently twirling by its stem. "Okay, bottom line. I don't think it's fair what your grandfather did to you. Disrupting your life like he has. I just don't think someone who is—forgive me—dead should be allowed to dictate his heir's behavior."

"So far we're on the same page. We both know that's exactly what he did."

Maddie met his gaze. "Yes. Speaking of legally, I didn't call Jim Thornton. No courage, I guess. I pretty much didn't want to hear his answer. So if he hears about your going, it won't be from me. I'm assuming he's not a stockholder and won't be there, right?"

"Right." As busy as his mind was with the myriad details of all the financial plates he had to get up in the air, Hank still worried what this decision in his favor had cost Maddie in honor and honesty. "So, are you okay with this decision, Maddie? I mean really? You don't look like you are."

She exhaled and looked away from him, closing her eyes and firming her mouth. From where he sat, she looked as if she were trying not to cry.

"Oh, man," he muttered too low for her to hear. "Maddie? Look at me." She did, her heart in her eyes . . . proud, defiant. Compromised. "Shit," Hank again muttered under his breath. "Look, forget it. I won't go. It's not worth it. Not with what I'm seeing right now on your face. You're right. It's only money. Just a deal. Who cares?"

Her stunned silence crept over them in much the same way that the evening's shadows were. Maddie's blue eyes stared holes in him. "Excuse me? You put me through hell for days with this decision—and now that I've made one you say forget it? Hank Madison, have you lost your mind?"

"Not yet. And yeah, somewhere inside me I know I have to go to New York and do this. It's not only my money—or yours—at stake here, but a lot of my investors' money, too. This whole deal is about jobs and economic growth. Gross national product stuff. But once I got to thinking about it, too, I realized that nothing is signed yet. Nothing's been done that's not undoable." He held her gaze, making sure he had her attention. "I want this deal, Maddie. Very much. But I don't want it at the expense of that look on your face."

Maddie's throat worked, her expression softened. He'd gotten to her. Then he realized how awful for her he felt inside . . . and knew the truth: she'd gotten to him. Something inside Hank died . . . and something else was reborn, something he couldn't name or even explore at this time. If ever.

"I appreciate your concern, Hank," she said. "But we can't lose sight of the important issues here. I mean about not upholding the will and then having to lie to Jim about it. For me, it was a case of 'do the means justify the end?' And I had to say yes. Which got me into situational ethics. God. And then I decided it's *not* the end of the world— unless you *don't* go. Like you said, it's jobs. And that makes it people's lives and livelihoods balanced against poor timing and a sweet old man's concerns for his grandson. Put like that, my decision was easy and could only be the one I came to."

Hank stared at her, seeing her in a new light. "Wow. I'm impressed. Do you have any idea how brilliant you are, Maddie?"

That earned him a smile. "You're just saying that because I gave you the answer you want."

Hank shook his head. "No. Now don't sell me short. I have never surrounded myself with yes-men. Or -women. I want to be told the truth straight up, no matter how much I might not like the news, and no matter what someone might think I want to hear."

"Very admirable."

"Hey, my first true compliment from Maddie Copeland." Hank was more amused than insulted. "You don't think much of me, do you? I mean for the most part."

"But I do. I think of you a lot." Her eyes widened. "I mean, I think a lot of you."

He stretched across the table to squeeze her hand affectionately. "And I think I liked your first answer better." His gaze met hers for an intense second, then he sat back, still feeling the imprint of her hand in his. "Can I ask you something now?"

Looking a little off kilter, and maybe a bit wary, she nodded. "Sure."

"What the hell do you really make of this will? I can't get a handle on it."

"Thank God. I thought it was just me. I think this whole thing isn't fair to you at all, Hank. Or to me. But here we are, and I think it's ridiculous. I can't believe Jim would even write it up. But the fact that he did makes me think there is something behind all this that has nothing to do with your taking a vacation."

Hank sat back, staring at her, admiring the quick intelligence that shone from her eyes. "I know where you're going with this. The other night out at the cottage, when we went looking for Beamer, you said something that makes a lot of sense."

"Well, please tell me. That will be a first."

"Hardly." Hank loved her self-deprecating humor. "You said you wonder if my grandfather did all this to get us together. You and me, I mean."

"Oh, God, I can't believe I said that." Maddie put a hand to her forehead and sent him a sidelong glance. "But yes, I said it, and you blew me off. You were right to. How conceited of me to even think it."

"Not at all. And I was just in a weird place the other night. But after thinking about what you said, I think it's something, well, to think about." Hank chuckled. "Could I be more vague?"

"I understand you. But I think I was wrong about that, Hank. I mean why would he do that? He didn't have to go to these lengths. He could have just brought you along to meet me at any point in the three summers he came here."

"That's true. Except being a workaholic, I probably wouldn't have taken the time. What a jerk, huh? My sick old grandfather." Hank stopped, took a breath. "Anyway, I certainly can't come up with any other reason why he'd choose Hanscomb Harbor, not that it's not wonderful. But I mean, you're here. Still, maybe this is something we can put on the back burner until everything else is settled. What do you say?"

"Okay. Gladly." Maddie smiled shyly at him.

"Good." Her smile pleased him to no end. It was such a simple expression. But it made his heart sing. He couldn't even say why. Nor could he remember ever dealing so gingerly with a woman before. This wasn't how he behaved. He usually moved in a much faster set, much faster women. Ah, but there it was. Maddie wasn't a fast woman. Or like any other woman he'd ever known. And furthermore, Hanscomb Harbor wasn't the big city. This was small-town America. Hank wondered if he was beginning to see inside his grandfather's motives here. *Next thing I know,* Hank thought wryly, *I'll be coming around in the surrey with the fringe on top and using terms like* court *and* woo.

"Hank, what would you have done if I'd come to a different decision?"

She'd certainly pulled him back to present times with that question. "I know where this is going. You think I'd just go do what I wanted anyway, don't you?"

"It crossed my mind, especially since you'd already said as much. And that being so, all I had to do was see if I could live with your decision, really. And it turns out I can."

"I'm glad, Maddie. But I wouldn't have gone if you'd had serious reservations."

"I do have serious reservations, Hank. But they're mine, not yours. So go to New York. Do what you have to do, and then get back here to your vacation. You have a cottage to repair and some relaxing to do."

To Hank's utter surprise, that all sounded appealing. Good God, he was loosening up. High spirits grabbed him. "Come on," he said, standing up and fishing some bills out of his pocket, which he tossed onto the table to pay for their drinks. "I promised you dinner. How do a hot dog and some cotton candy sound?"

"Wow," Maddie said, coming to her feet. "You really know how to treat a girl."

"Normally we'd get all dressed up and I'd take you out to a swanky joint. But since I'm supposed to be taking a load off and, from what I've seen, there are no swanky joints here, this is as good as it gets. But stick with me, baby, and I may even win you a great big teddy bear in the arcade."

Maddie sent him a look of mock outrage. "Excuse me, Mr. Macho? I have a pretty good arm myself. Maybe I'll win *you* a bear."

"Be still, my heart," Hank quipped, holding his arm out as she rounded the table and drew even with him.

For the second time this week, Hank put his arm around her, pulling her close to his side as they walked off. And for the second time, she didn't pull away. Still high on emotion and a renewed sense of well-being, Hank told her, "By the way, two things. The meetings in New York are set for next Friday, but I need to go to the city on Wednesday to make sure everything is still on track. How do you feel about that?"

She shrugged. "I said, do what you have to do."

"Good. And you're coming in Friday, right?"

She stopped. "Wrong. I am not. What do you need me for?"

"You're the acting chair, remember? You signed the papers at Jim's office on the day of the will reading."

"Oh, God. I can't. I have a fear of speaking in public. I couldn't even perform in drama productions in high school, Hank. I get sick in front of crowds. And I mean physically. I will lose not only my decorum but also my lunch."

"You can do this, Maddie. You have to. Your name right now is the valid one."

Maddie stared at the candy store directly in front of them. "I don't like this at all." She then directed her gaze to Hank. "You said there were two things."

"Yes. I don't want you worrying about Jim finding out. So I'm going to tell him myself. I'll call him once I get there."

Maddie clutched at his shirt. "Oh, Hank, don't. What if

he calls a default, or whatever it is he'd have to do?"

"I don't think he will. He was reasonable last time about my having to go to the office. We'll just have to take our chances, though. Besides, I think he'd find out anyway because there will be a huge media hype when this deal is inked. And since Jim is like family to me, I'd rather he know up front from me than find out from another source."

"Well, that's commendable." Maddie relaxed a bit and let go of him. "But that's what you need—more media attention." As if she didn't realize she was, she absently straightened and tugged at his shirt where she'd wadded it in her fist.

It was a small thing. But such an intimate gesture. You wouldn't touch someone like that if you weren't involved with him. Hank grinned down at Maddie. "I have a third thing to say, Maddie."

"I don't want to hear it."

"Sure you do. If I mess up before the six weeks are over—and I mean after New York and if all the quiet and clean air gets to me—and you end up with everything, then my plan is simple. I'll marry you to get it all back."

CHAPTER EIGHT

❦

THAT NEXT THURSDAY AFTERNOON, having been back in New York City since the morning before—back in his real life—Hank expected that he would have regained his equilibrium. After all, he was living again in his penthouse, he was at work, and things were crazy, hectic, and familiar. He'd expected that he could slough off his time in Hanscomb Harbor, that he could look at it as an interlude and nothing more. But it certainly wasn't working out that way.

His life here no longer seemed to fit. It was like a favorite jacket that came back shrunk or misshapened from the dry cleaner's. His life, it seemed, was tight at the shoulders and didn't want to button as easily as it used to. He'd thought that being away from Maddie, he would instantly become his old in-control self. And he was. To an extent. But he was also distracted. He'd thought that away from Maddie, he could again think clearly and would see that his attraction to her had been a summer fling. Something experienced, brief and intense, but soon set aside. Yes, away from Maddie . . . all he could think about was her, dammit.

Between bouts of paying attention to the crisis du jour or the meeting at hand, he found her on his mind, her face before him, her voice and her laughter teasing him. He could see her now, last weekend at that tavern. In that dress. The sunset behind her. Her blue eyes flashing. And then they'd been at the arcade. Damned if she didn't have a better throwing arm than he did. He had the teddy bear to prove it, too. She'd won it at the—

The door to Hank's lavishly decorated corner office opened and brought him sharply back to the moment. He couldn't believe this. Apparently he'd done it again—gone off to la-la land with his thoughts of Maddie. Trying not to look guilty, and at the same time reminding himself that this was *his* empire, Hank looked up from the complicated financial report he'd been studying. Okay, *ignoring*, since his thoughts had drifted to Maddie.

When he saw who was standing there, another jet of guilt shot through him, as if he'd been caught writing cute notes in class instead of paying attention to the teacher.

Sure enough, the enigmatic Ms. Smith stood in the doorway. His secretary, executive assistant, girl Friday, however she thought of herself, of eight years' standing. She looked like her name. Plain, tall, angular, buttoned down, her black hair pulled back in a tight bun, her no-nonsense black-framed glasses perched perfectly atop the bridge of her nose, her two-piece black suit as impeccable as her timing. She also insisted she be called "Miz" Smith. She scared the hell of out of everyone. Except him. So he told himself.

"Yes, Miz Smith? What can I do for you?" That was how it worked around here. She told him what was next in his day, and he did it.

"I have Mr. Thornton on the line."

Hank exhaled, then firmed his lips. He'd asked her to place the call to Jim and had felt somewhat like an escaped convict returning to the prison and alerting the warden that he had. Before he could reach for the phone, Miz Smith spoke. "Have you finished with that report, sir? I'll need to incorporate your changes before your meeting at four-thirty."

She said it as if she had much more important things to do in this business and he was such a hindrance. "Almost," he said, regarding the report in front of him. "I'll speak to Jim and then finish this."

She nodded and stood there, her hand on the doorknob.

"Yes?" He always expected some huge disclosure from her, but never got one. Maybe this time was different. She certainly looked ready to reveal something.

"It's . . . well, nice to have you back, sir. Line one," she said as she stepped back, closing the door behind her.

Hank blinked. That *was* huge, coming from her. A bit

encouraged, he grabbed up the phone and punched line one. "Hello, Jim. I guess you're wondering what a guy like me is doing in a place like this."

"You could say that." In a word, Jim's voice was grim. "I was surprised, let's say."

"Well, you shouldn't have been. You know me."

"Yes I do, Hank. But I thought hanging on to everything you have would mean something to you, too. I thought you'd at least try."

Hank gripped the handset harder. "I did try, Jim. And I am still going to try. My being here now is temporary and then I'll go back and finish my time."

"Does Maddie know you're here? Did you tell her?"

Hank thought about not giving her up, about saying she had no idea. But he knew her well enough to know that wouldn't work. She'd be disappointed in him, and she'd tell Jim the truth herself, anyway. "Yes, Maddie knows I'm here. I cleared it with her."

"You twisted that girl's arm, didn't you?"

"I did no such thing. And she's a woman, not a girl. All I did was tell her what was at stake and ask her opinion on what to do."

"Well, what the hell could she say to that, Hank, except what she did? And now you've both lost everything."

"Dammit, Jim, be reasonable. Let me explain."

"There's nothing to explain. The will is very specific."

"And unfair. And unrealistic. And very contestable. And yet I haven't. Have you asked yourself why?"

Jim had nothing to say to that. Hank began to hope. He was also determined to wait out his family friend and attorney. This was a classic example of whoever speaks next, loses.

"Why don't you tell me why, son."

Hank exhaled, surprising himself to realize that he'd been holding his breath. "Okay, my first thought was to contest it. But I didn't because for one thing I was so surprised by it, and for another you practically threw my luggage at me and flew me off to Hanscomb Harbor before I could think. Then when I did think about the will, I got to wondering what the old man was really up to."

"So Maddie had nothing to do with your wanting to stay there?"

"Yes, she had a lot to do—I mean no. This doesn't have to do with Maddie. Not my being here right now, I mean."

"Did you two fight?"

"No, Jim, we didn't fight. Why would we fight?"

"Maybe because she didn't want you to leave for the city. Maybe because she didn't want your actions to cause her to lose everything James left her."

Angry now, Hank jerked forward in his leather executive chair and perched his elbows atop his vast cherrywood desk. "Give me some credit, Jim. Damn. First Maddie, then you. You keep selling me short when it comes to things like behaving honestly and with honor. You make me sound like some ruthless corporate raider with no conscience. Is that how I come across?"

"You can. But not now. So Maddie put you through your paces, huh?"

"Hell, yes. She's tough. Made me sweat for days before she decided."

Jim chuckled. "She's quite the woman."

With that comment Hank's suspicions grew. Jim really wanted him to think Maddie was wonderful. Everyone did. Wherever he went in Hanscomb Harbor, the townspeople greeted him and told him something wonderful about Maddie. They were all crazy about her and wanted him to be, as well. It was a conspiracy. "Yes. Quite the woman. Everyone tells me so. But this isn't about Maddie, Jim. Not directly. This is about Madison and Madison. I think you can see that I was damned if I did and damned if I didn't. If I had stayed in Hanscomb Harbor, the deal on Friday would fall through. But if I came here, I could ink the deal but lose my inheritance. I had to make a choice."

"And you chose the company over your grandfather's wishes."

Christ. Agitated now, hot under the collar, Hank retorted, "Yeah, well, you can't miss what you never had."

"What does that mean?"

"It means I never had my grandfather's money, Jim. I don't need it, and I don't want it. But I did have the company. And yes, I know the company was part of the inheritance and now it's gone too because I came here to try to save it—"

"I see your point—"

"Do you, Jim? Really? Does any of this make sense? If it does, tell me what in the hell the old man was thinking."

"He wanted you to be happy."

"Happy? Do I sound happy to you, Jim? Or do I sound like I'm about to pop a vein in my head? Because that's how it feels."

"Hank, I think we can—"

"And you, Jim—are you going to be such a stickler that you can't see the position I'm in here? How many lives will be affected? I have good people who work for me, depend on me, Jim—"

"I agree. I think you should—"

"I can't just sit out in Hanscomb Harbor in shorts and sandals, walking on the beach, while this whole thing goes belly-up. What kind of an asshole would that make me?"

"The worst kind. I think you did the right thing in coming to the city."

"Well, I don't. Because I *had* to come to the city. I had to—" Hank cut his own words off and took a deep breath. "What did you say?"

"I've been *trying* to say I think you made the right decision in coming back to ink this deal on Friday and preserve your company."

Hank had to shift mental gears. He'd prepared for a bloodletting . . . and it wasn't happening. He still wasn't sure he had won, though. All Jim had said was he agreed with Hank's decision, and not that he was going to look the other way because he had. "I have to be here, Jim. This is my life, my decision. But I don't think Maddie should pay the penalty for something she had nothing to do with and couldn't prevent."

"I agree. She's a wonderful woman."

So they were back to that. "Point taken, Jim. You sound like her publicist. Is there a reason for that?"

"Oh, no, no. I just like her." He paused. "Do you?"

It was at that moment that Hank knew Maddie was right. The will, the money, the company's holdings, the riches, the cars, the real estate, all of it—none of it mattered. The only thing that mattered was what he thought of Maddie. "Yes, Jim, I like her. I just wish we'd met under other circumstances."

"What's wrong with these?"

"You're kidding me, right?"

"No. But just so we understand each other, you've violated the tenets of your grandfather's will. Maddie allowed it. You both lose. All the Madison and Madison holdings will now go into a trust neither one of you can touch."

Hank's heart plunged. He broke out into a sweat, felt weak. "Jim, for God's sake, man, have mercy. I thought you said you agreed with my decision to leave Hanscomb Harbor for this business deal."

"I do. But I'm also bound by the legal language in your grandfather's will."

"Which I could contest."

"You could."

"You know, Jim, this has made it pretty hard for me to mourn James Senior. I'm not over being mad and hurt and feeling a little betrayed here."

"I can see how you'd feel all those things. But you really shouldn't."

"And why is that?" Suddenly, to Hank's ear, what Jim *wasn't* saying was more important than what he was. "What's going on? You have something up your sleeve, don't you? Some loophole or something."

"No. No loopholes. No second chances. Nothing."

"Then what?"

"Well, like you, I thought your grandfather's will was

totally nuts. And I told him so at the time. An old man's last grasping at control and manipulation. I thought I knew him better than that. But then . . . he told me why he was doing this, Hank."

Hank's grip on the phone tightened. "Tell me why."

"I'm sorry, but that's for me to know and for you to live long enough to find out. So when James Senior told me, I realized he *was,* after all, the man I loved like a brother. So knowing what he hoped to have happen and why, I'm just going to pretend this phone call never took place."

Hank held his burgeoning joy at bay a moment longer. "I couldn't ask you to do that, Jim."

"You're damned right you couldn't. But I can choose to do it."

Hank laughed at this irascible old man he loved. "Jim, you're every bit the rebel that I am."

That seemed to please him. "Maybe so. Used to be, at any rate."

"You still are. But I don't want you to get into any kind of legal trouble. Mary would skin me alive."

"Well, then, we just won't tell her, will we? And hell, I'm not afraid of the Bar Association. What are they going to do? Slap me on the wrist? Disbar me? I'm nearly eighty years old and have all the money Mary and I could spend in three lifetimes. And I was interpreting the law before most of those ABA whippersnappers were even alive. Besides, they're afraid of me. So that's my decision, son. I'm going to look the other way. Take the spirit of the thing over the letter of it. But just this once. And because I do know the spirit of James's intention, there won't be another reprieve, I promise you."

Hank now allowed relief to sweep over him like a wave. He and Maddie weren't going to lose. Hank felt simultaneously sick and elated. "I won't need another reprieve, Jim, I swear it. After this, I stay put in Hanscomb Harbor for the duration of the six weeks."

"Duration? No, on second thought, I think I'll start the six weeks over when you get back there Friday evening or

Saturday. The timing on the first go-round after your grand-father's death was a surprise and not very fair to you. So we'll be prepared this time and give it a good, clean run."

Hank wanted to protest, then thought better of it—meaning, Maddie's beautiful, sexy face popped into his head. Six full weeks to concentrate on Maddie, once this week was behind him. "All right. Okay. I can do that. I can't wait to let Maddie know your decision. She'll be relieved. And happy."

"Good. She's a wonderful young woman. Very pretty, too. And smart. A business owner like yourself."

Here we go again. Hank grinned. All this Maddie-praising was starting to get funny, not that she didn't deserve every word of it. But Hank suddenly felt like doing a little bragging of his own. "She's also coming to the stockholders' meeting Friday. She's very eager to fulfill her obligations as chairwoman of the board."

That wasn't quite the truth but it should get Jim going.

"Admirable. Very admirable," he said. "Shows a sense of responsibility that seems to be lacking in some young people today."

"A veritable Girl Scout." This was becoming a game of one-upmanship.

"Sweet disposition," Jim countered. "But not someone to be taken lightly."

"I agree. You wouldn't want to take Maddie lightly."

"True. She's what we old codgers used to call the marrying kind."

Hank grinned and shook his head. That's exactly what this was—a game of one-upmanship. But he felt certain he had the ultimate compliment. "I don't know about marrying, but she is one hell of a kisser."

The surprised silence at the other end was Hank's reward. "You've kissed her?" Jim barked.

"Yes, I have."

Another silence followed this. "When?"

"In your office. On the day the will was read."

"You kissed her in my office on the day the will was read? Before you knew the details?"

Suddenly Hank felt as if he'd passed or failed some test. He couldn't tell which. "Well, I sure as hell didn't feel like kissing her after it was read. But why? What's wrong? What are you getting at?"

"Nothing." Suddenly Jim was a clam.

"That's it? Nothing?"

"Yes. You're two adults. It's not like I'm her father and I caught you two underage kids in the dark and necking on the front-porch swing."

Now it was Hank's turn to be silent.

"You're awfully quiet, Hank."

"I've got a lot to think about."

"True. That reminds me. Let me give you something more to think about."

"Great. Like what?"

"A bit of bad news."

Hank rubbed at his aching forehead. "Jim, for the last couple of weeks or so, there hasn't been any other kind. So what is it?"

"Not what. Who. Your mother isn't voting by proxy this time. She called me when she couldn't reach you. She's tearing herself away from Rodeo Drive long enough to come to New York—live and in person—for tomorrow's stockholders' meeting."

Hank's insides turned liquid. Lillian Elaine Smythe Madison was a hurricane. An overly dramatic force of nature who owned a fair percentage of Madison & Madison stock. And Hank hadn't yet told her about the will. Or Maddie and her part in it. All his mother knew was that James Senior had died. And now here they would all meet up on Friday. *Wonderful.* Hank slowly leaned over until his forehead rested atop his desk . . . much like a man about to be guillotined.

With the phone still at his ear, he said to Jim, "I'm a dead man."

"Not yet. But you will be. I don't envy you in the least,

son," Jim said, expansively, cheerfully. "Well, except where Maddie is concerned."

It was Friday, and Maddie felt sick. Her queasiness had nothing to do with her private Learjet ride into New York City that morning. It was the stockholders' meeting in less than an hour. She wasn't good in front of crowds. Never had been. That was why she'd taken that job in research at the Whitney Museum. So she could hide. And that was why she'd buried herself in Hanscomb Harbor after her jilting. So she could hide.

Life faced head-on just never turned out well for her. She thought back to herself as a little girl and skipping up to that strange dog that had bitten her. Not a good ending. She thought next of Stanton Fairchild, idiot doctor, and his leaving her in the lurch on their wedding day. Not a good ending. She thought of her parents coming to see her in New York at her insistent urging. She'd wanted them very much to see her Greenwich Village apartment and to see she was doing well. They'd been killed in a car wreck. *Not a good ending* didn't even begin to cover that one.

And then there'd been James. She'd befriended the man and then he'd died and left her everything. Not a good ending. And Hank. Not a good beginning. It was time to face it. She didn't do life well. What she did do well was hide—in back rooms, not boardrooms. She wanted her cozy little house and her safe little shop in the protective haven that was Hanscomb Harbor. She didn't want to be here in Midtown Manhattan inside this vast and richly appointed penthouse apartment that crowned the Madison & Madison Enterprises building.

Wow. A penthouse apartment. And she was inside one. She stroked her hands over the velvety fabric of the sofa cushions to either side of her. That was another thing. How could anything over five thousand square feet be termed an apartment? It was a city, and it needed street signs. It was a labyrinthine maze of breathtaking rooms that could trick you into thinking you were inside a villa on the Mediterranean, until you looked out a window onto Manhattan. Still, the tones and textures and fabrics reminded her of ancient, elegant times when women wore revealing togas and men rode about in chariots.

Maddie looked down at her modern black two-piece suit and matching pumps. She was so out of place here. Maddie shook her head. *James, my sneaky little friend, if you were here, I'd choke you.*

But James wasn't here. However, his grandson was. He'd just gotten off the phone with someone downstairs and was sitting down in the chair next to the sofa. "You okay, Maddie? You look nervous."

"I don't like being in front of groups. And the one gathering downstairs is the grandmother of all groups, Hank. But I'm not really nervous. I've got it all under control." To prove it, she immediately stopped twisting her purse strap around her fingers.

But Hank had noticed. He sat back, crossing an ankle atop his opposite knee. "You sure?"

No. "Yes. It's this place. It makes me nervous." Well, it was partly true.

Hank raised his eyebrows and then frowned at their surroundings. "Really? This place? Has something moved that shouldn't? Did you hear a twig snap or something?"

Maddie chuckled. "It wouldn't surprise me." She couldn't believe she was here with him. She'd missed him so much in the forty-eight hours he'd been gone. And that realization had upset her to no end. There was no way this was going to end well, "this" being how she felt about him. *I mean, look at him.* He was handsome, virile, capable, intelligent, and powerful. All that and more had been brought home to her today as she'd watched him in his environment and witnessed the respect and deference with which he was treated. What she had learned, again, was this man was not for her. Out of her league.

Maddie's gaze landed on him. He was watching her. "So I had a girl come in to help Celeste in the shop this weekend. Fran Dobson. She's nice. Has two kids. Twin girls

Babies, really. I figured she could use the money—and could keep Celeste from running amok. As if anyone can. And Beamer. She's fine. Celeste is keeping her for me while I'm here. She misses you. The dog, I mean. At least, I think she does. She hasn't really said."

Finally Maddie was at the end of her babbling monologue. It was Hank. He always did this—just sat and watched her and unhinged her. "What?"

Hank blinked. "I'm sorry. I was staring. So what about this place makes you nervous?"

It was Maddie's turn to blink. Had he not been listening to her? Did men ever listen to women? "What makes me nervous? Well, it's a three-day ride to the kitchen, for one thing," she said, trying to sound upbeat. "And for another, I just can't imagine living here. I mean, what does one person do with five thousand square feet of space?"

Hank frowned as he looked around, as if trying to see the penthouse through her eyes. "Beats me. I only stay here when I'm working late, but it's not really where I live."

Everything about him—his life, his lifestyle, the rich-and-famous part—said he was not for her. She needed to remember that. He'd never be happy in her world. And she would never be comfortable in his. No matter his offhand comment last weekend about marrying her. He hadn't been serious. Yet he was now staring again. Maddie smiled and raised her eyebrows, an unspoken question.

"I was just trying to picture you in the house on Long Island."

"Don't tell me it's mine."

"It is. You own it. Or will, when my six weeks are up. And now that Jim's chosen to pretend we aren't here to-day."

"That was amazing. I couldn't believe he did that. Wow. Thanks for calling me yesterday to let me know."

"You're welcome. Your Long Island house is bigger than this. Much bigger. And there are servants and acres of land and fleets of cars that go with it, too."

Maddie made a face. "Sounds complicated. I hereby give

it to you. It's yours. I don't want it. I have a feeling that servants—I can't even believe I'm saying that word in connection with me. Anyway, I think they would end up pushing me around just like Celeste does. Who needs that? I like it fine in Hanscomb Harbor."

Hank chuckled. "I don't blame you. I don't understand you, but I don't blame you."

Now, that was intriguing. "What's not to understand?"

"I think most people would jump at the opportunity you've been given to forever alter your life. Like they'd won the lottery."

"True. But I'm not most people."

"I've noticed that."

She couldn't tell if that was a good or bad thing. "So, Hank, tell me, are you happy with all this wealth?" Startled that she'd said that, Maddie popped a hand over her mouth and stared wide-eyed at Hank, who was laughing at her.

"It's okay. And the answer is a resounding 'I guess so.' Like you with your life, I've never known anything but this."

"Fair enough." Almost fearing his answer, Maddie nevertheless knew she had to ask it. She had to know. "Then could you be happy without it? Could you be happy, say, living a life of quiet desperation like most of the rest of the world?"

"No." Then he smiled. His high-wattage grin just about knocked Maddie off the sofa cushion she sat on. "But thank God—and Jim—I don't have to find out."

"Don't be so quick to speak. You still have to do your six weeks. Anything could happen."

"True. It could." He was totally relaxed here, yet he gave the impression of a crouching tiger. He had yet to look away from her and his dark eyes bored into her. He looked her up and down. "You look great, Maddie. I've always thought blondes dressed in black were sexy. Cool and mysterious."

An electric jolt of desire bolted through her, settling low down in her belly where a hot and heavy throbbing seemed

lodged. *Damn, damn, damn.* Jittery with nerves, Maddie
tugged at her short skirt and played off his comment about
blondes dressed in black. "As long as I look professional,
I'll be happy."

"Ah. Feeling overwhelmed?" he asked.

"Completely." She meant by him. Maddie couldn't pull
her gaze away from his. Suddenly the distance between
them seemed to narrow, though neither one of them had
moved. Or spoken.

The conversation petered out right there. Maddie
couldn't have been happier that it did. Every word between
them seemed to be pregnant with meaning and rife with
innuendo. She couldn't keep up. This female hormonal un-
dertow threatened to sweep her feet right out from under
her and carry her out to some lovesick sea where Hank
awaited her on a lush yet deserted island called Passion . . .
if there was a God.

Maddie took a deep breath. She stared at Hank still sitting cross-legged in the chair that perched conversationally
adjacent to where she sat on the sofa. "So," she blurted,
"why'd you bring me up here, again?"

He shrugged. "Mostly to get you out of the madhouse
downstairs for a few minutes. And to show you where
you'll be staying tonight. Burton's already stashed your
luggage in the master bedroom."

"Wonderful." Maddie studied the monument to Italian
architecture surrounding her. "Got a spare Sherpa guide on
you? I'll need one to find it."

Hank's chuckle eased her jitters. At least she could make
him laugh. "I'll show you where it is in a minute. Also, I
thought if you had any questions about the meeting, this
would be away from everyone where we can talk in private."

Talk in private? That sounded so intimate. Maddie's
heart beat a little faster, like it did right before a first kiss.
The tension, the tingly feeling, the giddiness. They were all
there—and she was doing this to herself because she already knew how Hank kissed. And she wanted nothing

more than for him to kiss her again. Yet she needed to stick to business. This was an important day for Hank. Even though he didn't show it, she knew how on edge he had to be. And yet he was taking all this time to calm her. How sweet. Then it suddenly occurred to her that of course he'd take this time to calm her. He didn't want her to blow this stockholders' meeting. And that was all that was behind this interlude. "So, is there anything else you need to tell me about today?"

Hank uncrossed his legs and sat forward in his chair. "No. I think I've run you through everything. But you're the virgin here."

Maddie swallowed, the word *virgin* pinging around in her brain. Not that she was, not in the biblical sense, but she may as well be, such was the deplorable state of her love life. That she now called it deplorable, though, was progress. So maybe she was over the hurt and could again want a man. No. This man. She was over Stanton and wanted this man—another rich one she couldn't have. Sobering. Maddie cleared her throat. "Okay, questions." Then the stupidest one she could think of just popped into her head and came out her mouth. "Do you think Adam had a navel?"

Hank narrowed his eyes and ducked his head, frowning at her. "What? Adam who?"

"Uh, the biblical one. You know ... Genesis. Adam. Never mind. Forget it." She felt like such a fool. "Do you think you could show me that bedroom now?" *Oh, way to go, Maddie. Take the man straight to the bedroom. It's the biggest day of his life and you're horny. Sexist pigette.*

Hank said nothing. So rich and charged was the air between them that Maddie could barely breathe, much less blink. Then suddenly he chuckled, his black eyes glittering like those of a pirate's. "Sure. I'll show you the bedroom." He got up from his chair ... just seemed to glide right out of it. Then he was on his feet and holding a hand out to her. "Just put yourself into my hands and I'll give you the guided tour."

Maddie almost whimpered with that. *Me. In his hands.* After a brief but ungraceful struggle between her skirt's fabric and the sofa's velvety cushions, neither one of which wanted to give, she came to her feet and took Hank's hand. The moment she touched him, her heart did backflips and pinged about in her chest. Her bones melted and she ended up a puddle at his feet. In her mind, at least. In reality, she walked alongside him and across the vast wasteland of the great room.

She couldn't have been happier being here with him like this. She couldn't have been more aware of his nearness, either. He smelled so good. And felt so warm. Capturing her attention, surprisingly, was his shoulder nearest her. Encased in a really expensive-looking suit coat, it was eye level to her and looked so broad and strong and capable. She wanted to lay her head on it and rest and know she was safe and protected and loved. Sudden and surprising tears pricked at the backs of her eyes.

"Just so you know," she felt compelled to say out loud, "I do know there's a lot at stake here today, Hank. And I am taking it all seriously. I want a good outcome. I just think if you brief me one more time on how difficult it can all be, I'll come completely undone."

"I think I knew all that, Maddie, but thank you for saying it."

With that he indeed gave her a guided tour. One after another, the rooms were staggering, yet understated and elegant. This was a world Maddie had never known. And didn't really want to live in. She meant it when she said wealth and all its trappings held no allure for her. She was like a 1970s flower child in that respect. Actually, she had been when she was a baby. Her parents had been hippies and had instilled in her some of those virtues. *Hippie virtues. Ha. Who knew?* But luckily for her, and themselves, they'd outgrown the era and gone on to be responsible adults and parents. And why was she thinking about all this now? Anything to keep her from latching on to Hank and climbing straight up him and wrapping her legs around his waist and kissing him full on the—

"And here's the bedroom," Hank announced, turning them into a breathtaking room fit for a sultan. "My bedroom, to be exact." And there he was . . . the sultan.

Maddie saw her luggage inside the doorway. Good manners pushed to the fore. She looked up at him. "Oh, I don't want to take your bed, Hank. Surely there's a guest room. I mean, where will you sleep tonight?"

He chuckled, leading her inside. "Now that's the sixty-four-thousand-dollar question, isn't it?"

Maddie felt stupid. The man could have a girlfriend. Or worse. A fiancé. A hot date. Two or three hot dates. A wife and three children. He'd never said. She'd just assumed he was single. He was single, wasn't he? Should she ask? *Don't you even dare ask, Maddie.* "I'm sure you'll find a corner or a doorway to curl up in."

"That was my plan." He let go of her hand and, with a grand sweep of his arm, said, "Amazing, huh? All this just for a place where you sleep."

"And other things." Again it was out before she could stop herself. When had she become this blurting imbecile? Could it be her closeness to him and being in the man's bedroom, for God's sake? Why wouldn't she be nervous?

"And other things," Hank said pointedly, grinning hotly down at her.

Maddie's breath caught. She had to step away from him. Now. So she went over to the bed and ran her hand over the quilted cover. "Wow. Soft. Nice. A girl could really feel snuggly and cozy in this bed."

Hank didn't say anything. Maddie turned around. He wasn't where she'd left him. Then she saw him. The thick carpeting must have muffled his steps as he'd walked away from her. He stood now, his back to her, in front of a bank of floor-to-ceiling windows. As she watched, he shoved his hands into his pants pockets. He looked such a sad, lonely figure. Maddie stared at his back and waited. For what, she didn't know. Within a few seconds, though, she realized that her gaze was wandering all over the man.

She tried to convince herself she was simply admiring a thing of beauty. Like a statue. A fully clothed statue. She'd always heard it said that the clothes made the man. Not in this case. The man made the clothes. Very arresting. His physique was athletic, broad-shouldered, well muscled. Powerful. His dark hair was freshly cut. His accessories impeccable. His white shirt snowy. And his dark suit fit him as if it had been tailor-made for him. It probably had. He looked nothing like the guy who had tied on an apron at her shop and helped Celeste with customers. Had that really been only a week ago? And had that man really been this one in front of her now? The two just wouldn't come together in her mind.

"You know, Maddie," Hank said suddenly, startling her back to the moment. He still faced Manhattan. "I could sleep here tonight."

CHAPTER NINE

FOUR SETS OF CARVED wooden double doors were open and ready to receive. Security guards stood attentively, insuring that only the invited entered. The accumulation of bodies packed the auditorium on the first floor of Madison & Madison Enterprises. Well-dressed bodies, to be sure. Busy bodies, too. Those who knew each other called out greetings or merely waved or discreetly nodded, depending on personality and worth. As people wiggled about impatiently in their seats, no small amount of whispering and covert staring raised the stakes as company officers and the board of directors came down off the dais to work the crowd, glad-handing, smiling, and dodging direct questions from the assembled stockholders.

The mood barometer wobbled somewhere between irritated crowd and budding mob. Why? Because the meeting was supposed to start in about twenty minutes and everyone had already heard the news about the Will, as it was being called in the business press, and how the company's leadership had changed hands, even if only temporarily. Confidence in the company was shaken. Huge sums of money were involved. And people were jittery.

They weren't the only ones. Elsewhere, behind closed doors in a private anteroom, Hank watched his chairwoman of the board hurry through the exit and head for the ladies' room for about the tenth time. What had he been thinking, to rattle Maddie as he had just before the meeting? *"I could sleep here tonight"? Where the hell had that come from?* But he knew. It came from being close to her. Wanting her had blindsided him. Just come out of the blue. As it did every time he was around her. He couldn't blame her for quickly exiting his bedroom upstairs or for preferring the company of strangers here downstairs.

Retreating to the white-clothed tables at the back of the room where coffee and water and tea were offered, Hank opened a bottle of water and wondered if he was a lost cause where Maddie Copeland was concerned. As if his water were a beer, Hank took a swig of it and gave vent to his thoughts. Okay, so Maddie turned him on. He didn't know why. She just did. Who could explain one person's attraction for a specific other? He certainly couldn't. Nor could he remember in his life ever before giving the concept this much thought.

So the hell of it was, he had no idea why Maddie seemed unique to him and held a singular attraction for him. Certainly there was a lot there to like. She was a blue-eyed, fair-skinned blonde of delicate features and slender grace. That always attracted him initially. But any woman, for him, soon paled if it turned out there was no intelligence and no wit to go along with the looks. In Maddie's case, there certainly was. And besides all that, she was a nice woman. Clean-cut all-American girl. The girl next door. Prom queen. The whole package.

Okay, so she wasn't hard to like. And she wasn't hard on the eyes. Yada-yada. Still, he couldn't account for why she, apparently above all other women, did it for him. Hank had known a thousand women who had going for them the things Maddie had going for her. But none of them had ever turned his head so fast that he got a crick in his neck. What was that all about? Hank cleared his mind, hoping for a glimmer of something. He stared at the framed painting hanging on the wall in front of him, only vaguely aware that it was a still life. Suddenly, in the act of raising the water to his lips, the answer hit him like a thump in the forehead. He was attracted to Maddie because she knew who he was and was totally unimpressed. Not that he was impressed with himself. But the tabloids certainly were. The entertainment shows were. The business world was. The general public was. But she wasn't.

Hank chuckled. *Good for her. Hell, good for me.* His next realization was the picture he had to make standing there in a corner of the room, with his back to it, drinking water, and laughing. If anybody came in, they'd think him demented. Or distracted. And they'd be right on both counts, Hank suspected. Maddie did this to him. It was the most amazing thing. Here finally was a woman who apparently wanted nothing to do with his world of wealth. She could simply walk away from it. She couldn't care less about his or anybody else's net worth. She knew who she was and was content to allow everyone else to be who they were, too. Live and let live.

Maybe that was why James Senior had come to like and respect her so quickly. She had simply liked him for who he was. That was rare in Hank's circle. And he felt a pang of jealousy. He wanted what his grandfather had possessed—a true friend. He wanted Maddie, among other things, to like him. How odd that was. And how simple, yet hard. Because he wasn't really certain that she did like him. He meant as a friend. Someone she could hang out with and just enjoy being around. Someone with whom she could share her thoughts and her hopes and her fears and her dreams.

Frowning, Hank rubbed at his clean-shaven jaw. *For crying out loud, I want Maddie to like me.* Even to his ears it sounded so elementary-schoolyard desperate. *Please like me. Be my friend.* But there it was. He'd never cared before if anyone liked him or not. He knew his place and his role in the public world. You were either "in" or "out" based on the state of your fortune and whether or not you were in favor with the power brokers. Or had the right lover. Or even the wrong one. It was an artificial world. He knew that. And he'd never really liked it, but he had moved easily in it. Not anymore. Right now what he wanted was "real." Whatever that meant. All he knew was Maddie represented that—the real world. She lived in it and maybe could show him how.

"Damn," Hank muttered. "Pull your head out, Hank. Think. You're giving Maddie way too much power here, buddy."

Now he was talking out loud to himself—and his life was in turmoil, his company was threatened, his fortune was shaky, his grandfather had lost his mind, and Maddie was at the center of it. Okay, this was better. This was thinking he understood. Maddie. He no longer thought her a gold digger, of course, but he reminded himself that he also didn't quite know the full extent of her involvement with James Senior in this debacle of a will. *Dammit, Grandpa.* Hank felt his heart throb fondly and with hurt. *Do you have any idea how much I love you and miss you and would like to kick your ass?*

"Hank, honey—"

"Jesus!" Hank jerked around to see his mother standing behind him.

"Not even close, sweetheart." Lillian Elaine Smythe Madison of Beverly Hills, California, inhaled deeply of her Sobranie cocktail cigarette. Her middle-aged, very pretty Irish face was puckered with worry. "What are you doing standing back here and talking to yourself? You're starting to worry me."

She eyed him critically, the tiger-mother in her quickly assessing his state of being. She turned her head slightly to exhale the smoke . . . and waited.

Hank studiously ignored a flush of embarrassment that heated up his cheeks. "You'd do better to worry about our chairwoman of the board."

Lillian Madison made a dramatic gesture. "Oh, that one. I do not believe any of this, Hank. You're an *employee*? You're *her* employee? Is that right? You work here for her?"

"Only temporarily. And you're not supposed to smoke in here, Mother. There are signs posted."

"The signs don't mean me. And we're alone, so I'm not bothering anyone. Now talk to me. You're an employee in your own company?"

Hank ignored her question, one she'd asked and he'd already answered about five times—in front of Maddie. Which explained why Maddie had gotten sick and left the room this last time. Instead, he frowned at the gold filter tip of his mother's European cigarette and the paper that wrapped the strong tobacco. Its blue color matched her outfit. "That's just what you need, Mother. A cigarette brand that color-coordinates with your wardrobe. Those damned things are going to kill you."

Hank watched his mother exhale a cloud of smoke over her shoulder and then eye the cigarette she held between two perfectly manicured long, slender fingers. "You've been saying that since you were a little boy."

"And I'll be right one day."

"No you won't. Smoking won't kill me before your grandfather's will does. Wouldn't you know that James Senior would go and do something this cockamamie and leave such a mess? What about your stock?"

She changed subjects as she did outfits. "I still have my stocks. And I'll have everything else back in six weeks."

"Good. Everyone is talking about it, you know. It's in all the papers now, that insane and embarrassing will."

"I know." Hank drank from his bottle of water. "I can't step outside without being followed and photographed."

Lillian shook her head, her expression sympathetic and exasperated. "You poor thing. And your grandfather was a crazy old coot. I loved him, but I always knew that about him. Honey, he was just impossible to be around. I couldn't take it anymore. Which is why I took you to the West Coast when you were a little boy."

Hank smiled sympathetically. He knew this story and how she felt guilty for not being here for James Senior at the end. None of them had been. Except for Maddie. "Grandfather could be difficult. But you did your best, Mother."

She nodded her agreement. "Well, I think as long as I'm here I'll go to this Hanscomb Harbor myself and just see what the big attraction is there."

Sheer gut-wrenching dread had Hank thinking a particularly pithy expletive. "I don't think that's a good idea, Mother. I don't see any need for you to go to Hanscomb

Harbor. You'd hate it." She meant Maddie and what was going on with *her*. And what James Senior's big attraction to *her* had been. "Maddie's not a gold digger, Mother. And you don't need to go there."

Hank heard himself defending Maddie. And realized he felt protective of her. In truth, his hair all but stood on end to think of Lady Lillian, as he called her, laying siege to Hanscomb Harbor and to Maddie. He wouldn't wish that on his worst enemy. And Maddie certainly wasn't their enemy.

Careful to keep her cigarette away from Hank, his mother put a hand on his arm. "We don't know she isn't a gold digger, sweetie. And I'm not going to spy on the girl, for heaven's sake. I'm going because I simply want to. But about that girl? From watching you with her, I don't think you're thinking clearly where she's concerned."

That stung. "What does that mean, I'm not thinking clearly?"

"Exactly what I said. You're not. Not where she's concerned. And I can see why. I'm not blind. But even that's not why I'm going to that little fishing village. Everyone is saying it will be the next place to go. Everyone is talking about it, honey. Like it's Newport, Rhode Island, or something." She shrugged. "I just want to see for myself."

No she didn't. Hank knew her that well. But Hanscomb Harbor overrun with the jet set? He could see it now. An unmitigated disaster. Nothing he could do about that, so he turned his mind to something more to the point today. Gossip. "What's all the other talk, Mother? The financial circles. What are they saying? Do they think Madison and Madison is down and out?"

Lillian Madison shook her head. "No. And that's because they have faith in you, honey." Her expression puckered. "But they don't in me. My God, you ought to hear the talk about me, what my so-called friends are saying."

Relieved over the vote of confidence in him and his company, Hank relaxed and grinned at his mother. She was such a contradiction. At once deep and shallow. Caring and casual. Concerned and blasé. "If they're talking about you, Mother, it's because you insist on giving them a lot of ammo. But if you ask me, you need new friends. Or your old friends should get jobs."

Lillian hooted at that. "Honey, they have jobs—keeping their husbands happy and producing their children to tie their men more closely to them. And staying slim and attractive. Those are full-time jobs. And this will thing. God. They've jumped on that like starlets on casting couches."

Now that they had moved on to country club gossip, Hank listened with one ear to his mother as he kept an eye on the room's closed door. Maddie wasn't back yet, and the clock kept ticking toward time to start the meeting. "So, tell me, Mother, how did Grandpa's will affect you? He didn't change anything in your regard."

Lillian rolled her eyes as if she were dealing with a particularly dim-witted child. "I know that, honey, God love the old loon. But it did involve you. And I'm your mother."

"How well I know that. But I don't know why you think you have to explain anything to them."

"You really don't?" She was quite indignant. "I just cannot let these bizarre stories going around about how we don't have any money rest unchallenged. They're saying James Senior left everything to a young blonde. Which he did. Now whether she's innocent or not, honey, this is the stuff of tabloid headlines. And I cannot have these false stories going around about me. The true ones are bad enough."

Hank bit back his grin. "Of course. I forgot."

Lady Lillian continued in her injured tone. "I swear those women are so shallow. And have such short memories. I mean, did I say anything when that old fart Clovis Martin got caught with his pants down in the coatroom and the woman on her knees worshipping him was *not* his wife? No, I did not. And Jackie Muncie—how about her? The woman has a drug habit. Why, she's on the preferred-customer list of all the pharmacies in Los Angeles. But have I ratted her out? No, I have not. And do I say anything when someone's newly wed daughter delivers a four-months-premature baby that weighs in at eight pounds? No, sir. But when it comes to *my* personal misfortune, does anyone cut me any slack? I can tell you they do not."

With sudden bemusement, Hank stared at his slender five-foot-four-inch mother as she took a drag on her color-coordinated Sobranie. Her red hair was perfectly coiffed. Her favorite day spa had her puffed and cremed and massaged to within an inch of her life. And her blue two-piece suit was without fault in taste, color, and fit. "Your personal misfortune? Again, nothing's changed for you."

"Then why is everyone up and down Rodeo Drive and all over Beverly Hills whispering around me and sending me flowers and offering condolences?"

"Because your beloved father-in-law died. Remember?"

"Oh. Of course. Poor James. Now tell me again why I can't go pay my respects at the cemetery in Hanscomb Harbor?"

"Because he wasn't buried, Mother. He was cremated."

She grimaced at that and waved away the smoke she exhaled. "There was something about a crab. What was that?"

"A lobster. His ashes are in a big ceramic lobster clock." Hank started laughing. It was suddenly funny—and wonderful.

"It's not funny, Hank." Lillian casually tapped her cigarette's precariously long ash into a water glass and carried on. "And they thought Howard Hughes was eccentric. Or Elvis. Ha. Those men were icons of rationality compared to James Senior. Your father certainly wasn't like that. Thank God. He was the practical one, God rest his soul. You take after him."

Hank's secret thought, as he gazed affectionately at his mother's face, was his own *Thank God.*

"But I swear," she was saying, "I don't even pretend to understand your grandfather. A ceramic lobster clock? Where is it? I'd like to see that."

"I don't know where it is," he lied. He had to convince her to go home. The last thing he needed during his six weeks in Hanscomb Harbor was his mother being there at the same time. Or even ever. The woman was a diva. Tremendously high maintenance . . . like a spoiled poodle. He loved her with all his heart, but she drove him and everyone around her crazy. She didn't know that about herself. She certainly wasn't vicious. Just rich and pampered—and every bit as loony as the rest of the Madisons. Except for Hank. He wasn't loony . . . he didn't think.

Hank turned to put the empty water bottle down and checked his watch. Ten minutes to go.

"Hank, are you listening to me?"

He gave his mother his attention. "Yes. But I need to go see about Maddie."

Lillian's light-brown eyes flashed with some emotion. "Maddie. That's a pretty name. And she's a pretty girl, isn't she?"

"Woman. She's a pretty *woman*. And yes she is."

"Woman? How old is she? Twelve?"

"I don't know. But I'm sure she's not twelve."

Lillian took another ladylike puff of her cigarette and stared past Hank. "This is just great. A twelve-pound, twenty-year-old blonde in charge of our lives and our fortune. All our hard-earned money. Just gone."

Hank stared at his mother. She was all about shopping, tennis, doing lunch at the country club, playing cards, gossiping, parties. She had no idea what the real world was like. But then he realized that she did. She was a Vietnam war widow. And she'd been a single mother and had never remarried. Hank's heart went out to her. Could he love her more? He shook his head, thinking he may as well get mad at a puppy. "It's not as bad as all that, Mother. And what hard-earned money? James Senior earned it. Not us. And he's supported me and you all our lives since—"

"Since your father was killed in Vietnam when you were a baby. I know, honey. I was there." She gave Hank an affectionate pat on his cheek. "Don't think for a moment that I didn't love James senior. I did. But I love you more. And I want you to be happy." She grimaced and tugged at her skirt. "My pantyhose are killing me." She then focused on her son. "Well? Go get that girl and let's get this damned meeting over with. I need to see how much money I'll have left. I just hope I don't have to marry one of those horny old rich men who're always chasing after me. They just won't leave me alone."

With that, she stubbed her cigarette out on a buffet plate and crossed her arms, clearly waiting for her orders to be carried out. She arched her eyebrows expectantly.

"Yes, ma'am," Hank said, laughing, his hands raised in surrender. "I'll go get Maddie."

But he hadn't moved a step before suddenly his chin and jaw were in his mother's clutches and she was turning him to face her. "Look at me." She scanned his features and dramatically dropped her hand to her side. "James Henry Madison the Third, you *are* under her spell. I can see it in your face. You haven't taken your eyes off that door since she stepped through it."

"I most certainly am not under her spell," Hank protested. "And the reason I'm watching that door is it's time to start the meeting. So go out there and entertain the troops as only you can." Hank gave his mother an encouraging and gentle push in the direction of the door that opened onto the auditorium.

Lillian teetered atop her high heels and finally got herself stopped. She turned to face him. "Where are you going?"

Hank sobered, readied for battle. "I have a sudden and uncontrollable urge to go to the ladies' room, Mother."

The door to the ladies' room swung open. And Hank Madison swooped in. Standing at the marble-topped vanity that featured four sinks, and clutching her damp white hand towel to her chest, Maddie gasped. So did the black-headed, tall, angular woman dressed in black—right down to her eyeglasses—standing next to her and closer to the male interloper.

"Mr. Madison!"

"Hank!"

The tall, twice-startled woman pivoted to face Maddie, who stared just as surprised back at her. Wordlessly, they both turned toward the amply identified Mr. Hank Madison. "What are you doing in here?"

Maddie and the other woman had spoken in unison, as if they'd rehearsed it that way. Again they exchanged glances with each other.

"Forgive me, Miz Smith," Hank said, heavy on the "Miz-z-z," and drawing their attention back to him. "I didn't know anyone was in here."

Maddie made a scoffing sound. "Oh, thanks. You knew I was in here."

Hank eyed her, said nothing to her, and spoke instead to Maddie's sink mate, who could have passed for little Wednesday Addams, now going by Miz Smith. "Would you excuse us a moment, please, Miz Smith? I need to speak privately to our new chairwoman of the board."

The woman hissed. In anyone else, Maddie knew, she would have recognized the sound as a sudden intake of breath. But in this woman, it was a hiss. Miz Smith zipped around once again to face Maddie, who had all she could do not to cringe. The woman's flat-black snakelike gaze whipped over Maddie and took her apart. Maddie swallowed and couldn't seem to blink as she stared up at the frightening lady.

"*You're* Miz-z Copeland?" You're *the Anti-Christ?* was what the woman's tone of voice made it sound like.

"Yes. Pleased to meet you," Maddie croaked out. She thought to offer her hand, but didn't, fearing the woman would bite it off at the wrist.

Miz Smith ignored Maddie's greeting and turned again to Hank, all calm and businesslike now, as if they were in his office and not the ladies' room. "I have everything set up, Mr. Madison. We're ready when *you* are."

"Thank you. I'll be right along."

Ready when you are. I'll be right along. That little

exchange wasn't lost on Maddie. It was as if she weren't even in the room. Okay, so no one wanted her here. Not Hank, his mother, Miz Smith, the other employees, or the stockholders. Where was the surprise in that? *Make it unanimous,* Maddie told herself, because she didn't want to be here, either. In fact, she was ready to flee right now. But to do so meant she would have to place herself in Miz Smith's reach. That wasn't going to happen. She would rather have ridden naked atop Beamer through the streets of Hanscomb Harbor.

Miz Smith quickly dried her hands and tossed the towel into the white wicker basket provided. She grabbed up her black leather notebook and papers from the shelf mounted above the sinks, and made for the door. She nodded conspiratorially as she passed by Hank and then exited. The door closed noiselessly behind her. Maddie tried to remember if the woman's reflection had shown up in the mirror in front of them.

Then, into the silence left by Miz Smith's exit, Maddie said, "Wow. It's nice to see Rosemary's baby all grown up and doing so well, huh?"

Hank chuckled. "She's not so bad." He looked around at this female territory he'd invaded. "Nice." Then he focused on her, his gaze roving over her face. "We need to go. We need to begin the meeting. How're you feeling?"

The meeting. Maddie's heart thumped. She put a hand to her rebellious stomach. "Like I could toss my toenails."

Hank winced. "Try not to."

"I think I already did." She tucked a lock of hair behind her ear. "So your mother is my new best friend, right?"

With a look of apologetic disbelief, Hank shook his head. "My mother is . . ." He looked around as if for inspiration, then sought Maddie's gaze. "Well, she's outrageous. You either love her or you hate her. She's my Celeste."

"Ah. I see. Thanks. That puts her in perspective."

"Good." His gaze traveled her length. "You okay? Can

we go now?" He indicated the exit door behind them. "They're waiting."

"Yeah, I know. That's why I'm in here. I told you I suffer from stage fright. And dogs. I'm afraid of them, too."

Hank tucked his hands into his pants pockets, looking conversational, as if they were standing around the water cooler in the office hallway. "Yet you overcame that fear and have Beamer."

"I was forced to have Beamer."

"And yet you did it."

"I get your point: I'm forced to chair this meeting today and I can do it. Look, I know how important it is to you, Hank. I do. And I want to do a good job. But would you just look at you?" She gestured toward him.

He frowned down at himself and then at her. "What about me?"

"You," Maddie said again as if her meaning were obvious. It was to her. His black and wavy hair. His high, wide forehead. The perfect eyebrows. His dark eyes. Aquiline nose. Those firm sensuous lips. The square jaw. "You're a Madison down to the bone. Rich, respected, in charge, capable. Those people out there will be expecting someone like you. And not like me."

"There's nothing wrong with you, Maddie." He smiled encouragingly. "Nothing at all. And looks can be deceiving. I'm not the least bit calm and collected, as you seem to think. In fact, I never am around you." He stepped farther into the washroom and leaned a hip against the lavish counter and crossed his arms over his chest . . . and stared at her.

Maddie didn't know what to do or say, so she smiled. "What?"

"Maddie, Maddie, Maddie," Hank said slowly, sensually. "I can't make you go out there. And right now I don't care if you do or if you don't. I'm happy just to be in here with you."

Maddie's heart leapt, her knees felt weak. She couldn't look away from Hank, but suddenly she didn't know what to do with her hands. She planted them at her waist, then crossed her arms under her breasts, then nervously smoothed her hair. This was insane. But could the washroom really be shrinking? It seemed so. It seemed as if Hank were getting closer and closer. She knew she hadn't moved. Then she realized that Hank had.

He approached her with a slow rolling gait that had Maddie involuntarily tensing and standing up straighter. She wasn't afraid of him. She just didn't know what to expect. When Hank stood directly in front of her, he looked down into her eyes. "I told myself I was coming in here to get you to go out there and chair that meeting. But that's not entirely the truth."

His voice, low and husky, enveloped Maddie. "Oh, God," she whispered. His nearness exploded the nerve endings throughout her. He stood so close to her that she could smell his aftershave. She could see the tiny laugh lines at the corners of his eyes, could see how long his eyelashes were.

A muscle in Hank's jaw worked. His black eyes narrowed sensually. He reached out, gripping her by her arms. "Maddie, I want to—"

"Me, too," she breathed, grabbing his tie and pulling him to her. She raised her face for his kiss. And Hank obliged, lowering his head until his mouth met hers.

The instant his lips touched hers, electricity popped through Maddie, weakening her knees, bringing her body alive. Her gasp was muffled by his lips being melded to hers. Hank's grip on her arms tightened. Maddie gave herself over to the moment and rested her hands against his chest. Hank responded by enclosing her in his embrace and deepening the kiss. Startling her was just how hungry she'd been for his kiss. She put everything she had into it. Passion. Need. Yearning. She was on her tiptoes, leaning into him, clinging to him. And he was holding her so tight she was certain a rib would crack. Their tongues darted about, dancing an intimate tango.

And then . . . it was over. Hank was pulling back, looking down at her, holding her once again by her arms, this time to steady her. With a hand over her heart, Maddie gasped for air and saw that Hank's breathing was just as labored, his eyes as glassy as she knew hers had to be. In a moment, he kissed her lightly on the forehead and stepped back. "Ready when you are."

"Okay," Maddie said, still shaky but tugging at her fitted suit jacket and smoothing her hair back. Hank waited wordlessly while she reapplied her lipstick. Then, with him at her side, she walked resolutely toward the exit. "I'm going to do this for you, Hank. But then you're coming right back to Hanscomb Harbor and putting in your six weeks."

"If you keep kissing me like that, it could be a lot longer," he said, grinning, his hand at the small of her back.

CHAPTER TEN

❦

TOPPING A SAND DUNE just above the shoreline, Maddie shivered and pulled her denim jacket closer around her. Here it was late August and yet summer seemed to have fled. Could it really have been only two days since the frightening board meeting that had gone—surprise!—smoothly? Friday had been hot and muggy. But today, Sunday, the wind was raw, the restive ocean was gray-green, and the rebellious waves punished the dun-colored sand. It was amazing. The tourists had left in droves. Hanscomb Harbor, for the most part, looked like a ghost town of its former self. Not that it was a bad thing to have one's town back to oneself. Although weather like this wreaked havoc with the local businesses' bottom lines, her own included.

Never mind about that. Focus, Maddie. Still standing atop the dune, she panned the beach, looking here and there and calling out, "Beamer! Where are you? Here, girl. Come here, girl. Good doggy."

And then she waited, listening, watching, and fighting the determined wind for control of her hair that whipped about her head and lashed at her face. "Doggone it," Maddie muttered. She then hollered, "I know you're out here, Beamer. I saw your footprints in the sand." Footprints? "Okay, pawprints. Whatever. Look, I don't have time for this, you great big furry ungrateful dog, you. If you don't come here to me right now this minute, I'm going to leave you out here. I swear I will."

She knew she wouldn't. And so did Beamer. What a name for a dog. Maddie recalled James saying he'd named her that because her doggy grin was as bright as a beam of sunshine. "Yeah, well, right now it's not."

Maddie thought back to her homecoming last Friday evening when Celeste, who'd not only minded the store but had doggy-sat while Maddie had been in the city, told her that Beamer had taken to jumping over the fence in the backyard and running off. Without fail, Celeste told her, she would find the golden retriever out here at the cabin she'd shared with her master for the better part of three summers. Maddie had sympathized with the dog at first, but now it wasn't funny. Not six times in two days. The magic was wearing off, especially in this weather.

Maddie grimaced, feeling the cold chafe her cheeks. Fisting her hand around the dog's leash, she tried to forget that she stood atop the very dune whose jutting tuft of sea grass had tripped her not too many nights ago when she and Hank had come here searching for Beamer that first time. And yet, here she was again and for the same reason, only she was now alone in her search. Alone and cold and wanting shelter and food and a hot cup of tea. Comforts.

"Beamer!" she yelled, frustration with the animal turning to anger as a first tiny drop of chilling rain hit her cheek and portended an unseasonal deluge. "Oh, just lovely. That's what I need. A good, cold soaking."

She looked over her shoulder to assure herself that her beat-up old Jeep Wagoneer, with its promise of shelter, was still there. It was. Right where she'd left it. *What do I think it will do—take off on its own? Leave me here? Hardly.* Still, she felt in her jacket pocket for her car keys. Her fingers closed around them, their familiar jangling weight reassuring her.

Just then a blast of wind pitched Maddie forward a few stumbling steps. "Whoa." She regained her footing and renewed her resolve. *I really ought to just leave the dog out here and see if she comes home on her own.* Another stinging drop hit Maddie's cheek and coursed down her face like a tear. She swiped it away. "Oh, like I'm really going to leave her out here," she fussed back at the gods who were messing with her.

"Come on, Beamer," Maddie yelled, hearing the whiny impatience creeping into her voice. "Let's go ho-o-me. We have food and a warm fire and books and things waiting for us. Here, girl. Come o-o-n-n."

Maddie listened. Still nothing. No response. She frowned, beginning to worry. Always before Beamer would come running. But not this time. Well, not so far this time. Maddie told herself that the golden retriever could be doing anything. Napping. Digging a hole. Following the particularly riveting scent of an especially revolting creature. Or maybe, on a more practical level, Maddie realized, it could be simply that the wind was carrying her voice in the other direction. See? The dog's being a no-show could be for any number of reasons. It didn't have to mean that something had happened to her.

Maddie marveled at her concern for the dog. For this dog. She still wasn't totally over her mistrust of dogs in general. But this representative of the furry, warm-blooded mammals was starting to grow on her. They'd come to an understanding of sorts, which went like this: Maddie stayed out of Beamer's three-fourths of the house (roughly defined as the second bedroom and all of the living room, the closed-in porch, and sometimes the kitchen), and Beamer did as she damned well pleased. It worked for them—as long as Maddie was quick enough to anticipate the dog and to move off the sofa or the bed or any given chair before Beamer could attack her and demonstrate her unconditional love of Maddie.

Truth to tell, even though she and Beamer were still essentially housemates and not soulmates, the dog's current behavior tugged at Maddie's heart. It was so human to go back to a place where you'd been happy. And yes it made her feel a bit inadequate to realize that the dog obviously couldn't wait to escape her current home and run back here. *The poor thing.*

Maddie shivered from the chilling wind and continued to pan the shoreline looking for Beamer. As she did, she suddenly realized she was staring at the cottage where James had stayed and then Hank had, however briefly. She hadn't heard from Hank, not since Friday, not since he'd said he could sleep there in that penthouse apartment. With her. He hadn't actually said *with* her, but it was implied. And what had she done? Fled. Got scared, got cold feet, and totally left town after the stockholders' meeting, running back to Hanscomb Harbor to sleep in her own bed. Alone.

Maddie could only shake her head in self-disgust. *So you weren't yet ready to deal with your feelings for Hank. Not under those circumstances, anyway. So what'd you do? You ran back here. To where you felt safe. Where you were happy. Just like the dog.* Maddie grimaced, not finding it the least bit reassuring that she had so much in common with, and could relate to, a canine. But there it was, the parallel between them.

The dog. That was it. What she needed to do here, she reminded herself, was find the dog. And she would. If only it didn't seem that Hank was everywhere out here. In her mind's eye she imagined the picture he would make if he were here . . . maybe barefoot, wearing a cable-knit sweater, his pants legs rolled up, walking along the beach, maybe picking up and examining a seashell. Maybe tossing a pebble into the water. His dark hair would be windtossed. Maybe he hadn't shaved that morning. Maybe his day-old beard gave him the rugged look of a sea captain. Maybe he would look up and see her and then the music would start and they would run toward each other and—

And maybe, just maybe, she'd been reading too many romance novels lately. "Another one of these corny things?" Lavinia Houghton always announced in an unduly loud voice when, red-faced, Maddie dared check one out of the library's vast supply. With her narrow-eyed reproving glare, the puritanical librarian would add, "They'll lead you down the garden path, missy. Just see if they don't. Many a young girl has been led astray by the wantonness between these pages." Which accounted for the dog-eared, oft-read appearance of the paperbacks, Maddie believed but had no courage to say. Still, maybe Lavinia was right. Maybe they were corny. Because those romantic images

that she'd just envisioned didn't happen in real life or to
real people.

They certainly never had to her. She never had happy
endings, much less beginnings.

With a shake of her head that Maddie hoped would dis-
pel her funky mood, she looked down upon the one-room
weathered-board beach cottages below. They were so pathetic as to be comical. The haphazard clump of cabins
owned by Mr. Hardy resembled, to Maddie's whimsical
eye, a tumble of toy cardboard houses roughly constructed
by some child's hand and then abandoned for the delights
of the arcade.

Well, standing there and staring at them wasn't finding
the dog. With a woe-is-me sigh, Maddie started down the
dune, recalling her slippery sandals of about a week or so
ago and pronouncing herself grateful this time for her lace-
up boots and jeans. Warmth and surefootedness were to be
prized in this landscape. So was patience. The sand beneath
her feet kept shifting, which meant Maddie achieved level
ground in an arm-waving stumble. Regaining a bit of her
footing and most of her dignity—and feeling now an increased patter of cold raindrops—she set off at a trot, heading in a straight line for the cottage she thought of as the
solitary one just before the sandy beach narrowed and disappeared around a rocky bend in the land.

Once at the slightly tilted beach house's side, Maddie
swung around a corner of it—and ran smack into a warm,
solid presence that gripped her by her arms.

An involuntary scream of surprise erupted from her. She
couldn't believe her eyes. But her heart did—and beat in a
wildly erratic manner just to prove it. In only a fraction of
a second her mind kaleidoscoped through scenes of last
Friday and how she'd fled for home following the stockholders' meeting because she couldn't come to grips with
Hank's—surely he'd been serious—proposition about
sleeping with her that night. She'd run away, behaving like
a jittery junior-high ninny unhinged by the prospect of her
first kiss behind the gym bleachers. The truth was she just

couldn't sleep with the man until all this crazy will stuff was over and done. To do otherwise would be self-incriminating.

"Whoa. Hey, Maddie, easy now. You're okay. It's just me."

Gasping for breath, Maddie stiffened and pulled back in his grip. "Hank Madison! What are you doing here? You just about scared the life out of me."

"I can tell. I'm sorry." He let go of her and shoved his hands in his jeans' front pockets. His half-zipped leather bomber jacket revealed a plaid flannel shirt underneath and the white vee of his T-shirt.

Could he be more sexy? Maddie fussed. Self-consciously she tugged at her waist-length denim jacket and then tried to smooth a hand through her wind-tossed hair. Too many tangles made it impossible. She must look a fright, she knew. No makeup. Her hair flung every which way like a fright wig. Her cheeks wind-reddened, no doubt. Her nose runny. She sniffed mightily ... always attractive ... and scrubbed her fingers under her nose, hoping she wasn't making it worse. "So what are you doing out here?"

The skies chose that moment to open up with a deluge of cold rain. "Trying to avoid the rain, for one thing." Hank quickly stepped under the wide overhanging eave of the screened porch.

Maddie followed him and happily crowded up against him. Behind him, she could now see his SUV that apparently the cabin's big boxiness had hidden from her sight when she'd been standing on the dune.

Hank put a sheltering arm around her, as if that were the most natural thing in the world between the two of them. "Man, it's really starting to come down now."

Maddie couldn't truly say that she'd noticed. All her sensory perceptions were busy soaking up the man in front of her. His clean scent. His body's warmth. The tone and timbre of his voice. The easy, confident way he held her. That jet-black hair. Those football shoulders—

"Come on." Hank's voice was raised in an effort to be

heard over the steadily drumming rain on the cabin's questionable roof. "Let's go inside."

That brought Maddie back to the moment. "Inside?"

"Yeah. We'll get soaked."

"You're staying in this place? I thought you'd be in town."

"No. I like it better here." Hank pulled a key out of his jeans pocket and turned away, heading for the screen door that would let them onto the porch.

She watched Hank open the screen door and saw him glance over his shoulder, obviously expecting her to be right behind him. She wasn't. He frowned, probably because she still stood where he'd left her. With her shoulders hunched against the cold and the rain, with her hands tucked into her jacket pockets, she watched him tromping back her way. She didn't move. She couldn't. Because she wasn't so sure she trusted herself alone with him . . . on a wild and rainy day like this . . . in a secluded cottage like this. The potential here had that romance-novel scenario written all over it.

"What are you doing, Maddie? Come on." He unceremoniously grabbed her by the stitched shoulder seam of her jacket and hauled her unresisting self along behind him. "You'll catch your death out here."

As he opened the flimsy screen door, Maddie balked and finally found her voice. "Wait. I can't leave Beamer. She's out here somewhere."

"No she isn't. She's inside."

"What? She's inside? How did she get inside? You mean I've been in the cold and rain calling for her and she's *inside*?"

"Yes, Maddie. The opposite of outside." Hank hauled her onto the porch before letting go of her. He stepped back and shook his head and ran his hands through his perfectly barbered hair. A very practical gesture to, no doubt, simply rid it of excess water. But the effect it had on Maddie was mesmerizing. She wanted to applaud and say bravo, even as she admitted that it was always the little things with him that got to her. The laugh lines at the corners of his mouth. The straight cut of his short sideburns. His long eyelashes.

"You hear that?" He jerked a thumb toward the closed front door. "I told you she was inside."

Indeed, Maddie heard the madly barking dog on the other side of the door. "Great. She'll maul me."

"That just means she's happy to see you," Hank said, grinning.

Maddie wasn't convinced. "Yeah, right. That's why she keeps taking off and coming back here. She hates me."

Shaking his head, Hank sent her a sidelong glance of masculine appreciation. "I don't see how anyone could hate you."

Tremendously pleased by his compliment, but striving to give nothing away, Maddie resorted to good manners. "Thank you. You're very kind."

He quirked his mouth in amusement. "Well, don't let that get out. It would ruin my reputation."

"Well, we wouldn't want that," Maddie quipped before returning to the business at hand—the dog's presence inside the cottage. "So, I guess you're the one who let Beamer in, right?"

Hank, in the act of fitting the key into the lock, stopped and looked her way, obviously hearing in her voice all her other unasked questions. "Guilty as charged. She just showed up right before I went into town for groceries. I looked around, realized she was out here alone. So I put her inside until I could get back. And yes, I know I should have brought her to you. But she put up quite a fight over not wanting to leave. And yes, I knew you'd come looking for her."

He'd kept Beamer here on purpose knowing she'd follow? How could she be anything but flattered? Trying not to preen, Maddie managed a chuckle and a bit of wit. "Well, that's all my questions answered. But just so you know, I didn't mercilessly leave her outside in this weather. She got out by opening the back door."

Hank's eyes narrowed. "The dog opens doors?"

"I can only assume because it was open and here she is, the stinker."

"Well, I'll be damned."

He was clearly impressed. Maddie fought a sudden urge to proudly blurt that she too could open doors and had been doing so for years.

But Hank saved her from that bit of imbecility by speaking first. "With her mouth, right? She doesn't use her paws but her mouth? To open doors?"

"I guess. I haven't actually seen her do it. I just know she does somehow."

"So you don't keep your doors locked?"

"Not all the time. This is Hanscomb Harbor, remember."

"Right. But that's amazing. About her opening the doors."

"Isn't it? And because she can, I get to chase about in the cold and rain looking for her." Maddie delivered all this with what she hoped was a brilliant smile. "Like now. And we're still outside."

"Oh, hell, excuse me. I got caught up . . ." Hank's voice trailed off and he met her gaze, his dark eyes conveying more than his words. "Okay, I got caught up in staring at you, Maddie. I'm glad you're here. Really glad."

Her breathing suddenly affected, Maddie stared round-eyed and said nothing as Hank turned the key in the lock and worked the doorknob at the same time. Nothing happened. With a glance her way, he then pushed against the stubborn door with his solid weight behind his efforts. The door still wouldn't give. Hank stood back and stared at it as if it had personally offended him.

His expression was comical, but Maddie wisely managed to maintain a sober countenance. "The wood's probably swollen with the damp," she offered in his defense. "The humidity makes it warp and hard to open."

"That makes sense." Then he pointed to the "In memory of James H. Madison, Senior" polished-brass plaque crookedly nailed to the vicariously hung door. "Did you do that?"

"No. Well, yes. In a way. I had Mr. Hardy do it." Hank

was frowning at her as if he needed further explanation. "He came to me after James died and said he didn't know what to do with the rent money James had paid him in advance for his six weeks here. I told him it might be a nice gesture to have a plaque made and put up. I hope that's okay."

Hank nodded. "Sure. Yeah. It's nice." He rubbed his fingers over the words engraved on the brass. "Probably the nicest thing about this place."

"Oh, I don't know about that," Maddie drawled without thinking as she looked Hank's handsome profile up and down. His eyebrows slowly rose as awareness flared in his eyes. Maddie could barely breathe. She feared a cloud of steam would rise from her damp clothes if they kept these hot-eyed stares going. "Uh, why don't you try that door again?"

"Right." But he didn't move. He continued staring at her, desire radiating from his dark eyes.

Maddie knew in her hotly thumping heart that if he made one move toward her, she'd go to bed with him. Just one move toward her, and she was going all the way. Friday she'd been totally silly about the whole issue. She wanted him. She was a consenting adult who was totally turned on by him. Forget all the legalities and uncertainties between them. Sometimes sex could make those things disappear. *Just one move, Hank, and I'm yours, baby . . .* She tried her best to convey that with her eyes.

But failed. Hank abruptly turned to the door and put his shoulder into his efforts, shoving hard against the stubborn wood. Maddie slumped. *Darn.* But the door burst open as if there'd never been a problem, taking Hank with it. Caught completely off guard, stumbling and cursing, he all but fell into the one-room interior.

Gasping, Maddie was right behind him. "Ohmigod, are you all right?"

In the middle of the room and dodging the jumping, playful, dry, warm, happy, barking golden retriever, Hank jerked to a teetering stop, whipped around to face Maddie, and struck what was to her a comically dramatic pose with his feet apart and his hands fisted at his waist. This was not the man of the thousand-dollar suits and the penthouse and the board meetings. That man had to be his evil, or at least his sober-minded, twin. Right now, this guy's expression was the exaggerated one of some silent-cinema romantic hero. "Why, yes I am. I meant to do that."

Maddie laughed at him. "You did not. You nearly fell on your face."

He arched an eyebrow nearly all the way up to his hairline, thoroughly impressing Maddie. "I did no such thing. What I nearly fell on was, in fact, my ass."

Maddie burst out laughing. And apparently offended Beamer. The dog, close by Hank's side, barked and barked at Maddie as if admonishing her not to laugh at her friend. Finding herself the least bit hurt in the pride area because Beamer hadn't rushed to her, Maddie fussed good-naturedly at the canine. "And what are you griping about, traitor?"

Beamer lowered her ears and managed to look guilty, if unrepentant.

"Well, I see you two have made your peace," Hank quipped, dropping his pose.

Maddie made a scoffing sound. "If you call her doing exactly as she pleases and my staying out of her way *peace*, then, yes, we have achieved that."

He waved her inside. "Come in, Maddie. Close that door, and I'll start a fire."

She couldn't resist. "And what will you start if I don't close it?"

That eyebrow went up again. "I'll start griping about the cold, most likely."

"I'd rather have the fire." Maddie closed the door, which muted the sound of the rain, but also blocked out most of what was left of the overcast afternoon's questionable daylight. That left it pretty dark inside the cabin. Sure, she'd been brave and wanton outside, but now she felt suddenly shy at being in such close and intimate quarters with Hank and a bed.

But apparently he wasn't afflicted by any such feelings because he was bustling about, opening the flimsy curtains that hung limply from slightly askew café rods. "There," he announced, "that's better." He rubbed his hands together as if satisfied with his efforts. "I'll go get some firewood off the porch." He headed in that direction, saying over his shoulder on the way out, "Have a seat, Maddie. Make yourself comfortable."

"Okay."

Have a seat. Maddie frowned as she panned the cabin's interior. It would have been a kindness to say the beach house was furnished in retro 1950s style. Only there was no style. And this stuff, given Mr. Hardy's penchant for . . . kindly put . . . economy, had probably been in here *since* the 1950s. The early 1950s.

Capturing Maddie's attention first was the old metal bed that sagged against the back wall. It sported a lumpy-looking mattress, graying sheets, and a stained bedspread. Maddie made a yuck face. Passion and desire had just taken a back seat to hygiene. She eyed instead the bedside lamp, torn shade and all, that teetered atop a red-painted crate of some kind. Turning around, she saw a dirty two-burner stove, a seriously stained sink with exposed plumbing, and a hulking monolith of an icebox crowding one wall. Adding to the kitchen area's charm was a chrome table with two matching chairs, the seats of which were covered by a red vinyl material. Cigarette burns and just plain old rips in the fabric completed the lived-in look.

Grimacing her distaste, Maddie turned her gaze toward the seating area. The torn and stained excuse for a couch didn't deserve further description, or to have a human sit upon it. As if that were her cue, Beamer climbed up on it and made herself comfortable. That explained that. An oval braided rug in front of the couch was no longer exactly oval or even braided. Okay, to be fair, not everything in the room was from the 1950s. Certainly, the Franklin stove sitting innocently against the far wall was from the *1750s*.

But all was not lost, for next to the kitchen area was a hopeful sign. A closed door. One that Maddie sincerely prayed, for Hank's sake, opened onto an indoor bathroom with clean and working plumbing. Completing this room's décor, and facing the couch, was a small TV atop a slightly adrift bookcase. It leaned to the left, whereas the cottage walls leaned to the right. It was enough to make a person seasick. No books resided in the bookcase. But it did boast a jumble of magazines, the nature of which Maddie felt no compunction to explore.

And here was something you didn't see every day. The TV proudly possessed rabbit-ear antennae. As expected, a folded square of aluminum foil, looking for all the world like a little shiny flag, had been mashed into place at the top of one antenna . . . and was even now slowly descending the antenna's length as Maddie stared at it. She had to stop herself from putting a hand patriotically over her heart and humming taps.

"So? What do you think? Just like home, huh?"

Maddie whirled around.

There stood Hank with an armful of firewood. Clutched in one hand was a rusty-looking can opener, the old pliers-like kind that was hand-powered. He waved this item at her and proudly announced, "Look what I found outside behind the wood crib. Pretty lucky, huh?"

"Lucky?" With dreaded certainty, Maddie knew Hank would be dead inside of a week, tops, out here. "Hank, you cannot stay in this beach house," she announced dramatically. "Not under any conditions. I had no idea these cottages were—and I use the word loosely here—furnished like this. Look at this place. What is Mr. Hardy thinking?" She stilled and stared soberly into Hank's dark eyes. "If you stay here one more day, you will die."

"I'll die?" Because he still held the firewood, Hank could only awkwardly toss the can opener into the big ceramic sink before advancing on the wood bin next to the Franklin stove. Concerned by Maddie's proclamation of doom, he looked all around the cabin's interior, but didn't spot any obvious or even potential threats. "What will I die from?"

"Can you not see?" She was clearly horrified. "Rust. And dirt. And grime. And germs. And other things, like dog hair."

Hank chuckled. "Come on, Maddie, I've been here for days. And if that combination could kill anyone, Stephen King would have already written a book about it."

"I'm serious."

"So am I." He bent over the crate and allowed the wood to roll out of his arms and into the slatted box. "There." Satisfied with his efforts, he straightened up and briskly rubbed his hands together. He smiled Maddie's way. "It's cold in here, isn't it? I'll get us a fire started and then we can—"

"Hank, that's exactly what I'm talking about. Have you ever started a fire before in your life?"

He was thoroughly amused, and a bit offended, to realize she thought him a pampered little rich boy who couldn't take care of himself. He briefly wondered if he should tell her about the mountain-climbing expedition he'd bank-rolled and participated in that had actually required a Sherpa guide. Or all the white-water rapids, in a kayak, he'd run on various continents. Or the cross-country skiing in Sweden. That month-long trek down the Amazon. The time he'd spent among the Aborigines in the Australian outback.

But then he thought of a better story. And scratched at his jaw as he pretended to think about her question. "Hmm. Have I ever started a fire? Oh yeah, I did. When I was nine. It was with my mother's lighter. We were at the country club. It was summer, and we were spending the day at the pool. There was a bunch of kids I knew, and I was trying to light a cigarette—"

"Wait. You smoked when you were nine?"

"Just that one time. It was a dare. A stupid-kid trick. Anyway, we were huddled in the dining room, just us kids.

It was between lunch and supper. None of the wait staff was around. So anyway, Tommy Jenkins jostled me and I missed the cigarette and got the curtains."

Maddie paled. "The curtains?"

"Yeah. And we were behind the curtains because we didn't want the grown-ups to catch us. Smart, huh? But it gets better. Also behind the curtains were plate-glass windows and everyone outside at the pool could see us."

Maddie was slowly shaking her head and staring at him as if he'd escaped a scientific lab somewhere. "Good God. Did anyone get hurt?"

"No. Some quick-thinking waiter was passing by with a couple pitchers of water and tossed it on the flames. And us."

"The flames? There were actual *flames*?" Her tone of voice said he was not helping his case any.

"Well, they weren't flames so much as . . . little ones. It was no big deal. No one was hurt. If you don't count my backside."

"Your backside got burned?"

"Blistered is more like it. By my mother. I learned my lesson. Or lessons. There were two. One, don't smoke. And two, never piss off my mother, especially in front of her friends."

Maddie tilted her chin up. "You're pulling my leg, aren't you?"

Hank held up both hands as evidence that he was not. "Swear to God. It's true. You can ask my mother." Time to come clean. "Who is here in Hanscomb Harbor as we speak."

Maddie tensed. "Say you're lying."

He shook his head. "Can't. She's here."

"Define 'here.' "

"Hanscomb Harbor. And don't ask where. You don't want to know."

"Oh, God. Okay, then why is she here?"

"Because she wanted to see for herself what the attraction was for my grandfather in this small town."

A silence stretched taut between them. Hank watched Maddie, seeing in her eyes the reflection of the wheels turning in her mind. He knew the moment she got it because she slumped. "We're not talking the actual geographical scenery here, are we?"

"No. We're not." Hank's smile was sympathetic.

"You know, Hank, very recently it has just started to totally suck being me."

"I understand. And it's all the Madisons' fault. I know that, too. And I'm sorry."

Maddie nodded absently as if benignly agreeing with him. Then she shivered. "We need a fire going in here." Her own words seemed to bring him into sharper focus in her sight. "A planned fire properly made in the wood-burning stove."

Hank crossed his arms over his chest. "I knew what you meant." Beamer backed him up with a resentful woof aimed her owner's way.

Maddie turned her pointing finger on the dog. "You're next, young lady."

Beamer lowered her ears and growled halfheartedly, as if she knew she had every reason to expect a dressing-down. Sure enough, Maddie began mock-seriously to chastise the dog. "How dare you open the door at home and get me out on a day like this and worry me like you did . . ."

Thoroughly enchanted with having her here, Hank took this opportunity to drink his fill of the blond and slender woman he'd spent many pleasurable hours with in bed . . . all of them in his head, unfortunately. Yeah, the fantasy sex had been great, but he'd also envisioned long hours of talking with her, of listening to her speak, of watching her movements and her expressions. The truth was, he found the thought of those activities with her just as sensual and intimate as sex would be. She excited him on every level. And that scared the hell out of him. Or should have. But didn't, which scared him worse.

Could he be more confused? What was it he wanted here? Something permanent? That would be the only kind a man could have with a woman like Maddie. As Jim Thornton had said, she was the marrying kind. The mother-of-your-children sort. Hank's bachelor's heart thumped its protest. *Damn. Am I sunk here or what?* He didn't know. But he did have an enforced six-week vacation to find out. Of course, a lot depended on Maddie's cooperation. And why would she? Hadn't the Madisons infringed on her life enough already? *True. So go slow here, Hank. Give her some time, some room. You need the same thing, too.*

Go slow? How? He was on fire for her. Just standing in the same room with her had him fisting his hands at his sides to keep from grabbing her and tossing her with him onto that damned rickety old bed in the corner. Going slow was going to be hard. Hank tried to ignore his body's willing response to that word. *Hard. Ha-ha. Funny.*

But he was a grown man. In control. And this was important. Maddie was important. He felt they had to get this right the first time out or say goodbye. And he didn't want that to happen. That was all he was willing to admit to right now, that he didn't want to *not* see her. It was a beginning. He liked that idea. A good beginning with Maddie. Right here, alone together on a rainy, windswept late-summer afternoon inside an isolated cabin at the beach. Just him and her. And Beamer, of course. In fact, Hank realized, he had Beamer to thank for getting Maddie out here.

And that was when Hank also realized something else. Maddie was done with her halfhearted harangue of the dog and was now standing in the middle of the room . . . staring at him staring at her. He jerked to attention. "You want to sit down?"

Before Maddie could respond, Beamer adjusted her position on the couch, reclining with much the same superior attitude as Cleopatra had probably employed. Hank met Maddie's bemused gaze. "I should have been more specific. So with the couch taken, I can offer you a kitchen chair or the bed." *Or the bed.* She'd already taken off once when he mentioned beds and sleep. Hank exhaled. *Go slow.* "Okay, never mind that. Can you stay for a meal?"

"You cook?"

He shook his head. "No. I heat. Remember, I have a can opener."

"If it's not the one you brought in with the wood, okay, yes."

Hank's heart soared. She'd stay. How hopeless was he to be so delighted? "I promise to use the new one I bought today," he said solemnly.

Now she looked uncertain. "Good. You really do want me to stay, right?"

"Oh, yeah. I want you to stay, Maddie." Hank felt certain he was dying here. Just standing here looking at her . . . the way she filled out her jeans . . . that long blond hair . . . her smiling face.

Go slow? What kind of a dumb-ass idea was that? Well, dumb-ass or not, he was stuck with it. Right?

CHAPTER ELEVEN

RIGHT. BECAUSE HERE THEY were, Hank lamented—he and Maddie, sitting innocently and fully clothed, opposite each other at the nasty little kitchen table. After unloading the groceries he had out in his SUV, he'd built a fire and had been cheered when Maddie had insisted on working side by side with him to whip up a damned fine meal of canned chili and saltine crackers. A suitable bottle of red wine rounded out their meal. Done eating now, Hank felt they were a bit more relaxed with each other, yet he couldn't take his eyes off her.

"Maddie," he said, eyeing her creamy-appearing neck and wondering idly what it would be like to kiss her there. "Do golden retrievers like chili? There's still some left in the pot."

Maddie raised a finely arched eyebrow. "I imagine golden retrievers love chili. But *should* you give her any is a whole other question."

"I'm guessing the answer to that would be no."

"Exactly. I haven't been the proud owner of a dog for long, but I don't think it takes much imagination to realize the, uh, end result. So if you give that dog as much as one taste of chili, I'll leave her here until the storm passes." She grinned brightly, meaningfully. "And I don't mean the one outside."

Hank grimaced. "Yikes."

They both looked at the dog sitting beside the table. Beamer looked from one to the other of them, a what-did-I-do expression on her face. Hank's chuckle joined Maddie's. "So what can we give her to eat?"

"Nothing now. She's terrible to beg. I'll feed her when I get home."

Hank nodded, leaning over to pat the dog's head and

ruffle her silky ears. "Sorry, girl. I've been overruled."
Hank sought Maddie's gaze, but got her profile as she, like
a mother whose child had just embarrassed her, watched
the disgruntled dog pad dejectedly across the room and flop
again on the disreputable couch. Maddie then swung her
gaze his way—and caught him staring. Hank couldn't for
the life of him look away or disguise his want for her. "I'm
glad Beamer jumped ship and got you out here."

Maddie's blue eyes widened. "Because it saved you another trip into town?"

"Hardly. You know what I mean."

Her face colored a bright pink. "I do." She seemed to
be having difficulty meeting his direct and hungry stare.
"And so am I. Glad, I mean. Although I could have done
without the wind and the rain."

"Yeah. It is pretty dramatic." She had Hank's heart beating now. It was so damned obvious that she wanted him
as much as he wanted her. He was about one second, he
knew, from shoving this table and everything on it out of
his way and making a grab for her. "Well," he added, "at
least you got some of my home-cooked canned chili. Not
too many people can say that. And it was nice to see a
welcoming face when I got here, even if it was a furry one."

Her chuckle was that of amused insult. "You mean the
dog, right?"

"No, I meant you," Hank countered, very seriously.
"You really do need to shave, Maddie." Then he chuckled.
"Of course I meant the dog. But this is a big breakthrough
for us, you know. Meaning I got through a bottle of wine
with you without me wearing any of it."

"Hmm. I must be slipping." She mimicked his posture
by sitting back in her chair and crossing her arms. "You
know, you said something earlier that keeps sticking in my
mind."

"Score one for me."

"No, seriously. About your mother. I asked you where
she was. And you said I didn't want to know. Guess what?
I do."

Hank very soberly shook his head. "Oh, but you don't. Trust me."

"Oh, but I do."

He shrugged his defeat. "All right. You'll know soon enough anyway." He settled into his chair and his story. "Lady Lillian—that's my mother—hated the accommodations offered in Hanscomb Harbor." Maddie made a *yikes* face. Hank nodded his agreement. "Exactly. Who's surprised? Her idea of roughing it is not having all-night room service in a five-star hotel."

"Neither of which we have here."

"Actually, you do."

"We do? Where? At one the bed-and-breakfasts?"

"Sort of."

Maddie raised her eyebrows. "Tell me, or I'll throw my napkin at you."

"Now I'm scared. She's staying with Celeste."

Maddie's eyes slowly widened as her mouth opened. She ducked her head the slightest bit and looked out at him from under her raised eyebrows. "You. Have. Got. To. Be. Kidding. Me."

"I wish I was. She's staying with Celeste."

Maddie shook her head disbelievingly. "How in God's name did this happen?"

"By accident."

"They say the same thing about nuclear mishaps."

"Yes, they do. Well, we'd tried every bed-and-breakfast. No dice. Turned her nose up at them. And she wouldn't even get out of the car at the Harbor Inn Motel. So I didn't dare bring her out here."

"Smart man."

Hank nodded. "I ended up—and you're not going to believe this—literally driving through the residential streets while she checked out the houses and passed judgment on them."

Maddie's eyes were now perfectly rounded. "Are you serious? She was just going to pick one out and go tell the owners she was here to stay?"

"Why do you think I call her Lady Lillian? She's like some queen from medieval times who just shows up and has to be entertained or else."

"My God. And she ended up with Celeste how?"

"Celeste didn't tell you she had a house guest?"

"No. When did this happen?"

"Yesterday."

"Oh. Okay. No wonder. I haven't talked to her. I gave her yesterday off since she covered for me on—" And there it was. Hank remained silent. Maddie averted her gaze, no doubt not wanting to say "Friday," the day she'd come back here, with no explanation to him, instead of staying in the city where he was. Suddenly animated and too cheerful and matter-of-fact, she met his eyes. "Anyway, I had Fran coming in Saturday. So I didn't need the help. And I haven't talked to Celeste." She frowned and tucked a lock of hair behind her ear. "So, what were you saying?"

Hank took pity on her. "I was saying there I was with my mother, on what I now know is the street where Celeste lives." Maddie nodded avidly that she was listening. "And Lady Lillian says, 'Stop here,' in front of this big house. After a day of this and driving all around, believe me, I stopped. She turns to me and says, 'I like this one.' "

"Hank, is your entire family insane?"

"Yes."

Maddie went on as if he hadn't spoken. "And your mother? She has no clue how the real world works, does she?"

"None. But if you have enough money, Maddie, you *can* be crazy. Yet it's called 'eccentric' and everyone indulges you."

Maddie nodded along with his explanation. "I see. So you knock on Celeste's door and . . . what?"

"She answers it. And I just about die."

"You may yet," Maddie assured him. "So you see it's her and, I guess, tell her what's going on. And she says . . . ?"

" 'Come in.' "

"Celeste? McNeer? Celeste McNeer? The one I know? The tiny, white-haired, foul-mouthed woman who works for me? She just says 'Come in' and is willing to indulge your mother? Just like that?"

"Close. But yeah, pretty much like that."

"They'll kill each other."

He shrugged. "Maybe not. They were having high tea when I left and working out the details of who gets the bathroom when."

"That's it." Maddie covered her face with her hands. "My name is Alice and I've gone down the rabbit hole. That's the only explanation that makes sense here, Hank." She flopped her hands onto her lap. "The only one."

He grinned at her. "I know. It's nuts, isn't it?"

" 'Nuts' doesn't even begin to cover it. And you? What were you thinking, leaving her there?"

"I was thinking my work here is done and—"

"No, seriously. What do you think is going to happen when they get around to talking about me? Celeste is my staunchest defender, Hank. You saw how she behaved that day you first came to my shop after your grandfather died."

Hank winced with guilt. "I remember. And I don't think I've apologized enough for my behavior that day, Maddie."

"Oh, forget that," she said dismissively, a hand held up as if to ward off further apologies from him. "That's nothing compared to how your mother thinks of me. What did she say about me in New York?"

Hank was not about to repeat his mother's description of Maddie. Something about a blond, twenty-pound, twelve-year-old in charge of their fortune. "She said you were pretty."

"Very diplomatic. But answer something else for me. When, and how, did *you* decide I wasn't a gold digger?" She closed her eyes and rubbed at her forehead. "I am beginning to hate that word."

"I don't blame you." Hank waited until Maddie looked up at him. "I got over it by knowing you, Maddie. Sure, when I first saw you, I thought I knew what was up."

"Why is that? Do I look like some kind of opportunist, Hank? I mean cheap? On the make? Overblown? That's how I picture someone you'd describe as a gold digger."

"Come on, you don't look like that at all. You're a young, beautiful blonde. But that's all some people need to see." Hank's face warmed as he remembered he had been one of those rush-to-judgment people. "And I couldn't have been more wrong, Maddie. All I had to do is get to know you better. Spend some time with you."

She raised an eyebrow, giving herself an arch look. "And ask people about me?"

He grinned. "I didn't have to. It seemed that everyone I met voluntarily sang your praises to me."

Now it was Maddie's turn to color. "Great. This town, I swear." She shook her head. "They love me. What can I say? It's a curse, being a nice woman."

Smiling, Hank indulgently watched her pick up her spoon and fiddle with it, dragging it idly through the remains of her chili. She again focused on him, the deep blueness of her eyes enough to arrest his attention. He always seemed to forget how blue they were. And how changeable. Maybe their color reflected her mood or what she wore. "So do you think your mother will come to the same conclusion about me that you did, Hank?"

This was starting to get uncomfortable. Hank could hardly defend his mother's behavior or her reason for coming here, but he also felt loyal to her. And to Maddie. Yet he feared she was right. His mother and Celeste would, no doubt, end up having words or worse if he didn't get a grip on this situation. Hank rubbed a hand over his face. *Great.* Suddenly, he was a man caught among a bunch of warring women. Four to be exact. Maddie. Celeste. His mother. Beamer. A bunch. *A chick fight waiting to happen.*

"Wow, you're quiet. That bad, huh?"

He shook his head. "Not at all. If there had been any way I could have stopped her from coming here, Maddie, I would have. I want you to know that. I used the whole trip here to tell her just how wrong she is about you. But she thinks she's protecting her baby boy."

Maddie sat up straight. "What? Now she thinks I have designs on *you*?"

Did she have to look so surprised and as if the whole idea were distasteful? Hank's ego went down in flames. This was great. His careless words would probably make her standoffish and even more reserved with him. *Damn, damn, damn.* But stuck now, he said, "She thinks— wrongly—that I'm next in line. Or in your sights."

Maddie's frown was that of insult taken. "Just grand. And you told her . . . ?"

"That she's wrong about you. But she insists on seeing for herself. And there really isn't anything I can do to stop her. She's an adult and can go where she wants. But the more I think about it, Maddie, probably the best place in Hanscomb Harbor for her to be is with Celeste. She'll certainly keep a lid on my mother's activities."

"If Celeste doesn't kill her first."

Hank spread his hands wide. "Hey, if she does, problem solved."

Tsking her outrage, Maddie leaned over the table to swat at him. She missed. "Stop that. That's terrible." She then sat back and gestured widely. "So, okay, how do you and I behave now? I mean, if she even sees us together, she'll think there's something going on between us."

"Would that be so awful?" Hank said quietly.

"Yes, it would," Maddie said instantly, to Hank's disappointment.

"Why?"

"With her money, she could use it to do a lot of damage here if she so chose. And the press is starting to show up. All your mother would have to do, to ruin my reputation, is talk to them."

Hank considered that and came up with a valid answer. "On the bright side, if you get some tabloid coverage, you wouldn't ever again have to worry about everyone thinking you're a nice woman."

Whoa. Her narrowed eyes said she didn't like that idea. "Is that supposed to be funny? Right now—with this crazy will and the news picking up on something this quirky— is the very time I need to be thought of as a nice woman."

"I know. I was only teasing. But, okay, what do you want to do about this crisis?"

Clearly disgruntled, she flapped her hands at him. "I don't know. We need to come up with something good, though."

Hank's hormones woke up and had him grinning. *We?* He loved the idea of "we." It was beginning to dawn on him too just how good a thing his mother's presence in Hanscomb Harbor could be. After all, he and Maddie would be forced to deal with her together. His mood brightened. The next six weeks were certainly shaping up not to be boring. And for once the light at the end of this tunnel having to do with Maddie might not be an oncoming train.

"What's so funny? I think we have a disaster on our hands, Hank."

"Not if we work together. Like we did at the stockholders' meeting. By the way, you were brilliant."

"Of course I was. You were sitting right there and whispering all the answers into my ear. And speaking of *by the ways*, congratulations on your business deal. I'm happy for you."

Hank smiled. "Thanks for letting it happen."

"Don't thank me. Thank Jim Thornton."

"Oh, believe me, I did. I sent him and Mary the biggest basket of flowers ever seen on earth."

Maddie made a face as if she were hurt. "I didn't get any flowers."

"You got chili—the gift that keeps on giving." Maddie's roll of her eyes had Hank chuckling. "But I'm just glad I have a good executive board to turn things over to for the next six weeks."

"That's got to be reassuring. I liked Hope Chesswell. She seemed very capable."

Hank nodded his agreement and was secretly pleased

with Maddie's assessment. "She is. That's why I made her my senior vice president."

He was further pleased to realize that he liked having Maddie to talk shop with. Normally he didn't like anybody in his business, so he didn't share it with anyone. But Maddie, thanks to his grandfather's will, already knew it and was involved. Or had been thrown into it, really. And yet she'd performed brilliantly at the meeting last Friday, despite her public-speaking fears. She'd also apparently overcome her fear of dogs. Hank cocked his head at an assessing angle. Maddie Copeland was a brave and interesting woman.

"*Anyway*," she said, giving the impression of being uncomfortable under his stare. "Your mother and Celeste. What do we do? Besides duck and run."

"Those are both good options." Hank rubbed his chin and stared at a point just to Maddie's left as he tried to reason out a course of action. "Well, I know my mother. And you know Celeste. What's your best guess?"

"I asked you first."

"All right." He shrugged. "I say we do nothing and it will work itself out."

Maddie eyed him levelly. "No doubt the very same plan offered by the city council of Pompeii a long time ago, Hank."

"You're probably right." Warming to his subject now, Hank moved his bowl to one side and crossed his arms on the tabletop. "Look, we both know the truth here. You're not a gold digger. And you're not out to take anything away from the Madisons."

"Thank you for that." Maddie nodded regally, causing a cascade of her golden hair to fall forward over her shoulder.

"Your hair is so beautiful." Hank stopped, hearing the words floating on the air between them. Had he really said that out loud?

Apparently he had, because Maddie stopped in the act of tucking the stray lock behind her ear and smiled shyly. "Thank you."

"You're welcome." Hank found her response endearing. He openly stared at the beautiful sight she made, even sitting here in this ratty cabin. She met his gaze, and the air crackled with unspoken desire. All Hank could think was there was a bed in the same room with them. Then reality set in, telling him there was also a big friendly dog here. And the subject of Celeste and his mother. That did it. Effective birth control. Thoughts of one's mother. Hank's desire level shriveled, but not so quickly as did a certain part of his anatomy. Physically uncomfortable now, he cleared his throat and shifted about in his chair.

With Maddie suddenly looking everywhere but at him, Hank felt it his duty to speak first. "My mother is really no threat, Maddie. If I thought she was, if I thought she was really going to cause some serious trouble for you, I'd put a stop to it, believe me. In a heartbeat. But I've dealt with her all my life, so I know how she is. She's here to make sure I'm okay. Nothing more. And I am. End of concern."

"I appreciate that, Hank. I really do. But I just wish I could believe it would be that easy. She was not amused by the whole idea of me two days ago."

"Well, you have to remember that she'd just been hit that day with all this will stuff. And remember how we behaved when we found out?"

Maddie's self-deprecating chuckle came accompanied by a shake of her head. "Only too well. I was a real princess."

"And I was an ogre. So, see? We got over it and we're doing better now. My mother will, too. She'll come around." Maddie opened her mouth as if to protest further. "Look, I should tell you how it is, Maddie. Lady Lillian is my mother and I love and respect her. But I'm also a grown man, and I'm not afraid of her. That said, I think I know her well enough to say she'll tire of this place inside of a few days and leave—if we don't give her a fight and a reason to stay."

Maddie firmed her lips together and nodded, obviously weighing his words. "I see your reasoning. I do. And I concede that you know her best. But from my angle, Hank, it's the idea of her being here and watching me that makes me uncomfortable. On the one hand I want to laugh because it's so silly and, okay, endearing that she'd be this worried about you. But on the other, I get the same feeling as I would with an IRS audit. You hate it and it makes you nervous and guilty, even when you have nothing to hide."

"You have every right to feel that way. Just as you have every right to handle her any way you see fit. I mean that. But I couldn't be more embarrassed that she's here and making you feel like you're under the gun."

"It's not your fault, Hank. You didn't do anything. And I guess you're right. She won't be satisfied until she learns for herself that I didn't do anything, either."

Hank shrugged and gestured toward her. "A pretty good assessment, I'd say. So we agree? There's not a thing either one of us can do until or unless she does something first, right? And if she does, we both step in?"

"Right."

Hank felt good about this. He and Maddie were working together. They had a plan of action. Or inaction, he supposed. "Remember, she may not do anything. I left her with Celeste, who certainly won't take any guff about you off her. Or probably won't leave her alone long enough for her to wander around Hanscomb Harbor unattended. Besides, I think it's more likely that the two of them will team up and take over the government."

That earned Hank a chuckle from Maddie. "And not a minute too soon, if you ask me."

Hank smiled expansively. "See? A bright side already."

The only bright side, come Monday morning at ten o'clock sharp—opening time at Maddie's Gifts—was the weather. The day dawned bright and warm. The air felt as if it had been washed clean by the wind-driven clouds that, like great sponges, had scudded across the sky in purifying swipes. Yes, the day promised to be beautiful. But not profitable. The unseasonable storm had taken its toll on fickle tourists who had left for home or warmer climes, taking with them their dollars and August's sales figures.

Maddie found herself thinking that maybe the decreased sales wouldn't matter—and caught her breath. That was twice this morning that the insidious thought had occurred to her. They were right, the people who said money corrupted. Going around her shop and opening the shutters and turning the Closed sign over to its Open side, Maddie invoked her work ethic, something she'd believed until now to be ingrained in her Yankee DNA. She told herself how dangerous it was to count on wealth she didn't have and may never get.

It was just so insidious, that much money. And unbelievable. She felt as if she'd been told she'd won the lottery . . . maybe. The maybe part came with Hank Madison. He had to do his six weeks uninterrupted before either one of them could win. If *win* was the right word. Maddie wrinkled her nose, thinking of earlier that morning and the first time she'd thought of the money and had balked at getting up and coming in to work. She'd caught herself mumbling into her pillow, saying, "I'm rich. I don't have to work."

But she knew that sentiment wasn't true. The rich were rich because they worked. Not because they didn't. Exhibit A was Hank himself. Look at the lengths his grandfather had felt he needed to go to get Hank away from work for only six weeks. That sobering notion had kicked Maddie out of bed—that and Beamer licking her face and whining to go out. Maddie had accused the dog of picking her moments to pretend she couldn't open the door and let herself out.

Maddie opened the cash register and readied the till for customers who probably wouldn't come today. Still, as she counted out the money, she told herself, *You're not lazy, Maddie. Or corrupted by money. You're suffering from sleep deprivation.* Maddie quirked her mouth irritably. *Ha. More like sexual frustration brought on by all those erotic dreams of Hank last night.* She sighed, feeling all dreamy inside. In her dreams, the two of them had done everything except sleep. Maddie exhaled a sharp, sensual *whew*, remembering how she'd tossed and turned and twisted her covers all about her while in the throes of the full-color images in her mind of Hank being in bed with her . . . of his hands roving tenderly over her . . . of him kissing her all over, but especially down there where he put his mouth—

The front door to the shop opened, setting off the maddening little bell above it. At the first note of the cheerful tinkling, Maddie's heart thumped madly and she jumped guiltily, fearing for one second that the merry music was instead an alarm sounded by the sexual-thought police.

Turned out, it was worse than that. In stepped Celeste, dressed in a blood-red polyester pantsuit. Right behind her was Lillian Madison, dressed to the elegant nines in expensive pastels that complemented her coppery hair and peaches-and-cream complexion. The two women were laughing and talking nonstop and just getting along great and having wonderful fun. Until they saw Maddie at the back of the shop. Instantly their conversation—the last words of which were spoken by Celeste and went like this: "And I swear I never saw Maddie look so . . ."—came to a screeching halt.

As the three women eyed each other, silence filled the shop and vied for space among the many souvenir items, which included postcards, gold nautical jewelry, and delicate handblown glass sea horses. However, for effect and sudden tension, the setting may as well have been the OK Corral.

"Adorable," Celeste said, finishing her last statement as she guiltily fingered her favorite pop-bead necklace and exchanged a glance with her companion-in-crime. She then smiled at Maddie. "I was just telling Lillian here about that time when you were four years old and had that dance recital and kept pulling your dress up and how everyone could see your frilly underwear. You never were one to stay in your clothes for long."

Maddie's knees locked. *Perfect. Just perfect. That's what Hank's mother needs to hear. I can't stay in my clothes.* With her face burning red-hot, Maddie refused to meet Lillian Madison's gaze. "Oh, Celeste. *Really.* You shouldn't have. You really should *not* have. I'm sure Mrs. Madison isn't interested in my little-girl antics."

"Why, sure she is," Celeste said, waving away Maddie's concern and heading behind a counter where her apron hung on a wooden peg. "I've been telling her about you, and she's been telling me about Hank. Now say hi to Lillian. I told her she could come in today and work with us. We can always use the extra set of hands."

"We can?" Maddie heard herself say, hating that her voice sounded so high . . . and panicky. It was worse than she'd feared. The woman wouldn't be all over town sowing discontent. No, she'd be right here doing it. Maddie fixed her gaze on Hank's mother, who smiled at her . . . like the Cheshire Cat. That was when Maddie knew she'd been right yesterday out at the beach cottage with Hank: she was Alice and she'd fallen down the rabbit hole.

"Well," she managed to chirp to Hank's mother, "as long as you're here, would you like a red apron? We all wear red aprons when we work."

"I won't need one." She began digging through her correct-name-brand handbag. "But I will need an ashtray."

"I don't have any. I don't allow smoking in the shop."

Hank's mother came up with a gold cigarette case and then smiled at Maddie. "I'm sure you don't mean me." She pivoted about, then pointed at a stocked shelf. "Oh, look. An ashtray." Sure enough, she picked up a souvenir crystal ashtray and held it up for Maddie to see. "How much, honey?"

"Fifteen ninety-nine."

Perfectly plucked light-brown eyebrows rose. "My. Pricey. Put it on my tab." She set it on a shelf conveniently close to her elbow. "You may as well start me one. I see a lot of things in here I like."

Maddie suspected she wasn't one of them.

By now, Celeste had on her apron and had stowed her purse in a locked cabinet in the stockroom. She was just coming through the curtain, which separated the back from the sales floor. "Lillian thinks I ought to get my hair cut, Maddie. She says this bun makes me look old."

"Well, you're not and it doesn't. I like you just fine the way you are. And I don't want you to change, Celeste."

The other two women didn't move. Or speak. Maddie wanted to cry. Could she have sounded more testy? she wondered. She couldn't believe her behavior in one way— here she was acting like some girl in junior high whose best friend had suddenly found herself a new best friend. But on the other hand, this was her shop and her rules and her town and her life and her reputation—Maddie inhaled sharply, pleading with the gods for calm. She closed her eyes and rubbed at her forehead.

And that was when the damned front door opened again and the stupid little maniacally tinkling bell chirped so happily and had Maddie ready to explode and maybe even spout a few choice curse words like Celeste always did when she heard the bell—

In walked Hank Madison. Dressed in jeans and a sky-blue knit shirt, the man stopped dead in the doorway. He took in the situation at a glance. Maddie knew because all color and expression left his handsome face. "Mother! What are you doing here—"

"What do you mean? I have to be somewhere—"

"Hank! Fancy seeing you here. Your mother and I had us a time last night at the Captain's Tavern—"

"The Captain's Tavern? You took my mother to the—"

"Hank, honey, did you know that there's a waitress there named Stephie who thinks you are so—"

"Not in front of Maddie, Lillian. You might make her jealous—"

"I am *not* jealous," Maddie jumped in. "Hank is his own man. He's free to do what he pleases with whom he pleases. I certainly have no claim on him. No designs and no intention of having ... any designs ... and claims on him . . ." Her voice petered out pathetically. Again her cheeks blazed hot. Maddie felt bad to see Hank looking so startled and a bit crestfallen. She hadn't really meant most of what she'd said. At least she didn't think she did. "I mean . . . he's certainly a nice man." She then realized he was in the room and that she should talk to him directly. "*You're* a nice man, Hank. You are. I just . . . don't think we . . ." *Dammit.* "I don't want to say anything more because right now I sound like an idiot."

Nobody moved or said anything. Not even to rush in with assurances that she wasn't an idiot. For her part, Maddie concentrated on dust motes dancing through a lemony shaft of sunlight that dappled the wood flooring.

Then Lillian Madison drew everyone's strained and grateful attention her way with a bit of unintentional theater. Without a word, and as if unaffected by Maddie's outburst, she snapped open her gold cigarette case and tapped out a long, thin pink-like-her-outfit cigarette. She put it to her lips, still managing to look like a lady, and expertly lit it with a matching gold lighter. She inhaled, put the lighter and cigarette case back in her handbag, elegantly exhaled, held the cigarette out between two long fingers, picked up the crystal ashtray, held it about chest-high, and finally eyed each of them in turn. Frowning, she focused last on her son. "What?" she wanted to know.

"Maddie has No Smoking signs posted, Mother."

Lillian sighed. "We've been through this already. She doesn't mean me. Look." She held out her ashtray. "She even gave me an ashtray. Credit me with *some* sensitivity, son." Then she looked him up and down. "I can't remember the last time I saw you looking so fit and relaxed. James Senior may not have been as crazy as we all thought he was."

"Not *all*." Everyone looked at Maddie. She felt so exposed, yet stood her ground. "I never thought he was crazy."

Lillian's chuckling snort brought all eyes her way. "I suppose you didn't. Just look at you. So pretty and blond."

Maddie knew she'd been insulted with compliments and her expression puckered. But Lillian Madison had already turned to her son. "So, what are you doing here bright and early, honey? Did you come to see what I might be up to?"

"No. Yes. Not really." Hank's gaze flitted to Maddie, leaving no doubt in her mind—or anyone else's, most likely—that he'd come to see her. Somehow, she felt vindicated by that. And happy. Hank focused again on his mother. "But what *are* you up to, Mother?"

She took a drag on her pink cigarette and turned her head to exhale the smoke. "I don't know about 'up to,' but I came here today with Celeste to work in Maddie's shop."

Hank made a scoffing sound of disbelief. "*You* want to work, Mother?"

Maddie saw Lillian Madison's chin come up and caught a glint of something in the older woman's eyes. Perhaps it was insult. Or hurt. Maddie felt her heart soften toward the woman. Go figure. That darned nice gene, no doubt. She then heard herself unbelievably coming to Hank's mother's defense. "Yes, she does want to work." A crazy idea popped into Maddie's head and had her grinning. "And I, for one, am grateful."

"You are?" Lillian, Celeste, and Hank asked in unison.

Maddie began untying her apron. "Yes, I am. In fact, I have so much else to do and have had such trying weeks lately that I think *I'll* take the day off."

"You will?" the threesome parroted.

"I will." Oh, boy, this felt good. Suddenly giddy and happy, Maddie slipped her apron over her head, hung it up, then smoothed her hands down her cotton flower-sprigged skirt. "Celeste, you're in charge. You have a set of keys, so lock up at day's end. I don't think it will be busy today since most of the tourists fled. But show Mrs. Madison the ropes. And you two have fun."

Over the two women's sputterings, Maddie turned to Hank, who'd crossed his arms and had a grin on his face and his eyebrows raised. Totally amused he was. "Your grandfather wanted you to learn how to enjoy life. So how would you like lesson one? I'm talking about a tour of Hanscomb Harbor and a picnic. With me, of course. And Beamer."

Hank chuckled and shrugged his football shoulders. "At last, Maddie. You've made me an offer I can't refuse."

CHAPTER TWELVE

THEIR FIRST STOP WAS Maddie's house to allow her to change clothes. She quickly removed her skirt and cotton-knit sweater and put on khaki shorts and a cap-sleeved, brushed-denim top. They leashed the happily barking golden retriever, left the house, and Maddie boldly looped her arm through Hank's as they walked down the slightly buckling sidewalk toward the town proper. She handed him the dog's leash. "Here. When she's this excited, she drags me all over the place. So, this is your day, Hank. What do you want to see first?"

He squeezed her hand where she held on to his arm. "I'd like to see you being this happy all the time."

Maddie laughed, drawing the attention of her neighbors, whom she waved to. "Morning, Mrs. Jessup, Mrs. Franks." To Hank, she whispered, "Poor old things. Their husbands died at almost the same time. Then they moved in together. Celeste thinks they poisoned their men, but I don't believe it."

Hank looked over his shoulder at the elderly widows who were digging in a garden. "Damn. Remind me to steer clear."

"I'll do that." Maddie sniffed the air, closing her eyes to get the full effect of the clean, slightly salty scent carried their way on a soft breeze. So invigorating. "Do you smell that, Hank?"

"Yeah. It was probably the dog."

She chuckled and shook her head. "I'm talking about the air. Isn't it great? So clean and fresh."

He leaned in close to her. Maddie felt his warm weight against her side and wanted to just bite him he was so wonderful. "I could describe you the same way," he said. "Clean and fresh."

Maddie pretended insult. "Well, great. You think of me as a dryer sheet?"

"A very pretty dryer sheet, though." Hank bent his head and kissed her lightly on the lips.

The casual intimacy of his kiss startled Maddie as much as it thrilled her. A kiss like that spoke of couplehood, of long-standing intimacy, of a free and easy association with each other. None of which they had. Suddenly she couldn't walk. She stopped and stared questioningly up at him.

Hank looked just as surprised by his behavior as she felt. He stood with her there on the tree-shaded sidewalk, right next to the full-service gas station, in plain view of everyone in Hanscomb Harbor who cared to look, and stared into her eyes. For her part, Beamer yawned mightily and stood around patiently—right between Hank and Maddie. An effective chaperone.

"I'm sorry, Maddie," Hank said, chuckling.

"For what?" She couldn't believe how affected and dreamy she felt. Nor could she believe how delicious it was to stand here this close to Hank Madison and feel his body heat and stare so intimately into his dark, dark eyes. The man remained startlingly handsome. Black neatly styled hair, high forehead and cheekbones, a straight patrician nose, wide generous lips . . . and he smelled *so* good. Maddie barely suppressed a sigh of the variety usually reserved for movie-star idols.

With a look of bemusement on his face, Hank scratched at his temple. "I guess I'm sorry for that . . . kiss."

Biting at her bottom lip, vaguely aware that she was playing the seductress, Maddie frowned. "You are? You're sorry? Are you sure?"

Hank looked at a loss for words. He fiddled with Beamer's leash. "I guess. I mean I shouldn't have done that."

Maddie tilted her head and arrowed him a look of invitation. She took no pity on the tall, dark, and handsome man she was slowly melting. "Really? Why not?"

Hank was now clearly confused by her behavior. "I don't know. I didn't even know I was going to do it."

"You didn't?" Maddie tucked her hair behind her ears and smoothed it back over her shoulders. She was only too aware of the effect her thick and curling, long blond hair had on men. And now she could only marvel at her bold self. *Look at me. I'm like some cavewoman hussy trying to attract herself a big old club-wielding mate.*

"Maddie, what's wrong? What are you doing?"

She shrugged. "I'm just standing here, Hank. What are you doing?"

"Trying to figure out what you're doing." He planted his hands at his trim waist and shifted his weight to one leg.

Maddie's breath caught. His unconscious masculine grace was almost poetic. Maddie could just see him in a toga and leaping up onto a chariot. *Look out, Ben Hur.* She started to speak, but Beamer caught her attention when she apparently gave up and sat down. "I think Beamer's trying to tell us something."

"Could be. So tell me what *you're* doing, Maddie. What's this all about?" He gestured to indicate all of the outdoors around them—and then her. "And you. What's this mood?"

Maddie smiled, leaning into him. "Do you like it?"

Hank frowned. "I think I do. But this isn't like you. I'd swear you were trying to seduce me. And I feel stupid just saying that."

Maddie quirked her mouth playfully and clasped her hands behind her back. "Well, you shouldn't. Because I just might be, you know."

"Seriously?" He liked that idea, said his arched eyebrows and the gleaming awareness in his eyes.

Now Maddie dissembled, playing the coquette. She turned and started walking . . . with a lot of sway in her hips. "I might be." Over her shoulder she said, "How am I doing so far?"

Hank laughed out loud and then applauded . . . softly, seductively. "Pretty damned fine, I'd say, Maddie Copeland. Pretty damned fine."

He tugged on Beamer's leash and he and the dog jogged to catch up with her.

A couple hours later, having completed the grand walking tour of downtown Hanscomb Harbor—one street, many stop-ins to chat with proprietors, introduce Hank, and lament over the fleeing of the tourists—Maddie now sat with him in the white-painted gazebo that decorated the town square. Every now and then someone would stroll by and wave at Maddie and she'd speak. But for the most part, they had the town and the middle of the day to themselves.

Basking in a light, warm breeze, they enjoyed their chicken pitas. Refusing to feel guilty for having dropped her Monday responsibilities, Maddie smiled with the deliciousness of the perfect day and tucked into her sack lunch from the walk-up take-out window at Papa's Diner. She leaned over to spread the waxy paper better so Beamer could scarf her own sandwich. Corned beef on rye. Frightening in its implications.

"We're going to pay for that sandwich later." Hank pointed to the dog's lunch.

"Who doesn't know that? But she loves it." Maddie glanced down at the golden retriever and saw her send Hank—Maddie would swear in a court of law—an ears-lowered, mind-your-own-plate-Buster look. Maddie chuckled, staring across the small circular enclosure at Hank, who sat opposite her. "I guess she told you."

Hank sipped at his iced tea and then said, "I guess she did. Sorry, girl." Then, holding his pita in his other hand, he sent Maddie an assessing look. "Look at your cheeks glowing and that big smile. You're the definition of having a great time. So what the heck made you just up and toss everything aside like this? I mean, I had to. We know that. But not you."

Maddie wanted very much to say it was because of him, because she wanted to be with him. But she wasn't quite brave enough for that, despite her earlier I-might-be-trying-to-seduce-you moment. "Actually, it was your mother."

Hank nodded. "A good enough reason. One I can certainly understand."

Maddie sent him an arch look. "Guess what? I think I like her."

His expression was one of pure disbelief. "You do not."

"But I do. It was something I saw in her eyes when you said you couldn't believe she wanted to work."

Hank sobered, really listening now. "Really? What did you see?"

Maddie shrugged as she picked out a bite of chicken and nibbled at it. "I'm not sure. It was like she was hurt that you would think she couldn't do it." Hank's expression fell. Maddie rushed on. "I could be wrong. It just, I don't know, made her seem more human to me. More real. It was like she suffered a moment when she feared she wasn't necessary. Or vital."

Hank seemed to have forgotten that he had an iced tea in one hand and a sandwich in the other. "Damn. All of that in one look? You really think I hurt her? I sure as hell didn't mean to. I was just surprised. She's never worked before. Never."

By now Maddie had swallowed her bit of chicken. "Really? I've never known anyone before who never worked. Wow."

"Well, don't be fooled. She didn't come here looking for work or to find herself. She knows who she is. What she wants to know is who *you* are and if you are any threat to her little world."

Maddie shrugged. "I'd probably feel the same way, put in her position."

Hank sat up straighter, as if he were surprised. "Would you look at you? Now you're looking for ways to like her. That's damned nice of you, Maddie."

She made a wide gesture with her hands, pretending insult. "There it is again. That mutant 'nice' gene. Well, I guess it's enough that Celeste likes her. And that you do." Maddie frowned. "You do like her, right?"

"Of course I like her. She's my mother." Then Hank

frowned, not quite looking at Maddie. "I guess I do. Yeah, I do." He grinned. "She drives me crazy." Then he sobered a bit. "What about your mother? Where's she?"

Maddie looked down at her lap. "She died five years ago in a car wreck. With my father." She looked up, meeting Hank's sober, stricken gaze. "Icy roads. They were coming to see me in Greenwich Village."

"I'm sorry, Maddie. I didn't know."

She smiled bravely, shrugging her shoulders. "It's okay. I cling to Celeste for someone to love and drive me crazy."

Hank nodded, setting down the remainder of his lunch and his drink. "I bet she does a bang-up job of that. So what were you doing in Greenwich Village?"

"I lived there while I went to college. Remember? We talked about this at the Captain's Tavern. I went to Columbia. Majored in art history. Then I worked at the Whitney Museum for three years in research."

He nodded. "Oh, yeah. It's all coming back to me. The sun goddess, right?"

"Right."

"Still, I'm impressed. All that art stuff sounds pretty interesting."

"Only to someone like me. And curators and collectors. And auction houses. And museums. Okay, a lot of people."

"So how'd you end up back here? Wait." He snapped his fingers and pointed at her. "That jerk doctor, right?"

Maddie felt her cheeks heat up. She put her sandwich down next to her on the narrow wooden bench. "Yes. That jerk doctor. The whole left-at-the-altar thing that's so tragic in movies." She rolled her eyes, trying to be brave and show she was over it. "It's not any better in real life, either. God. I just wanted to get away. I was so humiliated."

"I guess you were. I'm sorry that happened to you, Maddie."

She waved away his concern. "You poor man. Here I am trying to show you a good time on a beautiful day and you end up listening to my sob stories."

"Not at all. I don't see it that way." Hank leaned back,

putting a leg up on the bench, his knee bent, his hand resting lightly atop it, a relaxed pose that affected Maddie's breathing.

"So. What about you? What's your life story?" she chirped ever so brightly, trying not to stare openly at the powerful-looking muscles of his thigh under the confinement of his jeans.

"Not much to tell. Little rich kid. Country club existence. Private schools. Brat. Made my mother nuts. Never knew my father. He died in Vietnam when I was a baby."

"Oh, I'm so sorry, Hank. I didn't know. James didn't say much about his son, just about you. His little grandson, if you'll remember. I should have put two and two together to realize that you couldn't have been a little kid. But he was just always so glad that he had you."

Hank's black/brown eyes held a wealth of emotion. "He said that?"

"Of course he did. He loved you very much."

Hank nodded and looked down at his lunch. "I know he did."

Hank's comment proved to be an effective conversation ender. Not knowing what else to say or do, Maddie leaned over and fussed at Beamer for making such a mess of her lunch. She then picked out the remaining chicken in her own sandwich and hand-fed it to the golden retriever.

"You got over your fear of dogs pretty quick."

Maddie straightened up, wiping her hand on a napkin and glancing Hank's way. She then focused on the dog, who now stared at Hank, as if to say, "What's to fear?"

"She didn't give me a chance to be afraid, if you'll remember. She attacked me every time she saw me."

Hank nodded, putting his leg down and standing up to stretch. The man was poetic symmetry. Maddie watched his every move with hungry delight. "I can understand that urge," Hank quipped, grinning brightly, catching her staring. "I've had the urge a time or two myself where you're concerned."

With awareness flaring to a flame deep down inside her,

Maddie patted the dog's head and very primly said, "Well, we're all past that now."

"No we're not. Not all of us." Hank's gleaming eyes and arched eyebrows gave him the rakish appearance of a swashbuckling pirate. All he needed was a knife held between his teeth.

Totally embarrassed and excited by his innuendo, Maddie looked away, grinning. Hank came over to sit by her. Right next to her. Pressed up against her. He put his arm around her shoulders and crossed his legs, an ankle atop his opposite knee. "Ah, come on, Maddie, don't get shy on me. Where's that hip-swaying seductress from a few hours ago? I liked her."

"She went to the beach." It was the only ad-lib comment Maddie could come up with. Afraid she'd succumb to a fit of girlish giggles, she crossed her arms defensively and refused to look at Hank. All the while she felt naked somehow, even in her shorts and top. Being this close to Hank and with him coming on to her . . . God, it felt good. And scary.

"The beach, huh? Then that's where I want to go next. As soon as we finish our lunch."

As if those were code words for doggie scraps, Beamer immediately padded over to the other side of the gazebo and sniffed at Hank's sandwich. She licked it mightily and then threw him a can-I-have-it look over her shaggy, golden-furred shoulder. "Yeah, you can have it," Hank told her. "You've already had your dog lips all over it. Go ahead. Eat it."

She did.

"That dog is going to weigh three hundred pounds, Hank."

"Naw. We'll let her run it off at the beach." He got up and took Maddie's hand, pulling her to her feet. He didn't immediately release her hand, but stood there, only inches from her, staring at her mouth. Maddie forgot how to breathe. Then Hank roused himself. "Come on. We'll go get my Navigator. It's parked over by your shop. We'll

sneak around so my mother and Celeste don't see us and
put us to work. Then we'll ride out to the cottages. I'll
show you what I've already done to that old place since
yesterday. I think you'll be impressed."

As they gathered up their trash, leashed Beamer, and
exited the gazebo, Maddie wished she could tell Hank she
was already impressed. Impressed with the way he looked
in his jeans and knit shirt. Impressed with his muscled physique. Impressed with how he cared about his mother even
when she was being her most difficult. Impressed with how
friendly and down-to-earth he'd been this morning with her
friends and neighbors, all of whom were in awe of him. As
if he were their crown prince come down to walk among
the commoners.

But most of all, she was impressed with the way he
made her tingle all over. With the way he made her laugh
and smile and even cry sometimes. And the way he held
her. The way he kissed her. The way he made her nerve
endings dance with joy and anticipation. But more than any
of that, she was mostly impressed with how much he made
her want him. Just by being himself. She hadn't thought
that after the jerk doctor, Stanton Fairchild, she could ever
trust again, that she would even try again.

As they walked toward the boardwalk and the beach
beyond it, passing the sailmaker shop, the candy store, and
the Laundromat, Maddie looked up at Hank's striking profile. So classic were his features that she could see him as
the bust of a conquering hero. She sighed to herself. Did
she dare even try with him? He was wonderful in every
way. That was true. And he wanted her. That was obvious.
But did it go beyond that? Was she more than a summer
romance to him? A fling? Someone with whom he could
while away his enforced hours here and then forget when
he returned to his real life and his fast set?

Maddie hated her troubled thoughts on this bright and
heretofore lighthearted day. She didn't like these doubts.
Hated them. They were like storm clouds threatening a picnic. Yet she knew they were based on a self-preservation

instinct. The truth was, she just didn't think she could survive being used and tossed aside. Not again. And the heck of it was she had no reason—based on his behavior alone and not factoring in the will thing—to think Hank would do such a thing. But she'd been fooled before. All the way to the altar, in fact. And she wasn't about to let that happen again.

"So. What do you think? Just like home, right? I covered all the walls with this wallpaper that was already tacky on the back. Well, it's tacky on the front, too. I mean Conestoga wagons and westward ho? Please. But it was the only kind they had enough of at the hardware store."

"And that didn't tell you anything, Hank? But . . . wow. It's . . . nice. Great buffaloes. And are those Indians behind the rocks?"

"I think so. They're too small for me to be sure. I was thinking of getting the crew out here from *This Old House* to film my improvements. You know, before and after."

"Good idea. They should jump right on this."

She was so damned droll. Despite being excited and energized by her absolute femaleness, Hank had all he could do not to laugh. Not at her, but at her reaction. She had her hands planted at her waist and was valiantly looking around, serious and round-eyed. Hank raked his gaze over her, working his way up from her long and slim yet well-muscled legs, her gently rounded hips and accentuated waist, past the swell of her breasts, and up to her face. Her delicately boned features were frozen. She was horrified, and rightly so.

Hank knew his improvements, to use the term loosely, were awful. He'd never worked with his hands before. The wallpaper was lapped over in places, stuck together in folds in others, and some didn't line up exactly right, which made for some fantastic half-wagon/half-buffalo creatures. And one piece got stuck to the floor and there it still resided, as evidenced by Beamer's sniffing investigation of it. Hank bit back a guffaw at the dog's equally puzzled expression that innocently mimicked Maddie's. He made up his mind that if Maddie was going to give in to that mutant nice gene of hers and not tell him what she really thought, then he wasn't going to let her off the hook, either.

"And look over here," he said, directing her attention over to the corner of the one-room cottage that served as the living room. "I got some books at the secondhand store run by that small church with the tall steeple. Those are some nice ladies there. One of them gave me a prune Danish ring she'd made." The word "prune" smacked at Hank's polite sensibilities. "Not that I *needed* prunes," he added.

"Oh God, Hank." Maddie hurried to him and gripped his forearm. Her hand on his skin felt warm and firm. But concern edged her expression and her voice. "Hank, the church's secondhand store? Oh, honey. Prune Danish? It wasn't Mrs. Hardy, was it? The woman whose husband owns these cottages? Tell me it wasn't Mrs. Hardy and that you didn't eat any of it. When did you get the Danish? When? Think, Hank."

"What's the big deal?"

"It's big, Hank. Big. Think." She stepped back, crossing her arms under her breasts and eyeing him as if he had about three hours to live.

"Okay, I am." Concerned now, he cast about in his mind for the details. "Yeah, I went Saturday. I think. Yes. Saturday. And I don't know the lady's name. They weren't wearing nametags. But why? What's the problem?"

Maddie closed her eyes and rubbed her forehead. "Whew. You're probably okay then, since this is Monday. And it probably wasn't Mrs. Hardy. The big deal, Hank, is Mrs. Hardy, God love her, loves to cook and feed everyone. And every one of us, to a person, has had his or her stomach pumped as a result."

"Jesus."

"I remember invoking His name, yes."

"What does Mrs. Hardy do that makes everyone so sick?"

"We don't know. We've thought of sending a sample to

a lab somewhere to have it analyzed. But Mr. Canardy—he's our mailman—says we can't ship hazardous materials like that through the mail."

"Damn. Is she like those two little old ladies who poisoned their husbands?"

"We don't know they poisoned their husbands," Maddie chastised in a Sunday-school-teacher voice. "It's just that Mrs. Hardy is sweet and well-meaning, but she can't do much. It's a physical thing. So she cooks and gives it away and likes to feel needed."

Hank was appalled. "But if she's killing everybody—"

"No one has actually died." That defensive voice was back.

"But if she's making people sick, why would they sell her baked goods in the church store, for crying out loud?"

Maddie frowned at him as if he were simple. "Well, we wouldn't want to hurt her feelings."

That silenced him. He stared without blinking at Maddie. "It's that mutant nice gene, isn't it?"

She grinned somewhat sickly. "Afraid so. It's in the water."

"Well, thank God I've been drinking the bottled stuff."

Maddie eyed him about like a homicide detective would a suspect. "Did you eat the prune Danish, Hank?"

"No," he admitted. "I don't like pastry like that. But I just took it and then tossed it away out here."

"So you were being nice."

"I was not. You take that back."

"You were being nice. You didn't want to hurt her feelings. And I will not take it back."

Hank rubbed at his jaw and chin. "This is not good. I cannot turn up nice in six weeks. That would scare everyone at Madison and Madison. Our stock would surely drop."

Maddie was suddenly quiet and seemed to draw away from him, even though she hadn't moved. Hank looked into her eyes. "What?"

She roused herself, managing a smile that he could tell was forced. "Nothing. Why?"

"No, it's something. I said something about Madison and Madison, and you—Oh. I think I get it."

"You do? What do you think you got?"

"Six weeks. I'll be going back to New York. I won't be here anymore. And my little summer adventure will be over."

A fleeting look of pain crossed her face. "Your little summer adventure? Is that how you think of this?"

Too late Hank realized that somehow he'd stepped out onto a treacherous ice floe, not that there was any other kind. "Well, no. Not really. I was just being flippant. I meant it's easy being here. Easier than I thought. I thought I'd hate it. In fact, I was sure I would. But I don't."

She warmed a bit, relaxing her stance. "Really? You don't? Why not?"

Hank gestured an I-don't-know. "The town, I guess. It's nice here. The people are great. Friendly. Welcoming. I can see what my grandfather liked about the place."

"That's a good sign." Maddie's smile could only be called hopeful. "So we're beginning to grow on you?"

Hank crossed his arms over his chest. "Like a fungus."

"Lovely. I mean seriously: you like it here?"

"Yes. Seriously. This place could catch on and take off. Become a major upscale vacation destination."

Maddie drooped a bit. "Oh. You're talking about commercial viability. We'd hate that here, you know. It would ruin what makes Hanscomb Harbor so special."

"Or maybe it could only enhance it, Maddie. Like up in Newport."

She shrugged, clearly unconvinced. "I suppose that's possible. Still, I'd hate to see that happen. Hanscomb Harbor is a port, a harbor, a refuge, in more than one sense. And for more than a few people. We wouldn't like to see it overrun and ruined."

"Neither would I. And just so you know, I have no plans along those lines. And no desire to change even one thing here." *Most of all, you.* Hank heard himself talking advertising, but knew this wasn't at all where Maddie was coming from. She meant, was she the attraction here for him? *Hell, yes,* was the answer to that. Hank's pulse rate increased as awareness, never far below the surface where she was concerned, now flared in him, tightening his muscles. *Tell her,* his conscience urged. Hank exhaled slowly, feeling the weight of his desire.

Certain that his awareness of her radiated from his gaze, he held her blue-eyed attention—and took the plunge. "Maddie, you have to know that it's *you* keeping me here." He saw her eyes widen. "You have to know that the only reason I haven't contested my grandfather's will—and I could do so successfully—is because of you, so I can have an ironclad reason to be around you." She looked overwhelmed now. Hank didn't know what to do except keep talking. "I'm really looking forward to these next six weeks, Maddie. I've never felt this way before. Never. It's good. A good feeling. I have you to thank for that." Hank thought about that. "And my grandfather. It's going to be a great six weeks, me and you together."

Maddie didn't say anything. She just stood there. Hank searched her expression but saw nothing encouraging. *Oh, man, I've gone too fast.* Then he saw that tears stood in her eyes. Even Beamer knew something was up. The golden retriever gave up her investigation of the trash and padded over to nuzzle her nose under Maddie's hand. Maddie absently fondled the dog's silky ears and stared at Hank. He put a hand out to her. "Maddie? Are you all right?"

She shook her head. "No. I have to go, Hank. I'm sorry, but I just have to go. I don't feel well. Will you take me home, please?"

CHAPTER THIRTEEN

∽

ON THAT NEXT SUNDAY, the Reverend Hobbs preached a blessedly short sermon, the gist of which was his entire congregation needed to be aware that they were all going to hell. Then, in an effort to allow them immediately to begin to change their ways, he dismissed church early for once, admonishing them to repent. The chastised congregation, like ants swarming out of a disturbed nest, dispersed into the warmth of the late-summer day. As glad as anyone to be set free, Maddie inhaled deeply of the commingled noonday scents. "I love this time of year, Celeste."

"Well, don't tell me to breathe the air. You always say that. And then I always say, what choice do I have if I want to stay alive?" Celeste snapped.

Maddie exhaled, knowing what was wrong with her friend. "Okay. Can I say that this is a beautiful day?"

"What's beautiful? You're making me walk great distances to and from church. I'm an old woman, Madelyn Louise. This could kill me, you know."

"It's three blocks, Celeste. And it was your idea to walk. Now tell me you don't love this weather. For once I can't even smell the saltiness from the ocean."

"You watch—some stupid seagull will fly over and poop on us." At Maddie's tsk of annoyance, Celeste added, "Okay, okay, the air is fresh and crisp. Like a ripe apple with a big fat worm right in the middle of it."

Maddie grinned. "And who would the big fat worm be?"

"If you don't know, I'm not going to tell you."

After that, they walked along companionably silent, arm in arm, for several minutes. They turned left onto sunny, grassy Whaling Avenue with its row of picturesque New England–style homes. Celeste's two-story house, one of the showplaces of Hanscomb Harbor, sat at the other end of the long, curving residential block. And somewhere down there, inside Celeste's house, was Hank's mother. Maddie grimaced, hearing in her head the circling-shark cello music from the movie *Jaws*.

Just then, Celeste tugged at Maddie's sleeve to get her attention. "Did you hear what Lavinia Houghton, the patron saint of starched underwear, said about my new hairstyle?"

And there it was—one of the sources of Celeste's sourness du jour. "Yes, I heard her. But don't listen to her. I love your hair short, and I was wrong about your getting it cut, like Mrs. Madison suggested. It looks very fashionable."

"Oh, pooh on fashionable. That's what you say to old ladies. How about it looks bitchin'?"

"Bitchin'? Celeste, you have *got* to quit hanging out with Teddy Millicum." She didn't really mean it, though. Celeste and Teddy had a wonderful relationship. He visited her on a daily basis, and she provided positive attention for him that he didn't get at home. However, it remained Maddie's job to reinforce Celeste's notion that she was shocking.

"Hmph. I will do no such thing," Celeste announced. "I like Teddy. Besides, he gave me my new kitten, Bluebell. Now, there's a corker. The cat is actually blue. And she can already climb right up the curtains."

Maddie grinned. "You have that effect on a lot of people, too."

"Now you're just trying to cheer me up. But enough about air and Teddy and kittens. I want to talk to you about Hank."

Maddie's heart rate picked up, her cheeks warmed. Here it was—the other thing that had Celeste sour. "What about Hank?"

"I'm mad at him, that's what. What the heck is he thinking, sticking around in Hanscomb Harbor like this—and him a pampered city boy? He's lasted a week already and made me a loser in the betting pool down at the Captain's Tavern, I don't mind telling you."

Relieved that she was taking this tack, Maddie laughed.

"Celeste McNeer, here we are walking home from church and you're telling me you participate in gambling? Does nothing that the Reverend Hobbs has to say take with you?"

She waved that away. "I don't listen to him. Might turn me into another self-righteous prune pit like Lavinia Houghton."

"You? I don't think that's possible. So how long did you give him? Hank, I mean."

"Four days."

"Is that all?" Maddie walked along a few more steps before adding, "I put down some money on ten days."

Celeste stopped short, forcing Maddie to do the same since they were still walking arm in arm. They were in front of Mr. Bailey's house with its nautical rope fence. "Madelyn Louise, you're frequenting taverns and participating in gambling? Why, the next thing you know *you'll* be the one to prove the Reverend Hobbs right and go directly to hell."

Maddie grinned down at Celeste with her newly bobbed silvery-white hair and red lipstick—and neon-green dress under a demure lace shawl. "Why should you go to hell without me and have all the fun?"

Celeste reached up to pat Maddie's cheek. "You're a sweet young woman to think of me."

They started walking again, both waving at Mrs. Bailey, who was outside watering her flower garden. The woman was still wearing her nightgown and robe. Known around town as "that poor old crazy thing," she stared back at Maddie and Celeste as if she'd never seen them before.

"That poor old crazy thing," Celeste whispered to Maddie.

"I know. But she's harmless. And Mr. Bailey is good to her."

"He'd better be, or he'll have me to answer to."

"And nobody wants that."

Smiling, Maddie concentrated again on the day. Not the first hint of a breeze stirred the leaves. Bright sunshine smiled down cheerily upon her and Celeste. They'd already left the church crowd behind, so the only sounds were those of the occasional car that passed, the muted sound of children laughing somewhere nearby, and that of their heels striking the sidewalk.

Into the quiet, Maddie asked, oh so casually, "So how is Mrs. Madison doing? I mean, the two of you in the same house. What's she like? Is she a good guest?"

Celeste chuckled and smacked at Maddie's arm. "She's a terrible guest. Can't even work a microwave oven. Can you believe it? Never picked up after herself before now. But I like her. She's got a big heart, and she loves her son. She's definitely a hoot. I see a lot of myself in her."

"Heaven help us all. I thought she would have fled back to L.A. by now."

"Me, too. But she likes working in the shop."

"I know. My worst nightmare."

Celeste ignored her. "She talks to that lobster clock at the shop like it's James and cusses it something terrible."

"I've heard her," Maddie said stiffly. "I don't think that's very respectful."

"Maddie, honey, it's a lobster with a ticking clock in its belly."

Maddie fought the grin that wanted to claim her lips. "Maybe so. But it's also her father-in-law's last resting place, and she should show some respect."

Celeste gave Maddie her best scolding harrumph. "Don't get your knickers in a wad. She's just venting. Evidently the old boy used to give them all fits."

Maddie tried to be fair. "He did, from what Hank's told me. Certainly his crazy will proves it. I'll never understand that. Or why he dragged me into all this." Maddie was quiet a moment, then forced herself to say, "All right, I guess she's not all bad. I have seen Mrs. Madison dusting the silly ceramic thing and handling it carefully."

"She does. And here's another thing: she wouldn't let me sell it the other day," Celeste added, apparently in her newfound friend's defense.

Maddie rolled her eyes. "Celeste, you have got to quit doing that."

"A man was going to give me forty dollars for it."

"Forty dollars? Wow. That's a good price—" Maddie gulped back her words. "I mean, I don't care what anybody offers for it. No matter what else it might be, it's also an urn and it rightfully belongs to Hank."

"Then why don't you take it to him?"

Well, I've certainly stepped in it now. Here we go.

Sure enough, Celeste started in. "I can't imagine that there'd be all that much out at the beach in late August to amuse a person with Hank Madison's smarts and drive."

Maddie grimaced. "And yet there seems to be." She hadn't seen him since last Monday's picnic and drive and debacle. He hadn't come in to the shop, and she hadn't seen him around town. Not that she'd been looking for him.

"Sure seems to be a lot of reporters and cameramen in town. Good for the economy, but I hate all this commotion."

Maddie eyed Celeste. The darned little thing looked deceptively like anybody's sweet grandmother. "So much so that you gave ten interviews?"

Tottering along, leaning on Maddie's arm, she nodded. "I was trying my best to keep them away from you, dear. Can I help it if they've made me a media darling?"

"Dear God." Maddie remembered all too well the sudden infestation of the media this week. In fact, she couldn't believe that they hadn't attacked her the moment she came out of church today. Maybe they'd swarmed after Hank. Word of James's quirky will had gotten out in earnest. Then some tabloid reporter had followed Lillian Madison here, they now knew, and that was all it took. One picture. One rumor. And bam—Hanscomb Harbor was hotbed central. It was awful. And the crowning moment had been all those pictures of her and Hank around town last Monday. They'd been followed and photographed from a distance. How embarrassing. She'd hated seeing her life paraded through the tabloids.

There she and Hank and Beamer had been. Like lovers, the pictures made it seem. They'd been shot in the gazebo. Then outside her shop—which was now ground zero and mobbed with the curious. The very rich and curious. People of Hank's ilk. The nightmare was here—Hanscomb Harbor was the jet set's new playground. And those pictures of them walking Beamer on the beach. God. Like one big happy family.

"I *said*," Celeste fussed, pinching Maddie's arm and eliciting a yelp from her, "have you been out to the beach house to see him? And where's your head, girl? I've been talking to you."

Maddie rubbed her stinging arm and said, "I'm sorry. And no, I haven't been out there. You know what it's like for me right now. I can't go anywhere, do anything, without getting swarmed. Hank, either. We thought it best if we avoided each other."

"Oh, you did, huh? Yet no one's around now. Wonder if the new has worn off and they got their story and left?"

"That would be too good to be true. But I don't think so. I suspect something a little more tantalizing is going on with one of the real celebrities who are here. Maybe some movie star has been sighted doing something provocative."

"I hope it's Mel Gibson, and he's in a kilt."

Maddie nodded. "That would be good."

"Yes, it would. But I miss Hank. He hasn't been around since you took off Monday and left me and Lillian to fend for ourselves in the shop."

"Oh, fend for yourselves. You had three customers. And the two of you were playing bridge when I came back."

"Isn't that what a card table is for? And by the way, I'm disappointed in you. You may as well join Saint Lavinia Houghton in the Reconstituted Virgins Brigade."

It was Maddie's turn to smack at Celeste's arm. "I swear, Celeste McNeer, every time I think I've heard it all from you, you top yourself."

"I just speak the truth. Are you going to let that man get away from you?"

Maddie relived her humiliation of last Monday, of hearing Hank say what she'd feared—she was part of his six-week stay here and then he was gone. The ride back to town had been glacial and agonizing. "I don't think it's a matter of letting him get away from me, as you put it. He's not a prize, Celeste."

"That's not what the newspapers and magazines say. They say he's the world's most eligible bachelor. And the most sexy man alive."

Maddie exhaled. "He's all that and more, I'm sure. He's just not for me."

Celeste was uncustomarily quiet for several steps. Maddie heard a bird happily singing and waved at two boys who rode by on their bicycles.

"Why isn't he for you, honey?" This was Celeste's loving, nurturing voice, the one that invariably put Maddie in tears. Sometimes she forgot how much Celeste cared about her and worried about her. "I think he's perfect for you."

"Well, that's one vote. Come on, Celeste, you know how complicated this is. There's that stupid will that makes me look like a gold digger and also trapped Hank here. There's his mother, who hates me and thinks I'm after everything Madison. And there's the press looking for a hot story, just one picture of us together. You know . . . the big kiss. There's a huge bounty on that one. But it's one they won't get. Because it is not going to happen. So, given all that, why wouldn't we avoid each other? You tell me."

"That was a great speech, Maddie. But none of it matters. That's not what I'm talking about. I'm asking *you* how *you* feel about Hank. Period."

And there it was. The salt in the wound. Celeste could always get right down to the nitty-gritty with her. Maddie swallowed gathering emotion. "I don't know how I feel," she hedged.

"Ha. You do, too. You care a lot about him, don't you? More than you're willing to admit."

Maddie stopped and stared down at her elderly friend. "Well, if I won't admit it, according to you, you're not going to believe anything I might have to say to the contrary, are you?"

"No. Not until you say the truth, Madelyn Louise."

"I don't know what the truth is."

"You're as exasperating as hell, do you know that?"

Maddie raised her eyebrows. "We are not two blocks from church and you're already cursing."

Celeste screwed up her wrinkled little face. "It's your fault. So what do you intend to do, Maddie? Live out your life alone and tucked away here in this village?"

"Yes, I do." Maddie fondly pictured her tiny shop . . . her anchor, her one quiet place in a new and rocky world she didn't understand. But a world fraught with blind alleys that would undoubtedly lead to another unhappy ending. She didn't think she could take another one. So, against all that, it was her shop, her home, her friends, all of Hanscomb Harbor, the sameness and the familiarity that stood guard over her and kept her safe.

"Well, I think that's just plain ridiculous. You may as well dress all in black like Lavinia Houghton and go get yourself a job in her library," Celeste was saying. "You're only twenty-nine years old, Maddie. Too young to say your life is over. Look at me. Been widowed four times. You see me hiding? No, ma'am. There are some things you just have to leap into with both feet. Two of them are life and love." She thought for a second. "And money. That's three. And I guess that's all, too."

With that, Celeste pointed up the block. "Come on. I want to get home. My bunions are killing me. I need to get these shoes off." They started walking again. "It wouldn't kill you to be nice to Hank Madison, you know."

"Here we go."

"Did you two have a fight last Monday?"

"No. You have to have a relationship to have a fight. And we don't, so we didn't. Besides, if we had, it would have been in the tabloids."

"That's true. Do you care about him at all, Maddie?"

She exhaled. "I don't know, Celeste."

"Don't you think this would be a good time to find out?"

This brought them to Celeste's house. They stopped, standing outside her white picket fence's gate. Celeste gripped Maddie's arm and pleaded in earnest. "For the love of Pete, Maddie Copeland—do something. Grab this chance at happiness that's been laid at your feet, girl. Go after that young man."

Maddie heard the earnestness and the affection in Celeste's voice and in her plea. And it had her on the verge of emotional. "How, Celeste? How do I do that? And what if he doesn't want me? What am I supposed to do—lasso and hog-tie him like he's some prize steer?"

Celeste frowned in concentration, frightening Maddie into wondering if the woman was actually considering the viability of such a tactic. Celeste finally shook her head and said, "No. A steer won't do you any good. I believe steers have had their thingies nipped. I think what you want is a bull, dear, a real stud with all his parts in working order."

"Oh, for God's sake, Celeste. Look, maybe I'm one of those women just meant to be single. I mean, I've already been rejected once in front of a church full of people. You were there. And my other serious relationships—Wait. There weren't any. But the truth is, I don't need a man to be happy, Celeste."

"That's what all spinsters say, dear. But I'm saying you do need a man—you need *this* man. Why do you think James Madison went to all this trouble to get you two together? He wanted this match between you and Hank. He wanted it very much." Celeste's eyes widened. She popped a hand over her mouth.

And there it was. What Maddie had suspected all along. Anger exploded in her. "I knew it. I just knew it." She began pacing up and down in front of Celeste. "Ohmigod, it's true what they're saying in the tabloids. I'm a joke. A big fat joke."

Celeste wrung her hands. "Now, Maddie, calm down. You're not a joke. Nobody thinks—"

"Uh-huh. Everybody thinks, Celeste. Why do you think

my shop is suddenly so popular? I can't keep stock on the shelves. And it's certainly not because the whole world just realized they can't live without postcards and plastic molds for making sand castles. God, people are even *buying the bags* with 'Maddie's Gifts' on them. Buying them, Celeste. And *only* because I'm a scandal."

"It takes two to be a scandal, honey."

Maddie sighted on her friend. "You're absolutely right."

The next day, Monday, turned out to be Sunday's exact opposite. It was always a Monday, it seemed. Chilly, overcast, damp, glowering. The weather was proving to be as schizophrenic as Maddie's life suddenly seemed to be. The very air hung thick and oppressively heavy. And the leaves of summer seemed determined, before the end of the afternoon, to herald the approaching autumn by flinging themselves to the ground.

As if out of respect for their sacrifice, Maddie's Gifts remained closed and shuttered. It was supposed to be open, but she'd called Celeste and told her and Lillian not to come in today. What, she'd told Celeste, would be the point with hardly any stock to put on the shelves? Besides, Maddie didn't think she could endure the sight right now of one more slyly staring and smirking person bent on seeing her and having a Maddie story to share with the press.

On this dark day, then, one that matched her mood, Maddie set about viciously cleaning her shop. She ignored the repeatedly ringing phone, figuring it had to be some reporter or TV talk-show host or a member of the morbidly curious public. Instead, Maddie focused her energy on giving every shelf an angry dusting and the wood floors a cleaning they wouldn't soon forget. Through it all, Maddie talked to herself and argued right back with herself.

She fumed as she took stock of the depleted stockroom and recalled Celeste's revelations yesterday after church. James had set this all up. Well, of course she knew that. *The will. Duh.* Maddie hoisted an obviously overlooked box of trinkets to a higher shelf, thinking she could set them

out later. So, this was more about James wanting her and
Hank to get together than it was about James wanting Hank
to relax and enjoy life. Okay, so it could be about both
things, she supposed. And she didn't fault James for that.
He loved his grandson and wanted only good things for
him. But that was also the part Maddie didn't like. The part
where she came in.

She was one of those *things*. A *thing*. God, how politi-
cally incorrect. It hurt to think that James might have befriended her as a means to an end, a love interest for his
grandson. Couldn't he have just liked her for herself?
Surely he did. And shouldn't she feel complimented instead
of insulted that James had thought of her as someone he'd
want for a granddaughter-in-law? Unlike the jerk doctor's
family who treated her like a leper. Maddie rubbed at her
forehead. *Oh, I don't know. Maybe I'm going about this all
wrong.* What would be so horrible about being with Hank?
Well, nothing.

But only if it had been their idea, hers and Hank's. Now
it was like those guys who took out billboards to ask
women to marry them. Or the ones who ask on TV and
surprise the poor woman. Talk about pressure to say yes.
Maddie had always found those situations a bit painful to
watch and had hated the thought of something like that ever
happening to her. She'd wondered if the woman really
wanted to marry the guy or felt she had to say yes just
because of the pressure—the very public pressure—to do
so. Can't disappoint the audience or the ratings. Or even
break the guy's heart with that big an audience.

And now look at her. She had a world audience waiting.
It was as if this were Groundhog Day and she was the
groundhog. Everyone was waiting for her to come out of
her hole and tell them if they should be happy. She couldn't
believe that James hadn't, apparently, even taken into con-
sideration the fact that she and Hank might not suit each
other. Or maybe that one would and the other one wouldn't.
See? Now she didn't even trust her own instincts or even
anything Hank would have to say. And then to tie Hank's

entire inheritance to her like this. How in the world were she and Hank to know for sure what they felt? Or if they felt anything for each other?

Oh, stop it, Maddie, her conscience railed. *What did James do that was so horrible? He made you an extremely wealthy woman and brought a man into your life you could really come to care about. Ooh, how awful. Get over it. It's not like he locked you in a dungeon or took anything from you.*

Maddie angrily shoved the box of trinkets over on the same shelf. *So James didn't take anything away from me, huh? How about dignity? He certainly robbed me of that. He made me the butt of the town's joke. Hello, village in search of an idiot? Here I am. And how entertaining is it now for everyone as they all laugh behind their hands?*

It wasn't like that, Maddie. You know that. And Hank has already told you he cares about you. What's wrong with that? What's hurt here? Your pride?

Maddie's expression puckered. Yes. Her pride was hurt. What was so wrong with that? What's wrong with righteous indignation? What's wrong with wanting to be taken seriously? What's wrong with wanting to be left alone to live your life in quiet dignity?

Quiet desperation is more like it. This is the life you want? Hiding here in your house, afraid to go outside?

That was because of the reporters, Maddie assured herself as she snatched up the broom and switched and swished the poor concrete floor in the stockroom until she was choking and coughing from all the dust she raised. She worked it all over to the delivery door. *I am* not *afraid. I'm mad. I'm mad as hell at everyone, and I don't want to look at any of them. And yes, this is the life I want. It is still my life, even if everyone sees me as a joke. So leave me alone.*

Fine.

Fine. Maddie unlocked the solid door, jerked it open, remembered to look around—no lurking cameras—and then swept everything outside. She didn't normally do that. She usually swept the refuse conscientiously into a dustpan and dumped it in the trash bin. But right now she was in rebellion. Here, she was thinking, you want dirt on me? Well, here's some. Take that. She slammed the door closed, turned the dead-bolt lock, and shoved the broom into a corner. Planting her hands at her waist, she angrily observed her clean, neat surroundings. Was everything done? Had she cleaned the whole place?

Her eyes narrowed with a realization. No, she hadn't. There was one more thing she had to do. This remaining chore was something she'd needed to do for a long time. And today—a day without any sentimentality attached to it—was the day to do it. Maddie chewed on a fingernail as she thought. But what could she do with it? Where could she take the stuff? Hank Madison's face popped into her mind. Maddie smiled, somewhat like an executioner happy in his work might smile.

Reporters or no, and publicity be damned, she'd take it all to Hank. See how he liked that.

Thus galvanized, clinging to outrage and hurt, and denying that this was revenge and retribution, Maddie stalked across the stockroom, flipped the divider curtain aside, and stomped into her salesroom. Single-mindedly, like a ship under full steam, she headed for the jewelry counter . . . for the card table next to it. The card table underneath which sat that cardboard box of James's belongings from the cottage that Mr. Hardy had brought her and she'd all but forgotten. This same card table was also the one above which sat, on a shelf, that silly, stupid ceramic lobster clock that held James's ashes.

Maddie reached for it and tugged it down.

CHAPTER FOURTEEN

❦

MADDIE GRABBED HER RING of keys, pulled on her jacket, and carted the box outside. She called it very odd that there were no lurking reporters. What was going on? She shrugged away her concern, though. So they were gone. Like a case of the hives, they wouldn't be missed. Setting down the box on the musty earth, she locked the delivery door behind her, then pocketed her keys. She stood there a moment, feeling the cold in the air and eyeing the box of James's things. She looked to her Jeep Wagoneer parked a ways down the dirt drive. Did she really have the courage to do this?

She hesitated, wavering a bit. She leaned against the door behind her and lowered her head, staring at her lace-up boots. So, what was she doing here? What was her point? Did she just not want to see the obvious? And what was the obvious? That she and Hank had been manipulated by James's will into becoming a public spectacle? Surely James hadn't intended that. And Hank. In her mind, she saw him again after their chili dinner at the cottage. He'd walked her to her Wagoneer, put Beamer in the back, and then had opened and closed her door for her. Then she'd rolled down her window, he'd lingered, talking, and they'd had trouble saying goodbye. Like two silly kids on the phone playing "you hang up, no you hang up." Overall, the scene had been poignant, friendly.

Then there'd been that beautiful Monday last week. Why was it always Monday? Anyway, it had been beautiful—until he'd told her she was good for six weeks and then he was leaving. Maddie quirked her mouth. *Oh, come on. It's not like they're tearing up the roads between here and New York after that. He could come back. Or I could go there.* But what would be the point if he thought of her as a fling? She didn't think she could go throw herself at him, if that was how he felt. So it was better not to start. See? There was just nothing there. Hank had pretty much said she was a pleasant diversion to get through his enforced ordeal here before he could get back to his real life. How wildly complimentary was that? Even women who were one-night stands didn't like to think they were, she'd bet. Every woman wanted to feel—*deserved* to feel—that she was special, that she'd made that perfect guy fall for her on the basis of her own personality.

That's not how this was between her and Hank. At best, it had all the charm of an arranged marriage between reluctant strangers. And at its worst, it was, well, pretty much the same thing.

Maddie grimaced, her self-esteem further plummeting. *Could I be easier to manipulate? Just tug on my lonely heartstrings and watch me cave.* That was when she heard herself and felt nothing but disgust. She jerked away from the door and threw her hands up in the air, exhorting a cold and uncaring sky. "Well, you know what, James? You had no right to do this, my friend. I don't mind telling you, you made a mess down here. Just paved that road right straight to hell with your good intentions, buddy. And now it's up to me to straighten it out."

Having worked herself back into the proper frame of mind to complete her final task, and still clad in her dusty jeans and with her hair pulled back in a ponytail, Maddie picked up the cardboard box of James's things, atop which lay the stupid lobster clock, and strode toward her Wagoneer. This was right. This felt good. This had the ring of finality to it. *Goodbye, yellow brick road . . .*

As if reality and the present would intrude and try to dissuade her, the chilly air nipped at her nose and cheeks. Her fingers, wrapped around the square of cardboard, felt numb. And the box was heavy, as much from memories as content. Maddie drew in a ragged, emotional breath. Tears threatened. Her kind and sentimental heart wanted to cry. This was so hard. And James had been her friend. A real person. Sweet. Funny. A lonely little figure, sick and dying, who had loved simply to sit in her shop and work a jigsaw puzzle and talk to her and Celeste. He'd loved to bring her ice cream and then have dinner with her. Why was she so mad at him? The poor man was a victim of the saying that no good deed goes unpunished.

And now she carried in her arms James's old shirts and his shaving kit and the little gifts from her shop that he'd bought. She had his shoes, his battered old hat he always wore, and a framed picture of the two of them, taken at that silly booth in the arcade. Maddie tried her best not to cry, not to waver in her resolve. Until today, she'd never even gone through the box. Hadn't even looked in it or rummaged through its contents to see what James had kept.

But Beamer had. She'd pulled out that old sweater of James's and had dragged it off to add to her bedding. Okay, that had really gotten to Maddie. What Beamer had done was so human and such a statement of bereavement. Who with a heart wouldn't have been touched and saddened after witnessing that?

So today had been Maddie's turn to go into her darkened shop and face her conflicting thoughts. She'd lost a friend and gained . . . What? A dog. A ton of money. And a handsome guy. Maddie mentally scratched at her head. Why again was she mad at James? Oh yeah, she felt used. Used how? Then that old José Feliciano song came back to her. Something about if you're using me, then use me all up. She pictured Hank. And felt warm. In bed with Hank. For six weeks, if that was all they had. What would suck about that? But she knew. The aftermath would. The day he left. The day she felt cheap and knew she'd been a six-week stand. Hello, unhappy ending. When would it be her turn to get one right?

Today? No. Today wasn't so special. Then why was she so giddy about the prospect of seeing Hank? Why was her stomach aflutter and her hands shaky? All she was doing was taking his grandfather's things to him, things he had a right to have.

But she didn't believe her own motivation for a minute. Sure, she wanted to take Hank's grandfather's things to him. And sure she could have given them to Lillian Madison to give to Hank, but she hadn't. She'd kept them until she could get her nerve up to go see Hank herself. There it was: she wanted to see Hank Madison. Even with everything she knew about the will and James's intent and Hank's . . . whatever it was he felt, she wanted to see him.

Freakin' pathetic. That's what I am. Just throw myself at the man. Like Miss Prissy, that skinny, desperate hen in the Foghorn Leghorn cartoons. Well, that "happy" thought accompanied her to the back of her Wagoneer, where she set the box down. She fished out her keys, stuck the appropriate one in the lock on the tailgate, and turned it to lower the window into the tailgate frame. That done, she then lowered the tailgate itself. The devil was in the details, she fussed as she leaned over and hefted the box into her arms. She lugged it up onto the lowered gate and slid it across the Wagoneer's cargo bed.

A bit winded from her day's exertions, Maddie stood there, content to absorb her surroundings for a breath-catching moment. Her Jeep was parked in the grassy, rutted driveway that ran alongside her small house at the back of her shop. A rickety old one-car garage faced the Jeep and pleaded with Maddie to use it. At least that was one thing she hadn't fallen for. All she had to do was look at the garage's wormy wood to see the darned thing would collapse around her vehicle. And then what would she do? She didn't have the money to buy—Wait a minute. Yes she did. She had enough money—or would have soon—to buy a small country, if she wanted to. Or even a medium-sized one.

Maddie smiled diabolically. Okay, so maybe she would buy her own country. An island in the South Pacific would be nice. Maybe she'd live there as the queen of all she surveyed. That tropical image, with her in a grass skirt and a coconut bra, had her chuckling. Add Celeste to the scene and in the same outfit and it got downright hilarious. *Wait,*

Maddie admonished herself, *was that an old-people joke?*
Okay, maybe it was. Still, the concept that she could possibly command a monetary number with that many zeroes
in it boggled her mind. Maddie quickly shook her head,
telling herself that today wasn't the day for worrying about
how to spend Madison money. Today was the day to deal
with one particularly frustrating Madison.

Certainly, the chilly weather seemed to agree with her
timing. The afternoon's air was redolent with the pungent
scent of cold damp earth. There was also a sharp tang to
the air, a certain slant to the sun's light, and a bone-deep
awareness inside her that whispered winter would soon be
on its way. Only this morning frost had coated the ground.
It had melted into dew as the sun rose. But one day soon,
she knew, the frost wouldn't be so quick to melt. Or the
sun so eager to rise.

Suddenly a bit melancholy with knowing that by the
time that happened Hank would be gone, Maddie raised the
tailgate and locked it into place. She plucked her keys out
of the lock and told herself she was all done. She was ready
to go. Nothing to do but go. She stuck her hands in her
corduroy jacket's pockets and looked around her. Had she
forgotten anything? Like what? The route out to the old
beach houses where Hank was? Hardly. So, it was time to
go. Time to get on the road. Time to put one foot in front
of the other. Time to—

A sudden mournful howling behind Maddie made her
jump and chilled her to the bone. She jerked around and
stumbled against the Jeep at her back. She stared wide-
eyed, her heart pounding. It was Beamer. The dog was on
her hind legs, her front ones braced against the low wooden
fence that encircled Maddie's bit of backyard. The animal,
looking more wolf than domesticated pet right now, stared
unblinking into Maddie's eyes and then raised her head to
the skies, again howling—a long, ululating sound that
prickled the hairs at the back of Maddie's neck and sent
her skin crawling over her body.

"My God, Beamer, what's wrong?" Maddie didn't know what to do, or if she could even move to do anything. Then she knew. Without a doubt, she knew. It was the box. It represented James. And the dog smelled James's scent on his things. Maddie put a hand over her mouth. *Ohmigod, I didn't even think how this would affect Beamer. The poor thing.*

"Oh, Beamer, honey, I'm so sorry. You miss James, don't you?" Maddie walked toward the mournful dog. Beamer remained on her back legs, panting and whining and watching Maddie, who held a hand out to the golden retriever. "It's okay, Beamer. I know this is tough. And I know you hurt. But I'm just taking James's things out to Hank, all right? You have your sweater of his. So I think Hank should have something of his grandfather's, too. I know you're upset. But I really have to do this."

The dog cocked her head to one side and perked her ears up, considering Maddie. A bit encouraged, Maddie smiled. "There now. See? Good girl. That's a nice doggy—"

Beamer yapped suddenly and jerked her head up and howled for all she was worth. Startled, Maddie's old fears surfaced and she yelped and ran, not stopping until she was on the other side of the Jeep. Feeling a bit foolish, but more frightened, she peered at the dog from around the dinosaur vehicle's back end. With a perceived safe distance between them, and hoping the dog wouldn't remember it could jump the fence, Maddie scolded the animal. "Now, stop that, you hear me? You stop that right now. You scared me. Is that nice? I'm trying to do the right thing here and the least you could do is be supportive."

It's a dog, Maddie, she reminded herself. *I know that, but she still understands, I'll bet.*

Sure enough, Beamer eyed Maddie as if listening to every word. Then she dropped down from the fence and turned away, trotting for the other side of the yard. The animal passed out of Maddie's line of vision. "So there," Maddie marveled, coming out from behind the Jeep's protective bulk and putting her fisted hands to her waist. "I did it. Cool."

Victory was short-lived. What was the dog doing now? Maddie put a finger to her mouth and worried the nail. Though not completely convinced this wasn't some kind of a canine trick, Maddie nevertheless couldn't restrain her curiosity. She edged closer to the yard and craned her neck to see what, if anything, Beamer might be up to. But she couldn't see the retriever, not from where she was standing.

So, feeling somewhat like the witless heroine in the horror movies who always, always—unarmed and in her nightgown—went to check out the slithery, groaning, hideous noises in the basement on a dark and stormy night, Maddie sidled closer to her backyard's fence. She'd advanced about four or five steps closer when she suddenly remembered she never had happy endings.

Sure enough, in split-second sequences, the dog came trotting back into view, bunched her muscles, and went airborne, sailing effortlessly over the fence, her big furry body a projectile missile hurtling straight for a terrified Maddie. That old fight-or-flight instinct told her to choose. She did. She jerked around, running as fast as she could and screaming all the way. The hounds of hell were after her, she was sure of it. The dog was possessed. Any second now she'd be dragged down, killed, and devoured.

Completely panicked, she tore around the Jeep, up the driveway, turned right and flew past Maddie's Gifts, past the hardware store, and up the hill toward Cobblestone Drive.

On and on she ran. Only the steep angle of the hill, and a vicious stitch in her side, finally slowed her down and had her stumbling to a stop. Completely winded, and undevoured—and apparently even unchased by the dog since it was nowhere to be seen—she bent over at the waist and clutched her knees. As she sucked in great draughts of air, she stared numbly at a little tuft of grass clinging tenaciously to life in a crack in the sidewalk. She felt hot and weak all over, her nose was running, she was crying, her ponytail was hanging over her shoulder, she felt like the world's biggest coward, and—

Maddie turned her head. *Dammit.* A big, new, shiny SUV monster machine that had been wending its way down the hill was now pulling over to the curb on the opposite side of the road from her and slowing to a stop.

She wanted to scream. Throw a rock at him. Tell him to go away. But she couldn't catch her breath or straighten up, nor could she see a handy-sized rock. Worse, her sides were cramping and her legs were shaking with her exertion and her emotion. And now, here he was. *Are life and the fates just totally against me or what?* Maddie didn't have to look up to know who this was. This was a no-brainer. Hank Madison was riding to her rescue. Her knight encased in a vehicle of shining armor.

Sure enough, she heard the smooth, metallic motions of the machine's gears as he shifted his Navigator into park. She heard the driver's-side door open. Saw his jeans-clad legs as he stepped out onto the cobblestoned road. Heard the door being closed. And heard him call out her name and then, given the obvious sight she made, ask the world's dumbest question . . .

"Maddie? Are you all right?" It was a stupid question, Hank knew it. Of course she wasn't all right because here she was, around the corner from her house, alone, inexplicably halfway up a hill, and bent over and crying.

Without straightening up, she shoved her ponytail out of her face. Her puckered expression clearly said she agreed that his question had been the world's stupidest. "No, I'm not okay, Hank. Do I in any way look okay to you? I mean, do I really?"

Hank's frown punctuated his burgeoning alarm. What the hell had happened to her? He started to dart across the street, but a passing subcompact-sized car slowly climbing the hill prevented him from immediately going to Maddie. The driver, a sweet-faced, gray-haired lady Hank couldn't place, honked and waved first at Maddie, who ignored her, and then at him. He waved back, as much telling her to keep going as to return her greeting.

Hank then looked both ways. No more traffic. Apparently the lone designated vehicle for today's rush hour in Hanscomb Harbor had just driven past. Mindful of the slippery nature of such an uneven surface and how it could turn an ankle, Hank gingerly sprinted across the damp cobblestone road. Safely achieving the other side, he stepped up onto the curb. This put him right at Maddie's side. He bent over her, putting a comforting hand on her back and his other on her arm. "Maddie? What happened?"

He thought his tone of voice was tender and solicitous enough, but apparently she didn't because she said, "Don't you touch me, Hank Madison."

Surprised but ever accommodating, Hank took his hands off her. "All right." He stepped back, shoving his hands into the deep pockets of his lined nylon jacket. "So what's wrong?"

As he watched, Maddie walked her hands up her thighs and stood up straight. Her face was red, her nose was runny, and tears streaked her cheeks. Hank's heart ached for her. Looking very much like a little girl whose heart had just been broken, she swiped a sleeve under her nose and used her hands to wipe at her face. Her expression was a mixture of hurt and anger, seemingly aimed at him. "You're asking me what's wrong with me? As if you don't already know."

"I don't. If I knew I wouldn't be asking."

"What are you doing here, Hank?" Her bottom lip poked out in a serious pout.

Hank proceeded with caution. "Do you mean in a philosophical sense, the meaning of life?"

"No. Here." She sketched a big, angry arc in the air, as if to include the whole town. "Here. Right now. You know."

"But I don't. And Maddie, you're not making any sense."

She frowned, cocking her head at a disbelieving angle.

"I don't believe you. You know what I'm talking about."

He shrugged. "I really do not."

"Where are all the media today? Why aren't they here swamping us?"

"Oh. Them. I got tired of their constant harassment so I rented the Captain's Tavern for the evening and treated them all. Anything for an afternoon of peace. And maybe tomorrow they'll all have hangovers and won't get out of bed for a while."

She looked askance at him. "That was smart."

"And expensive."

Maddie stared mutely at him, her assessing, doubting expression making it clear that it had cost her big-time to say something nice about him. Hank withdrew a hand from his jacket pocket and scratched at his temple. It didn't itch, but he was just confused. What in her world here in picturesque Hanscomb Harbor could possibly produce this dire a result? It was akin to being cranky while at Walt Disney World. You just couldn't be. Then Hank came up with a possible candidate. "Hey, where's Beamer?"

Maddie tensed, her eyes rounded.

Bingo. Hank looked all around for the dog as he asked, "Did Beamer do something to you?"

"She howled. It was awful." Maddie seemed to come back to herself. She closed her eyes and held her head with both hands. Her chin trembled. "She howled and jumped over the fence at me. I really thought I was over being afraid of dogs. But I ran away like some scared little kid. How stupid is that?"

Relief coursed through Hank. She'd just been scared by the dog. That was all. Thank God. Still, he had enough sense not to let her see he thought her experience pretty much a two on a scale of possible tragedies, one hundred being the worst. "It's not stupid at all," he said supportively. "Not if you're already scared of dogs. Beamer is a big dog, and you could have been hurt. So you probably did the smart thing in running."

Maddie opened her eyes, revealing ice-blue irises that

saw right through him. "Oh, shut up. And quit trying to make me feel better."

A bit taken aback, Hank said simply enough, "Okay."

"And quit being so agreeable."

Well, how do you agree to do that without being agreeable? What do you say? Hank settled for "All right," but wisely said no more. Yet he had to fist his hands in his pockets in an effort not to reach out and try to comfort her.

God, he wanted so badly to take her in his arms and hold her. He wanted to tuck her head up under his chin and wrap his arms around her. She looked so sad and alone, even with him standing here in front of her. Something inside Hank melted at the sight of her hair coming undone from her ponytail. Fuzzy blond tendrils framed her face. Could she look more vulnerable or adorable?

She aroused such fierce protective instincts in him. If only she'd let him touch her. But she wouldn't. She'd already told him not to. And she'd told him last Monday to stay away from her. He hadn't understood why then, and still didn't. But he'd honored her wish. It had been hell, but he'd done it. And now, here she was. And all he could do was keep his distance and try to talk to her. This totally sucked. He tried another tack. "You want a glass of water or something?"

She looked at him as if he'd just offered to tear his arm out at the socket. "No, Hank, I don't. But what if I did? Are you going to tell me you have one there in your pocket?"

"Okay, so it was a stupid question. I'm just trying to help. You want to tell me about it? Or do you want me to just get back in my Navigator and go navigate myself right off the first high cliff I come to?"

She narrowed her eyes. "You'd do that for me?"

This sarcasm was really unlike her. "Okay, Maddie, this is more than the dog. You've been giving me grief since I got out of my car. What's really going on?"

She exhaled sharply. "Just get in your SUV and come to my place. And I'll show you what's going on."

"Fair enough. You want a ride?"

"No. I live just around the corner."

"I remember. But I was trying to be nice. So . . . see you there?"

"Fine." Without further ado or ceremony, she turned and walked away, heading back down the hill on the narrow band of sidewalk. Her steps were short and halting, owing to the steep grade.

Still worried about her emotional state, Hank stared at her back, noting her swaying ponytail, then her narrow feminine shoulders, the smooth swing of her cute behind, and the effortless stride of her long legs as she achieved more level ground. He watched her until she rounded the corner and the hardware store blocked her from his view. Hank shook his head, wondered again what the hell was going on, and then looked both ways up and down the road. No traffic. No surprise. He sprinted back across the road, got into his Navigator, started it up, put it in gear, and headed for Maddie's Gifts.

Somehow, he didn't think he was going to like what it was she had to show him.

In only seconds, Hank pulled into the narrow, grassy, wheel-rutted driveway next to Maddie's shop. He inched his vehicle up to the Wagoneer and stopped it about a foot from the other vehicle's nose. As he put his Navigator in park and killed the engine, he looked for but didn't see Maddie. He climbed out and closed the door. Then he saw her. Standing with her arms crossed, she was at the back of her beat-up Wagoneer. Eyeing the green simulated-wood-paneled vehicle as he walked along its side, Hank fought a grin. The woman would soon have most of the money in the Western Hemisphere and she drove this bucket of bolts. Ah, the eccentric rich.

He joined Maddie at the back of her Jeep, met her unhappy eyes, and then followed her gaze to the vehicle's interior. She lowered the tailgate to show him that the cargo space was occupied. "Well," he remarked, glancing over at Maddie, "I *was* going to ask—yet again—what's going on.

But now I see." He faced the Jeep's cargo bed. "Hello, Beamer. How you doing?"

Sitting nicely, Beamer was in the rear cargo compartment. She wore a dog grin and woofed her greeting at Hank. He noticed that she shared the space with a good-sized cardboard box, but didn't think anything about it—until, on a second glance, he saw the red ceramic lobster clock lying atop a bed of folded clothes. A feeling of fatalism assailed him. Hank pretty much knew what this was, but couldn't stop himself from asking, anyway. "What's all this?"

"It's everything I have of your grandfather's." Her face was absolutely expressionless . . . and unnerving.

Okay. This was a clue. All of his grandfather's belongings were boxed and in the rear of her car. "I see. Where were you going with it?"

"Out to your cottage."

Hank nodded but couldn't quite hold Maddie's steady gaze. Just seeing his grandfather's things like this made everything so real, the loss so new again. Emotion tightened in Hank's throat. He cleared it discreetly and said, "So apparently Beamer wanted to go, too. Am I right?"

Maddie nodded. "By all appearances."

God, he wished she'd yell or be sarcastic or tell him to go to hell. That he knew how to deal with. But not this blank staring and the monotonal, emotionless voice. "Why were you bringing me my grandfather's things?"

"Because I thought you should have them. He was your kin, not mine."

Oh, boy. Something major had happened. "He was your friend."

"So I thought."

"So you *thought*? Dammit, Maddie, talk to me."

She didn't even blink. "I am."

"No you're not. You're speaking to me, but you're not talking to me. Talk to me now, or I'm leaving and I'm not taking any of this stuff with me."

She shifted her stance, putting her weight on one leg.

"All right. Yesterday, Celeste told me everything. And I think you know what I mean by everything. So here I am—your sacrificial virgin."

Hank ducked his head. "My what? Come again?"

"Your sacrificial virgin. Figuratively speaking, of course. But you know all of this, Hank. One of two things is going on here and neither one of them is pretty."

"All right, I'll bite. What are the two things?"

Maddie's chin quivered as she sucked in a breath and appeared to struggle for control. "Scenario number one. Your grandfather befriended me because he wanted me for you—"

"What? That's crazy."

"Not so much. You yourself thought something like this was behind Jim Thornton's hints to you."

"Something, yes. But not a conspiracy, for crying out loud."

"Yet that may be exactly what it is. If he set this up like I think in scenario number one, then he left me everything that is rightfully yours, so you and I would be forced to meet and would hopefully fall in love and get married. How manipulative is that?"

"Pretty damned." Hank felt a bit numb, but not totally turned off by the whole idea, either. "Where are you getting all this, Maddie?"

"Mostly from Celeste, who has never lied to me. But the rest of it I came up with on my own."

Hank exhaled sharply and ran a hand over his jaw. "What 'rest of it'?"

"You tell me, Hank." Maddie's eyes were narrowed . . . and accusatory.

Why would she—? Suddenly, he got it. And didn't like it. "Oh, hold on. Do you honestly think I'd be in on something that . . . that screwball, Maddie? How could I be? I didn't know about the will until the same moment you did. And even if I had, *why* would I be? All I have to do is sit out here for six weeks and then go on with the rest of my life with everything back in place."

She closed her eyes and put a hand over her face, speaking through her spread fingers. "That's the part I hate the most. That you would toy with me."

Hank's chest tightened. "Toy with you? I have never toyed with you, Maddie. Never. I don't know what makes you think I have."

She dropped her hand to her side and stretched over the lowered tailgate. With her fingers, she snagged a corner of the box and pulled it toward her. Smoothly, she picked it up and, without warning, shoved it into his hands. "Here. This belongs to you. Take it and go. I never want to see you or that lobster clock again. And take the dog, too."

She made a move to step around him, but Hank, his arms wrapped around the box, purposely blocked her way. "Maddie, you are *so* wrong. You're wrong about me. And you're wrong to be doing this. You're not even in the ballpark with this behavior. Look, I don't know what's happened. But I know I didn't have any hand in it. I swear it."

"I wish I could believe you. But I know what James wanted. And I know what you said to me last Monday out at the cottage. And I know how your mother is not pleased with any of this and feels threatened. Well, I'm not happy, either. Maybe we were all used by James, I don't know. But really, Hank, when it's all said and done, none of it matters. It's just another day. And I'm sick to death of you Madisons and all your intrigue and the publicity. I mean, who needs it? I certainly don't."

This time, when she went to step around him, Hank let her go and turned to watch her. She stalked off, her hands in her pockets as she searched for, and then produced, a set of keys that fit the door on the side of her shop. She unlocked it, stepped through, and slammed it behind her.

Stunned, Hank swung his gaze to Beamer. The golden retriever arched her eyebrows dramatically. "What the hell did you do?" Hank asked her.

She whined and shifted about in the cargo hold . . . and then barked.

"Exactly," Hank said. "Well, thanks a lot. You and I

have just been told to get the heck out of Dodge because it's not big enough for the three of us."

Beamer again barked her agreement with Hank's assessment.

CHAPTER FIFTEEN

❧

CLAD IN HER THIN nightgown and curled up under the chenille spread, with only her nose exposed to the bedroom's cool air, Maddie snuggled back down into her warm cocoon after turning off the morning alarm. Not moving, she listened for a moment, as if for an intruder. She soon realized that the only interloper was the angry storm outside. It sounded absolutely deadly in its intent. Her next thought was a grateful thank-you that she wouldn't have to get out today in this viciously windy and rainy early-September weather.

Not so everyone else. Just past Labor Day, it was the first day of school. Poor kids. Poor teachers. She thought for a moment about not opening the shop. And then hated the very idea that she was even thinking that. *Here we go again.* She'd been over this before, this wondering how she was supposed to cling to her Yankee work ethic in the face of impending and tremendous wealth. Yep, it looked as if she would get the money and everything else James had left her. Hank was certainly seeing to that.

Two weeks had passed since she'd given him his grandfather's things, including Beamer. Well, give the man his due, he was hanging in there. And staying out of her way as she'd told him to do. Darn him. But the bottom line was it looked as if he'd do his six weeks, get his company back, and she'd get James's personal wealth. All they had to do then was sign the papers and go their separate ways. As if they hadn't already.

Maddie mugged a face. She would be incredibly wealthy in only a matter of weeks. A little over three. So why wasn't she ecstatic? Jumping for joy? Euphoric? Because she didn't want this inheritance to change her, not in a bad way. On the good side, she'd already decided to make huge charitable donations and get involved in funding worth-while projects. That went without saying. But she also caught herself daydreaming about whirlwind shopping trips, spending sprees on things like a house, car, boat, helicopter, airplane—No, wait. James had also left her all of those things. And a whole lot more. Maddie exhaled, feeling overwhelmed, if not totally daunted. But then she lost patience with herself. Why did she think she had to feel so bad about enjoying her bounty? Pleasure was not a bad thing, right? Right.

But not wanting to get up and go to work in the meantime was. *I don't have to. I'm rich.*

Well, there they were again, the insidious little devils. Sloth and laziness. Could the Reverend Hobbs and Lavinia Houghton be far behind with stern lectures on the evils of wealth? Maddie puckered up with defiance. *They're not my bosses.* Then she remembered two things. One, she was pretty much bound by civic duty to open her shop because it kept Celeste and Lillian Madison accounted for and not free to wreak havoc in the streets. And two, the Reverend Hobbs and Lavinia Houghton were currently not speaking to her. Maddie rolled her eyes, not even wanting to go there. The bake sale last weekend. *Lavinia Houghton meets Lillian Madison. Or, more accurately, Godzilla meets Mothra.*

Not that Lillian and Celeste hadn't joined up and fought the good fight. And not that the two women—*Go figure*—hadn't actually been defending Maddie when they got into a food fight with Lavinia. Yes, a food fight. Right there in the Fellowship Hall. Maddie could still hear Lavinia Houghton starting it by saying she would abide no slackers, rich or otherwise, in their midst, mind you. Maddie was the slacker and her not baking anything for the sale was the act of slacking. That remark had signaled "go" time. Two against one hadn't seemed fair, so Maddie had stepped in to try to stop it, only to be creamed with, well, a cream pie. Then, the "Rearend" Hobbs, as Lillian had taken to calling him, had waded in and gotten smacked with, ap-

propriately enough, an angel food cake. Just bounced off
the big, florid man, it had.

Reliving all that had Maddie laughing out loud, there
alone in her bed. Who would have thought that Lillian
Madison would come here and stay? The woman loved
Hanscomb Harbor. Not so much Maddie yet, but she was
thawing toward her. Some. Still, Hank's mother had relaxed, let her hair down figuratively, and found a home with
Celeste. And the two of them had teamed up and worked
tirelessly to terrorize the citizenry and the paparazzi. For
that second thing alone, Maddie believed, they had already
earned a special place in Heaven.

But open up the shop? Should she? Maddie frowned,
listening to the shrieking wind and pinging rain railing
against the windows. She couldn't imagine anyone braving
this weather in need of an emergency sea-horse brooch or
a severely discounted beach towel. So Maddie changed her
mind again and made a mental note that over her morning
coffee she would call Celeste, as much to check on her and
Lillian as to tell them not to bother coming in. They'd been
going to clear out the remaining seasonal stock today and
tidy the storeroom, but such chores were like ironing or
dusting. They could wait because certainly no one else
would do them for you.

Still, this meant that Maddie would spend the day utterly
alone, with only her own company. That was okay, she told
herself, despite the certainty that she would run into herself
around every corner. No matter where she went in her
house, it seemed, there she was. And there her thoughts of
Hank Madison were. How annoying, she tried to convince
herself. This wasn't working, so she beat herself up over
Beamer. She should kick herself for giving up the dog. That
had been wrong. So wrong. Her own stupid temper, Maddie
fussed. Poor Beamer, to be passed around so. How ashamed
was she? How many times had she picked up the phone to
call Hank, wanting to inquire about the dog? But she'd
hung up an equal number of times, too, before he could
answer.

She just couldn't talk to him. Couldn't hear the sound of his voice and not fall apart on some level. Why did the man have to be so obedient and honorable and keep his darned distance just because she'd told him to? Did he not know the first thing about pursuing a woman? Maddie thought about that and decided that, no, he probably didn't. A man like Hank Madison didn't have to pursue women. Probably all he did was snap his fingers and then choose from among the crowd. Well, then, she certainly had to be the exception, didn't she, having told him to go away after he'd told her he wanted to be with her?

Ha. Good for me. I stood my ground. Pride in that accomplishment lasted about two seconds. She slumped in her bed. *Yeah, I stood my ground. Alone. How stupid am I?*

Not in the least, she rushed to tell herself. Sure, Hank wanted to be with her—for six whole weeks. That had hit her like: hey, Maddie, be my summer fling, make these six weeks go by fast, and I'll make you a billionaire. Maddie pursed her lips. How insulting. Then she rapped her knuckles against her forehead. *And why in hell didn't I say yes? Six weeks are better than the current no weeks I now have.* Who'd said, " 'Tis better to have loved and lost than never to have loved at all?" Well, whoever it was, she knew what that meant now. Jump at the chance. Go for it. God, even Celeste had told her that much. Why hadn't she listened? Stupid pride. And morals. Values. Self-esteem.

Maddie covered her head with her pillow and cried out a very muffled, "Okay, I get the picture, all right? I'm not the six-week-stand type. And I'd hate me in the end. I know that."

She gave up her effort to smother her conscience and came out from under her pillow, brushing her hair out of her face and remembering what a stir her rift with Hank had caused in town. One benefit of it had been that even the most dogged of the paparazzi had finally left. No romance equaled no story and no pictures. And that meant no reason to be here. Good riddance. But not everyone had given up on them.

How many of Celeste's elderly friends, in the guise of browsers, had come into the shop to regale Maddie with their version of Hank's daily activities and then to gauge her reaction? Ten? Twenty? It had been like having the tabloid press descend on her again. Or like a soap opera. *The Days of Maddie's and Hank's Lives.* Even she had come to hate the sound of that stupid little tinkling bell over the shop's door. In fact, out of desperation and in an effort to stop the busybodies, Maddie had threatened to post a sign stating that no one over the age of sixty was allowed in the shop without having in tow a grandchild who had money and a mission. The visits had slowed to a trickle after that.

But those first few days after she'd told Hank to stay away had been very, very hard for Maddie. How her heart ached—no, *had* ached. It didn't anymore. She was over that—him—now. She was. Over it. Over him. Lying there in her bed, alone and curled up, Maddie wished her thoughts would just move on, would just leave the sight, the scent, the touch, the feel of Hank Madison alone.

She pressed her pillow against her ears as if that would stop the images in her head; would stop the raw desire, the want, the wish for more heated kisses; would stop the hot looks, the way he made her feel all tingly inside. The craving. Those unclaimed chances with him. The opportunities not acted upon.

"He didn't want *me,* all right? Not me. He wanted his life back. Not me," Maddie railed, hearing her voice crack, feeling the hurt in her heart. "Do you get it now? He didn't want me. So just stop it."

She didn't know who she was talking to, but still she waited as if expecting an answer. Or a rebuttal that told her she was wrong. Disappointingly, none came. Nor did the hurt lessen from having stated out loud what the source of her discontent was. She'd thought saying it, admitting it, would help. Or be cleansing somehow. It wasn't. *Great.*

I'm turning into the crazy old woman who talks to herself out loud when she's alone. All I need are thirty-four cats and a shopping cart to complete this picture.

Maddie sighed, thinking this was getting her nowhere. Neither was a constant mental replaying of that wonderful Monday when she and Hank had picnicked in the gazebo and then taken Beamer for a walk on the beach. That had been heaven. With that memory warming her, Maddie turned over in bed, snuggling even further into her cozy nest of covers. She closed her eyes, trying to blank her mind, to get back to that day. And then, suddenly, there he was. Hank Madison in all his masculine glory. Those dark eyes, the determined jaw, his broad shoulders and killer grin. He was magnificent.

But what really got to her the most was his "everyday person" attitude. The way he'd gamely taken up residence at that horrible little beach house and had set about making it better. That hideous wallpaper. Wagons, ho. And how he made her laugh that one day when he'd stumbled headfirst into the cottage. And the meal they'd shared together. How good he was with Beamer. How hard he worked to understand his grandfather's mind-boggling will. And how wonderful he'd been that one warm evening with that silly red apron on as he waited on her customers. What a man.

Maddie felt tears prick at her eyes. *What a man.* She sniffed and swallowed the emotion in her throat. *What an idiot I am to let him get away. I want him. It's that simple. And that hard.* She had no right, she told herself, to lie here and wonder in vain about him. After all, she kept throwing him back, pushing him away. How pathetic was it that all she had of him were memories? So what was he doing right now? she wondered. Probably sleeping. Did he sleep in the nude? Maddie shook her head, blocking that image from her mind. No sense going there.

She shifted about irritably in her bed. Why was she torturing herself with this? With Hank? She had a life without him. Hey, life was good. Her life was good. She was enjoying it—or would if she could stop thinking about Hank

Madison. If everyone would let her. God, she had days, whole days, when she knew that if he walked through the door of Maddie's Gifts, she'd say yes to anything he wanted from her and for whatever reason he wanted it.

Only he never did. He never walked through the door of Maddie's Gifts. And whose fault was that?

Later that morning, dressed in thick, droopy wool socks, her favorite ratty old paprika-colored sweatpants, a too-big denim shirt, and no makeup, Maddie stood with her back to the shop's door as she sorted through the mail Mr. Canardy had just dropped off. Bills. A catalogue. Some "Occupant" flyers. So . . . nothing exciting. *What did you expect—a love letter from Hank Madison?* Knock it off, Maddie warned herself.

Just then, behind her, the door opened and the little bell tinkled. Maddie turned, an expectant look on her face. "More mail, Mr. Canardy? I hope it's—"

She froze. The mail fell from her suddenly nerveless fingers. Envelopes smacked with a sick plop onto the newly polished hardwood floors. Maddie ignored the postal display in favor of running a quick mental scan over herself and how she looked . . . and how he looked. *Great. Dogpatch meets* GQ. "Hank Madison! What are *you* doing here?"

Hank, as if it explained everything, pointed to his confederates piling in behind him. "My mother called me and said she and Mrs. McNeer needed a ride in to work."

He's here. Hank's here. He's here. Maddie's mind stupidly repeated its happy refrain and would not work otherwise. "Your mother and Mrs. McNeer?"

"That would be me. Down here, honey. In front of the big man." The tiny, short woman to one side of Hank— sure enough, Mrs. McNeer—collapsed her dripping umbrella and glared up at him. "You're to call me Celeste. Every time you call me Mrs. McNeer, I think my last mother-in-law, the old battle-ax, is standing behind me."

"Yes, ma'am . . . Celeste," Hank replied obediently.

For her part, Maddie gave her head a quick Etch-A-Sketch shake to clear it of all the twisty little lines that kept her from thinking clearly. It worked. "Celeste!" she barked in annoyance. "What are you and Mrs. Madison doing here?"

Noisily digging in her big red leather handbag—no doubt for her cigarettes—Mrs. Madison, with a plastic rain cap over her peach-colored hair, said, "Lillian. Call me Lillian. We've talked about this before." She came up with her cigarette case. "Whew. I need a smoke. I swear it's coming down out there like a cow peeing on a flat rock."

That was the most unbelievable thing for her to say. Maddie joined Hank in staring accusingly at Celeste the Corrupter and the Unrepentant.

"What?" she wanted to know. But without waiting for an answer, she launched into Maddie. "And what do you mean what are we doing here? We work here." Celeste then directed her attention to Hank, who looked shell-shocked. "About my last mother-in-law, Hank. That was the meanest woman you ever saw. Everyone said she had the biggest set of brass bal—"

"Celeste," Maddie hissed, also noting the accusing glare Hank now directed his mother's way. "Stop that. Now listen to me. I know you work here. But I called you and told you not to come in today, that I wasn't opening the shop. Remember?"

"Of course I do. You think I'm senile just because I'm elderly, don't you? For your information, young lady, I tried calling you and you didn't answer. I got worried. And then Hank drove by, and I flagged him down and told him to give us a ride over here."

"That is *not* how it happened," Hank said, coming to his own defense and pointing at Celeste. "They called me and—"

"Shhh, honey," his mother said, putting a hand on his all-weather jacket's sleeve and shaking her head no. "I want to hear this."

She meant Celeste, who was still getting on to Maddie.

"So you can just sue us for worrying about you when you didn't answer your phone."

Maddie crossed her arms under her breasts and smiled knowingly at her friend. No one had to tell her this was a matchmaking setup. "I didn't answer it because it didn't ring."

That got her. Celeste stared blankly for a moment, then blurted, "Damn bad weather. Must have messed up the phone lines. And say, if you aren't open today, how come the door is unlocked and you're here? Are you trying to cheat us out of our hard-earned wages?"

"Do I look like I'm dressed for work? Mr. Canardy came by with the mail and I—Oh, never mind that." She rounded on Hank, drinking in her fill of the man, all rain-wet and tall and clean-smelling. "I'm really sorry about this, Hank. You were obviously set up by these two. I told them not to come to work in this storm."

He ran a hand through his hair, raking away glistening drops of water. "I believe you. But I just do what I'm told." He grinned, a killer sexy grin that showed white and even teeth. "It's easier."

Maddie damned near whimpered. She had to stiffen her knees against the urge to jump into his arms and wrap her legs around him and kiss him hard, right in front of his mother. "Yes. I know. You do exactly what you're told. Even when you shouldn't, probably."

"What do you mean by that?" Oh, he *so* knew. His eyebrows were arched and his dark eyes gleamed with an awareness that said *You've missed me, haven't you?*

Though her mouth dried and her bones melted, Maddie managed to raise her chin a regal notch. It would have had more impact if she hadn't been dressed like poor old crazy Mrs. Bailey. "Nothing. I don't mean anything."

"Ha. She means she missed you," Celeste supplied to Hank. Maddie froze, her mouth open. "Close your mouth, Maddie. It makes you look simple, hanging open like that." She then turned back to Hank. "She's also mad. Probably because I brought you here when she looks like a ragamuffin."

"I am not mad, Celeste," Maddie blurted. She felt her cheeks warming with that lie. "I'm just surprised, is all. I wasn't expecting to see you." She darted her gaze to Hank's handsome face. "Any of you. Especially you. And yet, here you are."

"Here I am," Hank repeated, his slow grin easily holding Maddie's gaze.

Neither one of them—Maddie or Hank—had moved, Maddie knew that rationally. Yet she felt as if she were on Rollerblades and someone had shoved her in his direction. Any second now, she would smack right into him. She couldn't look away from him. He was here. He was really here. The electricity, the attraction, the awareness, they were overwhelming. Happiness thrummed through Maddie's veins. Her pounding pulse seemed centered somewhere underneath the front of her sweatpants.

Just then, Celeste walked between her and Hank, right through their charged field of sensual awareness. Maddie half expected the tiny little woman to be zotted and fried like an insect that collides with a bug zapper. But no such luck. Oblivious—or pretending to be—and already removing her rain cap and slicker, Celeste idly commented, "He has nowhere to stay, dear. His cottage flooded in this weather. I told him he could stay here with you."

That broke the trance. Alarm bells, whooping sirens, and clanging gongs of warning exploded through Maddie's head. "What?" She whipped around to sight on Celeste. "With me? He can't stay here with me."

"Of course he can." On her way to where her red apron hung from its peg, and with Lillian now on her heels, Celeste told Maddie, "The motel and the Wainwrights' bed-and-breakfast are full, dear. And he can't stay out at Cotton Hardy's rat trap. One more night in that drafty old cottage and the man will catch his death of pneumonia. So here he is. He'll stay here with you."

Maddie's mind began whirring again. "No. He can't."

She then remembered he was in the room and swung her gaze to him. "You can't."

He opened his mouth to say something, but Celeste beat him to it. "Hank is staying here with you. And Lillian and I are here today to work. Hank can help us, too. We can use a good set of strong arms around here. Heavy lifting is what men are best at, you know."

"Second best," Lillian piped in, grinning, leaning now against the jewelry counter and smoking.

Maddie ignored her, favoring instead Celeste the Matchmaker. "He's not staying here. And you're not working today. Neither is he. If you're so worried about him, he can stay with you. Your house has four bedrooms."

"Excuse me?" This was Hank. "If I could—"

"Not now, Hank, dear," Celeste cut him off sweetly. She turned back to Maddie, her entire demeanor self-righteous. "Hank can't stay with me. I have Lillian with me. And Bluebell, my kitten." Celeste's puckered expression said that she'd covered only three bedrooms and knew it. "And the fourth one is my sewing room."

"You don't sew."

"I could."

"He's not staying here." Maddie leaned in toward Celeste. "I'm a single woman." As if that were a shameful secret. "His being here would compromise me. And start the rumors again. People would talk."

"Not Lavinia Houghton, I'll bet." This was Lillian off in her corner. "She's probably still picking coconut out of her hair."

Celeste and Lillian whooped it up at that, cackling and nodding their heads.

"If you'll just let me say—"

"In a moment, Hank. Hush, now." Celeste again cut him off and turned to Maddie. "Like it or lump it, Maddie, you've got a houseguest."

"I really hate to keep interrupting—"

"Then don't!" Maddie and Celeste shrieked at Hank.

Silence reigned in Maddie's Gifts.

As usual, Celeste recovered first. "Hank, why don't you go get your luggage and the dog while Maddie and I—"

"The dog?" Maddie was further horrified. "He has the *dog* with him?"

"Yes, I do," Hank answered for himself, now speaking rapidly as if fearing he'd be cut off again. "She's in the car and it's cool and running, so there's no need to call the SPCA. But look, I speak English, I am present, and I'm an adult. It is *me* we're—okay, *you're*—talking about here. Still, I would appreciate it if you would let me have my say."

"Now I think *he's* mad," Celeste observed.

"He is," his mother confirmed. "A tantrum's not far behind."

Ignoring the hecklers, Maddie waved a hand at Hank, as if bestowing permission. "All right, fine. Go ahead. You have the floor. What is it you want to say?"

"Thank you," he said pompously but politely. Then a slow grin lit his features as he stared Maddie's way. "So, which bedroom is mine?"

The spare one was his answer to that. The guest room. Talk about winning a battle but not the war. Talk about all being fair in love and war. This was war. Didn't know about love. But it was hell, Hank knew that much.

Separated from Maddie's bedroom by a narrow hallway that may as well have been the width of the Grand Canyon for all the access Hank figured he'd have to it, his assigned bedroom was roughly the size of his shoe closet at home. Occupying the space with him was a tiny little square of a frilly-curtained window; a closed door that no doubt opened onto a minuscule clothes closet; a mint-green-painted three-drawer dresser at the foot of the bed; and a skinny oak nightstand with a bitsy lamp beside the bed.

He felt like giant Gulliver among the teensy Lilliputians. Huge. Like the bed. A wall-to-wall double bed whose dimensions precluded using the closet or closing the door to the hallway. No swing room. So, okay, the tweedy Berber carpet, what little of it he could see, was nice. And the décor was at least inviting, if terribly feminine.

So, Hank concluded, scratching his head, the only way to move around the room would be to slither between pieces of furniture. But no. He'd run the risk of wedging himself between the heavy furniture and the solid wall. He could see Maddie having to call the fire department. No way. Hank puzzled this one out, deciding that, essentially, he would have to stand on the bed and command the room from there. Which he couldn't currently do because Beamer, the eighty-pound golden retriever, was already stretched out there and regarding him with a look that clearly said she thought him an interloper.

"What are you looking at?" Hank challenged.

Raising only her majestic head, the elegant dog grunted and woofed at him. Encouragement? Or warning? Hank suspected the latter, but told himself he could do this.

Trial and error told him that kneeling atop the bed, at its foot, put him within easy reach of the narrow three-drawer dresser that stubbornly squatted on its allotted two feet of floor space and resisted cooperating. Hank had quickly realized that should he brave the five or so inches of clearance between bed and dresser by standing on the carpeted floor and actually pulling out a drawer, he could very easily, given the gymnastic contortions that would have been involved, cut off his oxygen. It just wasn't worth it because he could only use the top two drawers, anyway. The third one, totally blocked by the bed's frame, remained pristine and inviolate. No sense even trying that one.

How hard could it be? Hank fumed. All he wanted to do was put his underthings, socks, shirts and the like, in a drawer. He'd had no idea that such a mundane task could require the kind of brainpower and planning as would a trek to Machu Picchu. Wasn't it enough that he'd already had to referee Maddie's and Celeste's argument over where he'd stay? Wasn't it enough that he'd already had to drive Celeste and his mother home and then come back here— all in the wind and rain? Yes, it was enough, and he was now in no mood for mishaps. Hank gripped the top dresser drawer's round, blunt knob and yanked it open.

Mishap.

The whole drawer came out in his hand, spilling a bunch of feminine sweaters onto the end of the bed and over Hank's thighs. "Well, son of a bitch," he muttered as he sat back and stared at the mess. He looked over his shoulder at the dog. "You better not be smirking."

Before he could decide if the golden retriever was or not, he heard, "I see Beamer's made herself at home. I should have warned you she slept in here."

Maddie had sought him out. Alight with pleasure that she had, Hank pivoted to see her in the doorway. "That explains it. I'll probably have to fight her for the bed."

"Most likely." Maddie didn't say anything else. Hank stared at her staring at him. The air thickened with an unspoken something that felt a lot like desire. Maddie cleared her throat and pointed at him kneeling there on the bed and awash in her sweaters. "Did you find anything to your liking? Maybe that red one with the pearl buttons?"

So she was going to keep things light. Hank scooped up the sweater she'd described and held it up in front of him, looking down at it draped over his chest. "I don't know. I think red makes my butt look big."

Grinning, shaking her head, Maddie leaned against the doorjamb and crossed her arms. "Men. You are so shallow, to allow your self-worth to be determined by the size of your . . ." Her face turned bright red. "Well, your butt."

Laughing affectionately at her, Hank experienced an overwhelming desire to leap across the space that separated them and take her in his arms and kiss the hell out of her. Even in sweatpants and a big denim shirt, she was gorgeous and wonderful. Warm and witty and funny. And here he was with her. He intended to be the best houseguest ever and maybe even try to cut through all the red tape in their lives that kept them apart.

"I'm sorry about the size of the room," she said, frowning as her gaze panned the small space. "It never looked this small to me before I saw you in it. You just seem to fill a room with your presence." Her attention came into sudden sharp focus. Her eyes widened. "Uh, why don't you give me those sweaters?" She held her hands out to receive them. "I am such a bad hostess. Let me have them. And then I'll clear out those other drawers for you, too."

Hank held up a staying hand. "No. I can get all this. Don't worry about it."

She lowered her arms to her sides. "But you're the guest here. You poor thing. Look at this room. I'm sure you're used to better."

"Maddie, it's okay. You don't have to do anything special for me. You weren't expecting me. I mean, who the hell knew every room for rent in Hanscomb Harbor would be full? I should have called you first. But I didn't. So I'm the beggar here and not about to be choosy." Now that didn't sound right. "Not that this isn't nice. It is." Kneeling there, he gave the bed a test bounce that earned him a warning *grrr* from Beamer. "Well, I like it," he told the grumpy dog.

"You're a nice person, Hank, do you know that?" Maddie said. "Your mother did a wonderful job of raising you."

Thoroughly heartened as well as embarrassed, Hank shrugged away her compliment and tempered his words with a teasing grin. "She had a lot to work with."

"I can see that."

She liked him. Affected more than he thought he would be, Hank put the sweater down and sank back on his haunches, resting his hands on his thighs. He couldn't take his eyes off her or forget for one second how close she was. Or how they would brush against and by each other in this cozy little house. How long, he wondered, could he resist his impulses where she was concerned? Not long, he figured, male libido being what it was. Suddenly feeling he needed to say something, because she certainly wasn't helping being this close to him and a bed. "The truth is, this is pure luxury compared to some places where I've had to lay my head down for the night."

Interest sparked in her blue eyes. "Really? That sounds intriguing."

"Well, it's really pretty *National Geographic,* but I've slept in a small boat as we motored down the Amazon. That was pretty rough. And scaling Everest. You'd be surprised to know there're no five-star hotels at the top of that thing."

She straightened her stance. "Shut up. You have not done those things."

"Have so."

"Wow. You work hard even when you play. I've hardly ever left New England. And you've been everywhere."

"Just about." *But nowhere I've liked better than right here with you. Tell her that out loud, coward. No, the time isn't right.*

"So," Maddie said, signaling an end to this moment. "If you'll hand me those sweaters and the stuff from the other drawers, I'll leave you to your unpacking."

"If you insist. But I'm keeping the red one." Hank scooped up the sweaters, only to be hit with the perfumed scent that wafted from them. A sudden exciting weakness melted his bones. Maddie had worn each of these garments. He wanted very much to hold them to his nose and breathe deeply of her scent. But he figured she'd probably call the police if he did anything that shocking. So he dutifully handed them to her, his hands brushing over her outstretched arms as they transferred the load between them.

Hank surprised himself by clutching at Maddie's wrists and holding her wide, blue-eyed gaze. The sweaters provided the only cushioning that kept their bodies apart. "You're not going to run me off this time, Maddie."

She lowered her gaze as if suddenly shy. But then looked up at him from under her eyelashes, giving him a look that boiled his blood. "I'm not going to try to, Hank. Not this time."

CHAPTER SIXTEEN

HER ARMS CROSSED, AND hugging herself, Maddie stood peering out the window of her kitchen door. It was lit up inside against the bruised and glowering clouds that for two days now had denied the sun and waterlogged the citizens. Just awful weather. Outside, the cold rain had slacked to a drizzle, but the weather folks said more was on its way. Yet here she was, Maddie thought, grinning, lucky enough to find herself in an intimate cocoon of warmth with the one person who, at least in her book, could give cabin fever a whole new meaning. If only he would. If only she could let him.

In the backyard, the tall trees, with drenched leaves and drooping branches, appeared to be pouting. Beamer too was insulted by the whole thing. Outside to tend to her business, and under Maddie's watchful eye, the dog gingerly picked her way around the puddles until she could find decent grass. Sniffing out a select spot, she looked pointedly back at Maddie as if to tell her she wished some privacy, please. Shaking her head, Maddie looked in Hank's direction and rubbed at her arms. "I am so cold. Whatever happened to all that global warming we keep hearing about?"

Off to her right, seated at her drop-leaf kitchen table, Hank idly flipped through a dog-eared women's magazine. "It flew south to Florida."

Maddie grinned, seeing her reflection in the window's glass. "If we had any sense we'd join it there."

Several images kaleidoscoped through her mind. Bikinis, palm trees, pink hotels, white-sand beaches, pretty drinks with umbrellas, Hank at her side . . . and one room or two? Aha. There was the rub. *Down, kaleidoscope.* In Maddie's frustrated estimation, they seemed destined to wallow in a mudhole of unspoken desires. Yes, she saw the looks he gave her. And yes, she sent him her own fair share. After all, she was a healthy female with all the urges of a woman her age. So what was he waiting for? Her? And what was she waiting for? Him?

It would seem so. A part of her wanted to turn to him and say, "All right, big boy, let's get it on." Maddie felt her face heat up with merely thinking something like that. She knew herself only too well: she might think these sexy, very forward things, but she could never say them. She always envied women who could and who wore their sexuality like perfume. Maddie just couldn't do it. She was way too conservative. And frustrated as a result.

"I take it we're not going to Florida?"

With a guilty start, Maddie pivoted to face Hank and strove to keep lightness in her voice. "No."

"Damn." Teasing though his words were, his dark eyes glittered with something stronger than humor.

Maddie's pulse leapt in response. He was so handsome. And exciting. And even a bit dangerous-looking. Like a pirate. Or Rhett Butler. Or Zorro. Or maybe like the men who'd played those characters, she supposed. "Florida was fun to think about, wasn't it? A girl can always dream."

"So can a guy. Okay, aside from Florida, what do you want to do?"

Climb all over you. Maddie sucked in her breath, afraid for a second that she'd blurted that out loud. "Uh, I don't know. What do you want to do?"

"I don't know. Put on wet suits and swim around in your backyard?"

Maddie chuckled. "God knows we could. All this rain."

"Maybe we ought to be working on an ark, then."

She pretended to seriously consider that. "No. I don't know how to measure cubits. And all those animals." She gave a shiver of mock horror. "The mess."

"That's true. How about we play checkers?"

She made a scoffing sound. "You're no challenge. I keep beating you." With that, she opened the door for the dog to come in.

Accompanying Beamer was a wet, whipping wind that scurried across the warm kitchen floor and elicited yelps from Maddie and Hank before she could get the door closed. Hank snapped his fingers and clapped, calling the dog to him. Maddie successfully, but just barely, fought her urge to respond and run over to him. Instead, she indulgently watched Beamer, with wet paws and a big doggy grin on her face, trot over to Hank. Whereupon he lavished praise on her and dried her furry feet with an old towel Maddie kept in the kitchen for that purpose. Ruffling the dog's ears, Hank caught Maddie's attention. "You don't *beat* me at checkers, by the way. I let you win."

Mock outrage was called for. "You do not. I beat you fair and square every time. So does Beamer."

Hank shrugged. "Two out of three. She's not so smart. Hey, want to go see my mother and Celeste?"

Well, she certainly hadn't expected that. *Go see his mother and Celeste?* The man was really desperate for something to do. Was he bored silly being here with only her? How ego-deflating. "Sorry. Can't. They've gone to the beauty shop this afternoon."

Hank sat up, shaking his head in disbelief. "In this weather? Are you serious? Here we are, not getting out. Having the good sense not to get out, I should say. And those two are going to the beauty shop? It's weather like this that blows ships off course."

Maddie grinned, loving his easy moods and sense of humor. "I know. But you obviously don't understand the sacred nature of beauty-shop appointments, do you?"

"Apparently not."

"It's a girl thing."

He held his hands up as if in surrender. "Enough said." He turned in his chair to sadly watch Beamer pad down the hall. "Great. There she goes. Right to my bed."

His bed. Maddie had to look down, knowing she was guilty of leaving her bedroom door ajar at night, hoping to hear him snore or breathe or just turn over in the bed. But mostly, in the middle of the night, he fussed at the dog,

Beamer growled at him, and then Hank ended up on the sofa. But still . . . he was here. And now they were rained in together in her tiny little house.

Hank spoke again to Maddie, inviting her to meet his gaze. "At least tell me that my mother is driving and not Celeste."

"Your mother is driving, and not Celeste."

"Are you just saying that to make me feel better? Or do you know?"

"I *don't* know, and it *was* to make you feel better."

"Well, you could have lied again. Because now I don't feel better."

"Sorry. I'm sure they'll be fine. It's not a long way."

"Those two don't need a long way to get in trouble." With that, Hank got up and went to the refrigerator, opening it and staring at the contents.

Maddie's breath caught. This was such an intimate act. She couldn't believe it. Yes, she certainly enjoyed watching him, a picture of inherent grace as he leaned over and peered inside at the shelves of offerings. But what was quickening her woman's heart was the realization that you didn't do what he'd just done—go into someone's refrigerator—unless you felt you were at home and were completely comfortable. Still standing by the door that led out into her backyard, Maddie leaned against it and crossed her arms, wondering if he realized what he'd done. Or if his act was as unconscious as it had appeared.

Either way, this was heartening. He was comfortable here and with her. She had ample evidence of that, she realized as she mentally followed a common thread that ran through their days of enforced togetherness. She meant the way they talked. And what they talked about. She marveled at how "everyday" their conversations were; at how domestic intimacy had woven its way through their words; at how their talks had the feel of those of a long-married couple chatting idly about the weather and people they knew in common.

The odd thing was that they had yet to discuss Maddie's

angry scene when she'd dumped into Hank's arms her revelation about his grandfather's intent with his will, as well as the man's ashes, his belongings, and even his dog. Not that she wanted to bring up such an embarrassing example of her temper's excesses. And not that she hadn't been wrong about what James had hoped might happen here. She wasn't. But good manners dictated that she should at least apologize for the way she'd told Hank and how she'd treated him that day.

That darned James and his damned will. It was funny that, after all the hoopla, what the will had boiled down to was one simple statement: Hank had to do his time, she had to verify it, and then they both got their lives back and she got a lot of money. Okay, she was underplaying it here because there remained the not-so-simple part. The one where James had set them up to hopefully fall in love. Maddie quirked her mouth in defeat because that didn't seem to be happening.

And there was no sense in going down that road. What had James been thinking, that sweet, silly old man? Didn't he know he couldn't orchestrate love? It just had to happen. You either felt it or you didn't. Okay, sure, you had to meet first. And yes, she and Hank probably would never have met without James's outrageous will. This line of reasoning had Maddie frowning. *Wait a minute. So all James did, really, was introduce us, right? He played matchmaker. And the rest is up to us.*

Hank cleared his throat discreetly, but the sound pulled Maddie out of her enlightening reverie. To her surprise, he was no longer in front of the refrigerator but had sat down again at the table and had an open soda in front of him. "You were really out of it there for a minute, Maddie. Where'd you go?"

"I took that trip to Florida," she quipped, seeing Hank with new eyes. And the two of them in a new light. As an intimate possibility and not a legal liability.

"You went there without me? Damn." He sipped from the aluminum can. "So. Has the mail come yet?"

Perfect. Something to do instead of standing here and staring at him. Maddie headed across the kitchen. "I don't know. I can go look."

Hank held up a staying hand. "No. It's okay. I just like to hear Mr. Canardy whine and gossip. Hey, did you know that a Mrs. Svensen is down in something he called her weak spot? What is that, anyway?"

Suddenly, with talk of her friends and neighbors, they were back on an even keel. Maddie relaxed, chuckling at Hank's frown of confusion. "Oh, God, her weak spot. Nobody really knows what it is. Or wants to. But you're beginning to sound dangerously like a Hanscomber, do you know that?" *And do you like that, Hank? Could you be happy here with us? I promise we just look crazy on the outside, but we're good and real on the inside.*

Hank was shaking his head. "I've suspected it. This place is addictive, Maddie, as it turns out."

He likes it here. Maddie instantly brightened and felt silly for simply standing in the middle of her kitchen in her jeans and a sweatshirt. She crossed her arms, as if that solved everything. "I thought you'd hate it here."

"So did I. But I don't." The way his gaze traveled up and down her, shivering her, told her she had a lot to do with his liking this town. Nothing could have thrilled her more.

"I'm glad," Maddie told him. "Because I really thought it'd be harder on you to slow down than it seems to have been so far."

"Again, so did I. But this place is so damned interesting. Or maybe it's the people. No wonder my grandfather fit right in. Everyone here is nuts. Or quirky. In a good way. Like characters in a book."

"Thanks."

"I said in a good way. But I don't really mean you." His expression sobered. "Maddie, you're the most *real* person I've ever met. I mean that. Hell, you've met my mother and you knew my grandfather." Hank shook his head. "It was always something with them. I think now that it wasn't that I didn't want to relax and take life easy. It was more that I didn't dare. How could I? I had family acting up all the time. And I had the company and the tremendous responsibility it is. Which I love, don't get me wrong. And I want it back. I can handle that. It was the personal stuff that killed me. I never had time for myself to find out who I was or what I liked or who liked me—"

Hank stopped and stared at her. "Will you listen at me going on? I don't do this, open up like this." He held up the can of soda for her inspection. "What the hell is in this stuff?"

This was the conversation Maddie wanted to have—the one where she got to know him. She took the few steps necessary to put her at the chair opposite his and pulled it out, sitting down. "I put truth serum in it."

He chuckled. "You know, I about half believe you."

"Smart man. But really, Hank, go on. I want to hear what you have to say. What you think. I really do."

He pulled back a bit and set the can down, appearing reluctant to meet her gaze. "Why is that?"

Maddie considered his posture, his expression, everything he'd just said. A sudden insight struck her. "Hank, you poor thing. You never knew who you could trust, did you? Who you could count on? My God." Maddie sat back in her chair, recalling her warm and loving family. "How frightening for you. But that's really what it comes down to, isn't it?"

Suddenly Hank seemed vulnerable, young. Hurting. It was fleeting. He shrugged it off. "It wasn't all that bad. I did okay."

Maddie wanted to hold him in her arms and comfort him, but she suspected he wouldn't appreciate such a mothering impulse from her. "I think you did better than okay. Like you said, I know your mother and I knew James. For all their being really out there, they love you. I can see that. Your mother talks about you constantly. James did, too."

Hank chuckled, looking shy. "Great. Between the two

of them, I suppose by now you've heard all the things I wouldn't ever tell on myself."

She had, but she thought she'd let him preserve some of his dignity. Some. Not all. Grinning, Maddie leaned forward over the table. "I know your mother's pet name for you is Hanky-Wanky."

With his face bright red and Maddie laughing gleefully, Hank surged to his feet, looking around the kitchen. "Where are the sharp knives? Can I borrow one, please?" He unbuttoned his sleeves and began rolling them up. "I am now morally obligated to end my life."

"Sit down." Maddie waved him back to his chair. "I won't tell anyone." He assessed her expression for sincerity. She grinned brightly. But he sat anyway, sipping the soda and staring at her over the can's rim. "I am loving this, Hank. Our talking. We haven't done this before, just sit and get to know each other. And that's the thing. I mean, I don't *know* you. You know what I mean?"

He shook his head as if she'd said something mind-boggling. "No. What was the question again?"

"There wasn't one." Suddenly feeling the moment was here, and it was a pivotal one, Maddie looked down, fiddling with the same magazine that Hank had been thumbing through a little bit ago.

"Maddie?"

She met his gaze, entranced by the gleaming lights in his black, black eyes. She couldn't even see his pupils. "I think I owe you an apology."

"You do? For what?"

"For that day I dumped all that stuff on you. I mean about your grandfather. And all his stuff. And Beamer. God, poor Beamer. I'm just sorry, Hank."

"Maddie, you don't have to do this—"

"But I do. I think that day, my reaction and my behavior, well, they're here in the room with us. Between us. Holding us back. At least I feel they are. And I'm sorry. I was just overwhelmed that day. And hurt and embarrassed by what Celeste had told me. I couldn't even begin to imagine what you must think. Well, I knew what you thought. That I was an opportunist preying on an old man, yada, yada. So does your mother. Or she did. I don't know if she still does. She did defend me in a food fight. But then to find out that everyone was right and James did want me and you to . . ." Maddie hesitated. She couldn't say "fall in love." So she said, "You know. Well, I just lost it. But maybe not for the reason you might think."

There. She'd said it. Or had talked all around it. Maddie took a deep breath, held it, and then exhaled slowly. "Say something, Hank. You're completely unnerving me."

Hank rested an elbow on the table, cupped his chin in his hand, and stared into her eyes. "I think I would love to have happen what my grandfather wanted to have happen, Maddie, if you would."

Okay, there. Now he'd *really* said it. Taut seconds passed while Maddie gazed into his eyes. Longing seized her. She tucked a lock of hair behind her ear. "You would? I mean you do? You want that?" She sat back, actually feeling how wide her eyes were at this moment. "Wow." Then she recalled that day in the cabin. His whole six-week-hot-and-heavy thing. Her eyes narrowed. "Want *what* exactly to happen, Hank?"

He shrugged and gestured broadly. Maddie was captivated. Her heartstrings fairly vibrated with their own symphony of desire. Could the man be more sexy? A woman didn't stand a chance. His close-fitting jeans that hugged his muscled thighs. The chambray shirt that highlighted his broad shoulders. That tantalizing peek of his T-shirt underneath. Helplessly, she stared, feeling like a child gazing longingly into a toy store's display window and sighing over coveted treasures she could never possess—

"I guess I don't know," Hank said, popping Maddie's sensual bubble. "I mean here we are. Together. Alone. With about three weeks of time to kill."

Maddie felt cold and wanted to cry. She was like the smitten heroine in a historical romance novel who'd just found out that because of class differences she was only good enough to be the mistress but not the wife. It hurt. Her chin came up. "I'm not that kind of girl, Hank."

He frowned. "What kind of girl? What are you talking about?"

Just as Maddie gathered her courage and opened her mouth to tell him what she thought and how he hurt her with his let's-have-an-affair-but-nothing-more line, the phone rang, startling her into jumping up. Its harsh, loud tone fairly squealed "Emergency!"

Hank glanced over at Maddie when she turned in her passenger's seat to address his mother and Celeste sitting behind them in his Navigator. "Thank *God* no one was hurt."

Hank adjusted his rearview mirror so he could a little more discreetly see the backseat occupants. There was Celeste, a sour look on her face. She folded her hands together reverently and directed her gaze upward. "Thank you, God. Although I would have been a lot happier if You hadn't let it happen in the first place."

Hank heard his mother snicker and saw her actually poke Celeste in the ribs with her elbow. It was like she was a little kid. He didn't know what to think of this side of her. All his life she'd been this dressed-up L.A. lady who divided her time between the country club and the shops on Rodeo Drive. All her life she'd worried about appearances and being part of the "in crowd," and what people thought of her. Uptight. Sometimes superficial. Bitchy. And now look at her . . . happy, sweet, cheerful, dressing down. Working in a gift shop. Getting in food fights at churches. Talking about cows peeing on flat rocks.

Hank shook his head. There was definitely something in the water.

But apparently today Maddie hadn't yet had her ration of happy juice. Because, stern of expression like a scolding mother, she shook a finger at Celeste. "Being irreverent is no way to show your gratitude for a good outcome."

"Well, excuse me, Pope Lavinia Junior. Just look at my hair. Stuck flat to my head. You're not the one who just paid big money to have your do done, only to have it ruined by a thunderstorm that made all the roads slippery, now are you?"

"No, but neither would your car have ended up in a ditch with the possibility of both of you being injured, or worse, if you had stayed home today and not gone to the beauty shop."

Hank knew what this was. Blasphemy. A moment of silence . . . stunned, accusatory . . . followed. Hank hunched his shoulders as if expecting a blow. No way in hell was he saying anything. He just held on to the steering wheel with both hands and kept the heat and the windshield wipers going. Parked at the side of the road, he valiantly watched the emergency personnel—a tow-truck driver and two policemen—performing their thankless jobs.

"I cannot believe you said that, Madelyn Louise Copeland." Celeste's tone was injured. "Here I am a poor old woman, all beat up and bruised, and you're going to deny me my one pleasure in life."

She was neither beat up nor bruised. Would Maddie fall for that? Hank glanced over at her sweet blond loveliness. She'd fallen for it. Her expression stricken, she reached in the back and took hold of Celeste's hand. "Oh, I'm so sorry, honey. I don't know what I was thinking. You're absolutely right, of course. Beauty-shop appointments are sacred obligations, not to be missed, not even for snow or rain or dark of night."

That was when Hank made his mistake. "I thought that was the postal service creed."

Maddie and Celeste and his own mother looked at him with who-asked-you expressions on their faces. From the back of the Navigator, Beamer chimed in with a woof that clearly said whose side she was on.

"Right." Hank decided he stood a better chance outside in the driving rain. "I'll just go see how long they're going to be."

"Good idea," Celeste said. "Tell that silly goose Chief Brickman that he can reach us at the Lobster Shack."

Sucked right in, Hank repeated, "The Lobster Shack?"

"Yep. Fanny Nordstrom—she's my beautician—told me it's going to be open tonight. Storm or no, people have to eat. So that's where you're taking me and Maddie and your mother for supper."

Over everyone's exuberant jubilation, Hank said, "I am?"

Celeste looked at Lillian Madison. "Is your boy simple? Or did I not speak English to him?"

Lillian, of the delicate Irish features and also ruined hairdo, nodded. "I believe you did."

Everyone looked at him again. "So, the Lobster Shack it is." Then he thought of something else. "What about Beamer? Do we need to take her home first?"

"No. She can go. They know her there. James used to take her there."

"Now, that sounds just like that old coot." That was his mother.

And that was Hank's cue. He opened the door and got blasted with wind-driven rain. Wearing a heavy fisherman's slicker, he quickly stepped out and closed the car door behind him. The very atmosphere was a shock to the system, much like Mrs. Svensen's earlier phone call to tell them that Celeste had ditched her car in front of her house. Hank shivered as a determined wind whipped the rain against him. The drops pinged and stung like needles. He felt as if he'd been tossed into a huge blender filled with frozen-margarita ingredients and the setting was "puree." Worse, the sky—the color of slate and resembling a slab of granite—hung low and thick about him. No amount of bulky or waterproof clothing stood a chance of keeping him dry and warm for long.

The scene before Hank as he made his slip-sliding way across the street was one of flashing lights, emergency vehicles, and bundled men scurrying adeptly about. A day not fit for man or beast. Yet, here were representatives of both species. A scowling tow-truck driver, whose black dog sat serenely in the warmth of the truck's cab while the man—

an order of beings allegedly more intelligent—worked in the rain. Two police officers—the entire force, as Hank understood it—also worked the scene. One directed traffic that consisted of an occasional car creeping by with a curious driver. The other officer had his hands full with crowd control, the crowd consisting of a handful of hardy residents of Passaquat Drive who'd braved the elements to see the car in the ditch in front of the Svensen house.

Hank hurried up to the policeman in charge of traffic flow, of which there was none at the moment. So, essentially, the armed man was standing in the middle of the slippery street and doing nothing. Hank got his attention and had to yell over the wind. "Excuse me? Is it okay if I take Mrs. McNeer and my mother away now?"

The barrel-shaped man with a bulbous nose gave Hank the once-over. "Well, I don't know. That would depend on who you are."

It was hard to talk with the driving rain and wind in his face. Hank turned his back to it and tried again. "Hank Madison."

"Oh, pleased to meet you. I'm Chief Brickman." Again Hank underwent the man's scrutiny, only this time it was a friendly one. "So you're James's grandson, then? I've heard a lot about you."

No doubt. "Yes. That's me. Look, if you're through here with them, I'd like to get them someplace dry and warm. They've suggested the Lobster Shack."

Wearing a fur-lined green nylon cap with the earflaps down but not fastened, the bundled-up chief of police rubbed at his cold-reddened nose. "So the Lobster Shack is going to be open tonight? I wondered."

This was quite the conversation to be having at an accident scene and—again—in the wind and the rain. "Well, that's according to . . . someone at Mrs. McNeer's beauty shop."

"That'd be Fanny Nordstrom. She always does Mrs. McNeer's hair. Fanny's a big girl, mind you. Nice. Got two kids. Husband's a lobsterman. Good to her and the kids . . . but kinda strange-looking."

Hank nodded, happy in the bad weather just to assume that the policeman meant Fanny's husband was actually a man who made his living lobstering . . . and was not actually a lobster-slash-man. "Good. Well, anyway, that's where we'll be if you have questions or need Mrs. McNeer or my mother."

"Okay. Maybe I'll see you there. The missus likes lobster well enough."

Hank could only nod to that as he endeavored to put an end to this bit of business before the wind swept him away. "Where will Mrs. McNeer's car be?"

"Be?"

Hank's heart sank. They'd hit a snag. "Yes. When you tow it away, where will it *be*?" Freezing his ass off, and getting wetter by the second, despite his heavy rain gear, Hank hopped from one foot to the other.

"Be, huh?" The policeman regarded Hank a moment, then twisted his body to peer at the tow truck. He shifted back to stare rather blankly at Hank. "It'll *be* at the end of the tow hook, I suppose."

All right, it was too cold and wet to do this. Surely there was only one garage in a town this size. "Of course," Hank said affably, remembering that he was an outsider and this man was armed and probably thought him as dense as Hank thought he, the officer, was. "Well, see you later. Thanks."

Chief Brickman waved a big, gloved hand at him. "You're welcome there, young fella. By the way, it's nice to have you in Hanscomb Harbor and seeing our Maddie. She's a good girl, and we all love her. Had her share of hurt, though. We want to see her happy. So you be good to her, or you'll answer to us all."

That stopped Hank. Celeste had pretty much given him the same speech and warning when she'd called him the other day to give her and his mother a ride to Maddie's. Hank met the chief's eyes, a light brown replete with sincerity and friendliness. *Well, I'll be damned.* He had the town's seal of approval to court Maddie. An old-fashioned term, but one that fit this place and its people. Suddenly filled with warmth and a sense of well-being, Hank gave the officer an informal salute. "Will do, Chief."

To Hank, the restaurant appeared to be under siege, surrounded as it was by weather-ravaged but serviceable cars, trucks, and SUVs, all haphazardly spaced. The vehicles appeared more abandoned than parked in the dark and rainy lot. And the Lobster Shack itself turned out to be just that— a shack where they served lobster. Wood-constructed, the squat building didn't look like much from the outside. It sat at the end of Harpoon Avenue where it intersected with Queen Street on the way to the beach. But going inside was like going home. Warm air redolent with home cooking and buzzing conversation, punctuated by laughter, assaulted Hank's ears. Bustling waitresses carrying heavy trays cheerily greeted each newcomer and directed them to the few empty round tables covered with red-checkered tablecloths.

But Hank's party was apparently special. When they walked in the door, they got a hero's welcome. Everyone stopped, stared, and then clapped and cheered, calling out their relief that no one was hurt in the accident. Obviously local news traveled fast here. His mother and Celeste took all the attention as their due. But they'd no more than gotten inside the door before Beamer proved her favorite-customer status. Everyone cheerily petted her as she politely ambled by, followng a waitress named Sandy over to an alcoved area away from the human diners. A plastic bib with a big red smiling lobster adorning it—much like the ceramic one which held his grandfather's ashes—was put around her neck and she was served the same lobster (shelled for her), new potatoes, and coleslaw that everyone else got.

As luck or design would have it, the table at which they were seated commanded the middle of the large dining room. Talk about living—or dining—in a fishbowl. People at the surrounding tables had no compunction, either, about turning around to speak and to comment on what was good tonight on the menu. As it turned out, the lobster was. So that was what they ordered and, also wearing bibs, ate and ate until they were stuffed. Hank couldn't remember when he'd had a better time, better food, or better company. Especially Maddie's. It might be raining and miserable outside, but inside here, with her at his side, it was warm and wonderful.

She was quite something. And he wanted her. In all ways, he suspected. In his life, his bed, his heart. Could that be true? Had his grandfather known exactly what he was doing and that Maddie would be the one for him? He couldn't have. He just couldn't have. And yet . . . seeing her here tonight with the townspeople who were her friends only made him want her more. He wanted this feeling more, too . . . this acceptance and camaraderie. He'd never had that before, not as an adult, not after he'd become someone to be sucked up to and maybe feared, someone who never knew if people liked him for himself or his power and his money.

He thought about his life in New York City. He thought of the penthouses, the private jet, the parties, the women, the job, the responsibilities, all the meetings, the worries, the hundreds of people who depended on him. The sheer isolation. That was the oddest part. He had everything, yet he had nothing. Not what really counted. The connection. The caring. The trust. The friendships. Those things he found here. Not in New York City. His real life. He'd only been gone from it for a few weeks.

But would he ever be happy in that world again? Had he ever been? He then called to mind the first time he'd come to Hanscomb Harbor. He'd told Jim he hated it and couldn't imagine ever spending any time here. Jim had told him never say never. Hank remembered dismissing that, but now he admitted that Jim had been right. Because here he was, and he loved it.

These people simply didn't care about his net worth,

only his worth as a person. Was it this spirit of kindness that had brought his grandfather here over and over? Surely it was. And surely it had been the sweet woman now at Hank's side who'd kept his grandfather coming back here. Because, God knows, she certainly kept him coming back, even after telling him to go away. Well, he'd tried that, and he hadn't liked it, not one bit. Being away from Maddie was like being away from the sun.

Hank settled his gaze on her, content to watch her sitting sideways in her chair, her back to him, and chatting with some high school friend of hers she'd introduced to him, only he'd already forgotten the woman's name. Then, as if it were the most natural thing in the world for him to do, he draped his arm across the back of Maddie's chair. He knew she had to feel the weight of his arm across her back. Across the table from him, Celeste winked at him and his mother raised her eyebrows speculatively, her gaze darting from Hank to Maddie and back to him.

But he had eyes only for Maddie as she pivoted in her chair until she could see him. She met his gaze, her blue eyes questioning his intent, revealing a struggle of emotions flickering there. Hank smiled, said nothing, but his heartbeat seemed to stop, to hang in the balance. Would she disapprove of his intimate gesture? Ask him to remove his arm? Her expression softened but into a frown of uncertainty. Following it instantly was a smile of what he wanted to believe was approval. Hank's heart soared as she then casually resumed her conversation with the other woman.

How was it possible to be this happy? Hank wanted to jump up and shout his joy, just punch the air with his fist and yell, *"Yeah!"* He could only conclude that either the close and steamy air in the Lobster Shack was inducing euphoria, or again it was the water. Or could it simply be that this feeling of possessiveness of and connection to Maddie was real? He didn't know. But he did know he was satisfied on a soul-deep level in ways he never had been before. And he wanted to do whatever it took to keep this feeling. It was like he'd met her . . . and come home.

He told himself he must have done something right in his life to be here at this moment and with her. This observation put him in mind of someone he loved and missed, someone who, as it might turn out, had done something good in his last moments of life to make this moment possible. Warmed with a rush of emotion, Hank smiled secretively and arrowed a message upward. *Thank you, Grandpa. Just . . . thank you.*

A few of the local men came over to the table, their arrival putting Hank back in the moment. Introductions were made all around and the men pulled up chairs close to Hank and began talking fishing and football with him. As if they did it every day. Hank couldn't believe how this made him feel. Pleased. Very pleased. And relaxed. A part of something bigger than himself. A community. He now realized that men in New York and around the world he'd thought of as friends were actually business acquaintances, people who courted him because they wanted something from him. Hell yes, he'd done the same thing with other industry leaders. But these men of Hanscomb Harbor wanted nothing beyond simple male camaraderie. It was great. Satisfying somehow to belong like this.

A sense of well-being washed over Hank. His acceptance here, he knew, had to do with Maddie. She was a hometown sweetheart, and he was associated with her. Hank liked that. He liked it a lot. And kept his arm possessively around her shoulders. He couldn't seem to keep his gaze from lighting occasionally on the back of her blond head, either. Or his hand from fondling a long, soft lock of her hair.

Man, this was heaven. But could he make it last? He didn't know. Because he and Maddie had yet to discuss what she'd meant earlier when she'd looked hurt and had said she wasn't "that kind of girl." What kind of girl did she mean?

CHAPTER SEVENTEEN

❦

AT FIRST MADDIE DIDN'T know what had awakened her. She lay in a curled-up ball under the covers. Her first thought was it had to have been the storm. She listened but heard nothing . . . and quirked her lips in relief. The storm had evidently blown over. That was good. So what time was it? She rolled over in bed until she could see her bedside clock. The glowing digital numbers told their own story. Three forty-three A.M. Maddie groaned. What *was* this sleeplessness of late? Why couldn't she rest, get a good night's sleep?

Her libido answered for her: because Hank is just across the hall in his bed. Smiling secretively, Maddie gathered a pillow to her chest and allowed herself to picture that . . . Hank in bed, that gorgeously muscled body all stretched out and relaxed . . . she sighed. And wondered if Hank was sleeping. In the nude. Maddie blinked and shook her head. *Stop that. No wonder you can't sleep.*

She forced herself to be serious. Hank. What was she going to do about him, Mr. We Have Three Weeks of Time to Kill?

Maddie lay still, staring at nothing, yet seeing the night-gray shadows of her familiar furnishings. *He wants to have an affair with me. That's it. Then back to the city he goes. And me? I stay here.* So what would be so awful about that? What if she did have an affair with him? Maddie thought about that. What would she have left when he left? A ton of money and total devastation of her heart. She made a face that said even pursuing this line of thinking was lowering her self-worth in her own eyes. She simply couldn't do as Hank seemed to want. Because she wasn't the free-and-easy, sassy kind of hip modern woman who wore short skirts and strappy sandals and moved confidently from one affair to the next with her heart unaffected.

No, it was her lot in life, no matter what Hank Madison thought of her, to be the marrying kind. A throwback to another era. An anachronism. *Great.* Maddie snorted, very unladylike. *Marry who? No one's knocking on my door begging me to marry him. And I only got jerk-doctor Stanton as far as the altar before he bolted, the pathetic loser. Which pretty much made me one, too.*

That hurt. *What is wrong with me? Why am I like this? I want to be happy. I do. It's just that darned "no happy endings" rule that seems to control my life. Everyone I love dies or leaves me. No wonder I'm afraid to get close to anyone. No wonder I—*

Maddie sat straight up in bed, staring blindly into the shadowed darkness that contrasted with her moment of enlightenment. "Ohmigod," she whispered, clutching at her covers as sudden insight washed over her. "It's not *life* that won't give me happy endings. It's *me* who won't take another chance on them. It's *me* who won't let anyone get close enough to even try—because I'm afraid of losing them. God. What an emotionally stunted little coward I am. No I'm not. I've had some real losses. It's no wonder that I'd be gun-shy. Who wouldn't be? But still . . . I had no idea. I'm a coward."

This was such a revelation. Had there ever been, she wondered, someone more afraid than her to risk her heart? Someone more afraid than her to act on faith and step out over the Abyss of Love? God, what a clam she'd been all these years, just hiding here in the wet sand of a lonely shore when her problem was *so* fixable. All she had to do was tell Hank how she felt about him and tell him she deserved more than an affair.

Her heart thumped heavily, hopefully. That was it. Take her chances. Risk her heart. Only then would she be truly alive. No. She couldn't do that. Wait. Yes she could. Her thoughts collided with each other in their rush to be heard. That was true courage, they shouted—the willingness to take the chance. *But what if it doesn't work out?* It doesn't matter. It's the willingness to risk being vulnerable and getting hurt that counts. It says you're alive. *The willingness to act even though it may not work out? Oh, I don't know if I can do that.* Coward. Maddie slumped with the weight of her troubling epiphany. Then she gathered courage to her as she had the pillow. *Okay, what I have to do, then, is let go of old fears and embrace new opportunities, no matter their outcome.*

It wasn't as if she hadn't known all this before. It was more like she'd anesthetized her senses to the truth of it. Like she'd squelched thoughts of love and happiness, had convinced herself she wasn't supposed to have them, instead of admitting to herself that she longed for them yet feared she may never have them. So sad. How bitter she could have become. But then, Hank had come into her life, thanks to James. *Sweet James.* He'd given her so much. She meant his friendship and then this chance at happiness with his grandson. What a great gift, more so than any amount of money could ever be.

Maddie concentrated now on thoughts of Hank. She wanted him. And he wanted her. What she didn't know was if she needed him. She believed she did. Need and want were two different things, she knew that. And need trumped want in the love department. Need. Did she have it for Hank? That bone-deep, aching, longing, hot, powerful, driving *need* to be with him? "Ohmigod, come on," Maddie railed out loud. "Won't somebody answer me? Hello, up there? Have want and need come together for me in the person of Hank Madison?"

Just then, the hallway was flooded with a white and blinding light. Stunned into jerking upright, her heart pounding, Maddie couldn't move her limbs. She blinked and sucked in a disbelieving breath, absolute fear and certainty assailing her. Was this a for-real heavenly revelation? Would there be celestial music? The fluttering of angelic wings? A deep and booming voice?

The quick answer to that was . . . the deep voice of a very earthly presence who had obviously flipped the hall light on and was now standing in her bedroom doorway, flanked by a yawning golden retriever. "Maddie? Did I hear you call me? I would swear I heard you say my name. Are you all right?"

The obvious answer was "Yes." And the obvious behavior was an apology that got him to go away because of how mortified she was that he'd heard her talking out loud to herself—and about him. But none of that came out. "No, I'm not all right, Hank," she said, sitting with her legs spread, but under her covers, and flopping her hands down in front of her. Even to her own ears she sounded pouty and put out with him, mainly because she was.

"You're not okay? Then what's wrong? Are you sick?"

"No." With the light behind him and her room still in the dark, Maddie had no idea how much of her he could see. She brushed her sleep-mussed hair back from her face and tugged at her nightgown's neck.

"You're not all right and you're not sick." Following his recap, Hank leaned a shoulder against the doorjamb and crossed his arms over his chest. His bare chest, Maddie suddenly noticed. His bare muscular chest with the fine line of dark hair that met and proceeded down his flat belly, only to disappear under the band of his boxer shorts. Which were the only article of clothing the man had on.

"What are you, then?" he asked her, drawing her attention to his face, which was totally in shadows.

"Wide awake now and over it."

"Me, too. Wide awake. But over what?"

Apparently seeing where this was going, or that it was going nowhere, Beamer turned around and wandered off in the direction of the kitchen.

Maddie shrugged. "Over everything."

"Such as?"

Maddie exhaled, reaching down deep inside herself for the courage to take the plunge. At the end of this conversation, she and Hank would either be trying to have something together. Or they'd be done with each other. It was so very scary. She couldn't even have said for sure if her heart was actually beating, or if it was waiting for a sign that said it would have a reason to go on beating. "You, Hank," Maddie heard herself say. "I'm over you."

"Me?"

"Yes. You. And you did hear me say your name. But I wasn't calling you or talking in my sleep like you probably thought. I said your name because I'm mad at you."

"At me? What did I do?" He pulled away from the doorjamb and pointed behind him. "I was across the hall in bed—"

"You don't think I'm the marrying kind." Maddie felt hot and sick all over. There. She'd said it.

And it had stopped him. Hank planted his hands at his trim waist. "I don't—You're not what?"

"The marrying kind. But I am." Maddie still couldn't believe she was actually speaking her mind for once. Or was it her heart? "Instead, you think I'm the mistress kind. Well, I'm not."

"I have no idea where this is coming from, Maddie. Like yesterday, there in your kitchen right before the phone rang. You said you're not 'that kind of girl.' Is this more of that?"

"Yes. And let me remind you, I'll soon be in the same class as you, you know."

"The same class? Maddie, what the hell are you talking about?"

"The money. The will. I just can't do it, Hank."

"Do what?"

How could he not know what she meant? "Have an affair with you, what else? God, Hank, pay attention. I just can't do that. It's not me."

"Well, that's fine because I don't remember asking you to have an affair with me, Maddie." He chuckled, but it wasn't from anything being funny. "Did you maybe dream that?"

"No. And you did too say it. How about all that 'we have six weeks together' stuff? Huh? And then the 'three weeks to kill'? What was that if not an invitation to an affair? It's like 'be with me now because tomorrow I leave for the war.' Well, our mothers and grandmothers may have fallen for that, but not this generation."

Hank stared at her as if he'd never seen her before. "Are you sure you're awake? That you aren't talking in your sleep right now? Because none of this is making sense."

With a sigh of disgust, Maddie made a dramatic show of pinching herself and then waiting. Nothing happened. She shrugged. "Apparently I'm awake. But *you're* the one who's dreaming if you think you can have a wham-bam-thank-you-ma'am kind of relationship with me, Hank Madison."

"Jesus, Maddie, I never said that was what I wanted. You misunderstood me when I said we had six weeks, then three. I meant we should use the time to get to know each other. To see if there was anything there we could build on. I never meant an affair or a one-night stand. How long have you been stewing over this?"

Her answer was simple. "Since you said it, obviously."

He didn't actually move, but Maddie detected a subtle shift in his weight, a tensing of his posture. "I don't believe this. You waited this long to say something? Hell, Maddie, all you had to do was ask me what I meant."

"Yeah, right. Like that's easy to just pop into a casual conversation with someone you barely know. What was I supposed to say? 'So, Hank, I hardly know you but I think I'm attracted to you, and you are to me, and since you as much as said you think I'm easy and want to have an affair with me to ease your six-week burden of having to be here and not work yourself into an early grave so you can get all your money back and go right back to working too hard. Well, okay, sure, here I am, your willing vessel, your good-time party girl, let's do it.' " Maddie crossed her arms. "I don't think so."

"Are you kidding me? Is that how I came across to you?"

He was so startled and angry that Maddie realized she'd probably really read him wrong. Struck shy with guilt, she lowered her gaze and suddenly found her hands to be of great interest to her. Sitting there in the semidark, with it being not yet four o'clock in the morning, she picked at her fingernails and shrugged. "Maybe."

"Maybe, hell." His chuckle this time *was* warm and *did* have to do with funny. Maddie's heart thumped hopefully. "I cannot believe this. I mean, Maddie, all of this. Me and you." She raised her head, daring a sidelong glance at him standing there in the doorway. "Yeah. Everything. Together. Us. Me and you."

"Really?"

"Christ, I have no credibility here. How did this happen?" He scratched at his temple, looked around him as if he'd lost something, then faced her again. "You know what, Maddie? I think right now you're pretty vulnerable. I think it's the middle of the night and here we are, two healthy adults who are very attracted to each other."

"So far, so good. But . . . ?"

Sure enough, "*But* I don't want to take advantage of you—"

"What if I want to take advantage of you?" Maddie caught her breath. And heard Hank do the same. She clapped a hand over her mouth. Had she really said that out loud? She flashed a mental image of short skirts and strappy sandals. Sassy. Confident. Take what you want. What you need. Yeah, baby. She threw her covers back.

Hank drew back, pointing at her. "Stop that. Cover yourself."

Maddie ignored his orders as she slowly, sensually slid over to the side of her bed, allowing her gown to ride up her thighs, all the way to her hips. She knew she had good legs . . . and now was the time to use them.

"I mean it," Hank said. "I'm warning you, Maddie Copeland. Don't start something you can't finish."

Maddie stood up beside her bed. Her nightgown's silky material flowed around her like water, the hem swishing to its proper place at her ankles. "What makes you think I can't finish it, Hank?"

A modest, conservative tiny corner of Maddie's brain

held its ears and shrieked. Where had this vampy seductress voice come from? But the rest of her brain, the part connected to her heart said . . . you go, girl.

"Maddie, what are you doing?" Hank demanded, still standing in the doorway and clearly agitated.

She walked toward him. "Right now I'm walking toward you."

"I know that. I can see that." The man looked behind him. For reinforcements? To see if he had a clear path of retreat?

"What's the matter, Hank?" She stopped right in front of him and smoothed her hands up his chest. He felt just the way she knew he would . . . warm, solid, his skin's scent so clean yet musky. Intoxicating. "Don't you want me?"

"Jesus." Hank grabbed her arms and held her out, away from him. He leaned down until his face was even with hers and then peered deeply into her eyes. "Are you sure you're awake? I've never seen you act like this. This isn't like you."

Instantly angry, Maddie snapped out of vamp mode and actually stomped her foot. "Dammit, Hank. I'm awake and I know what I'm doing. Being *me*, acting like myself, has gotten me nowhere. *This* is what I want." She pointed to him and then to herself as best she could with him still holding her arms. "I want you, Hank." She stared up into his dark eyes. "Do you understand? I've been taking the high road and trying to be good and do the right thing. And what has it gotten me? Nothing. Nada. Zip. Nil. The big zero. Well, I'm not satisfied with that anymore. I want you, and I want you now."

Hank chuckled. It sounded warm and encouraging. He gently shook her, no more than waggling her shoulders. "What am I going to do with you?"

"Exactly what I hope you're going to do with me. And me with you. That 'us' thing you talked about. I'm acting on it."

Hank let go of her as if she were hot. "I was wrong,

Maddie. This cannot happen." He turned away from her and rubbed at his forehead. His other hand gripped his waist. Then he looked up toward the hallway's ceiling and the light . . . and shook his head. "I can't do this."

His words shattered Maddie. Her heart broke, falling in pieces to the floor. She thought surely she could hear its tiny tinkling little shards, like bits of fragile blown glass, striking the hardwood floor in notes almost musical. She gulped back a sob. And boy, if she'd thought telling him she wanted him was the hardest speech she'd ever made, then she'd been wrong. Because saying the things she was getting ready to say was pure hell and mortification. "Look, it's okay. Really. I obviously misread the signs. I'm sorry."

She had to swallow the thickening in her throat. Hank chose that moment to turn around and face her, his expression a hard frown. Maddie darned near lost her courage, but plunged onward. "How embarrassed am I. You poor man."

He gestured with his hands out to his sides, palms toward her. "*Now* what the hell are you talking about?"

"You. And how you can't do this. You're not attracted to me. I didn't—"

"What? Not attracted to you?" Now he was mad at her. "Are you kidding me? I'm absolutely crazy mad about you. I'm so all-fired *on fire* for you that it's a wonder that damned bed across the hall hasn't burst into flames."

Maddie's eyebrows rose almost of their own volition.

Hank took off, pacing up and down the lighted hallway like a man possessed. "*Not* want you? Maddie, I've damn near had to bite my tongue off to keep from saying something stupid to you like how much I want you. I thought you'd think, yeah right, buddy, this has to do with your grandfather's will. When nothing could be further from the truth." He'd completed a circuit of the short hall and begun another one.

"That's what I meant when I said I can't do this. When it happens, it has to be pure. Nothing to do with the will. When all that's over, Maddie. Only then. Because then it would be as equals. A 'want to' thing only. Nothing that can be taken wrong or seem suspect. Do you understand? Like I'm seducing you to insure I get back my inheritance. I couldn't risk that. Not with you. You're different. You are the marrying kind. Who doesn't know that? So feeling that way, but with you so close, I damn near had to tie my hands behind my back, if I could accomplish such a thing, to keep from grabbing you to me and kissing the hell out of you. And at night? Oh, let's don't even go there. Knowing you're right across the hall and I can't even come into this room? All I can do is lie there and picture you in that thin gown—which, by the way, you look great in—and your body underneath it and, damn, just torture the living hell out of myself and feel so hot that I'm in a cold sweat and have to grip the goddamned sheets and just hold on." He began a third circuit.

Maddie wasn't sure she'd even blinked yet. All she could do was marvel at the wonderful things he was saying and drink in the heart-stopping sight he made pacing, half-naked, up and down her hallway at four in the morning.

"And the cold showers? Damn. I think I could live naked on an ice floe, I'm so used to the cold now. I don't think I'd even feel it. And why do you think I've been working so hard on that cottage out at the beach? I'll tell you why. Sexual tension. It builds entire cities. I believe it because of the way I feel about you, and the frustration of not being able to do anything about it. Ho-ho, I could carve—by myself, with one hand tied behind my back, and using a toothpick—an entire village out of the side of a Swiss alp. And you know those Anasazi ruins? The ones in the side of that cliff out in Arizona? Ha. They're no mystery. That was some poor guy who couldn't have the woman he wanted. Hell, he had to do something."

It was at the beginning of his fourth lap that Maddie stopped Hank with a hand on his arm and said, "Hank? I want to go to bed with you."

He was still wild-eyed and revved up. He blinked, shook his head. "What?"

Maddie chuckled. Could he be more adorable, more handsome and sexy in his blue boxers, standing right here in her silly little hallway with the almost threadbare runner and literally declaring himself to her? Maddie felt so powerful—and turned on. "I said, Hank, that I want to go to bed with you."

He frowned, looking as if he were trying to understand a foreign language he couldn't quite grasp. "You do?"

"Yes. I do. I'm saying yes, Hank. To you. Right now. To us." She pointed to her rumpled bed and added, "In there. Now. Me and you."

Hank turned around to stare into her bedroom . . . he took a long time to do it, too. Maddie used the time to note the athletic musculature of his neck and fine, large bones of his shoulder. Hank suddenly faced her again. "Okay," he said.

Maddie smiled, holding her arms out to him, stepping into his embrace. "Okay. Good."

Hank couldn't get her to bed quick enough. Breaking their embrace, he picked her up—her weight was next to nothing—and carried her to her bed, placing her gently atop it. He leaned over her, his fisted hands braced against the mattress and to either side of her. Staring into her incredible blue eyes, not able to get enough of looking at her sweet face, he said, almost conversationally, "Maddie, I have waited for this moment for so long that I'm afraid this isn't going to be pretty."

She chuckled softly. "Good. I don't want it to be. Pretty is for the movies. I want the real thing." Her expression became slanted, seductive. "I want hot, and sweaty and good. Total body contact."

Grinning, his gaze roving down her sultry length and then back up to her movie-star face, Hank assured her, "I can do that."

"Yeah?" Maddie reached up a hand to cup his neck and pull him down to her. "Let's see you, big boy." Then she kissed him hard enough to bruise his lips.

Hank couldn't have been more turned on, more hard, more on fire. Still with his mouth locked to hers, he lowered himself atop her, stretching out his length to cover her with his body. When she broke their kiss, Hank rolled to the other side of her and quickly tugged his boxers down and off his body. Maddie just as energetically shed her nightgown and panties. With no more preamble or finesse than that, Hank rolled toward her and Maddie turned to him, opening her arms to receive him.

"My God, you're beautiful," Hank breathed, almost frozen at the sight of her pink and lovely nakedness. She was perfectly formed. Not a blemish to mar her image.

"So are you, my fine man." She squeezed the muscle of his arm and rolled her eyes in a girlish and silly manner.

"Stop that. You'll embarrass me." Grinning, shaking his head, and still lying beside her, Hank let his hands rove over her soft shoulders and down her ribs, to the curve of her waist and over her hip to her thigh in wonder. She was truly magnificent, everything he had dreamed, everything he had pictured. He met her eyes, finding them languid with desire. Her mouth curved up in a smile of welcoming that caught Hank's breath and had his heart bursting with sudden emotion. He cupped her cheek, running his thumb over the delicate curve of her jaw. Then the sudden urgency of intense desire seized him, making his voice husky. "Maddie, I can't wait. I'm sorry."

"Well, I'm not." She chuckled, a seductive sound from the back of her throat as she shifted her weight in such a way that encouraged him to move up and over her. At the last moment, she hesitated, a hand against his shoulder, stopping him. She lowered her gaze as if suddenly struck shy. "Hank . . . honey," she all but whispered, "I . . . I'm so embarrassed is what I am . . . but I'm, well, ready for you already. This has never happened to me." She now looked into his eyes, her expression of want melting him. "It's you. You're doing this to me. I want you and in ways I've never wanted another man. I swear it."

Hank's breath caught. "God, Maddie, I feel the same

way about you. I can't even imagine wanting another woman like I want you. Keeping my distance has been killing me." With that said, and needing no further urging from her, he peppered her face, her neck, her jaw with nipping kisses. He then quickly obliged her, moving atop her and settling himself in her loving embrace.

Maddie immediately opened herself to him, putting her arms around his neck, pulling him down for a soul-searing kiss of such sweet sensuality that Hank was inside her before he was even conscious of having made the move. But inside her, he was. And nothing had ever felt better. Nothing. She was heaven. Hot, slick, tight, inviting. Moaning with desire, with intense need, Hank had to break their kiss before he passed out.

Gulping in air, hearing her do the same, Hank realized he was already steadily thrusting and thrusting, moving in and out of her with the age-old rhythm of lovers everywhere. Clutching her to him, his every muscle rigid with effort, Hank concentrated solely on satisfying her. Moaning, Maddie raked her hands through his hair and nipped his neck, his shoulder, and his collarbone with biting little kisses . . . and whispered the universal sounds of love, urging him on and on. Now almost mad with desire, Hank kept up his pounding pace, feeling the heat, feeling the tension in her body, feeling her inner muscles clamp around him and claim him. Shattering sensations exploded through Hank.

He knew the exact moment when Maddie reached her climax . . . she stilled, held him in place, tensed, gasped, called out his name—a long, spiraling cry erupted from her. Like a raging bull, Hank intensified his thrusts, quicker and quicker and quicker until he exploded inside her, until his body spent itself atop hers . . . until he could no longer hold himself rigid, until he collapsed atop her, a dead and sated weight. She whimpered, going limp, breathing hard. Hank swallowed, knew he should roll off her, but he didn't think he was able. He truly was not able to move. But his skin slick and his temperature still high, Hank somehow found the strength to dislodge himself from her and to shift himself to her side. He still had an arm across her ribs and a leg thrown over her thighs.

"Damn," was all he said.

"I'll say," Maddie replied, holding his arm to her chest. He could feel her heart racing, knew every breath she took.

Several minutes passed in which Hank felt his pulse slowly returning to normal, felt his nerve endings settling down. A loving lethargy seized him. He could barely think, yet he could hardly not.

Their first coming together had been cataclysmic, earth-shattering. The want, the need, the pent-up frustration, the weeks of holding back . . . it had taken over and the result, he told himself, had not been a pretty picture. Their bodies had collided and an act of pure sex had taken place. A hot and heated one, yes. Satisfying . . . oh, baby, yes, Hank verified for himself. But not pretty. And not like he'd wanted it to be with Maddie. She deserved better. More romantic.

He smiled at her lying there on her back, her perfect, beautiful body naked and sated and glistening. The sheets were everywhere. Hell, it was a damned wonder they weren't shredded and the mattress wasn't in the closet. Hank tugged his arm from Maddie and slid his leg off hers. Turning on his side, he propped his elbow up so he could support his head with his hand and see every creamy inch of her. "Maddie, honey, you're everything I thought you would be. You are so damned beautiful."

"So are you." Smiling, her eyes half-closed, she turned to him, putting her slender arm around his neck and tugging his head down so she could kiss him. Just before his lips met hers, Maddie gripped his face in her hands, her mouth not even an inch from his and whispered, her breath warm on his lips, "I want you, Hank. Again."

"Oh, Maddie." The words were no more than a sigh as he claimed her mouth and his tongue found hers. Lying half across her now, Hank eagerly returned her kiss, one that instantly deepened with hunger and ardor, one that made up for all the lost time and the empty nights. His

arms slipped around her shoulders and waist. He pressed
her to him, feeling the sweet fullness of her breasts pressed
against his chest. Her moan in his mouth as his tongue
danced with hers, as she moved her head to better accom-
modate his mouth, ripped through Hank, hardening him.
He lifted his mouth from hers and looked down at her, at
the slender, pink, delicateness of her, the aching fragility
of her, the sweet blond beauty of her. "I don't think I can
wait, Maddie. And I want to. I want you to have . . . I don't
know . . . music and roses and romance—"

"I'll have all those, Hank. One day I will. We will. But
now, for tonight, I want only you. I need only you." With
that, she gently pushed him off her, urging him onto his
back.

Hank complied and she rewarded him with her hands
and lips roving over his body even as she pulled herself up
and over him, her long blond hair falling forward as she
lowered herself, hips first, then belly, then breasts, on top
of him. Her smile was that of the seductress. Hank could
barely breathe. He was damned near gasping as Maddie
showered his neck, his shoulder, then his chest with sweet
little nipping kisses. She inched herself lower and lower
down him, her mouth never leaving his skin, her hands
never still.

Hank had taken all he could. "Maddie, ohmigod," he
gasped, gripping her under her arms, pulling her up his
length and gently depositing her on her back on the bed.
And there she lay smiling softly, proud and posing for him.
Hank's breath damn near left him. As if in a trance he
hoped never to awaken from, he lovingly caressed Maddie's body, his gaze following his hands' path. The sweet
mounds of her breasts captivated him. So round and firm.
Lying beside her, scooting down some, Hank lowered his
head and captured a nipple, gently sucking it and nipping
it until it was an erect bud, no less hard with desire than
he was. Maddie's moan was his reward, and his body
throbbed. He quickly moved to her other breast, giving it
the same loving attention.

She cried out, arching her back, and with her hands on his shoulders, pushed him down lower on her. Hank needed no further urging. He shifted his weight and eased himself atop her, sliding down, down until he could kiss her concave and creamy belly, her belly button, her soft-skinned, gently arching pelvic bones, and finally . . . he was where she wanted him, where he wanted to be. Hank drank slowly and steadily of her womanhood. Maddie's breath caught, she tensed, she called out his name, thrashed her head from side to side. Hank held her to him, showing no mercy. He knew the moment she was there, that she achieved her climax. The shuddering, undulating waves held her rigid and in their thrall. Hank damn near exploded with her. When she was gasping and limp, wet with her need, Hank pulled himself up her and, with her eagerly urging him on, settled himself in the circle of her hips and entered her, his entire length sliding into her inviting wetness.

His satisfied moan matched hers. For long seconds, Hank didn't move. He held his weight off her, but leaned down to kiss her passionately. Maddie's hunger matched his. But only when he felt her hips begin to move did Hank begin to do the same, matching his thrusts to hers. In this way, they coupled, a loving give-and-take that joined their bodies in the ancient ritual of mating. Their pace increased, smoothly, rhythmically. Hank's muscles tautened, he waited for Maddie, felt her body tighten around him. Felt her legs go around his hips, felt her hands tightly gripping his biceps. Maddie's body pulled him into her and held him there. A cry escaped Hank.

Then Maddie made that sound at the back of her throat that Hank had been waiting to hear, the one that told him her moment had arrived. She arched her back and tensed her thighs against him. Hank felt the ripples tearing through her and thrust harder and deeper . . . until he joined her in the long, slow, heated fall of agonizing sensation that pinned them to the bed and to the moment. When it was done, Hank collapsed atop Maddie, unable even to spare her his weight. But she seemed to welcome it, holding him close, her arms up under his and stroking his back. She planted feathery kisses along the ridge of his shoulder. And breathed in concert with him. Hank felt her heart beating against his, its thrumming pace as ragged as his own.

Nothing ever, at any time in his life, with any woman, had ever felt like this. This was magic. And this was good. This was right and beautiful and—

Someone with a big slurpy tongue was licking his arm. Hank jerked up. "What the hell?"

"What's wrong?" Maddie cried, tensing under him.

"Her," Hank tattled, nodding his head to indicate she should look to his right, her left.

In the dawn's gray light, Maddie turned her head to see the culprit. "Oh, for heaven's sake."

There, beside the bed, was of course Beamer. Her big face, grinning, wonderful dog-breath and all, with lolling tongue and brown eyes alight, her ears held at neutral, was about two inches from the lovers. She woofed. Enough of this foolishness. It was time to get up. The sun was coming up and a girl needed her breakfast.

There was no way they could go back to sleep, anyway. Too excited, too adrenaline-pumped. Besides, it was already six A.M., so what was the point? Dressed again in her nightgown, with a silky matching robe over it, Maddie made a pot of strong coffee and fried up a pan of thick bacon. For his contribution, and dressed now in a white T-shirt and jeans, Hank worked over a pan of a dozen eggs he was scrambling, half of which had Beamer's name on them. With toast and homemade jam—*not* from Mrs. Hardy's kitchen of death—topping it all off, they sat happily around the drop-leaf table and ate and talked.

"Wow, Hank," Maddie teased, not able to get enough of looking at him. "A man who's great in bed *and* he can cook. I've hit the jackpot."

"Don't get too excited," he said, sipping his coffee, yet still managing to send her an arch expression. "Breakfast is about the extent of my talents in the kitchen." He grinned devilishly. "Well, my culinary talents, that is. Later on, if you want, we could test the sturdiness of this table or those countertops."

Maddie feigned shock, even while feeling her cheeks warm up at the very notion of Hank sweeping everything off the table or a counter and taking her atop them. "Hank Madison, I'm shocked at you."

"And titillated by the idea, right?"

Grinning stupidly, she looked away, shaking her head. "Yes. Totally."

"So, while we're on the subject, there's something we *didn't* do that we need to talk about, Maddie."

She showed him her best aghast expression. "Hank, please. Are you insatiable?"

"No. Well, yes. Sometimes. But I mean safe sex."

His words cured her hots and left her cold and gaping at him. "Ohmigod, I never even thought about that."

"Neither did I." Hank looked sheepish now. "But you should know that I'm okay. I've always before used condoms. And I—oh, hell, Maddie, I hate this. I've been tested. Pilot's licensing, et cetera. What I'm trying to say is I'm clean."

"You're a pilot? I didn't know that."

"Yeah. Not commercial. Private." Hank reached across the table to affectionately squeeze her hand. "Focus, honey."

"Right. Okay. Me too. Clean, I mean. Stanton always used a condom. And I haven't been with anyone else since." Maddie found that talking about this, she couldn't quite hold Hank's gaze. She resorted to tucking her hair behind her ears to keep from looking directly at him. "That said, can we *not* talk about this anymore?"

"We have to. Two words: birth control. I'm hoping since I was stupidly condomless that you practice some?"

Maddie's eyes rounded. "Ohmigod, Hank. No. I cannot believe this. In this day and age. But no. I had no reason to. Until you. Until now."

It loomed there between them like a blinking neon sign:

Baby. Baby. Baby. The word actually pulsed with a life of its own. And echoed.

Maddie watched Hank set his coffee mug down. He picked up a piece of bacon, bit off a portion, and chewed it . . . all while staring at her. He swallowed and said, "This is your call, Maddie. I'll support whatever you want to do."

She stared at him. That wasn't exactly the loving declaration she suddenly realized she'd wanted. As if a baby with her would be the end of the world? No, in his defense, she argued with herself, he was being practical. And supportive. And PC. And clinical and cold. Well, so could she. "I don't know what I want to do, Hank."

He nodded, his expression that of a veteran poker player. "All right."

Oh, had the room cooled. Maddie felt the distancing begin. The pulling away. It was only normal, she tried to tell herself. She'd read that somewhere. After making love, many couples fussed with each other. It was a way of reestablishing boundaries after such profound intimacy. Well, normal or not, it felt terrible. Like a betrayal somehow. Which was really ridiculous because the odds were more in favor—given her quick mental calculations of her last menstrual cycle—that she would get a negative response on a . . . a pregnancy test. She winced, more mentally than physically. She could barely even think those two fateful words, much less stand Hank's quietness. Of course, she hadn't said anything, either. But she didn't feel it was her place to do so.

"Maddie, we should really talk about this."

She crossed her arms, suddenly defensive, self-conscious. "I don't think there's anything to talk about."

"I do. We didn't use protection. You could be . . ." He inhaled, exhaled deeply. "Pregnant."

God, he would hate having a baby with me. Didn't that tell her everything she needed to know about how much he cared? Or didn't care? What had all that in the hallway been about? If you loved someone and wanted to commit to them, wouldn't the prospect of a baby, an expression of that love, make you happy? Once again Maddie had to gather her courage and step out over the Abyss of Love—and actually say something. "Would that be so awful, Hank, if I was?"

He shrugged. "You tell me. As they say, it's your body."

She crossed her arms and leaned over the table. "As *they* say? Do you know how cold that sounds? How impersonal? This is me and you. Admittedly, if asked to define right now what you and I are to each other, I probably couldn't. But, still, Hank . . . it's me and you. And we have that whole hallway speech of yours and what we just did in my bed. Am I right?"

"Yes you are. And because of all that, I don't want to get this wrong now." He looked around the kitchen as if he searched for something he'd lost. Then he focused on her. "Look, the storm's broken. So maybe we should take some time, not say anything more right now. Maybe I ought to see about going back out to the cottage on the beach. Maybe give us each a little space. Work some things out in our heads."

The big kiss-off.

Her emotions on a roller-coaster ride, Maddie made a show of not bolting from the table, although that's exactly what she did. She headed purposefully for the sink as if she meant to wash the dishes. With her back to Hank, and hurting inside as she hadn't since her parents had been killed in that car wreck, Maddie plugged the sink, squirted soap into it, and ran hot water. But it was nowhere near as hot as the scalding tears that filled her eyes. She refused to cry. Absolutely refused. She kept her back to Hank and fought for control. He didn't say anything. Neither did she.

Finally, when she thought she safely could, she turned around and played at nonchalant. "Sure. That's a good idea. Why don't you do that—go out to the cottage? But this time, leave Beamer, okay? This is her home."

"All right." He wiped his mouth and stood up. He cast a glance her way, opened his mouth to say something, but closed it. Then he tried again. "I'll just go pack and . . .

leave." His black eyes were edged with some strong emotion. "I'll call you, Maddie. I will."

She nodded, quickly looking away and hugging herself. "Sure."

With that, Hank left the kitchen and strode down the hall.

Maddie exhaled and looked over at Beamer, whose head and tail were drooping. "Oh, you poor thing. Come here. It's okay. You didn't do anything wrong." Snapping her fingers, Maddie called the dog to her. Beamer padded over, tail wagging slowly. Maddie squatted down in front of the golden retriever and got her face washed for her efforts. "Thank you. I needed that." She ruffled the dog's warm silky ears and hugged her thick furry neck. "I can't believe I was ever afraid of you."

Beamer woofed her understanding.

Maddie nodded. "If only it was that easy with people. You wouldn't believe how stubborn and silly we can be."

CHAPTER EIGHTEEN

❧

"OHMIGOD, YOU'VE HAD SEX with my son."

"Ohmigod, you've have sex with her son."

Maddie now knew the meaning of "frozen tableau." Because here one was. Lillian Madison's loudly blurted pronouncement, on the crowded sales floor of Maddie's shop, and Celeste's hooting confirmation, had stopped her in her guilty tracks—and all the customers in theirs. Maddie'd only just showered and talked herself into carrying on with her day and had stepped into view of the public. Like an actress onto a stage. On cue, her eyes widened and her cheeks warmed. But she forgot her lines.

Not so her customers. "Bravo!" "My, my." "Way to go." Comments like that came her way from several sophisticated upscale customers who turned to her and applauded her in a discreet yet sly way. A few other shoppers of the real kind hustled their children out the door. One of those, a little boy about four years old, asked his mother what sex was. Whatever the woman's answer, it was lost as the door closed behind them.

"Uh, her son is thirty-four. He's not a . . . boy or anything. He's a man," Maddie felt stupidly compelled to—Hello!—verify for them all. *That's it. Add fuel to the fire.* Her gaze darted over the staring crowd, then landed on some bins of merchandise. "Oh, look, there's a special on these items over here," she desperately improvised, pointing to them. "Half off. Your choice. Feel free to help yourself."

Because there is a God, that started a stir and got everyone moving again. Stung, weak-kneed, her stomach roiling, Maddie grabbed her red apron off its hook, tied it on, and worked her way through the upscale crowd—yes, upscale, the new shoppers. Suddenly Maddie's Gifts was *the* place to shop. You were simply no one if you didn't have something from Maddie's Gifts. She remained a celebrity in the right circles. She was famous for being a scandal. Lovely. And now Lillian had certainly raised the bar on tabloid coverage, hadn't she?

Like an avenging angel, Maddie determinedly wedged her way over to Lillian at the cash register and stood four-square in front of the older woman, the avowed mother of Maddie's recent bed partner. Lillian, perfectly coiffed as always, and adorned in diamonds and silk, had a beringed hand clapped over her mouth. Her brown eyes held remorse and said her blurted assessment had been accidental yet honest.

"I cannot *believe* you said that," Maddie hissed in a whisper of indignation, her hands riding her waist.

Lillian recovered, stuck her hand in a pocket of her red apron, fumbled around, and turned to Celeste. "Smoke break." She held up her cigarette case and lighter as proof. She then nodded her chin in the direction of the sales floor. "Can you handle this, Celeste? I'm taking Maddie outside."

A dart of disbelief lodged in Maddie's heart. The woman meant to take her outside—and do what? Beat her up?

"Sure," Celeste the Traitor said, pushing Maddie toward the door. "You go on now, honey. And keep your dukes up."

Her dukes? Maddie then realized that she'd unconsciously fisted her hands. She immediately relaxed them, splaying her fingers wide. But they stubbornly re-formed fists. "All right. You bet I will. This conversation has been a long time coming, and I mean to have it now."

Celeste's expression fell. "How come I have to miss all the good stuff? Can't I come outside with you?"

"No," Maddie said in unison with Lillian—then stared at her in surprise. Hank's mother wanted this, too. Maddie recovered and said, "After you."

Lillian raised a perfectly plucked eyebrow and tamped a cigarette out of its pack. "Age before beauty?"

"Sure. Whatever." This was just what she needed to take

her mind off her other problems, Maddie told herself. A good fight with Hank's mother. Maddie waved her hand, indicating that Age should indeed precede Beauty.

That happened and the two women stalked through the shop, heading for the front door. Maddie didn't know about Lillian Madison, but she was very aware of the slanted looks and sly smiles coming their way from the customers who were only now getting what they'd come to Maddie's Gifts for: a tantalizing scene worthy of front-page, above-the-fold headlines. Ones that could supplant any star's latest alien-baby story. A few of the bolder ones fell in line behind Maddie.

But Celeste put an immediate stop to that by yelling, "Stop right there. I will personally shoot any customer who leaves this store before I tell them they can."

They evidently believed her because they all stopped, like in a game of red light/green light. Those in the way of the advancing, red-aproned women did, however—as noted by a logical information-processing part of Maddie's brain—step aside and merely watch with hungry longing as the redheaded woman in the lead jerked open the beveled-glass door and set off the merrily tinkling bell above it. It closed behind her and Maddie with what Maddie thought of as ironic finality. Meaning the public was inside in a private place, while this very private scene would take place outdoors in public. It was funny, the things the brain would notice at the most intense moment in someone's life.

Like the weather. Maddie's senses told her the day was beautiful. Warm. Windless. Green leaves showed signs of aging into spectacular reds and yellows and oranges. Somewhere, lost in the high branches, birds sang. Nearby, children laughed. Cars made their way down the street. Ocean-salt–tinged air filled her lungs. Maddie breathed in great draughts of it. She had a feeling she was going to need all the lung power she could muster.

Lillian marched around to the side of the shop, to the narrow alley and driveway that defined the boundary between Maddie's shop and the drugstore next door. Finally, Hank's mother stopped. She pivoted around with admirable military smartness, faced Maddie, and held out her cigarette case. "Smoke?"

She said it like *choose your weapon*. "No, thank you."

"Mind if I do?" She already had the cigarette she'd tamped out of its pack inside the store held between her lips and was lighting it.

Maddie watched the process. "No. They're your lungs."

Lillian eyed her over the cigarette. "You sound like Hank."

Maddie had no response to that.

Lillian inhaled, smoothly removed the cigarette from her mouth, exhaled over her shoulder, away from Maddie, and said, "Sorry about that comment inside. But so . . . you and Hank."

"Yeah. Me and Hank," Maddie parroted, feeling defensive, squeamish, brave, scared, guilty, defiant. "As the whole store now knows. But how'd you know?" Surely Hank hadn't run to his mommy after leaving Maddie's house about three hours ago.

Lillian Madison shrugged. "I just know. I'm a woman, too, honey. We know these things."

Maddie frowned. She was a woman, too, but she didn't know these things. She couldn't look at a freshly scrubbed, fully clothed woman, like she was right now, and tell she'd just had sex.

"And I'm a mother," Lillian added, as if that explained everything. She took another puff on her cigarette, and sent Maddie a sidelong glance. "So where is he? Where'd he go?"

How did she do this? Then Maddie realized Hank's Navigator was gone from her driveway, which she and Lillian were now standing in. "Back out to the cottage at the beach."

"God," Lillian snorted, exhaling smoke. "Rat traps."

"Ramshackle."

"Bacteria on the hoof."

"Total disasters."

"And he loves it out there, doesn't he?"

That surprised Maddie. She caught a fleeting look of something vulnerable in Lillian's expression, of some hurt or fear. "Yes. He does."

Hank's mother, a slim, pretty, and, Maddie suspected, very complicated woman, turned her head, so as not to look at Maddie. "Look, honey," she said, tapping the ash off her cigarette. She was actually fascinating to watch as she smoked, Maddie decided. She made all the attendant ritual of its motions and gestures graceful and fascinating. Like performance art. "Let's get something straight," Lillian said, drawing Maddie's attention to her face. Maddie saw nothing of this woman in Hank. He obviously took after the Madisons. "I can be a complete diva. I know that about myself. I'm also an elitist snob and a pampered rich bitch. It's protective coloration for living in Beverly Hills."

Maddie wasn't about to acknowledge any of that, not by word or gesture. She just stared and realized her cheeks felt flushed and her stomach a bit sick. Where in the world was this going?

"But things are different here. I'm different here. I sure as hell never got into a food fight at a church, or anywhere else, before in my life." She chuckled to herself as if reliving the experience and feeling proud of herself. Then she eyed Maddie. "But more importantly, my *son* is different here."

Ah. This was where they were going. Maddie nodded. "I think James was hoping he would be happy here."

"Yes. James. I think he was hoping Hank would be happy here with *you*, Maddie. And the old coot was right. For whatever reason, you make my son happy."

The fabric of Maddie's heart tore a tiny bit. She made a self-deprecating sound, almost a chuckle. "Not so much today."

"I know. Obviously something happened. And he's gone back out to that cottage that surely houses somewhere in its many funguses the cure for a major disease." Again she said that as if talking to herself. Maddie bit back a chuckle that surprised her. She hadn't ever thought to be amused by Lillian. Maddie realized she'd been wrong about something else, to think there was nothing of Lillian Madison in her son. Hank's dry wit surely came from his mother. Lillian shook her head and got back to the subject. "Anyway, I won't ask what. It's not any of my business."

But she wanted to know. She wanted Maddie to tell her what had happened. It was there on her face. Maddie purposely said nothing.

Lillian again took an elegant drag off her dwindling cigarette, exhaled, and looked down at the ground, idly toeing the dirt around with her low-heeled pump. "All right. I can respect that. You know, Maddie, I came here to expose you as the gold-digging opportunist I believed you surely to be." Maddie fought a defensiveness that invaded her heart. "But it didn't take me long to find out that you're not. Celeste certainly set me straight in a hurry. As did everyone else in town I met." She arrowed an assessing glance Maddie's way. "Hanscomb Harbor is a magical little place, isn't it?"

Thank God. A sufficiently neutral topic. "Well, it was. Before all the hoopla and headlines. Before the invasion of paparazzi and the jet set."

"Yes. My world. My people."

Oops. Maddie felt her cheeks burning.

"Don't worry. Your town will survive. I know these people. Their sort, anyway. They'll soon tire of the game and move on to the next big thing."

"Well, it can't be soon enough to suit me."

"I feel the same way. Which tells me they *were* my people, but not anymore. Like I said, I'm different now."

"You seem happy. More relaxed," Maddie ventured, trying to find the vein they were mining conversationally out here in the open air of an alleyway.

"Yes. I'm thinking about moving here for good."

Maddie's stomach plunged. "Good. We'd love to have you."

Even Lillian didn't believe her. She chuckled and poked at Maddie's arm, which made Maddie laugh with her. "Nice try, Maddie, I appreciate the effort. But we both know better. Still, I'll do my darnedest to be a good Hanscomber. I'm certainly interesting enough to fit right in, don't you think?"

"Especially with Celeste." Maddie put her hands behind her back and leaned against the sun-warmed wood wall of her shop and looked around. "Hank says there's something in the water."

"Well, I'll be sure to drink plenty of it."

Maddie glanced over at Lillian, who, with the toe of her shoe, was now grinding her cigarette butt out on the moist ground. She was quiet, but seemed to be waiting for Maddie to speak. What could she say, except the truth? "It's not good right now between Hank and me, Lillian. And I don't know how this is going to work out. Or if it even will. If it doesn't, will you still want to stay here?"

Lillian nodded, then exhaled and crossed her arms under her breasts. She looked away from Maddie, out toward the ocean that shimmered just across the street and down the slope from Maddie's Gifts. "I know how hard this is for you, honey. You didn't ask for any of this. And the Madisons are a tough lot to deal with." She turned her head until she was looking into Maddie's eyes. "But I just want you to know that, well, I'm on your side. Woman to woman."

Sudden and unexpected tears pricked at Maddie's eyes. She had Hank's mother's approval. Maybe too late. Maybe when it didn't matter. But it was approval, nonetheless. "Thank you."

Lillian squeezed Maddie's arm affectionately. "You're welcome."

Sitting alone for the moment in Jim Thornton's office as he conferred with Mrs. Crane at her desk in the anteroom, Maddie relived her memories of being in this astoundingly ornate office a little over six weeks ago. Again she saw

herself spilling that wine on Hank. Then she suffered mentally through the reading of James's disastrous will. When
she looked back on it now, on all the drama, the tears, the
laughter, the hurt, the misunderstandings, she could only
ask herself, what had been the point of all that living and
loving? Of waking her up from her dream, of pulling her
out of her shell? So she could be shown how pathetic her
life was? So she could have yet another unhappy, unsatisfying ending?

Maddie wanted to slump with the ironic futility of it all.
After all, here she sat—alone—in a leather chair that faced
Jim's big desk, and all she could do was stare like a zombie
at the diploma- and award-laden wall behind it . . . and
wonder where Hank was right now. He'd done his six
weeks, the last three of which she hadn't seen him or talked
to him. Sure, he'd called as he said he would. And she'd
talked to him then. Again she could hear herself saying that
maybe he'd been right, that they shouldn't have done anything about their attraction until they got through the legal
flaming hoops. So why didn't they cool it now and catch
up again after all the signing had been done, she'd said.
And he'd quickly agreed.

And then the torturous three weeks had passed . . . and
then another one. And still, as of today, no word from
Hank. His mother said nothing. Celeste said nothing. The
three of them just kept working and pretending that everything was normal. And sure enough, as Lillian had pre-
dicted, life in Hanscomb Harbor had returned pretty much
to normal. It was again the sleepy little fishing village an-
ticipating autumn and pumpkins and cider.

Maddie rubbed at her aching neck and sighed, focusing
as always on Hanscomb Harbor, her anchor. She missed
the little harbor town, even though she'd only left there that
morning and would return this evening. It wasn't so much
that she minded being away from home. It was more that
she minded being here in New York City where *he* lived.
Where *he* breathed the same air that she did. But here she
was because she'd seen no sense in delaying this chore for

even one more day. So here she was, waiting to sign away her interest in Madison & Madison Enterprises. Here she was waiting to take control of the fabulous wealth that James had left her. And then she and Hank could go their separate ways. As if they hadn't already.

Maddie frowned. How did something like that happen? One minute you were hot and heavy, the next cool and distant. She shrugged her shoulders, there alone in Jim's office. Sometimes some things just didn't work out and it was nobody's fault. It seemed relationships that reached a fever point as quickly as theirs had were destined to cool. Too hot to handle. Too hot not to cool. How sad was that? About as sad as this moment when there was nothing dramatic to mark its passing. There should have been. It seemed only fair. All her other unhappy endings had been over-the-top dramatic. Left in the lurch at the altar in front of a sympathetic yet embarrassed crowd. A car wreck with twisted metal and horrible headlines. James's passing. Hank's passing out of her life. Thank God she'd had her period, then, right?

The door to the office opened. Maddie struggled hard to keep her rising emotions off her face. She didn't want Jim Thornton, who'd just come back in with Mrs. Crane on his heels, to know how much she was hurting.

"I'm sorry, Maddie. Client emergency. Just let us get these documents in order, and we'll be ready for you to sign." He sat at his desk and Mrs. Crane stood next to him. They both looked at her, waiting.

Maddie waved a hand their way. "Take your time. I'm fine."

No, I'm not. Maddie put a hand to her temple. *Stop it right now, Maddie. You tried. You gave everything you had. It just didn't work out. So sign the damned papers and get out of here. Then you never have to feel anything again.*

Jim Thornton nodded at Mrs. Crane and she gathered up some papers and left. Maddie was now alone with a somber, unhappy lawyer. One whose sad, heavy-jowled face said he felt the failure of James's grand design the same as she did. It was sad, actually, very anticlimactic, that with only the stroke of a pen, of ink flowing across the bottom of a page on a line indicated by the single word "signature," it would all be over and done.

Jim pushed the documents across to her and showed her where to sign. With no fanfare and no delays, Maddie signed. Then, pen still in hand, she gazed at the letters that formed her name. Madelyn L. Copeland.

So simple, so quick, so surgical. It was done. The die was cast. The act completed. She no longer had any say, legal or otherwise, in Madison & Madison Enterprises, Inc. Hank had his life back. And she had hers. The pen, it turned out, was mightier than the sword. And usually drew more blood.

"And here too, Maddie, if you would," Jim said, putting another legal document in front of her and indicating the appropriate line. He continued to speak low and soft, as if out of respect for someone in the room who was dying. Someone was, but only inside where you couldn't see, where it never showed, where Maddie kept her hurt. She signed without comment and sat back, waiting for further direction from Jim.

"That's it. All done." With short pudgy fingers, Jim rubbed at his forehead. The poor balding man had an acre of forehead forested with freckles atop his too-big head.

When he didn't say anything else, Maddie broke the silence. "Is that all? Am I free to go?" She felt as if she were a prisoner who still couldn't believe she'd earned her freedom. She certainly didn't feel as though she were free. No, she felt anything but free. She felt strangely burdened. Weighted down. As if some prankster had glued her to her chair.

"What the hell happened, Maddie?" Jim blurted. "How'd it all fall apart? You and Hank were so perfect together."

Maddie blinked in surprise and stared at him.

"I'm sorry. I had no right to say that. Look, you want a drink? I know I sure do." Without waiting for her answer, and with his features set in stubborn lines, he pushed his chair back and stood up. "Come on. Let's go sit over there. I'll get us something stiff and we can talk, friend to friend."

Rising from her chair, but not so sure she wanted to have this conversation, Maddie nevertheless shrugged. "All right."

"Good. What can I get you?" Jim was on his way to the wet bar. With his suit coat off, he looked downright grandfatherish in his white shirt and red suspenders that struggled to hold his slacks up.

"Rum and Coke is good." Maddie trailed after him, veering off to the seating area, where she sat on the sofa. Unbidden flashbacks assailed her. Spilling her purse. Shoes off. Hank coming in. Startling her. Spilling wine on him. Maddie wrenched the emotional memories to a halt. And got up, moving to one of the opulently upholstered Queen Anne chairs that sat at either end of the low coffee table. In this office, it wouldn't have surprised her to find out the chairs had actually been Queen Anne's.

"Here you go," Jim said, handing her a short crystal tumbler. He had an identical one in his hand. He chose to sit at the end of the sofa closest to her.

In silence Maddie sipped at her beverage and watched Jim doing the same with his. He looked her way and caught her staring. "Good stuff, huh?"

"The best. God bless the Bacardi family." The rum warmed her stomach, and the glass gave her something to do with her hands. Maddie crossed her legs and perched the tumbler atop her knee, holding it in place with both hands. She cut her gaze to the closed double doors to Jim's ornate office.

"Hank's not coming. His presence wasn't required."

Maddie focused on Jim. He'd thought she was looking for Hank. She had been, but only sort of. "I wasn't looking for him."

"I know. Maddie, this sucks."

She chuckled. "I'm sorry. That word coming out of your mouth is totally unexpected. Celeste's, yes. But not yours."

Jim grinned. "I've said a lot worse. So how is Celeste?"

"Well, if you ask her, she says she's still kicking, only not so high. But she's fine. She has a new short hairdo, a wild kitten named Bluebell, and a new friend in Lillian."

"Go figure. I never saw that one coming. But when I've talked to her, Lillian seems to be thriving there. I'm glad."

"Yes. Me, too. She's out in L.A. right now, closing things out there. So Celeste took the time to visit her niece's family in Indiana. There's a new baby named after Celeste. She went there for the christening."

"Another Celeste? From the stories Hank and Lillian have told me about her, and from what I saw of her that one time, well, God save us all." Jim downed a good portion of his drink.

"Amen." Maddie sipped at her drink and eyed Jim, wondering when he would come to the point. Or if he had a point. Maybe he simply wanted to visit with her a bit. Why'd she think everything had to have a point?

"So, Maddie, what'd you do with Beamer for the day? I'm so glad that at least the two of you found your way together."

"Me, too. It wasn't easy, but I persevered since it was what James wanted." Instantly self-conscious, Maddie looked down at her drink.

Jim coughed and sniffed and said nothing. What could he say? Her words hung between them like pregnant pigeons. Left unsaid was that James's wish had also been that she and Hank be together. But they weren't, and Jim knew it.

"So, Maddie," Jim said a little too loudly, "Beamer is where?"

"Teddy Millicum—a local teenager—is looking after her. He has Celeste's kitty, too, while she's away." Talking about her hometown friends put Maddie more at ease, and she found herself chatting. "Teddy's a good kid and likes to take Beamer for long walks. They go to the park at the town center. It's good for both of them. And this way I don't worry what he and his girlfriend are doing alone together. The last thing his or Millie's parents need to have right now is a grandchild."

Jim's face crumpled, much as if he'd experienced a pain.

Alarmed, Maddie pushed to the edge of her chair. Quickly, she set her drink on the coffee table and put a hand on the elderly attorney's arm. "Jim, are you okay? What's wrong? Do I need to get someone?"

"No." He put his hand over hers and squeezed affectionately. "I'm fine. I didn't mean to scare you. I'm sorry, Maddie. Really. Sit back. Enjoy your drink." She did, and he continued. "It was just all that talk about grandkids, I guess."

"I'm so sorry. I had no idea. I didn't..." Her voice trailed off because she really had no clue why that would upset him.

Jim waved her apology away. "Oh, don't worry about it, Maddie. It's not your fault. Or your problem." His voice was brusque with barely contained emotion. "It's just that..." He paused, staring at her for long moments that left Maddie feeling diminished somehow, as if she personally had let Jim down. "Well, as you know," he began again, "Mary and I have no children. And this is silly, but we got caught up in thinking... well, we thought you and Hank... we hoped that..." His voice trailed off. He looked desultorily at the drink in his hand.

Maddie blinked rapidly, trying to squeeze back the tears as she held tightly to the chair's arms. "You hoped that Hank and I would... give you a sort-of grandchild?"

Jim sat back abruptly, crossing a leg over the opposite ankle and clearing his throat, just generally trying not to look emotional. "Silly, huh? We're not even related."

"Sure you are. What's blood? We have friendship. And I think it's very sweet, Jim. I really do. You and your wife, from what Lillian and Hank have told me, would make— would have made—" Maddie gritted her teeth against the scream of hurt and frustration that wanted out. "Could this *be* harder, Jim? I'm trying to say that you will make wonderful grandparents. Maybe Hank will find someone . . . and can give you that grandchild."

"We don't want someone. We want you." The hard-shelled, no-nonsense, world-renowned attorney, like a pouting child, sat forward, plunked his drink down, pulled a handkerchief from his back pants pocket, and blew his nose heartily. As he refolded the no-longer-so-crisp square of linen and repocketed it, he downplayed his show of emotion. "It wasn't so much for me as Mary, you understand. Bless her heart, she had you already expecting by next Christmas and was planning a party and even the baby's nursery. She even bought a little book of names for babies."

Oh, God. This moment, for Maddie, would have been more bearable if Jim had simply beaten her with a stick. As it was, Maddie's heart swam in tender and wretched sympathy. On an impulse, she got up and hugged Jim's neck and kissed his forehead. "Poor Mary," she said, meaning *poor Jim.* "How sad she must be. Tell her I'm sorry, will you? I never wanted it to end this way, either."

Overcome, Jim simply nodded but then caught her wrist as she straightened up. "What did happen, Maddie? Why did it end with you and Hank? I know you don't owe me the first explanation, and you can tell me to go to hell. I'm just asking friend to friend. I care a great deal about you, as much as I do about Hank. And like him, you're hurting a lot worse than you'll let on."

Maddie's heart leapt at mention of Hank. *He's hurting?* Would he be hurting if he didn't care? Maddie stared blindly at the thick carpet as it blurred and shimmered through her unshed tears. With Jim still holding her wrist, all she could do was stand there and sniffle and shrug her shoulders. Jim released her and Maddie took her seat. She plucked a tissue out of a handy box on the table and wiped at her eyes. Jim held her drink out to her. Maddie took it and raised the glass to her lips.

Feeling a bit restored after a few sips, and with the tissue and the tumbler still in her hands, she faced Jim again. "Jim, I don't mind talking to you. And I don't want to hurt your feelings. But I know you talk to Hank. Just promise me you won't repeat any of this to him."

His expression earnest and unoffended, Jim raised his right hand. "I swear I won't. I've been off the clock since we left my desk. This stays between me and you."

"Thank you." Maddie drew in a relieved breath and exhaled softly. "I don't know what happened, Jim. I really don't. No, I'm lying. I do know. It just got too hard. Hank and I met and collided. It was that will. The mistrust. The suspicions. The defensiveness. It was always there between us. We just kept starting and stopping, starting and stopping, until we finally just stopped."

Jim nodded. "Like a car with engine trouble."

"Exactly."

"What? You couldn't take it to a mechanic?"

Maddie chuckled. "If only it had been that simple."

Jim leaned forward. "It is, Maddie. It's that simple. I know it and James Senior knew it." He gripped her hand, squeezing it earnestly. "Maddie, go back to Hanscomb Harbor. Today. Right now."

Taken aback, Maddie said, "I am."

"Stay there."

"I will. I live there. Jim, what is this?"

"I want that happy ending, Maddie. It's what's supposed to happen."

"Well, it's what James wanted to happen, but—"

"So do you. And so does Hank."

"I don't know how you can say that with any certainty, Jim—"

"But I can, Maddie. I can. And you'll see, too. You and Hank being together is *supposed* to happen."

"You keep saying that. I think you need to explain yourself."

Jim sat back and grinned. "No. It's best if James Senior does."

This was getting scary. "Jim," Maddie said very placatingly, about like she would to a knife-wielding crazy man. "James is dead. James cannot explain anything."

Jim shook his head. "That's where you're wrong. He can. He did. It's in a letter."

"A letter? What letter?"

"One I wasn't supposed to tell you or Hank about until after the six weeks."

Her heart pounding, Maddie scooted to the edge of her seat. "Where is it? Give it to me."

"I can't."

"Why not?"

Jim nodded, smiling secretively. "Go home, Maddie. Go to Hanscomb Harbor . . . and wait."

CHAPTER NINETEEN

ॐ

"I LOVE YOU, AND I am never going to go away again."

This was everything Maddie wanted to hear, only the speaker who was hugging her was all wrong. It was Celeste, who had just returned from her niece's house in Indiana. When she'd called to say she was home, Maddie had closed the shop, thrown on her jeans, and called to Beamer. Then the two of them had experienced a pleasant walk over here. And now, while Beamer cast a wary eye toward the second riser of the white-painted stairs that led up to the second floor, which was where the bright-eyed kitten Bluebell stood eyeing the golden retriever right back, Maddie followed Celeste into her cozy living room.

Once they were settled in, Maddie questioned Celeste about her opening remark. "Why aren't you ever going away again? Didn't you have a nice time?"

Celeste waved that away. "Too many kids running all around the house and making noise. No wonder I keep them half a continent away. But Celeste Junior is, of course, wonderful. She's just like me. Never complains."

Maddie pitched forward, coughing, nearly choking on her own saliva. Beamer padded over quickly and poked her dog nose into Maddie's face. Fighting tears, Maddie sat up and gave the dog a reassuring pat to the head.

"You all right?" Celeste barked. "What's wrong with you? Catching a cold? Before I left, I told you to wear your sweater of a night if you went out."

"I don't have a cold," Maddie rasped out, watching the baby cat ambitiously clawing her way up the side of Celeste's favorite reclining chair.

In the next instant, the literally blue kitty bounded over the arm and sailed into Celeste's lap, eliciting a surprised whoop of joy from her owner. "I think I missed Bluebell as much as I did you."

"I'm very flattered. So did you have a nice ride from the airport? I would have come to get you, you know."

"Oh, I don't like to be a bother. Besides, Teddy didn't mind. He rearranged his after-school work schedule and got a baby-sitter for his little sister and borrowed his mother's car after he took her to work, so it was no trouble. Mrs. Millicum walked home. It was a pretty day for it. Won't hurt the lazy cow any to get some exercise."

Maddie blinked. "Well, as long as it was no trouble for him."

"He said it wasn't. I heard from Lillian. She'll be back here next week."

"Yes. She called me, too."

"You like her, don't you?"

Maddie smiled. "Sure. But not as much as I like you."

"Ha. Flattery will get you nowhere. So, did you get that autumn display in the shop's front window yet?"

"I did. Last week, in fact, after I got back from New York City."

Celeste lowered her gaze and concentrated on petting the cat in her lap. "So you went through with it."

"It wasn't a matter of going through with it, Celeste. It was just the next step. The final step."

Maddie's best friend now focused on her. "I guess you haven't heard from Hank?"

"No, I haven't. And I don't expect to, either."

"Maybe. Maybe not."

"What's that supposed to mean?"

Celeste's eyes widened innocently. "Nothing. I didn't mean anything by it. You want some tea?"

"Sure."

"Good. Will you fix me some, too, when you get up to make yours?"

Maddie knew she should have seen that one coming. Laughing, she got up and impetuously hugged Celeste, who protested as hard as she hugged Maddie back. "I love you, do you know that?"

Celeste preened and straightened her fluorescent green sweater about her. "Well, of course you do. What's not to love? Now go see about the tea before I die of thirst." Maddie started to move away from her chair. "Hot tea, mind you. Not too strong. Lots of sugar."

"I know, Celeste," Maddie sighed, already on her way to the kitchen. "Like you like your men. Hot and sweet."

"That's right. How do you like your men, dear?"

Maddie turned around and came back into the living room. "Around, Celeste. I like them to be *around*. I like them to want to be around me, mostly."

"So you don't want one who has to work and travel all the time. You want one to hang around the house all day in his underwear and watch TV and drink beer and belch?"

"Dear God, no. Surely there's a compromise in there somewhere. I mean, he could at least be on the same continent, don't you think?"

"I think all the time, honey. So where's Hank right now?"

Maddie shrugged. "I don't know. How would I know?"

Celeste grinned and looked guilty and conspiratorial.

Maddie's heart thumped erratically, but a sinking feeling in her stomach also weakened her knees. "Celeste McNeer, what do you know?"

"I know plenty."

"And you better spill it right now." Maddie sat down heavily on the sofa. "What is going on here? If you don't tell me, I'll—"

"Now, calm down, Maddie." In a huff, Celeste pursed her lips and stroked her kitty and wouldn't look at Maddie. "You're so suspicious of everyone lately, dear. I think you're getting paranoid."

"Ha. With good reason. Shall we talk about my last couple of months?"

"No. It's boring. It's past. Over and done. I want to talk about today."

"What about today?"

"About a phone call I had today when I got home."

Maddie eyed her friend with deep suspicion—and a ton of hope. "From who?"

"Mr. Cotton Hardy."

"Oh?" Synapses in Maddie's brain began firing. Cotton Hardy. The cottage. Hank. "What did Mr. Hardy have to say?"

Celeste narrowed her eyes. "When'd your voice get that high and squeaky? You sure you're not getting a cold?"

Maddie cleared her throat. "I'm not getting a cold. What did Mr. Hardy want?"

"Well, I can tell you one thing. It's a good thing he didn't want a cup of tea because around here he'd never get it."

"And neither will you until you tell me why you're being so secretive."

Insulted, Celeste put a hand to her sweater-covered bosom. "Secretive? I am not. You been hanging out with that Lavinia Houghton while I was gone?"

"Lavinia Houghton doesn't hang out. Or talk to me. But if you don't spill what it is you're trying so hard not to tell me, Celeste, I'm going to tell her who it was who sent her that anonymous package from Frederick's of Hollywood. And had it delivered to her at the library during the children's hour."

Celeste's sweet little birdlike face blanched. "How'd you know about that?" Then she pursed her lips in irritation. "I mean, I don't know what you're talking about. I've been in Indiana for a week, only to come back and have you accuse me of such a thing. Why, I just can't believe it— and me an old lady." Maddie raised an eyebrow at Celeste. Celeste caved, sitting forward eagerly. "What'd the old girl do?"

Every bit as titillated as Celeste was, Maddie leaned forward. "Well, Mary Kitchener had her two kids there and told me all about it. She said Lavinia opened that package and held up those crotchless panties and very nearly had a heart attack. Screaming and cursing your name. Right there in the quiet library. She scared the little children into crying for their mamas. It was great, Celeste."

Celeste whooped with glee, startling the kitten in her lap into jumping down and taking off for the hallway. Beamer barked and followed curiously. From around the corner came a sudden hiss, followed by a sharp canine yap, which immediately preceded Beamer's hurried reappearance in the living room. The dog, a bit ruffled but not bloodied, obediently sat by Maddie, ears perked as she stayed alert for any sudden tiny cat sightings from the hallway.

Laughing, petting Beamer, Maddie sat back and crossed her legs. "So. What were we talking about? Let's see . . . Cotton Hardy's call to you, right? And now that you know that I know about Lavinia and Frederick's, you can just start talking. Come on, speak to me, girlfriend. Cotton Hardy, yada-yada. Go from there."

Celeste huffed up like her kitten. "Oh, all right. Cotton Hardy sad he couldn't reach you at your place, so he called me looking for you. I told him you were on your way here, so he gave me a message for you."

Suddenly afraid, and her heart thumping with hope—when would it ever learn?—Maddie put her hands over her ears. "On second thought, I don't want to hear this. Whatever it is, it's not going to be good. I can tell."

"Suit yourself." Celeste readied herself to stand up. "I think I'll make me a cup of hot tea."

"No. Tell me. I'll listen, I swear I will. What did Mr. Hardy say?"

"Well," Celeste began, settling back into her chair and drawing her sweater around her. "He said the strangest thing happened today. He said he went out to work on those old beach houses of his and right there in James's old cabin was . . ." Grinning, she eyed Maddie. "Now what was it? I forget what he said."

"Damn you, Celeste, don't make me shake it out of you. What? What was out there?"

"Well, right there on the kitchen table was a big bouquet

of flowers with a little card addressed to you."

"To me?" Maddie parroted, not daring to hope.

"Yes. To you. Why else would he have called? There was something else, too. That damned stupid lobster clock thing was next to the flowers. He said he was through for the day out there but to tell you he'd leave the place unlocked for you, if you want to go get them—Maddie! Wait! Where're you going? Wait for me. Come on, Beamer, I'm not about to miss this. Maddie, wait up! We're going with you."

Hank figured if he were a man to bite his fingernails when he was nervous, he'd have them bit off up to his elbows by now. As if to prevent that possibility, he stood with his arms firmly crossed. Standing outside the brass-plaqued Madison cabin but inside the screened and shaky front porch, he stared out at the ocean's frolicking waves. At a time like this perhaps he was supposed to think of the timelessness of the vista. Blue sky meeting blue-green ocean. As he watched, the occasional gull dipped and wheeled, its trademark cry combining with the *whoosh-whoosh* of the waves and the briny sea air. Other than that and him, though, the place was deserted. Isolated. No beachcombers. No Hanscombers. Just him. And his hopes. And his fears.

A perfect time for pondering life's mysteries and secrets and possible purpose. A perfect time to believe you were the last man on earth. Hank's chuckle was more a grunt than a laugh. *The last man on earth*. Which made him perfect for Maddie, actually, since she'd said she wouldn't have anything to do with him if he was the last man on earth. *Be careful what you wish for, Maddie. You just might get it.*

Hank sighed, coming back to reality. What would Maddie do? That was the big question. Or would she do anything? That was an even bigger question. Would she leave him standing out here, his heart pinned to his sleeve? It's what he deserved but couldn't stand to think might be his fate. Surely his grandfather couldn't have been so wrong about the two of them. As if needing reassurance, Hank felt for the folded envelope, still sealed and safely tucked in his oxford shirt's pocket. The two names, his and Maddie's, were written in his grandfather's own hand. One of the last things the old man had done before he'd died.

What could the letter contain? What words of wisdom would James Senior have to impart at this late date? And shouldn't there have been two letters, one to cover each possible ending, a good one and a bad one? But no, there was only the one envelope. *Wherever you are, Grandpa, I hope to hell—or heaven—you knew what you were doing. Because I sure don't.*

Hank turned his head, marking the lowering sun's progress. With the uneven rows of cabins essentially acting as sundials, he checked the steadily elongating triangles of shadow left in the sand. The wedges of black were deeper now . . . longer . . . mocking. *God, it's true. Nature doesn't give a damn what humans are going through. It marches on, relentless, oblivious.* And yet, he'd been marking the passage of time by the lengthening shadows because that was easier than constantly staring at his watch and fretting every passing minute. He figured about an hour had passed since he'd had Mr. Hardy call Maddie, then Celeste, before leaving for home and his supper.

Hank finally looked at his watch. A demoralizing mistake. *Yeah, an hour and about four lifetimes have passed.* At this rate, he knew, he'd have himself worried into a bleeding ulcer if Maddie didn't show up soon. What if she didn't show up at all? Not having the first clue how long "at all" might be in real time or his heart's time, Hank had to ask himself how long he was prepared to wait, how much time would have to pass before he called it, like a rained-out game.

He didn't know but it wasn't time yet to give up. He comforted himself by recalling that all Mr. Hardy had been able to do was leave a message for Maddie. What if Celeste had forgotten to give it to her? Unlikely. So what if Maddie decided to just blow him off? She could. But Hank didn't think she would. If nothing else, she'd be curious about the flowers and the lobster-clock urn.

Okay, so where is she, then? In his mind, he tried to picture what she might be doing, what might be taking her so long. Had she driven to Celeste's? Or had she and Beamer walked? Had she taken Beamer at all? Would Maddie take time to go home, change clothes, and do makeup and hair? Maybe she'd walked to Celeste's and then had to go home and get her car. Maybe she'd needed to get gas in her car. And since Celeste had just gotten in from Indiana, maybe Maddie was helping her unpack first. Maybe Celeste was tired and Maddie had stayed with her and didn't want to—

The sound of someone driving up the road that led out to the cabins caught Hank's attention—and his heart's. With his pulse accelerating, he didn't move to go see who it might be, but he did attune his hearing. Up on the road behind the cabin, someone had just stopped on the proverbial dime—and gotten nine cents' change, by the sound of the protesting tires. Hank's heart beat even faster, his pulse pounded at his temples. Feeling damp with emotion and a bit weak-kneed, he closed his eyes, took a deep breath, and steeled himself for this to be anybody, not necessarily Maddie. And not necessarily Maddie with good news for him. She could, after all, have come out here to tell him to kiss her sweet behind . . . which he'd be more than happy to do, but in a good way.

A car door opened . . . then closed. Then silence. Hank strained his hearing to see if he could detect footsteps coming his way. Impossible to do in this sand. So, he waited, hoping, praying that he wasn't too late, hadn't been so stupid that he'd let this one chance at happiness slip through his fingers. If this didn't work, then he didn't know what else to do, how else to be.

Hank tried to calculate the distance from the road's end to the cottage's door. He'd walked it many times. It wasn't that long a walk. Yet no one had appeared. She had to see his Navigator parked on the side of the cottage. She now knew he was here. Or maybe his hearing was playing wishful-thinking tricks on him and he hadn't really heard someone drive up. No, he'd heard someone. But where was she?

He could go see, of course. No he couldn't . . . he couldn't get his feet to move. And so he waited right where he was. God, how he'd missed Maddie, how he'd wanted her, how he'd longed for her touch, to hear the sound of her voice, to feel her smooth skin against his body. Her kiss. Just the sight of her delicate blond loveliness that framed a soul so sweet and pure would be enough to bring him to his knees. One glance and he would give her everything that had ever been his or would be his . . . starting with his heart, which beat only in her presence.

Suddenly Hank heard himself and had to laugh. When had he gotten so sappy and poetic? But what was so sappy, really? Too many men, himself included until recently, he admitted, equated love with weakness and committing to one woman with being tamed or caged, like some lion whose freedom had been denied him. *Lion? More like a chest-beating gorilla.* While that might sound big and brave and macho, what really brought a man to his knees was being without the woman he loved. And Hank had been without Maddie for a month now. By his own calculations, then, he should be facedown in the dirt.

"Hank?"

His heart damned near stopped, then all but lurched out of his chest. Hank turned to face her. Standing outside the porch and framed in the screen door, she stood in sunshine, so bright and radiant a picture that he feared his mind was playing tricks on him and she was only a vision, not flesh and blood. But a vision wouldn't need to shade her eyes from the sun, would she?

"Maddie. You came. I wasn't sure you would."

"I wasn't, either." She had on jeans and a pink vee-necked sweater. Her blond hair hung in loose waves about her shoulders

"Well, still, I'm glad you did." It was all he could choke

out before clearing his throat and trying to get a grip on his emotions.

As if suddenly uncertain, she lowered her gaze and fiddled with the screen door's rusty latch. "I confess that I didn't know you'd actually be here in person until I saw your Navigator."

Hank's chest hurt, felt tight. "Would you have come if you'd known I would be here?"

She raised her head and squinted against the sunlight that seemed determined to shine on her. "I don't know."

"An honest woman. I like that." He was dying. He was standing here and dying right in front of her. "I got the message you left on my machine. About there not being a baby. I'm sorry, Maddie. For the way I acted about that. I was just . . . stupid, I guess. And happy. Which surprised me. But I didn't want to say how much I wanted something like that to happen, I didn't want to get attached to even the idea of a baby . . . not if you didn't want that."

"Oh, Hank. I gave you no credit, did I? I should have known that was how you'd feel."

"No. I should have said."

"So should I, about how I felt. I was upset because you weren't happy. Then I felt the burden of the possibility, and how I would feel. And then it just got complicated, didn't it?"

"Yeah. But there isn't a baby. So would you like to come in out of the sunshine?" Then he heard himself. "That didn't necessarily follow. And would probably be more compelling if it was raining, I suppose."

"Maybe." Still, she opened the screen door and stepped inside. It banged closed behind her, making her jump. "I forget that thing doesn't work right."

"I don't think anything out here does. So . . . how've you been, Maddie?"

She shrugged. So slender, so delicate. Yet much stronger than he'd ever be. "Okay. You?"

Awful. Just plain awful. And worthless to anybody, in-

cluding myself. Awful and worthless. "Oh, I'm okay. Everything treating you good?"

"Sure. Even your mother."

"Scary. I told you it's in the water."

Then she looked inside the open door to the cabin. Her gaze lingered there. Still without looking at him, she said, "The flowers are beautiful."

"Thanks. That lady who runs the flower shop here is a drill sergeant."

With some visible effort, as if she were sad yet something was funny, Maddie grinned at him. "She's Lavinia Houghton's sister."

"Yikes. So this will be all over town. Me. The flowers. You."

"Exactly. I see you brought the stupid lobster clock, too. You know, I've actually missed it. Go figure. So, I guess it's my turn for custody of it?"

Hank paused before answering. "If that's how you want it."

Maddie's chin quivered, a sob escaped her. She struggled for control. "No, Hank, it's not how I want it. Nothing is how I want it. Not one living thing is how I want it."

"I'm sorry, Maddie. I really am."

She slumped where she stood. "I know. I'm sorry, too, Hank. I don't know what else to tell you." Then, as if the dam of her emotions had broken, Maddie flooded him with words. "Will you listen to me? I don't even know what I mean. Sorry for what? What are we sorry about? There were never any promises between us. No commitment. God, we were forced together by an absurd will pressed on us by a sweet, sweet man who loved us both and wanted us to be together. We can't say we didn't try. But it doesn't look like that's going to happen, does it?"

Just then a car's horn blew several long blasts.

Maddie put a hand to her forehead. "And that would be Celeste. She and Beamer are in the car and are obviously impatient."

"Either that, or they can't stand the suspense." She

hadn't come alone, was all he could think. So she could make a quick getaway if she wanted? Great. Hank's pride got out the bricks and the mortar and threatened to build a wall, but he resisted. "Maybe they're wondering 'will they or won't they?' "

Maddie cocked her head at a questioning angle. "Will we or won't we what?"

She was so close Hank could smell her perfume. He knew in his soul how her skin smelled, how her body's chemistry worked with this particular floral scent. He swallowed, wanting so very much to take her in his arms. If he could only hold her, maybe he could breathe. "Are you serious? You don't know?"

"Oh, Hank, I do and I don't. I don't know why this has to be so hard. People get together and stay together all the time. Every day. All around the world."

"I know. So why can't we, Maddie?"

Her features crumpled as if she were about to cry.

Hank took a step forward, his hand held out to her. "Maddie?"

She held up a hand to stop his advance. "No, Hank. Don't. If you touch me I'll fall apart, I swear I will."

"Maddie, if I don't touch you, I'll fall apart."

Her chuckle was a bit watery. "Well, we have a real problem then, don't we?"

Hank shrugged and spoke with soft sincerity. "Nothing we can't work out. I swear to you, Maddie, things are different now. I'm different."

She cocked her head at a questioning angle. "Really? Just all of a sudden? How?"

Hank exhaled. "In a lot of ways. And not all of a sudden. Over the course of the past several weeks. Being here. Being with you. It's changed me."

"Damned water."

"Then we should bottle it and sell it." Hank took a leap of faith. "Maddie, I want us to have a happy ending."

She held up a hand. "Oh, wrong phrase. I never have happy endings, Hank. But as silly as it might sound, as fairy tale–like as some would say it is, I want one, too. Just one. But you've got the wrong girl here. I don't have them."

"Never?"

She shook her head. "Never. You know my background. In fact, last week, in New York, I dubbed myself the 'Not the Happy Ending Princess.' "

"Sounds grim."

"I know. It seems, Hank, that if I achieve anything with people, I'd have to call them workable solutions. They seem to be all that I can manage."

"Sounds to me like settling. Very depressing."

She crossed her arms, managing to look conversational. "Isn't it, though?"

"Maddie, things *have* changed. I've changed. I wish you'd trust me."

She dropped her pose. "I kept trying to, Hank. I did. I thought when we were together that just maybe this time . . ." She stopped, lowering her gaze. Waiting, slowly dying, Hank could only stare at the uneven part in her hair, which made her seem achingly vulnerable. Like a little girl that life and love had batted around freely.

Maddie drew in a breath, again met his gaze, and continued. "Well, I thought just maybe. I thought if I really tried hard, you know. If I gave it everything I had, gave you everything I had, just quit thinking and worrying so much and gathered my courage and made the leap—"

Interrupting Maddie was the smoothly metallic sound of a heavy vehicle being started up. Her eyes widened, her mouth opened. Hank tensed right along with her. He stared at her, and together, they said, "Celeste!"

The one word was enough to propel them into motion. Maddie whipped around, Hank right on her heels, and pushed open the old screen door. Together they tore around the cabin's corner, ran by Hank's Navigator, and then . . . stopped dead and stared in shocked surprise. Celeste had turned Maddie's Wagoneer around and was already tearing up the highway on her way back to town. Celeste waved a hand out the lowered window on the driver's side. And Beamer's big dog head was stuck out the passenger's side. Her long ears ruffled by the breeze, she barked her good-bye.

Hank couldn't stop the grin that quirked the corners of his mouth. *God love you, Celeste.* He looked down at Maddie.

She wasn't amused. She'd planted her hands at her waist, her eyebrows were lowered in an angry frown, and she looked ready to stamp her foot. Her hair ruffled, and pink-faced with temper, Maddie turned her gaze up to Hank. "She stole my car. And my dog. I cannot believe she did that. Now how am I supposed to get back to town?"

Totally in love with her, and about one second away from dropping to one knee and asking her to marry him, Hank grinned down at Maddie. "You don't know? Isn't it obvious?"

Maddie stared blankly at him . . . then slowly got it. Her color heightened even more. "Oh." Then she chuckled and stared at her rapidly disappearing vehicle. "Well, that little stinker."

"Yeah," Hank said, feeling butterflies in his stomach and tremendous gratitude in his heart for the car-and-dog thief that was Celeste. "That little stinker."

"So what do we do now?"

"Come back to the cabin with me, Maddie. I want to *talk* to you."

CHAPTER TWENTY

❧

"I LIKE THE WAY you talk, Hank."

"Yeah? I like the way you talk back."

Maddie chuckled. The whole world, when viewed from the safety of Hank's arms, was a warm and wonderful and welcoming place. Maddie had learned that last summer. And she'd thought, until today, that she'd never know it again. She knew now that, before, she hadn't put Hank first, and he hadn't put her first. Could it happen again? Afraid that it could, she said, "Hank?"

Hugging her naked body to his side where they lay together in the rickety old bed of the beach cottage known locally now as the Madison Cottage, Hank answered, "Yes?"

"I'm scared."

"Of what? That you'll get cooties from this bedding?"

"No, silly." She playfully swatted at his muscled and bared chest, one she never tired of caressing. She then thought about cooties. "Ohmigod, maybe I should be." Her alarm had her trying to sit up, but Hank held her firmly and intimately in place. Maddie still managed to brace herself on her elbow. She tucked a lock of hair behind her ear. "You don't think we actually could, do you?"

"It's a little late to worry about that. We've been in this bed for about an hour. But are you itchy? Do you feel bugs crawling on you?"

Suddenly she did. They were everywhere. In a panic brought on by the mere suggestion, Maddie began scratching. "I will just die if I get cooties."

Hank laughed and pulled her down for a quick kiss. "I'm only teasing you. I got fresh bedding from Mr. Hardy. I think we're adequately protected, even beyond our other forms of protection."

Satisfied—in all ways—Maddie again curled up beside him, resting her head at the crook of Hank's shoulder and his chest. She loved the scent of him. Clean, male, sensual. His aftershave added a citrus-tinged musk that always fired her senses.

"So tell me," Hank said conversationally as he stroked her bare skin from waist to hip. "What has you scared?"

Maddie blinked, reveling in his nearness, their closeness. Now she hated like anything to bring up her fears. "I don't know if I want to tell you. It feels so good to be here with you, Hank. It really does. But every time we start talking, we start walking—and always in opposite directions from each other."

"Not naked we won't. So here's the deal. We can't get dressed until everything is out in the open. No naked pun intended. So, do we have a deal?"

No way was she going anywhere naked. Then her sex-sated mind treated her to a romantic picture of herself and Hank strolling hand in hand, au naturel, upon the beach outside. Savoring that image, Maddie sighed, yet agreed. "Okay, deal."

"Good. So you're scared because . . ."

Banishing images of beach strolls, Maddie focused on the important moment at hand and steeled her courage. "I'm scared because . . . well, I'm afraid we can't make this work between us, Hank. I mean I know we're good together, even beyond the physical aspects—which, by the way, are wonderful. But we also talk and laugh and, I feel, respect each other. Those things are important."

"So far I agree. I would also add that you're a gnawing hunger in my belly. But I think right now what I'm feeling is actually a gnawing hunger in my belly."

Maddie chuckled, hearing herself how his stomach was growling. As if having found its kindred spirit, her stomach growled right back at him. "How flattering for us both, huh? Okay, so basically we get along. We have fun. And all that's good. But we had all that going for us before,

Hank. Yet we couldn't make it work. Who's to say that won't happen again?"

In the silence, she could now hear Hank's heart beating. Maddie closed her eyes, concentrating on the sound and trying to imprint on her soul its reassuringly repetitious sound. Hank shifted his position, as if to signal his coming answer. "*We* say it won't happen again."

"You sound so sure."

"I am. Well, no I'm not. I'm sure I want it to work, I know that much." He kissed her forehead. "But maybe we *should* have a little fear. You know, something to keep us constantly aware that it could go wrong if we don't keep trying."

"That's true."

"Exactly. You'd think at our ages that we should have already realized that much."

"Oh, I don't know. History books and novels are full of examples of people who should have known better but didn't. So maybe it's not age as much as it is learning from each relationship. But that's the part that scares me. I've never had a relationship that lasted for very long. So all I know is how one ends badly, Hank. I hate that about me. And it worries me for us."

Speaking of her fears had Maddie cupping Hank's cheek to draw his gaze to hers. "Please tell me there's an us here to fight for."

Hank took her hand in his and kissed her palm. "There is, Maddie. We're definitely an us worth fighting for." His expression became thoughtful, introspective. "Now, that's interesting. And maybe that's the point here for both of us, the lesson we need to learn."

"What is?"

"That we keep coming back to each other. That we do keep fighting, or want to, at any rate, for what we feel for each other. Before you, Maddie, I can tell you that the minute a woman got serious about me, or things got otherwise complicated, I was outta there, using work as an excuse to distance myself."

"You did that with me, too."

"Yes. And I was stupid. I'm sorry. I've certainly suffered for it. And it didn't work. Because here I am, coming back because the old ways weren't working. Pretty much, my heart was telling me something my brain hadn't yet figured out."

"And what was that?"

"That it's different—no, I'm different—with you. Hell, running away is the last thing I want to do. Or work. I can't think. I can't concentrate. Nothing satisfies me. I don't want to be anywhere but with you. Now, that's got to mean something." He paused, staring at her as if waiting for her to say something. She didn't. "You're supposed to jump in right here and say it does mean something. Because if it doesn't, then I have to get up and walk into the ocean and just keep going."

Maddie's heart soared. She tugged her hand out of his and pulled herself up on an elbow. Staring down at him, she ran her hand over his smooth-shaven jaw and down his muscular neck. "It means something, Hank. It means everything. I read a saying the other day that had a big impact on me. Some man—I forget who—said that love isn't difficult, but when we think it is, it's usually because we're loving ourselves too well. Isn't that a wise insight?"

"Profound, too. I like it. It makes me feel guilty, but I like it."

"Me, too. I thought about it a lot. And I just want to say . . . well, I want to say—" She took a deep breath, stepped out over the abyss, and allowed her heart to pour out its words. "Hank, do you know how much I love you? Do you have any idea? I don't give a damn about me, about anything but you. I'm every bit as bad as you are. Nothing and no one but you can make me happy—not now and not ever." She rested her head against his warm chest and hugged him. "Just you. I only want you. I love you."

Hank lifted her chin. Maddie stared into his black eyes and saw a look of wonder had claimed his face. "Maddie, do you realize that's the first time you've said you love me? And I've never told you. So here it is: I love you, Maddie Copeland. With all my heart and soul. I have to have you in my life, that's all there is to it. And I think everything else is possible if we love each other well enough."

"Oh, Hank, this is everything I could have ever wanted. I think I'm going to cry."

"I might join you," he said drolly, "because, I don't know about yours, but my last month has been hell."

"You poor thing. I'm so sorry."

"No need to apologize. I've been the idiot. After my six weeks were done here, I took off for Europe, telling myself I could get you out of my system. The joke was on me. All I wanted to do was say to hell with it and come grab you up."

"Hank, there were only about four weeks in this past month where I wished you would. I had the same urge to run to you. But I didn't know where you were. So I just gave up and figured you knew where to reach me."

"Yes, I did. Right here in Hanscomb Harbor, which by the way has been a major part of my thinking."

Maddie stilled, not sure she wanted to hear his next words. What if he wanted her to leave here? She loved Hanscomb Harbor. The old defenses reared their heads— and Maddie recognized them. Instantly she squelched her selfish desires and prepared herself to put Hank's wishes first. This was the new way. Unselfish giving. "So, what about Hanscomb Harbor?"

"I think we should live here. Buy some land. Build a house."

Maddie stared at him, her mouth suddenly dry, her heart pit-a-patting. "What are you saying?"

"I'm *saying* I think you should marry me and we should live here."

Maddie could barely swallow. "What?"

Hank chuckled and spoke louder. "I think you should marry me and we should live here in Hanscomb Harbor."

"You do?"

"I do," he said in a normal tone of voice. "I guess I should get used to those two words: I do. So will you?"

Maddie sat up, pulling the top sheet modestly over her breasts. "I don't know."

Hank sat up, too. "You don't know? Did I miss something? Why don't you know?"

"I'm scared."

His elbows resting atop his sheet-covered knees, Hank stared at her, his expression incredulous. "Talk to me, Maddie."

She twisted until she could throw her arms around him. Hank held her tightly. With her head nestled against his neck, she cried, "I love you, Hank. I'm sorry. I know love is chancy at best. I know it's a big leap of faith. I know all that. But Hank, I need something, okay? I don't think I could stand it if you stuck me here in a house and went about your life. It's my biggest fear and yet that's essentially what we've been doing. And it sucks. We've both said we hate it, and yet—"

"Maddie, listen to me." Hank pulled her arms from around his neck and held her back so he could look into her eyes. "Everything is different. When I came back from overseas, I reorganized my company. Turns out, it was the easiest and the best thing I ever did because it was so well run and because I do have good people. You've met them. So I put them in charge. And hell, I can commute. I do have a jet. And a helicopter. New York's not that far. And I don't have to go in every day, either."

"I do not believe this is you talking. James Senior just rolled over in his grave. Or urn."

"I'm sure he did. But thanks to my grandfather I've learned I *can* work and step back some and have a life, too. So he gets his wish. No more Mr. Workaholic Madison. And you're stuck with me around the house. Or working in your shop, if you want." His expression became faraway, wondering. "I think I've developed a thing for those little red aprons."

Maddie smacked at him. "Stop that." But his was the

most unbelievable speech she'd ever heard. And because it was, Maddie said, "I don't think I believe you, Hank. About not working so hard. Or even playing so hard. Are you sure you can and not explode? It's hard to change your nature. And I'm not really sure I want you to. I mean, this is the you I fell in love with."

He smiled at her. "You are so beautiful, Maddie. But I learned something else about myself. It wasn't that I couldn't take it easy and slow down and enjoy life. It was that, before you, I had no one to slow down for or with. But now I do. I have you."

"Oh, Hank, that is so great."

"I think so." He chuckled. "Although they might not at Madison and Madison. Which is now the daily headache of the very capable Mrs. Chesswell. I am now the chairman of the board, and she's the president. I bumped everyone on the board of directors up one notch. And I even gave Miz Smith to the new president."

Maddie recalled the black-wearing snippy woman she'd met in the ladies' room that day of the stockholders' meeting . . . and made a face. "Poor woman. I mean Mrs. Chesswell."

"She can handle her. And it's only for a while. I'm thinking of asking the scary Miz Smith to run our lives from here. What do you think? You know, the secretarial stuff. The details. Letters. Travel. Upcoming meetings we have to attend. I think we can hold a lot of them here. The board would like that, I'll bet, now that Hanscomb Harbor is a hangout of the rich and famous, which includes us, of course."

"Hank, this is overwhelming. It's like winning the lottery and finding out you've inherited Shangri-la, too. Good Lord, I'm going to have people. And Miz Smith. And bodyguards. What about them?"

"George and Burton? They'll be around, chauffeuring and piloting. Guarding us. So . . . will you marry me?"

Maddie had been so invested in listening to him that she almost missed his proposal that he slipped in again. With thrilled happiness coursing through her veins, she never-theless shrugged dramatically. "I don't know."

Disbelief sobered Hank's expression. "You don't know?"

"No." She fought a grin. "I need time to think."

As if wounded, Hank sank back against the pillows. "While we're young, Maddie." Then he raised his head and met her grinning gaze. "So, I've talked to my mother."

Maddie grinned. "Have you?"

"Yes. She tells me you gave her James's house on Long Island."

"Her and Celeste. They're such fast friends now that I thought they should have a second house. A small vacation home. I'm hoping their antics can draw some of the tabloid heat off us."

"You're brilliant. And very generous. Besides, Gerta can keep an eye on them for us and warn us if they break free."

"That's true. But what worries me more than those two is what happens if Lavinia Houghton bonds with Miz Smith? Can you see that? They'll institute a scorched-earth policy that will leave us all crispy critters."

"We'll just have to avoid church bake sales. Now, let's talk money. I was thinking—"

Maddie put a hand over his mouth. "No. I want you to listen to me now." When she saw in his eyes that he would, she lowered her hand. "Just hear me out. Hank, I want to keep in my name what James left me. I want my money to stay separate from yours. I'm not saying this well, but I want us both to have, I don't know, freedom, I guess. Our own independence."

Hank looked troubled. "A way of walking away, you mean?"

"No. A way of staying together, Hank. Being together because we want to be. Not because we have to be. Not because of legal and financial intricacies. But only because we love each other. And love each other like two people who don't have a dime or a possession between them. Just themselves. Equals. Only in that way will I not be afraid.

Only in that way can I make a big leap, Hank. Does that make sense?"

His expression relaxed, and he nodded. "Actually, it does. I was going to say something along those lines about the money, too. About how I think my grandfather wanted you to be on a par financially with me so you didn't feel secondary or intimidated or whatever you would have felt."

"All those things, actually."

Hank took her hand and kissed it. "I think I understand. And I can honestly tell you, Maddie, that on every level you leave me in the dirt. You are the best person, the nicest woman, I know."

She grimaced. "Oh, everyone says that to me. How nice I am. Vanilla ice cream. Boring."

Hank laughed affectionately at her. "Maddie, you're about as boring as that lobster clock over there."

With Hank, Maddie focused on the big ugly red ceramic clock urn sitting on the table in front of the flowers. "Ohmigod, Hank, I forgot the urn. That's really James over there. I mean we're going to do this, aren't we?" Gripped with sudden fervor, Maddie held on to Hank's hands. "*James*, Hank. He brought us together. We're doing what he wanted, aren't we? It worked. Ohmigod, it worked."

Hank sat up. "You're right. It did." He divided his gaze between Maddie and the lobster clock. "You think he knows? I mean about us, right now, somehow? Up there, I mean."

"Oh, I hope so. He deserves to know." Suddenly troubled, Maddie's features registered her concern. "Hank, have you worked through your emotions about him not . . . well, telling you he was dying? I would hate for you to still have hard feelings."

"I don't," Hank said quietly. "I think I understand a lot more now. I talked a lot with Jim. And he said my grandfather didn't want me to see him weak and sick like that. It was his silly pride, Maddie. Another lesson in there for me, right? I can keep my pride and live alone and die the same way. Or I can come down out of the towers of big business and live. At least, I think that's what he might have meant."

Maddie nodded. "I think you're right. He used to tell me to quit being afraid of love. Just take a leap and live. And look at me—I did. And it was with you. How sweet and loving of him to worry about us so." Then she thought of something else that animated her. "Ohmigod, Hank, Jim has a letter. It's from James and it's to us. We can get that now and open it."

"Wait. Does that mean you're saying yes to me, Maddie? You know, you haven't said it yet."

Maddie smiled and cupped his cheek with her hand. "Yes, Hank, I will marry you. And we will have a big wedding and invite all of Hanscomb Harbor. Celeste will be my matron of honor. And Beamer will be our canine of honor."

"I think you ought to ask Lavinia Houghton to be your maid of honor."

"You're just being bad now. And your best man will be . . . ?"

"Jim, of course."

"An excellent choice. He'll be so pleased." A loving warmth swept through Maddie. Emotion and tears of joy threatened to swamp her. "And you and I will have a long and happy life together and give your mother and Celeste and Jim and Mary the grandchildren they want—or deserve, however they want to see it."

Hank stared at her. "I love you, Maddie." Then he looked up to the cobwebbed ceiling of the ratty old cottage they inhabited. "Hey, up there, thank you, Grandpa, for this most precious woman. I will always treat her like the treasure she is." Hank met Maddie's gaze, his dark eyes glittering. "I have a surprise for you. I've got the letter."

Maddie smacked at his arm. "You're lying."

"I am not. Jim gave it to me when I told him I was coming here. Where's my shirt?"

With Hank hot on her heels, Maddie jumped out of bed and helped him hunt for it. Embarrassingly enough, their clothes were everywhere, a telltale trail that led straight to the lumpy-mattressed bed.

"Here it is," Maddie cried out triumphantly, standing over by the kitchen table and holding up his light blue oxford shirt.

Hank, magnificently naked and unconcerned, padded over to her. "In the pocket. Look in there. I folded it up."

With due reverence, Maddie pulled the envelope out and unfolded it. "I feel as if we should have some sort of official ceremony for this. Music or something. A drumroll."

"Darn. I left my bagpipes in the city. You want me to hum something appropriate? Or get out two spoons and play them solemnly?"

Maddie laughed at him. "No. Don't be silly. Here." She held the letter out to him.

As if under arrest, Hank held his hands up and backed away. "Not me. You open it. He was your friend."

Maddie advanced on him, the letter held out like a weapon. "And he was your grandfather."

Hank stopped. "That's true. Give it here. I'll open it."

Maddie pulled it back. "No. I want to."

Hank grinned, folding his arms over his bare chest. "How'd I know? Go ahead, then. Open it."

Maddie exhaled and stared solemnly at Hank. "Here I go . . . opening it." Her hands suddenly shaking, she pulled at the sealed edge on the back of the lined envelope, tearing it open. Her heart in her throat, she reverently lifted the flap and pulled from it a single, trifolded piece of paper. Barely able to breathe, her heart beating too fast, Maddie straightened it out. Sure enough, James's handwriting. She read his words. Her breath caught. She looked up, seeking Hank's gaze. "Hank, this can't be. You are not going to believe this. It's crazy. Ohmigod. Look."

His expression apprehensive, Hank came to her side. "What are you talking about? What can't be?"

Blinking back tears, her chin trembling, Maddie practically danced in place as she held the letter out to him. "This. Take it. It can't be. Read it."

Frowning mightily, Hank took the paper from her, watched her dance in place . . . and then read. His mouth dropped open, he stared at Maddie. "Son of a bitch," he shouted. "You're right. How could he know? He couldn't. It's impossible. And spooky."

Proving it, his eyes widened like a spooked child's on Halloween. Maddie watched Hank pan the cabin's interior, as if he thought they weren't alone. His gaze lit on the lobster urn, then Maddie. "There's no way he could have known it would end like this. None. And that other stuff he wrote? We didn't even know. Not until this minute. No way, Maddie."

"I know." Flapping her hands, Maddie was all but on her tiptoes now. "This is so—is there a word for it? Unbelievable. Absolutely unbelievable. I don't even know whether to be scared or uplifted, Hank. He wrote this before we'd ever met."

"I know." Hank again read his grandfather's words.

That was when Maddie stopped, sobered, and suffered a clear, lucid moment. "For God's sake, what are we doing? It's like James is right here with us. Put on some clothes."

As if they were teenagers caught by their parents, and with her scalp tingling from a mixture of excitement and righteous fright, Maddie grabbed up pieces of clothes, sorting hers from his, tossing him his, and quickly shrugging into her own. And Hank—the letter held between his lips— was right behind her, dancing and twisting until he was more or less clothed.

That accomplished, they stood in the cabin, facing each other. Maddie could barely catch her breath, so agitated was she, so full of disbelief. Hank's heightened color and breathing said he fared no better.

Maddie gnawed at her thumbnail. "I feel like I should make the bed."

Hank had to take the letter out of his mouth before he could answer. "It's a little late for that."

"True." Maddie paused, then leaned in toward Hank, pointed at the lobster clock, and whispered, "Do you really think he's here right now?"

"I'm not going there, Maddie. I'm really not. I'm just going to accept. How about you?"

"Me, too. I accept."

"Good. Me, too."

"You already said that, Hank."

"Good."

Then . . . Maddie stared at Hank. He stared back. But Maddie proved to be the first one not able to stand the suspense. "What should we do now?"

"I don't know. What do you want to do?"

"I don't know."

"Good."

"Hank, we're losing it."

"I know."

"Don't say 'good' again."

"I wasn't going to."

"Good." Suddenly Maddie's mood brightened a bit. "You know what? We shouldn't be scared. Because this is really great. There's no way James's wording is accidental. Or even a good guess."

"That's true. But he couldn't have known, Maddie. So, what do you think it is? Divine? Providential? Something from the Great Beyond?" Hank's expression was as sincere and hopeful of a rational explanation as was his tone of voice.

"I don't know. But there are things in that letter James couldn't have known when he wrote them. He couldn't have. And I can't explain it. Can you?"

Hank rubbed absently at his chin. "No. But let's try not to overthink this." Then he did. "The way I see it is we've been through a lot of hell, but we made it. We'll just focus on that. I think my grandfather saw in us what we couldn't see in ourselves. I think he knew we'd see it in each other if we got together. And I think he counted on us having the courage to keep fighting to get it right. I believe we finally have. And I think he always knew we would, so he just anticipated us."

"Okay. Maybe. That's good. I like that. Anticipation." Calmer now, more willing to consider Hank's explanation, Maddie smiled at him, hoping even a tenth of the love she felt for him shone through. "And you explain the stuff in the P.S. how?"

"I don't. Just leave it, okay? Accept that it is in there and it happened."

Maddie nodded. "Okay. Good. So when did you get so wise?"

"Are you serious? About five minutes ago when I read this." He held up the letter.

Maddie nodded. "You're absolutely right. I mean, look at us. Here we are, the two of us handed a great big silver lining. And what do we do? Start looking for clouds. For explanations."

"Well, no more. Come here, you." Hank held his arms out invitingly, and Maddie walked into his embrace.

"God, Hank, I love you," she murmured, reveling in the warmth and the solidity of his body as he pressed close to her. "Is it possible to die of happiness? I could, you know. Right now. This minute. Because you feel heavenly to me."

"I'm glad, but don't you dare die. You're not getting off that easy. You're going to stick around here and enjoy me for a long time, dammit."

With that, Hank held her out from him and looked down into her eyes. His expression serious now, he said, "Maddie, I hope to make you forget those clouds that worry you. I can't say enough how convinced I am that this outcome has been inevitable from the moment we met. And I think, even before you and I met, that my grandfather saw in you the same qualities that he knew I could and would come to love."

"Oh, Hank, do you really think so?"

"I do. I also think that all my grandfather did was give us both a chance, the opportunity, to get it right. And we did. That's what we need to realize. We did it, Maddie. We broke through—"

"You're right. We did." Overcome with that exciting realization, Maddie felt tears prick her eyes. "James made this possible, Hank. Not with his money or power, things I never wanted anyway. He knew that. He just used them to set us on the path that would lead to this moment. He was a dear, sweet friend to me. And how I love him for that."

Her expression intensified. "But not like I love you, Hank. What I feel for you is completely beyond anything I ever dreamed I could ever feel for anyone. I will always love you. And I will try my best to make you happy."

Hank's frown was a pout. "Well, great. That was a beautiful speech. Thanks a lot. You didn't leave me anything to say but the lame 'Me, too.'" He grinned. "So . . . me, too. I love you, Maddie."

Maddie pulled him to her for a soul-searing kiss. Then, together and as one, they again read James's final yet astounding message to them both.

To Maddie and Hank, the two people I love most in the world.

I knew you could do it. Hank, I see so much of myself in you (and so much that is better) that I now entrust you with my most precious friend—Maddie. I know you will love her and see in her all the qualities I saw. And to you, Maddie, my sweet friend, I leave you my beloved grandson. After today, honey, you are no longer the Not the Happy Ending Princess.

Congratulations to you both. This is the happy ending you both (and I) deserve.

Love,
James (aka The Old Man)

P.S. Don't forget to put fresh water out for Beamer. And keep Lillian and Celeste away from bake sales. Oh, and thanks for the brass plaque on the cottage door there. That was a nice touch.

Read Cheryl Anne Porter's

BOLD NEW SERIES

About Three Passionate Sisters
And The Men Who Capture Their Hearts!

HANNAH'S PROMISE
NOMINEE FOR THE BOOKSTORES THAT CARE
"BEST LOVE & LAUGHTER ROMANCE" CATEGORY

After she finds her parents brutally murdered, Hannah Lawless travels to Boston, vowing revenge on their killers. When sexy Slade Garrett joins her crusade, Hannah may have found her soul-mate—or the heartless villain she seeks . . .

JACEY'S RECKLESS HEART

As Hannah heads East, Jacey Lawless makes her way to Tucson, in search of the scoundrel who left a spur behind at her parents' murder scene. When she meets up with dashing Zant Chapelo, a gunslinger whose father rode with hers, Jacey doesn't know whether to shoot . . . or surrender.

SEASONS OF GLORY

With Hannah and Jacey off to find their parents' killers, young Glory is left to tend the ranch. And with the help of handsome neighbor—and arch enemy—Riley Thorne, Glory might learn a thing or two about life . . . and love.

Our Husband

ACCLAIMED AWARD-WINNING AUTHOR OF
Manhunting in Mississippi

STEPHANIE BOND

"Compelling, absorbing and rich."
—*Publishers Weekly*

Fate has just thrown a curve ball at the women in Ray Carmichael's life—all three of them. When they meet at his hospital bed, they discover they're all married to the same man. And when Ray suddenly dies, the police suspect that one of these spunky ladies has committed murder. Now they're three women left with a man's betrayal—and worse, each other. But one thing they each insist—they didn't kill Ray. What can they do? Something outrageous and probably impossible: stick together to catch a murderer . . .

"Treat yourself to an evening of memorable characters." —Susan Andersen, author of *Baby, Don't Go*

"A rollicking first novel that's got everything—humor, romance, suspense, and not one but THREE memorable heroines! Great fun!" —Jane Heller

AVAILABLE WHEREVER BOOKS ARE SOLD
FROM ST. MARTIN'S PAPERBACKS

A hot, hilarious novel about small-town secrets,
big-time betrayals,
and the redemptive power of love,
laughter and chocolate brownies.

TELL ME LIES

Jennifer Crusie

"Jennifer Crusie presents a humorous mixture of
romance, mystery, and mayhem."
—Susan Elizabeth Phillips, *New York Times* bestselling
author of *Nobody's Baby But Mine*

"[Crusie] has a wicked sense of humor, keen insights into
the complexities of modern relationships, and a way of
making her characters seem genuine and her stories
real…A wonderfully fresh, funny, tender, outrageous
story that will delight fans of the comic mystery….Crusie
is definitely one of a kind."
—*Booklist*

AVAILABLE WHEREVER BOOKS ARE SOLD
FROM ST. MARTIN'S PAPERBACKS